Frederick W. Hutton

Manual of the New Zealand Mollususca

A systematic and descriptive catalogue of the marine and land shells, and of the

soft mollusks and Polyzoa of New Zealand and the adjacent islands

Frederick W. Hutton

Manual of the New Zealand Mollususca
A systematic and descriptive catalogue of the marine and land shells, and of the soft mollusks and Polyzoa of New Zealand and the adjacent islands

ISBN/EAN: 9783337392161

Printed in Europe, USA, Canada, Australia, Japan

Cover: Foto ©Andreas Hilbeck / pixelio.de

More available books at **www.hansebooks.com**

𝔈olonial 𝔐useum & 𝔊eological 𝔖urbey 𝔇epartment.

JAMES HECTOR, M.D., C.M.G., F.R.S.,

DIRECTOR.

MANUAL

OF THE

NEW ZEALAND MOLLUSCA.

A SYSTEMATIC AND DESCRIPTIVE

CATALOGUE

OF THE

MARINE AND LAND SHELLS, AND OF THE SOFT
MOLLUSKS AND POLYZOA OF NEW ZEALAND
AND THE ADJACENT ISLANDS.

BY

FREDERICK WOLLASTON HUTTON, F.G.S., C.M.Z.S.,

Professor of Biology, Canterbury College, New Zealand University.
(Late Curator of the Otago Museum.)

𝔓ublished by 𝔈ommand.

WELLINGTON :

PRINTED AT THE OFFICE OF JAMES HUGHES, LAMBTON QUAY.

1880.

PREFACE.

———::———

AN accurate knowledge of the affinities and distribution of the recent Shells of New Zealand is a very necessary element in the Geological Survey of the country, as it must form the basis of our Tertiary Geology, upon the correct decyphering of which many questions of the highest interest depend ; such, for instance, as the former distribution of land, of ocean currents, and of temperature in the Southern Hemisphere, and the true nature of the agencies which have operated in producing the Auriferous alluvia or Gold Drifts.

Shells afford the most reliable data for Palæontologists ; but before the extinct shell fauna can be utilized, the recent shells of the area must be thoroughly determined. The preparation of the first Catalogue was beset with difficulties, which were explained in the preface to that work ; but, as was then anticipated, its publication has led to a vast improvement in our knowledge of the subject.

The consent of Government was, therefore, readily given to the printing of the present work at the public expense, the compilation of which has been an entirely gratuitous service on the part of Professor Hutton.

This MANUAL is not, however, merely a new edition of the Catalogue by the same Author which was issued by this Department in 1873, but it embodies and replaces the following works, all of which are now out of print :—

1. Catalogue of the Marine Mollusca of New Zealand. By F. W. Hutton. Wellington, 1873.
2. Critical List of the Mollusca of New Zealand. By Ed. Von Martens. Wellington, 1873.

3. Catalogue of the Land Shells of New Zealand. By J. C. Cox. M.D., F.L.S. (of Sydney.) Wellington 1873.

The information contained in these works, together with much that is new, is now presented in a convenient form for reference, and it is hoped that the present Manual will be of service to teachers of Natural History as a text book in a department of New Zealand Zoology that is particularly adapted for training students in the art of collecting and classifying natural objects.

JAMES HECTOR,

Director.

Colonial Museum,

Wellington. February 1st, 1880.

CONTENTS.

————::————

ERRATA.

Page 4, line 10 from bottom, and elsewhere—for Lamark, read Lawarck.

,, 38, line 18 from bottom—for Diplommautina, read Diplommatina.

,, 81, line 20 from bottom—for Monguin-Tandon, read Moquin-Tandon.

,, 85, line 4 from top—for *Vernetus*, read *Vermetus*.

,, 125, line 5 from bottom—for Handcock, read Hancock.

., 130, line 19 from top—for Lutariinæ, read Lutrariinæ.

,, 155, line 2 from bottom—L. lactea. This is a Lucina and should have followed L. divaricata.

BIBLIOGRAPHY.

——::——

Linnæus.—Systema Naturæ, 12th edition   1766
Chemnitz.—Conchylien Cabinet, 12 vols.   ... 1769-95
Martyn.—Universal Conchologist, 4 vols.   1784
Lamarck.—Animaux sans Vertebres, 7 vols.   ...   1815-22
Quoy and Gaimard.—Voyage of the Astrolabe, Zoology   1830
Gray, J. E.—Yate's New Zealand ...   1838
,,   Dieffenbach's New Zealand   1843
Reeve, L.—Conchologia Iconica, (20 vols.)   ... 1843-78
Gould.—Expedition Shells, 8vo., Boston   ...   1846
,,   American Exploring Expedition ; Mollusca   1852
Adams, A.—Proceedings of the Zoological Society   ... 1851-56
Hombron and Jacquinot.—Voyage au Pole Sud   1853
Deshayes.—Proceedings of the Zoological Society   1853
Pfeiffer & Dunker.—Malako. Blatt.   1861
Zelebor & Dunker.—Verh. z. b. Wien   1866
,,   ,,   Reise der Novara   ...   1857
Pfeiffer.—Monographia Heliceorum Viventium (6 vols.)   1868
Frauenfeld.—Verh. z. b. Wein   1869
Martens.—(Shells brought home by Captain Cook) Malako. Blatt.   1872
Hutton.—Catalogue of the Marine Mollusca of New Zealand   1873
,,   Catalogue of the Tertiary Mollusca of New Zealand   1873
Martens.—List of the Mollusca of New Zealand   ...   1873
Smith.—Voyage of the Erebus and Terror ; Mollusca   1874
Hutton.—Revision des Coquilles de la Nouvelle-Zelande, Journal de
           Conchyliologie   1878
Tenison-Woods.—On some fresh water shells from New Zealand. Pro.
           Lin. Soc. of N.S. Wales, iii., p. 135 ...   1878

As well as many smaller papers referred to in the text.

Dr. H. Filhol has also published a paper on the shells of Stewart Island, which, unfortunately, I have not seen.

LIST OF ABBREVIATIONS.

—::—

A.N.H.—Annals and Magazine of Natural History.

An. s.v.—Histoire des Animaux sans Vertebres.

Ann. d. Sci. Nat.—Annales des Sciences Naturelles; Zoologie.

C.M.M.—Catalogue of the Marine Mollusca of New Zealand.

Cat. Tert. Moll.—Catalogue of the Tertiary Mollusca and Echinodermata of New Zealand.

Conch. Ic.—Conchologia Iconica.

Jour. de Conch.—Journal de Conchyliologie.

M.H.V.—Monographia Heliceorum Viventium.

Mal. Blatt.—Malakozoologische Blätter.

P.L.S.—Proceedings of the Linnean Society of London.

P.L.S. of N.S.W.—Proceedings of the Linnean Society of N.S. Wales.

P.Z.S.—Proceedings of the Zoological Society of London.

Q.J.M.S.—Quarterly Journal of Microscopical Science.

Verh. z. b. Wien.—Verhandlungen der Zoologisch-botanischen Gesellschaft in Wien.

U.S. Ex. Ep.—United States Exploring Expedition; Mollusca, by Dr. Gould.

SYNOPSIS OF THE FAMILIES.

————::————

Class—Cephalopoda.

Class—Gasteropoda.

Class—Brachiopoda.

Shell of two valves, placed dorsally and ventrally.

Class—Polyzoa.

Animal composite ; mouth surrounded by tentacles.

Order—GYMNOLÆMATA.—No epistome. Marine.

Sub-order—CHILOSTOMATA.

(*a*). Cells more or less ovoid ; mouth less than the diameter of the cell,
furnished with a moveable lip.

1. Polyzoarium of distinct pieces connected by flexible joints.

2. Polyzoarium continuous throughout.

* Flexible, never adnate.

** Rigid, adnate or erect.

Sub-order—CYCLOSTOMATA.

(*b*). Cells tubular ; mouth of the same diameter as the cell, without any
moveable lip.

Gasteropoda

1. Shell regularly spiral.

(a.) *Shell fusiform, tapering to each end.*

		Page
Anterior canal straight ; aperture entire behind	· MURICIDÆ	46
Large, canal short, with few varices	· TRITONIDÆ	63
Shell notched in front	· BUCCINIDÆ	52
Columella curved to the right	· APORRHAIDÆ	67
Columella, plaited	· FASCIOLARIIDÆ	59
Shell thin, keeled	· TRICHOTROPIDÆ	68

(b.) *Shell convolute, the aperture nearly as long as the shell.*

* Spire moderate.

Spire covered with enamel	· ANCILLIDÆ	58
Aperture wide, columella plaited	· VOLUTIDÆ	61
Aperture narrow, columella plaited	· MITRIDÆ	60
Columella plaited, outer lip thickened in the middle	· MARGINELLIDÆ	62
Columella plaited, aperture rounded in front	· ACTÆONIDÆ	119
Columella plaited, spire short	· AURICULIDÆ	32

** Spire very short.

Aperture with a recurved canal	· CASSIDIDÆ	65
Aperture large, without canal	· DOLIIDÆ	65
Shell inversely conical	· CONIDÆ	41
Shell thin, swollen	· APLUSTRIDÆ	120

*** Spire none.

Oval ; aperture narrow	· CYPRÆIDÆ	66
Small, cylindrical	· CYLICHNIDÆ	120
Small, last whorl expanded	· PHILINIDÆ	122
Moderate or large ; inflated	· BULLIDÆ	121

(c.) *Shell turreted or elongate.*

Outer lip indented near the suture, canal long and straight	· PLEUROTOMIDÆ	42
Whorls ribbed, sutures deep	· SCALARIDÆ	69
Aperture channelled in front	· CERITHIIDÆ	73
Aperture with an oblique notch in front	· TEREBRIDÆ	41
Spirally striated, aperture rounded	· TURRITELLIDÆ	83
Small, aperture entire, columella plaited	· PYAMIDELLIDÆ	72
Small, aperture entire, columella smooth	· RISSOIDÆ	80

(d.) *Shell globular, or turbinated.*

Polished, aperture semicircular	· NATICIDÆ	70
Aperture semicircular, columella flat	· NERITIDÆ	89
Shell thin, blue	· JANTHINIDÆ	70
Aperture rounded, not pearly inside	· LITTORINIDÆ	78
Aperture rounded, pearly inside	· TROCHIDÆ	90
Whorls flattened, not pearly	· AMPHIBOLIDÆ	35

(e.) *Shell conical, with a flat base.*

Shell not pearly inside	· SOLARIIDÆ	70
Shell pearly inside	· TROCHIDÆ	90

(f.) *Shell boat shaped.*

Interior with a shelly process	· CALYPTRIDÆ	86

Lamellibranchiata.

INTRODUCTION.

THE present catalogue will be found a great improvement on the last, both in completeness and in accuracy of nomenclature. This is owing partly to the publication of Dr. v. Marten's "critical list," and of the Mollusca of the Voyage of the Erebus and Terror; and partly to the improvements that have taken place in the Libraries and Museums in New Zealand during the last six years. It must still, however, be regarded as only a precursor of a monograph.

More than sixty species are now catalogued for the first time, and probably but few omissions will be found. Many of the species however here recorded will, no doubt, prove to be identical, while many others will be shewn to have been put down to New Zealand by mistake. Not much dependence can be placed on the localities in Mr. Cuming's collection, and some of those of Mr. Strange appear to me very doubtful. I have, however, thought it better, as books of reference are scarce, to give the original description in nearly every case, so that others, as well as myself, may form an opinion as to what should be regarded as synonymous, and what species should be struck out of the list.

No doubt the catalogue will want a great deal of revising in the generic names attached to the species. Hardly any of the animals have been examined, while it is often impossible to feel sure of the systematic position of a shell without a knowledge of the animal. Most of these observations can only be made upon the living animal, and as the Molluscan fauna of New Zealand differs very much in different localities, the correct systematic position of a large proportion of our shells can only be attained by the united efforts of many observers. To assist in this part of the work I have given, in the description of families and the genera, an account of the external characters of the animals belonging to them. These descriptions are taken almost entirely from Adam's "Genera of Mollusca," 1858; but the families have been grouped together on a more modern system.

A

A very large number of the species have been figured by Reeve and Sowerby, in the Conchologia Iconica, and others in the Voyages of the Astrolabe, the Erebus and Terror, the Voyage au Pole Sud, and the American Exploring Expedition, under Captain Wilks. In addition to these I have given references to figures in Adams' "Genera of the Mollusca," Woodward's "Manual of the Mollusca," and in Dr. Chenu's "Manuel de Conchyliologie," as these works are easily procurable. Several interesting remarks on the habits of some of the species, by Mr. Bidwill, Dr. Stanger, and Dr. Dieffenbach, will be found in the appendix to Dr. Dieffenbach's "Travels in New Zealand."

A list of shells found at Great Omaha, in the Auckland District, has been given by Mr. Kirk in the Transactions New Zealand Institute, 1872, p. 367 ; another of those found at Auckland by Mr. Cheeseman, in the same publication for 1875, p. 309, in a paper containing many valuable notes on the habits of the species; and the shells of Otago have been catalogued by myself in my report on the Geology of Otago ; Appendix, C (Dunedin 1875.) Many additions to the Molluscan fauna of Otago will, however, be found in this catalogue. Unfortunately I have not seen Dr. H. Filhol's paper on the Mollusca of Stewart Island, nor M. Jouan's essay on the fauna of New Zealand, published in the Mémoires de la Société des Sciences Naturelles de Cherbourg, t. xiv. (1869.) Much still remains to be done towards working out the geographical distribution of the species; and lists would be particularly valuable from Napier, Taranaki, Wellington, Nelson, Hokitika, and Banks Peninsula. For much information respecting the distribution of our shells in Australia and Tasmania, I am indebted to Mr. T. W. Bednall, of Adelaide.

The better the fauna of New Zealand becomes known, the more prominently does it stand out distinct from that of any other country ; and this is particularly the case with the shells. Formerly a list of New Zealand shells shewed a large proportion of tropical forms found in Australia and Polynesia, but the localities of most of these are now known to be inaccurate. Out of be   ' 350 and 400 species, which the New Zealand fauna really contains,   ' is only evidence of about 64 being found anywhere else, and in ver   of these cases have New Zealand specimens been compared with for   nes, the identifications having generally been made by description   figures only. The following is a list of the 64 species to which I 1

Argonanta tuberculata
Spirula peronii
Siphonaria sipho
Trophon paivæ
Neptunæa dilatata
Euthria antarctica
Polytropa textiliosa
,, succincta
,, striata
Tritonium australis
,, spengleri
,, olearium
Ranella leucostoma
,, vexillum
Dolium variegatum
Cassis pyrum
,, achatina
Trivia australis
Janthina communis
,, exigua
Littorina cærulescens
Nerita atrata
Bankivia varians
Halotis rugoso-plicata
Tugalia parmophoroides
Patella magellanica
Chiton sulcatus
,, glaucus
Lepidopleurus longicymbus
Tonicia undulata
,, lineolata
,, atrata

Bullina lineata
Bulla oblonga
Saxicava australis
Corbula zealandica
,, erythrodon
Anatina tasmanica
Myodora ovata
Chamostræa albida
Zenatia acinaces
Tellina deltoidalis
,, ticaonica
Chione strutchburyi
Callista multistriata
Lucina divaricata
Diplodonta globularis
Kellia cycladiformis
Mytilicardia excavata
Barbatia pusilla
Pectunculus flammeus
Nucula strangei
Mytilus magellanicus
,, latus
,, edulis
Crenella impacta
Modiola australis
Pinna zealandica
Pecten australis
Vola laticostatus
Lima angulata
,, japonica
Placuanomia ione
Ostrea edulis.

The following eight genera are peculiar to New Zealand, and to them may perhaps be added, Waltonia,

Laoma
Janella
Konophora
Latia

Potamopyrgus
Anthora
Cryptoconchus
Vanganella.

It is very different with the Polyzoa, for out of the 100 species here catalogued, 69 are already known to occur elsewhere; but even in the Polyzoa we have three genera which, so far as yet known, are peculiar to New Zealand. They are Onchopora, Muscaria, and Cintipora.

MAORI NAMES.

I have been able to collect only the few following Maori names for our shells :—

HAKARI, Artemis subrosea and Tapes intermedia
HOHE-HOHE, Tellina alba
HUAI, Chione stutchburyi
KAIKAI-KORORO, Chione costata
KOKOTA, Mesodesma nova-zealandiæ
PAKIRA, Myodora striata
PAWA, Haliotis iris
PIPI, Mesodesma novæ-zealandiæ, and Chione stutchburyi
PUKAURI, Chione yatei
PUREWHA, Modiola areolata
PURIMU, Cardita australis
TUA-TUA, Mesodesma spissa
WAHA-WAHA, Psammobia stangeri.

MOLLUSCA OF NEW ZEALAND.

Class—Cephalopoda.

HEAD large, separate from the body. Eyes large, lateral. Ears developed. Mouth with two horny or shelly jaws with fleshy lips, and surrounded by eight or ten fleshy arms, or numerous tentacles ; furnished with an entire or slit tube, or siphuncle, used in locomotion.

ORDER—OCTOPODA.

Body short, rounded ; head large ; eyes fixed ; arms eight, all sessile ; no internal dorsal shell.

FAMILY—OCTOPIDÆ.

Body naked ; arms tapering, with short sessile cups.

Genus, OCTOPUS*—Cuvier.

Arms with two rows of cups ; body round, without fins.

O. maorum, *sp. nov.* Body oval, rounded behind, smooth below, roughened but not tuberculated on the back. Head slightly granular. Arms long, tapering, dorsal pair the longest, ventral pair the shortest ; web broad, smooth. Cups in two rows, close, elevated ; those of the eighth or ninth rows the largest, gradually diminishing both ways ; those on the dorsal arms largest, twice the diameter of those on the ventral arms. Dark gray, paler below.
Dunedin.
This species attains a large size.

Genus, PINNOCTOPUS—D'Orbigny.

Body oblong, with broad, lateral, wing-like expansions, which extend in front and enfold all the body ; arms very long, with two rows of slightly prominent cups.
New Zealand only.

---

* Dr. Gray, in the catalogue of the Cephalopoda in the British Museum, gives New Zealand as the locality of *O. lunulatus* Quoy et Gaim. This is an error, it should be New Ireland.

P. cordiformis, *Quoy, Voy. Astrolabe,* ii., *p.* 27, *l.* 6, *f.* 2; *Adams, Gen. Moll., pl.* 1., *f.* 3; *Chenu, f.* 35. Body orbicular, tubercular, winged. Arms nearly equal in length, the lateral ones shortest. Reddish brown; arms with pale blue lunules.

FAMILY—ARGONAUTIDÆ.

Body of female covered with a thin shell; arms tapering, very unequal; cups prominent, in two series. The two dorsal arms webbed at the extremity.

Genus, ARGONAUTA—Linnæus.

Shell one-celled, thin, transparent.

A. tuberculata, *Shaw.* *A. nodosa, Solander, M.S.S.* : *A. tuberculosa, Reeve, Conch Icon., f.* 1 : *Chenu, f.* 45 ; *A. oryzata, Meush.* Shell compressed, sides with transverse plications, which are longitudinally tuberculiferous; keels two, with compressed tubercules. White, brownish on the spire, where also the keel tubercules are blackish brown. Five or six inches across.

North Island, sometimes as far south as Wellington. Indian Sea. South Pacific. Chili. Tasmania. South Australia.

Animal.—Body oblong, rounded behind, smooth, spotted with violet: eyes large, prominent; siphuncle united to the base of the arms by a lateral membrane; arms tapering, except the dorsal pair, which are palmate at the end, these are the shortest, the next pair to them the longest, and the others graduated; the lowest pair are keeled on the outside; membrane small, all the arms equally webbed ; cups large, less than there own diameter apart, in two rows, with a single row of rather smaller cups round the mouth.

Chatham Islands. As the shell of this animal was not obtained, I refer it doubtfully to this species, as it differs from Dr. Gray's description.

ORDER—DECAPODA.

Body oblong or cylindrical ; head smaller than the body ; eyes free in the orbit; arms ten,—eight sessile, two tentacula, elongated ; fins developed ; an internal shell, occupying the middle of the back.

FAMILY—ONYCHOTEUTHIDÆ.

Fins posterior, dorsal, angular ; eyes naked ; ears with a longitudinal crest ; shell horny, lanceolate.

Genus, ONYCHOTEUTHIS—Lichtenstein.

Fins terminal, broad, together rhomboidal ; sessile arms angular, cups in two alternating lines ; tentacular arms with a rounded group of small sessile cups, and two series of claw-like hooks on each club. Shell lanceolate, pennate, tip acute ; end produced, narrow ; sides dilated, thin, with a central longitudinal keel contracted at the end.

O. bartlingii, *Lesueur ; Gray, Cat. Moll. Brit. Mus. Cephalopoda, p. 54; Chenu, f. 74.* Body elongate ; back with a central transparent line over the keel of the shell ; sessile arms slender ; tentacular arms with six large hooks. Shell dark brown, with a short central keel above and a ridge beneath. (Gray.)

Auckland. Wellington. Indian Ocean.

Genus, OMMASTREPHES—D'Orbigny.

Fins terminal, broad, together rhomboidal ; sessile arms subulate ; tentacular arms scarcely enlarged at the end, both they and the sessile arms with cups and horny rings. Shell horny, flexible, narrow, gradually wider above, terminated by an expansion that forms a conical cavity : a central and two marginal ribs.

O. sloanii, *Gray, l.c., p. 61.* Body cylindrical ; fin rather more than one-third the length of the body ; sessile arms compressed, cups equal, oblique, in two rows, higher side of rings with acute teeth, lower smooth ; tentacular arms slightly keeled externally, cups of lower part small, in two rows, of middle part in four rows ; rings with distant teeth all round. Colour purplish, caused by minute dots placed close together ; beak black. (Gray.)

Bluff to Auckland. Indian Ocean.

FAMILY—LOLIGIDÆ.

Fins either posterior or lateral ; eyes covered with skin ; ears with a transverse ridge. Shell horny, lanceolate, pennate, or spathulate.

Genus, SEPIOTEUTHIS—Ferussac.

Fins extending the whole length of the back ; sessile arms unequal, with two rows of cups ; tentacular arms long, club enlarged, cups in four rows. Shell pennate, lanceolate, narrow in front and with a central keel.

S. lessoniana, *Féruss : Gray, l.c., p. 80.* Body elongate, spotted with violet ; fins dilated posteriorly ; sessile arms elongate, cups oblique, rings with distant acute teeth : tentacular arms bluntly clubbed, cups large, very oblique, rings with distant acute curved teeth ; buccal membrane with cups. Shell lanceolate, broadest in the middle, outer edge not thickened, central rib broad, extented in front, one-fifth the length. (Gray.)

Bay of Islands (Antartic Expedition.) New Guinea.

S. bilineata, *Quoy and Gaimard, l.c.,* ii., 66, *t.* 2, *f.* 1 (?); *S. major, Cat. Mar. Moll. of N.Z.* Body cylindrical, attenuated behind ; fins rounded, fleshy, most dilated in the middle of the body ; buccal membrane without cups ; sessile arms rather short, order of length, 4, 3, 2, 1, cups large, rings with short blunt teeth on the higher side ; tentacular arms strong, with cups and rings like those of the sessile arms. Shell lanceolate, widest at about two-fifths of its length, edge not thickened, central rib broad, extended in front about one-sixth of

its length. Yellowish white, spotted with violet ; length of body sometimes 13 inches, perhaps more.

Wellington to Auckland.

There is nothing in Dr. Gray's description of *S. major* in his catalogue of Cephalopoda that does not also answer for this species, but the
description is too short to feel confidence in the identification.

FAMILY—SPIRULIDÆ.

Body sub-cylindrical ; eyes covered with skin, and with a lower
eyelid. Shell calcareous, internal, spiral, chambered, chamber traversed
by a ventral siphon.

Genus, SPIRULA—Lamark.

Body oblong; fins two, small ; sessile arms with numerous cups ;
tentacular arms long. Shell thin, involute in the same plane, whorls
separated from each other, septa concave outwards, with a funnel-
shaped siphon on the inner side.

S. peronii, *Lamark ; S. australis, Lam ; Lituus lævis, Gray,
l.c., p.* 116 ; *S. australis, Owen, Voy. Samarang, Moll., p,* 13,
pl. 4, *f.* 2 ; *Woodward, Manual of the Mollusca, pl.* 1, *fig.* 9 ; *Chenu, f.*
166.

Mantle smooth.

Animal very rare. Shells abundant on sandy beaches, Bluff to
Auckland.

For a description of the Anatomy, see Owen's Zoology of the
Voyage of the Samarang, Mollusca ; and Annals of Natural History,
5th series, vol. 3 (1879) p. 1.

Class—Gasteropoda.

HEAD distinct, with eyes and tentacles. Body usually protected by a conical more or less spiral shell, often furnished with an operculum.

ORDER—PULMONATA.

Air-breathing, herbivorous gasteropods. Hermaphrodite. Breathing organ an air sac, lined by vascular network, and closed in front, situated behind the heart. Larva without any conspicuous velum.*

Sub-Order—Stylommatophora.

Eyes on the end of stalks, or processes of the body wall. No operculum. Terrestrial.

FAMILY—OLEACINIDÆ.

Lingual teeth numerous, in more or less curved rows; the central teeth inconspicuous, the marginal aculeate, or with a single long recurved apex. Head short; tentacles moderate, situated below the eye-peduncles. Body spiral, protected by a shell. Pulmonary opening on the right side, beneath the margin of the shell. Foot elongate, narrow, simple posteriorly.

Sub-Family—Helicellinæ.

Mantle-margin included. Shell discoidal, or trochiform, umbilicated, usually thin, many whorled; peristome straight, acute.

Genus, PATULA—Held.

Shell umbilicated, depressed, discoid, or turbinate, rugose or costulately striate; whorls equal or gradually increasing; aperture lunately rotund; peristome simple, straight, acute.

A. Umbilicus, narrow.

P. chordata, *Pfeiffer; Malak. Bl.* viii., 1861, *p.* 147; *M.H.V., vol.* 5, *p.* 72, *No.* 200. Shell sub-perforate, globosely-turbinated, thin, somewhat closely covered with cord-shaped ribs, not shining, marbled minutely with whitish and reddish; spire convexly conical, somewhat sharp; whorls 5, convex, the last slightly inflated at the base; aperture a little oblique, lunar; peristome simple, straight, margins remote, columellar margin slightly reflected at the perforation.
Diam., greatest, ·15 ; least, ·14 ; height, ·12. (Pfr.)
New Zealand (Hochstetter).

---

* *Siphonaria* and *Gadinia* have a gill in the pulmonary cavity, and are thus passage forms between the Pulmonata and the Branchiata.

This shell differs from its near ally, the *H. iota*, Pfr., by the turbinated spire, and by the almost closed-up perforation.

P. iota, *Pfeiffer; P.Z.S.,* 1851; *M.H.V., vol.* 3, *p.* 69; *vol.* 5, *p.* 114, *No.* 465; *H. pilula Reeve, f.* 809. Shell perforated, sub-depressed, thin, closely ribbed, not shining, yellowish horny, rufous spotted and reticulated; spire shortly-conoidal, somewhat acute; whorls 5, rather convex, gradually increasing, the last not descending, rounded; aperture a little oblique, rotundly-lunar; peristome simple, straight, margins distant, columellar margin arcuately ascending, sub-dilated above, open.

Diam., greatest, ·16; least, ·14; height, ·1. (Pfr.)
New Zealand. Queenstown (F.W.H.)

P. dimorpha, *Pfeiffer: P.Z.S.,* 1851; *M.H.V., vol.* 3, *p.* 68; *vol.* 5, *p.* 114, *No.* 457; *Reeve, Conch, Ic., f.* 775. Shell perforated, depressed, thin, very closely striated and somewhat closely so with thread-like ribs, a little shining, diaphanous, pale horny, minutely rufously-tessellated, and at the suture ornamented with rufous spots; spire scarcely elevated; whorls 5, rather convex, the last not descending, rounded, higher than broad; aperture sub-vertical, lunar; peristome simple, straight, with the basal margin somewhat bent backwards, columellar margin callously-reflected above, almost concealing the perforation.

Diam., greatest, ·34; least, ·3; height, ·2. (Pfr.)
New Zealand (Strange.)

P. hypopolia, *Pfeiffer: P.Z.S.,* 1851; *M.H.V., vol.* 3, *p.* 68; *vol.* 5, *p.* 114, *No.* 459; *Reeve, f.* 787. Shell very narrowly umbilicated, depressed, thin, very closely ribbed, silky, horny-cinereous; spire little elevated, convex; whorls 5½. slightly convex. the last not descending, more convex at the base; aperture a little oblique, broadly lunar; peristome simple, straight, columellar margin arcuated, slightly reflexed above.

Diam., greatest, ·26; least, ·24; height, ·13. (Pfr.)
New Zealand (Strange.)
Queenstown, Dunedin, Oamaru, Lake Guyon (F.W.H.)

P. decidua, *Pfeiffer: P.Z.S.* 1857, *p.* 108; *M.H.V., vol.* 4, *p.* 71; *vol.* 5, *p.* 137, *No.* 606. Shell umbilicated, depressly-turbinated, thin, sculptured with membranaceous, deciduous, fine ribs, horny-yellowish, obscurely and angularly streaked with reddish; spire somewhat regularly conoidal; whorls 5, rather convex, slowly increasing, the last not descending, sub angulated at the periphery; umbilicus narrow, pervious; aperture oblique, lunately-rotund; peristome simple, straight, margins converging, columellar margin slightly expanded.

Diam., greatest, ·14; least, ·13; height. ·08. (Pfr.)
New Zealand.

P. celinde, *Gray; P.Z.S.,* 1849, *p.* 164. *Helix Celinde, Pfr., M.H.V., vol.* 3, *p.* 125; *vol.* 5, *p.* 202, *No.* 1132; *Reeve, f.* 799. Shell sub-perforated, rather depressed, membranaceously-plaited, pale brown; spire canoidal, rather acute; whorls 5, firmly pressed together, the last sub-carinated, not descending, rather convex at the base, impressed in the middle; aperture oblique, sub-triangularly lunar; peristome sublabiated, margins remote, joined to a small callus, somewhat straight, basil margin somewhat straitened.

Diam., greatest, ·16; least, ·15; height, ·09. (Pfr.)

Auckland (Greenwood.)

P. zic-zac, *Gould; U.S. Ex. Ep.,* xii., *p.* 41, *f.* 44; *Pfeiffer, M.H.V.,* i., *p.* 116 *and* v., *p.* 173; *Cox, Aust. Land Shells, p.* 18. Shell small, rounded, depressed, pale straw-colour, painted with small oblique lightning-like brown lines, and furrowed with acute, closely set reflected hairy plates; beneath convex, perforated with a large step-like umbilicus. Whorls 6, convex, narrow; aperture sub-circular, sub-angulated at the base; lip simple, reflected near the umbilicus.

Diam., ·3; height, ·18. (Pfr.)

Gould first gave New South Wales, and subsequently New Zealand, as the habitat of this species. It does not appear to have been again recognised in either country, but probably New Zealand is the correct habitat, and it must have been collected at the Bay of Islands.

P. kappa, *Pfeiffer; P.Z.S.,* 1851; *M.H.V., vol.* 3, *p.* 154; *vol.* 5, *p.* 246; *No.* 1506; *Helix collyrula, Reeve, l.c., f.* 811. Shell umbilicated, depressed, ribbed, ribs bearing hair-like filaments, not shining, horny, obscurely variegated with rufous; spire extremely short, rather convex; suture impressed; whorls 5, rather convex, gradually increasing, the last not descending, rounded; umbilicus narrow, previous; aperture vertical, depressed, lunar; peristome somewhat simple, margins remote, the right margin straight, basal margin shortly reflexed, columellar margin obliquely ascending.

Diam., greatest, ·21; least, ·2; height, ·12. (Pfr.)

New Zealand (Strange.)

Distinguished by its hairs.

B. Umbilicus wide.

a. Upper surface convex.

P. varicosa, *Pfeiffer; P.Z.S.,* 1854; *M.H.V., vol.* 3, *p.* 97; *vol.* 5, *p.* 153; *No.* 762; *Reeve, f.* 824. Shell umbilicated, depressed, very thin, finely striated, varicosely-angled with distant ribs, not shining, fuscous; spire slightly elevated, obtuse; whorls 4½–5, flattish, the last not descending, depressed, flattish at the base; umbilicus moderate, pervious; aperture small, oblique, lunar; peristome, simple, straight, columellar margin above very slightly reflexed.

Diam., greatest, ·14; least, ·13; height, scarcely ·08. (Pfr.)

New Zealand (Strange.)

P. tiara, *Mighels; Boston, Proc..* 1845, *p.* 19; *Pfr., M.H.V., vol.* 1, *p.* 85; *vol.* 3, *p.* 98; *vol.* 5, *p.* 156; *No.* 783; *Reeve, f.* 611. Shell umbilicated, slightly convexly depressed, somewhat thin, above arcuately-striated, luteous, adorned with lightning-like rufous streaks, rather shining; spire clearly arched over, obtuse; whorls 6, rather convex, slowly increasing, the last somewhat tapering, not descending, slightly striated beneath; umbilicus large, conical, exceeding one-third of the diameter; aperture oblique, lunately-rounded, sub-opalescent within ; peristome simple, straight, margins approximating, right-margin arcuated in front, columellar margin not reflexed.

Diam., greatest, ·32 ; least, ·28 ; height, ·16. (Pfr.)

Bay of Islands, New Zealand (Hochstetter.)   Kaui, Sandwich Islands (Mighels.)

P. coma, *Gray; Dieff. Trav., vol.* 1, *p.* 263 ; *Helix coma, Pfr., M.II.V., vol.* 3, *p.* 99 : *vol.* 5. *p.* 156, *No.* 792 : *Reeve, f.* 796 ; *Voy. Erebus and Terror; Moll., pl.* 1, *f.* 3. Shell umbilicated, depressed, rather thin, obliquely closely ribbed, slightly shining, pale fuscous, sub-radiated with brown spots ; spire a little elevated, flatly convex ; whorls, 5, rather convex, slowly increasing, the last obscurely angled, not descending anteriorily ; umbilicus broad, conical ; aperture diagonal, lunately-rotund ; peristome simple, straight, margins slightly convergent, upper part somewhat bent backwards.

Diam., greatest, ·28 ; least, ·24 ; height, ·12. (Pfr.)

Auckland (Greenwood and Sinclair ;) Wellington and Lake Guyon (F.W.H.)

Perhaps *H. diemenensis,* Cox (A.L.S., p. 20) is the same. *Patula consimilis* (Pease) from the Society Island is also closely allied.

P. tau, *Pfeiffer; Malak. Bl.,* viii., 1861, 148 ; *M.II.V., vol.* 5, *p.* 159, *No.* 809. Shell broadly umbilicated, depressed, rather thin, above marked with somewhat apart rib-like plaits, rufous, tessellated with whitish ; spire slightly elevated, crown minute ; whorls 5, rather convex, slowly increasing, the last tapering, not descending, slightly striated beneath ; aperture small, slightly oblique, lunar ; peristome simple, straight, margins hardly converging, columellar margin not dilated.

Diam., greatest, ·12 ; least, ·1 ; height, ·04. (Pfr.)

New Zealand (Hochstetter.)

P. gamma, *Pfeiffer; P.Z.S.,* 1851 ; *M.H.V., vol.* 3, *p.* 100 ; *vol.* 5, *p.* 159, *No.* 808 ; *Helix buccinella, Reeve, l.c., f.* 821. Shell umbilicated, depressed, thinnish, very closely striated with rib-like striæ, diaphanous, pale horny, rufously clouded ; spire very slightly convex ; suture impressed ; whorls 5, rather convex, slowly increasing, the last not descending, convex beneath ; umbilicus broadish, conical ; aperture sub-vertical, rotundly-lunar ; peristome simple ; straight, margins converging, regularly arcuated.

Diam., ·12 ; height, ·05. (Pfr.)

New Zealand (Strange.)

Queenstown, Dunedin, Preservation Inlet (F.W.H.)

P. egesta, *Gray; P.Z.S.,* 1849, *p.* 166 ; *Pfr., M.H.V., vol.* 3, *p.* 102 ; *vol.* 5, *p.* 164, *No.* 842 ; *Reeve, l.c. f.* 798. Shell broadly umbilicated, depressly semi-globose, rather solid, regularly spirally-furrowed, and strengthened with strong longitudinal plaits, distantly placed, dilated into sub-triangular, membranaceous, deciduous lamellæ, black-rufous ; spire short, convex, above depressed ; whorls 5½, convex, the last tapering, generally inclining downwards ; aperture small, a little oblique, lunately circular ; peristome simple, straight, margins closely united.

Diam., greatest, ˈ17 ; least, ˈ16 ; height, ˈ1.   (Pfr.)
Auckland (Sinclair and Greenwood.)
Distinguished by its spiral grooves.

B. Upper surface flat or concave.

P. obnubila, *Reeve, l.c., No.* 792, *pl.* 130 ; *Pfr. vol.* 3, *p.* 633 ;
vol. 5, *p.* 164, *No.* 844 ; *Helix sigma, Pfr.* Shell umbilicated, depressed,
intensely fuscous, throughout decussated with impressed spiral furrows
and oblique striæ ; spire depressed ; suture distinct ; whorls 5, flatly-
convex, the last rounded ; aperture lunar; peristome simple, acute.
Height, ˈ14. (Pfr.)
New Zealand.
Distinguished by its spiral grooves.

P. anguiculus, *Reeve, l.c., No.* 802, *pl.* 131 ; *Pfr., M.H.V., vol.*
3, *p.* 634 ; *vol.* 5, *p.* 173, *No.* 920. Shell umbilicated, depressed,
sub-discoidal, brownish, adorned with sub-remote rufous streaks ;
suture of the spire impressed ; whorls 5, rotundate, longitudinally very
finely striated with rib-like striæ ; aperture sub-circular ; peristome
thin, margins closely united.
Height, ˈ1. (Pfr.)
New Zealand.

P. ide, *Gray ; P.Z.S.,* 1849, *p.* 166 ; *Pfr,, M.H.V., vol.* 3, *p.* 108 ;
vol. 5, *p.* 172, *No.* 911 ; *Reeve, f.* 789. Shell umbilicated, depressed,
thin, arcuately-ribbed, pilose, pale horny, radiated with brown ; spire
flat, sub-impressed in the middle ; suture impressed ; whorls 5½, rather
convex, slowly increasing, the last somewhat rounded, not descending ;
umbilicus moderate, pervious ; aperture slightly oblique, rotundately-
lunar ; peristome simple, straight, margins very remote, columellar
margin short, greatly arched.
Diam., greatest, ˈ32 ; least, ˈ28 ; height, almost ˈ16. (Pfr.)
Auckland (Major Greenwood.)

P. eta, *Pfeiffer ; P.Z.S.,* 1851 ; *M.H.V., vol.* 3, *p.* 107 ; *vol.* 5, *p.*
173, *No.* 922 ; *H. corniculum* ; *Reeve, f.* 826. Shell umbilicated,
depressed, finely striated with rib-like striæ, silky, waxen ; spire flattish ;
suture impressed ; whorls 4, slightly convex, the last more broad, not
descending, depressed ; umbilicus rather broad, perspective ; aperture a
little oblique, lunately sub-circular ; peristome simple, straight, margins
closely united.
Diam., greatest, ˈ12 ; least, ˈ1 ; height, ˈ05. (Pfr.)
New Zealand (Strange.)

P. zeta, *Pfeiffer ; P.Z.S.,* 1851 ; *M.H.V., vol.* 3, *p.* 109 ; *vol.* 5, *p.*
173, *No.* 919 ; *Helix infecta, Reeve, f.* 808. Shell very broadly umbilicated, depressed, sub-discoidal, rather solid, somewhat closely strongly
plaited, not shining, pale yellowish, tessellated with large chestnut spots ;
spire flat, submersed in the middle ; suture deep ; whorls 5½, very
narrow, convex, rather swollen, the last not descending, somewhat

tapering, strengthened beneath with fine plaits ; aperture a little oblique, smallish lunately circular; peristome simple, straight, margins closely united.

Diam., greatest, ·14 ; least, ·13 ; height, ·06. (Pfr.)
New Zealand (Strange.)

Sub-Genus, *Flammulina—Martens.*

Periphery rounded ; whorls rapidly increasing, generally painted with brown waved stripes.

A. Edge of the aperture thickened at the base.
a. Imperforate.

P. venulata, *Pfeiffer; P.Z.S.,* 1857, *p.* 108 ; *M.H.V., vol.* 4, *p.* 163 ; *vol.* 5, *p.* 232, *No.* 1395. Shell imperforated, depressed, thin, closely plicately-striated, downy, variegated with corneous and reddish markings, disposed in streaks and spots ; spire slightly elevated ; whorls 4½, convex, gradually increasing, the last not descending, impressed in the middle of the base ; aperture vertical, elongately-lunar; peristome simple, right margin straight, basal margin somewhat reflexed, columellar margin bent downwards, subcallous, adnate.

Diam., greatest, ·24 ; least, ·2 ; height, ·12. (Pfr.)
New Zealand.

b. Umbilicate.

P. portia, *Gray; P.Z.S.,* 1849, *p.* 165 ; *Pfr., M.H.V., vol.* 3, *p.* 154; *vol.* 5, *p.* 246, *No.* 1505 ; *Reeve, f.* 806. Shell umbilicated, depressed, thinnish, sculptured with closely-set elevated, sub-arcuated plaits, covered sparsely with rather rigid hairs, horny, variegated with rufous spots and streaks ; spire short, convex; whorls 5½, rather convex, regularly increasing, the last somewhat inflated beneath the suture, not descending anteriorly, sub-compressed at the base about a moderate, pervious umbilicus ; aperture oblique, rotundly-lunar ; peristome simple, margins nearly united, the upper part arcuately protracted below the insertion, the basal part shortly reflexed, ascending obliquely to the umbilicus.

Diam., greatest, ·32 ; least, ·28 ; height, ·16. (Pfr.)
Auckland (Greenwood and Sinclair.)
Dunedin (F.W.H.)
I have followed Adams in including this and other species in the genus Patula, but I believe that most of them will be found to belong to the family Stenopidæ.

B. Edge of the aperture simple.
a. Imperforate.

P. omega, *Pfeiffer; P.Z.S.,* 1849, *p.* 127 ; *M.H.V., vol.* 3, *p.* 33 ; *vol.* 5, *p.* 54, *No.* 63 ; *Helix compessivoluta, Reeve; l.c., f.* 791. Shell imperforate, depressed, rather smooth, covered with a fuscous-horny epidermis ; spire slightly elevated, reddish on the crown ; whorls

4, flattish, rapidly increasing, the last hardly more rounded at the base, impressed in the middle; aperture oblique, lunately-oval; peristome simple, straight, basal margin slightly arched, reflexed above, adnate in the umbilical region.

Diam., greatest, ·38; least, ·28; height, ·14. (Pfr.)

New Zealand.

Wellington (F.W.H.)

P. tullia, *Gray; P.Z.S.*, 1849, *p.* 165: *Helix Tullia, Pfr.*, *M.H.V., vol.* 3, *p.* 35; *vol.* 5, *p.* ·55, *No.* 75; *Reeve; f.* 1460. Shell imperforate, depressed, thin, closely-ribbed, diaphanous, tessellated with pale-yellow and rufous; spire slightly convex; whorls 5, rather convex, narrow, the last not descending, obscurely angled at the periphery, impressed in the middle at the base; aperture sub-vertical, lunar; peristome simple, straight, basal margin slightly arcuated.

Diam., greatest, ·18; least, ·16; height, ·08. (Pfr.)

Auckland (Greenwood.)

b. Umbilicate.

P. lambda, *Pfeiffer; P.Z.S.*, 1851; *M.H.V., vol.* 3, *p.* 84; *vol.* 5, *p.* 143, *No.* 653; *Helix ignijlua, Reeve, f.* 774. Shell umbilicated, sub-conoidly-depressed, thin, somewhat smooth, now and then sculptured with spiral striæ, slightly shining, diaphanous, fulvous, chestnut-spotted; spire sub-conoidal, rather obtuse; whorls 5, rather convex, the last not descending, obscurely angled at the periphery, convex beneath; umbilicus moderat, conical; aperture oblique. lunately-rotund, within shining; peristome simple, straight, margins closely united, columellar margin sub-dilated above, expanded.

Diam., greatest, ·51; least, ·43; height, ·28. (Pfr.)

New Zealand.

P. biconcava, *Pfeiffer; P.Z.S.*, 1851; *M.H.V., vol.* 3, *p.* 109; *vol.* 5, *p.* 173, *No.* 917; *Reeve, f.* 810. Shell umbilicated, depressed closely arcuately-ribbed, opaque, horny-yellowish, rufously streaked; spire concave; whorls 4½-5, narrow, the last but one convex, the last rounded, not descending; umbilicus broad, perspective; aperture sub-vertical, higher than broad, lunar; peristome simple, straight, right margin sub-arcuated in front.

Diam., greatest, ·2; least, ·17; height, ·08. (Pfr.)

New Zealand (Strange.)

Wellington (F.W.H.)

Sub-Family— Vitrininæ.

Animal too large entirely to enter the shell. Mantle margin more or less produced, reflected over the sides, or sometimes entirely covering the shell. Tail often obliquely truncate, but not furnished with a caudal gland. Shell thin, usually horny and transparent: aperture very wide.

Genus, VITRINA—Draparnaud.

Mantle with the front edge greatly extended, and covering the neck often as far as the tentacles. Tail very short, shell pellucid; whorls

few, rapidly increasing, the last dilated; peristome thin, simple, acute. Animal too large entirely to enter the shell.
World wide.
In the type species the lingual teeth are 100 rows, of 75 each; the marginal teeth with a single long, recurved, apex.

V. dimidiata, *Pfeiffer; P.Z.S.,* 1851, *Cat. Pul. Brit. Mus.,* 71; *Reeve,* 72. Shell much depressed, periphery ovate, very thin, sculptured with minute arcuate striæ, silky, shining, pale horn colour; spire nearly flat; whorls two and a quarter, which are open beneath, and with a narrow membranaceous edge; aperture horizontal, as large as the whole shell; peristome simple, with regularly curved margins.
Height, ·05; greatest breadth, ·2; least breadth, ·14. (Pfr.)

V. zebra, *Le Guill; Rev. Zool,* 1842, 136; *II. zebra, Pfr., Cat. Pulmonata in Brit. Mus.,* 70; *M.II.V.,* 2., *p.* 809, 5. *p.* 20. Shell rounded, umbilicated, depressed-convex above, more convex beneath, hyaline, ornamented with obliquely wavy flamelets of white and chestnut; whorls 4, thinly striated above; aperture rather dilated; umbilicus very small.
Axis, ·2; breadth, ·3. (Pfr.)
Auckland Islands only.

Genus, DAUDEBARDIA—Hartmann.

Eye-peduncles short; tentacles rudimentary; pulmonary orifice on the right border of the mantle, a little posterior; body elongated, greatly developed. Shell on the hind part of the body, perforate, horny, depressed, paucispiral, horizontally and rapidly involute, last whorl very large; aperture oblique, very wide. Animal too large entirely to enter the shell.
Europe.

D. novoseelandica, *Pfeiffer; M.II.V., vol.* 5, *p.* 10, *No.* 10. Shell imperforated, greatly depressed, ambit oval, rather solid, sculptured with distinct striæ of growth and radiant impressed lines, fulvous; spire small, occupying one-eighth of the entire length of shell; whorls, 2½, the last laterally sub-compressed; columella thickly callous above.
Height, ·1; length, .4; diameter, ·27. (Pfr.)
Waikato.

Genus, HYALINA—Ferus.

Tentacles short; lateral teeth of tongue aculeate.
Mantle thickened, and slightly reflected; tail obliquely truncated. Shell depressed, vitreous, shining, umbilicated; whorls regularly increasing, the last not descending at the apertute; aperture rotundately lunar; peristome thin, straight.
Eupope. N. America. W. Indies.

H. corneo-fulva *Pfeiffer Malak. Bl.,* viii., 1861; *M.II.V. vol.* 5, *p.* 145, *No.* 673. Shell umbilicated, sub-orbicular, depressed, thin, faintly finely striated, most distinct at the suture, shining, pellucid, horny-fulvous; spire slightly elevated; suture impressed; whorls 5, rather convex, regularly increasing, the last depressly-rotund; umbilicus narrow, pervious, scarcely exceeding one-sixth of the diameter; aperture a little oblique, rotundly lunar; peristome simple, straight, margins remote, columellar margin accurately bent downwards, slightly dilated above.

Diam., greatest, ·4; least, ·32; height, ·15. (Pfr.)
Bay of Islands, New Zealand (Hochstetter.)

H. novaræ, *Pfeiffer; Malak Bl.*, viii., 1861, *p.* 148; *M.H.V., vol.* 5, *p.* 169, *No.* 882. Shell somewhat narrowly umbilicated, depressed, thin, somewhat smooth, finely striated at the suture, pellucid, shining, pale, yellowish-horny; spire flat; suture simple, scarcely impressed; whorls 4, rather convex, gradually increasing, the last depressed, not descending; aperture somewhat greater, slightly oblique, lunar; peristome simple, straight, margins sub-converging, columellar margin above shortly expanded.

Diam., greatest, ·23; least, ·2; height, ·08. (Pfr.)
Bay of Islands, New Zealand (Hochstetter.)
N.B.—Very closely allied to *H. remota*, Benson, from St. Helena.

FAMILY—HELICIDÆ.

Lingual teeth in numerous straight transverse rows, equal, uniform, and with the edge-teeth serrated or dentate. Head well developed; mouth with a horny upper jaw; eye-peduncles and tentacles retractile under the skin. Margin of the mantle not extended, nor produced into lobes; pulmonary orifice on the right side, under the edge of the shell. Foot elongated, not glanduliferous. Orifice of reproductive organs at the base of the right eye-peduncle. Aperture closed by an epiphragm during hybernation.

Sub-Family—Succininæ.

Tentacles short and thick; foot broad. Shell thin, horny, ovate, or oblong; spire small; aperture large, oval; columella simple, not truncate anteriorly; peristome acute.

Genus, SUCCINEA—Draparnaud.

Animal nearly retractile within the shell. Shell imperforate, oval, horny; spire short, last whorl large; aperture wide, oblong; columella simple, acute; peristome simple, acute.
World wide; sub-aquatic in habit.

S. tomentosa, *Pfeiffer. P.Z.S.,* 1854, *p.* 297; *M.H.V., vol.* 4. *p.* 814; *vol.* 5, *p.* 33, *No.* 108; *Reeve, Conch Icon., No.* 81. Shell oblongly-conical, thin, covered with downy hairs, not shining, pellucid, pale horny; spire conical, acute; whorls 3, the second convex, the last three quarters of the entire length of the shell, attenuated at the base; columella sub-callous, slightly plaited, arcuated; aperture a little oblique, sharply oval, somewhat incumbent; peristome simple, rather expanded.

Length, ·3; diam., ·2; height, ·15. Aperture, length, ·23; breadth in the middle, ·16.(Pfr.)
New Zealand (Strange.)

C

Sub-Family—Achatininœ.

Shell more or less conoidal, solid, the last whorl usually very ventricose, aperture wide ; columella usually more or less truncate at the fore part ; outer lip generally simple and acute.

Genus, TORNATELLINA—Beck.

Shell imperforate, ovate or sub-trochiform ; aperture semi-lunar ; columella tortuous, truncated ; margins unequal, the columellar uni-lamellated, the external plicated within.

Europe. S. America. Polynesia.

T. novoseelandica, *Pfeiffer ; P.Z.S.,* 1851 ; *M.H.V., vol.* 3, *p.* 524 ; *vol.* 6, *p.* 263, *No.* 22. *Elasmatina reclusiana, Gray, P.Z.S.,* 1849, *p.* 167, *not of Petit.* Shell oblongly-turreted, thin, smooth, shining, fulvous-horny; spire turreted ; rather acute; whorls 5, somewhat convex, the last one-third of the length of shell, rounded at the base ; parietal fold deep, moderate ; columella callous, white, upper portion torturously-subtruncated ; aperture hardly oblique, somewhat ear-shaped ; peristome thin, acute.

Length, ·13 ; breadth, ·07 ; aperture, length, ·07. (Pfr.)
New Zealand (Strange.)

Sub-Family—Buliminœ.

Eye-peduncles and tentacles well developed ; foot elongate, pointed behind. Shell ovoid, conoidal, or turreted ; aperture longer than wide ; columella arcuated, not truncate anteriorly.

Genus, PLACOSTYLUS—Beck.

Shell imperforate, oblong-conic, rugosely striated, last whorl a little shorter than the spire ; aperture oblong-oval or irregular ; columella tortuous, arcuately plicate ; peristome thick, reflexly expanded, the margins united by a shining tuberculated callus, the columellar dilated, appressed.

Australia. New Caledonia.

P. bovinus, *Bruguière ; Coll., No.* 368 ; *Petit Journ. Conch.,* 1853 ; *Crosse, Journ. Conch, vol.* xii., 1864 ; *Pfr., M.H.V., vol.* 6, *p.* 82, *No.* 721 ; *Bulimus Shongii, Lesson, Voy. de la Coq. : Reeve, Conch, l.c. f.* 159 ; *Pfr., M.H.V., vol.* 2, *p.* 140 : *A. auris-bovina, Lamark ; L. fibratus Martyn.* Shell imperforate, oblongly-conical, solid, rugosely-striated, covered with an olivaceous-rufous epidermis, banded by whitish at the suture : spire conical, rather acute ; whorls 7, convex, the last shorter than the spire, sub-compressed at the base ; columella arcuated ; aperture oblongly-oval, within cherry-red, sub-caniculated at the base ; peristome very thick, armed at the base with a moderate tuberculous callus, margins united by a callus, columellar margin dilated, prominent.

Length, 2·55 ; diameter, 1·05 : aperture, long. 1·1 : broad, ·5. (Pfr.)
Hokianga to North Cape.

P. novoseelandicus, *Pfeiffer : Malak. Bl.,* viii., 1861. *p.* 149 ; *Crosse, Journ. Conch.,* xii., 1864 ; *Pfr., M.H.V., vol.* 6, *p.* 83, *No.* 722.

Shell imperforate, ovately oblong, solid, irregularly rugosely striated, fulvous-brown, occasionally streaked with chestnut ; spire ovately-conical, flesh-coloured on the upper portion, apex rather acute ; suture ragged, widely margined with white ; whorls 6, moderately convex, the last equalling the length of the spire, sub-attenuated at the base ; columella vertical, scarcely torturous ; aperture sub-vertical, rhomboidly-semioval, within yellowish-white ; peristome thick, white, margins united by a white callus, the right margin rather expanded, slightly arcuated, within the upper part slightly sinuous, basal and columellar margins dilated.

Length, 3·05 ; diam., 1·22 ; aperture within, length, 1·37 ; breadth, ·58. (Pfr.)

Wangaruru, near Bay of Islands, New Zealand (Hochstetter.)

Note.—Eggs testaceous, oval, length, ·27 ; young shell, sub-perforate, thin, pale-horny.

P. antipodum, *Gray; Dieff. Trav., vol. 1, p.* 247 ; *Revue Zool., 1844, p.* 373 ; *Pfr., M.H.V., vol.* 2, *p.* 227 ; *vol.* 6, *p.* 153, *No.* 1304 ; *Voy. Erebus and Terror, pl.* 1 *f,* 5 *g.* Shell oblong, imperforate, smooth, pale fuscous, covered with pale-fuscous opaque epidermis, variegated profusely with dark lines, principally at the suture, apex obtuse, rubicund ; whorls rather convex; aperture ——; peristome ——? ; specimen not adult ; whorls 4, the last 1 inch in diam. ; axis, 1 inch (Gray.)

Bream Head and Whangarei.

Probably the young of the last species. Said by Gray to be allied to *B. fulgetans,* Brod, from the Philippine Islands.

Sub-Family— Pupinæ.

Tentacles rudimentary, minute, or entirely wanting. Foot short, obtuse, or pointed behind. Shell cylindrical, or fusiform ; whorls numerous, narrow, equal ; aperture small, frequently with elongated teeth or thin laminæ ; peristome generally non-continuous.

Genus, PUPA—Draparnaud.

Shell rimate or perforate, cylindrical or oblong ; aperture rounded, often toothed ; margins distant, mostly united by a callous lamina. Animal with a short foot, pointed behind ; lower tentacles short.

Widely distributed.

P. novoseelandica, *Pefiffer; P.Z.S.,* 1851 ; *M.H.V., vol.* 3, *p.* 530 ; *vol.* 6, *p.* 299, *No.* 76 ; *Reeve, Conch, l.c. f.* 126. Shell perforated, sub-cylindrical, thin, obliquely closely ribbed, deep fuscous, variegated with straw-coloured spots, principally about the impressed suture ; spire as it proceeds upwards scarcely attenuated, apex sub-rotund ; whorls 7½, rather convex, the last dot reaching to one-third of the entire length of the shell, rounded ; aperture sub-vertical, semi-circular, toothless ; peristome, simple, straight, margins remote, columellar margin slightly dilated above.

Length, ·18 ; diam., ·08 ; aperture, length, ·05. (Pfr.)

New Zealand (Strange.)

Sub-Family—Helicinæ.

Shell globular, or convex ; spire short, the last whorl much larger than the others, composing nearly the whole shell ; umbilicus covered or open; aperture regular, semi-lunar, generally without teeth; peristome thickened or reflexed.

Genus, HELIX—Linnæus.

Shell imperforate, or with the umbilicus covered, more or less globose; whorls convex, the last large, ventricose, deflexed at the aperture; aperture lunately orbicular; peristome patulous or reflexed, columellar margin dilated, callous.

Sub-Genus, Rhagada—Albers.

Shell imperforated, somewhat globose, rather solid, striated, whitish, banded; whorls 4½-5½, regularly increasing, rather convex, the last slightly descending in front, convex at the base; aperture exceedingly oblique, lunar; peristome lipped within, somewhat expanded.

H. reinga, *Gray; Unpub. List N.Z. Shells, pl.* 1, *fig.* 11, 12; *Pfr., M.H.V., vol.* 1, *p.* 289; *vol.* 5, *p.* 302, *No.* 1965; *Reeve, f* 772. Shell perforated, perforation covered, globosely-depressed, rather solid, obliquely finely striated, whitish, adorned with a single chestnut-coloured band, and with many orange-coloured lines; spire sub-elevated; whorls 5½, rather convex, gradually increasing, the last convex beneath, descending anteriorly; aperture very oblique, narrow, sub-triangularly lunar; peristome shortly expanded, within white-lipped, columellar margin straightish, obscurely and obtusely unidentated.
Diam., greatest, ·59; least, ·51; height, ·4. (Pfr.)
New Zealand.

Sub-Genus, Rhytida—Albers.

Shell umbilicated, thin, convexly-depressed, undulatingly wrinkled or striated; spire slightly elevated; whorls 4-5, flattish; umbilicus broad, funnel-shaped; aperture oblongly-ovate; peristome simple, sharp, margins converging.

H. greenwoodi, *Gray; P.Z.S.,* 1849, *p.* 165; *Pfr., M.H.V., vol.* 3, *p.* 156; *vol.* 5, *p.* 247, *No.* 1520; *Reeve, f.* 434. Shell umbilicated, convexly-depressed, thinnish, throughout very closely rugosely-granulated, slightly shining, fuscous, with an olive-green tinge; spire smallish, convex, rather obtuse; suture impressed; whorls 4, rather convex, rapidly increasing, the last large, strengthened at the periphery with many elevated, obtuse, backwardly-descending bands, anteriorly descending, a little convex at the base, sub-compressed at the entrance of the chestnut-coloured, funnel-shaped umbilicus; aperture very oblique, oblongly-oval, within shining, whitish; peristome simple, margins closely united, superior portion straight, bent backwards, inferior portion thickish, dilated and reflexed towards the columella.
Diam., greatest, ·93; least, ·75; height, ·47. (Pfr.)
Auckland.

H. dunniæ, *Gray; Ann. and Mag. Nat. Hist., vol.* 6, 1841, *p.* 317; *Pfr., M.H.V., vol.* 1, *p.* 207; *vol.* 5, *p.* 256, *No.* 1587; *Reeve, f.* 425; *Voy. Erebus and Terror, Moll., pl.* 1, *f.* 7. Shell umbilicated, depressed, fuscous, keeled, irregularly granularly striated; spire slightly elevated, obtuse; whorls 4, flattened, the last slightly descending anteriorly, convex beneath, compressed around a moderate, funnel-shaped umbilicus ; aperture very oblique, irregular, transversely oblong, laterally spread out ; peristome simple, superior margin depressed, dilated in front, columellar margin shortly reflexed.

Diam., greatest, ·95 ; least, ·79 ; height, ·43. (Pfr.)

Nelson. Bay of Islands.

Sub-Genus, Thalassia—Albers.

Shell scarcely perforated, orbicularly conoidal, thin, pellucid ; whorls 5-6, slowly increasing, the last angulated or carinated, the base at the perforation impressed ; aperture diagonal or slightly oblique, more or less angularly lunar ; peristome simple, sharp, columellar margin somewhat reflected.

A. Shell trochiform.

a. Umbilicus narrow.

H. regularis, *Pfeiffer; P.Z.S.*, 1854, *p.* 50 ; *M.H.V.*, *vol.* 4, *p.* 33 ; *vol.* 5, *p.* 86, *No.* 277; *Reeve, Conch, Icon.,f.* 1259. Shell perforated, the perforation partially covered, regularly coniform, thin, very minutely striated, pellucid, viscously glossly, luteous, horny ; spire conical, rather acute ; suture scarcely impressed ; whorls 6, flattish, slowly increasing, the last not descending, acutely keeled, flattish beneath ; aperture diagonal, depressly-securiformed ; peristome simple, straight, margins remote, columellar margin dilated above, sub-adnate. ·

Diam, ·12 ; height, ·12. (Pfr.)

New Zealand.

H. heldiana, *Pfeiffer*; *P.Z.S.*, 1851 ; *M.H.V.*, *vol.* 3, *p.* 60 ; *vol.* 5, *p.* 87, *No.* 279. Shell perforated, minute, trochiformed, thin, smooth, shining, fulvous-horny ; spire conical, rather obtuse ; suture impressed ; whorls, 5½, somewhat convex, the last keeled, not descending, slightly more convex beneath ; aperture slightly oblique, depressed, angularly lunar ; peristome simple, straight, margins remote, columellar margin very shortly somewhat reflexed.

Diam., ·08 ; height. ·06. (Pfr).

New Zealand (Strange.)

H. conella, *Pfeiffer, Mal. Blatt.* viii., 1861, *p.* 147 ; *Mon. Hel.* v., *p.* 86. Shell sub-perforated, conoidal, carinated, thinnish, sub-acutely striated, minutely tessellated with horn colour and reddish markings ; spire convexly conoidal, with the apex rather acute ; suture marginated at the periphery, and slightly convex at the base ; aperture oblique, sub-angularly lunar ; peristome simple, straight, margins remote, briefly reflexed and arched over at the columellar margin.

Diam., ·18 ; height, ·11. (Pfr.)

Kakepuku (Hochstetter.)

H. pœcilosticta, *Pfeiffer; P.Z.S.*, 1851 ; *M.H.V.*, *vol.* 3, *p.* 59 ; *vol.* 5, *p.* 89, *No.* 301 ; *Reeve, f.* 815. Shell perforated, trochiformed, thin, closely plaited, fulvous, rufous-spotted, diaphanous ; spire convexly-conical, apex rather acute ; suture margined ; whorls 5¼, narrow, somewhat convex, the last keeled, not descending, flat beneath ; aperture

a little oblique, depressed, angularly lunar; peristome simple, straight, columellar margin ascending, callously-reflexed.
Diam., ·16; height, ·13. (Pfr.)
New Zealand.

H. erigone, *Gray; P.Z.S.*, 1849, *p.* 165; *Helix Erigone, Pfr., M.H.V., vol.* 3, *p.* 60; *vol.* 5, *p.* 86, *No.* 278; *Reeve. f.* 817. Shell perforated, conical, thin, smooth, keeled, pellucid, fulvous, obscurely streaked with red flame-like markings; spire conical, rather acute; whorls 6-7, slightly convex, the last flattish beneath the sub-acute keel; aperture a little oblique, depressed, sub-angularly lunar; peristome simple, straight, columellar margin short, sub-callous, rather reflexed.
Diam., greatest, ·1; height ·08. (Pfr.)
Auckland (Major Greenwood.)

b. Umbilicus broad.

H. alpha, *Pfeiffer; P.Z.S.*, 1851; *M.H.V., vol.* 3, *p.* 112; *vol.* 5, *p.* 183, *No.* 981; *Helix stipulata, Reeve, f.* 813. Shell umbilicated, conical, keeled, obliquely finely striated and distantly lamellarly-ribbed, variegated with brown and yellow streaks; spire rather convexly-conical, apex rather obtuse; whorls 5½, slightly convex, the last not descending, acutely denticulately keeled, flat at the base, sub-angulated at the moderate, pervious umbilicus; aperture diagonal, somewhat hatchet-shaped; peristome simple, straight, upper margin short, basal margin arcuated, sub-vertically ascending towards the columella.
Diam., greatest, ·17 : least, ·16; height, ·12. (Pfr.)
New Zealand (Strange.)

H. beta, *Pfeiffer; P.Z.S.*, 1854; *M.H.V., vol.* 3, *p.* 112; *vol.* 5, *p.* 183, *No.* 982; *H. barbulata, Reeve, f.* 814. Shell umbilicated, trochiformed, keeled, thin, arcuately strongly plaited, fulvous, broadly spotted with chestnut; spire elevated, convexly-conical. rather acute : suture margined; whorls 7, narrow, flattish, the last somewhat receding, not descending, ciliated towards the keel, slightly convex at the base ; umbilicus narrow; aperture oblique, angularly-lunar; peristome simple, straight, basal margin regularly arcuated.
Diam., greatest, ·13; height, ·13. (Pfr.)
New Zealand (Strange.)
Queenstown, Dunedin. (F.W.II.)

B. Shell turbinate.
a. Umbilicus narrow.

H. ophelia, *Pfeiffer; P.Z.S.*, 1854, *p.* 146; *M.H.V., vol.* 4, *p.* 29; *vol.* 5, *p.* 80, *No.* 241; *Reeve, f.* 1345. Shell perforated, turbinately depressed, thin, under the lens irregularly marked with hair-like striæ, not shining, diaphanous, horny, marked with narrow reddish streaks; spire rather convexly conoidal, crown small, fine, somewhat acute; whorls 5, flattish. rather prominent. gradually increasing, the last not descending, sub-angular, flattish at the base; aperture oblique, rotundly-lunar, within shining ; peristome simple, straight, margins slightly converging, basal margin rather constricted, columellar margin bent downwards, near the very narrow and pervious umbilicus, shortly reflexed.

Diam., greatest, ·32 ; least, ·28 ; height, ·18. (Pfr.)

New Zealand (Hochstetter). Australia (Pfr.) Cape York, North Australia (Edwards.) Cox, Austr. Land Shells, 1863, p. 35.

Probably a mistake in the New Zealand habitat.

H. zealandiæ, *Gray ; Dieff. Trav., vol.* 1, *p.* 247 ; *Helix Zealandæ, Pfr., M.H.V., vol.* 1, *p.* 81 ; *vol.* 5, *p.* 85, *No.* 226 ; *Reeve, f.* 780. Shell perforated, depressed, turbiniformed, pale horny, pellucid, variegated with rufous spots, minutely finely striated ; spire convex ; whorls 5, flattened, the last keeled, convex ; umbilicus deep ; peristome simple, acute.

Diam., greatest, ·38 ; least, ·36 ; height, ·22. (Pfr.)

Auckland (Major Greenwood.)

H. fatua, *Pfeiffer ; P.Z.S.,* 1857, *p.* 107 ; *M.H.V., vol.* 4, *p.* 30 ; *vol.* 5, *p.* 80, *No.* 243. Shell perforated, turbinated, thinnish, irregularly finely striated, somewhat shining, fulvous ; spire conoidal, rather acute ; whorls 5-5½, moderately convex, the last not descending, periphery sub-carinated, rather convex at the base ; aperture a little oblique, lunar ; peristome simple, straight, columellar margin somewhat rigidly bent downwards.

Diam., greatest, ·2 ; least, ·10 ; height, ·9. (Pfr.)

Taupiri, New Zealand (Hochstetter.)

H. antipoda, *Homb. and Jacq., Voy. Pole Sud, Zool.,* v., *p.* 18 ; *pl.* 6, *f.* 13-16 ; *Pfr., M.H.V., vol.* 4, *p.* 111 ; *vol.* 5, *p.* 182, *No.* 972. Shell narrowly umbilicated, globosely-conical, above striated, shining, grey, rufous-streaked ; spire conoidal, rather acute ; whorls 5½, flattish, the last keeled, slightly descending, convex at the base ; aperture hatchet-formed ; peristome simple, straight.

Diam., greatest, ·32 ; least, ·28. (Pfr.)

Auckland Islands.

b. Umbilicus broad.

H. aucklandica, *Le Guill ; Revue Zool.,* 1842, *p.* 140 ; *Pfr., M.H.V., vol.* 1, *p.* 119 ; *vol.* 5, *p.* 182, *No.* 973. Shell orbicularly-conoidal, thin, small, pellucid, shining, yellowish-brown ; whorls 6, depressly sub-convex, striated, evenly painted with longitudinal, equidistant, scarlet spots, the last keeled, above marked with transverse, obscure fine striæ, beneath more convex, spotless, deeply umbilicated ; aperture sub-rotund, anteriorly sub-angulated ; peristome acute, fragile.

Diam., ·28 ; height, ·16. (Pfr.)

Auckland Islands.

H. sciadium, *Pfeiffer ; P.Z.S.,* 1857, *p.* 108 ; *M.H.V., vol.* 4, *p.* 112 ; *vol.* 5, *p.* 183, *No.* 979. Shell umbilicated, conoidly semi-globose, rather solid, sub-arcuately striated, fulvous, obscurely variegated with reddish ; spire convexly-conoidal, rather acute at the apex ; suture margined; whorls 5½, slightly convex, the last not descending, acutely keeled at the periphery, at the base a little more convex; umbilicus almost equalling one quarter of the diameter; aperture slightly oblique, angularly lunar; peristome simple, straight, columellar margin slightly expanded.

Diam., greatest, ·21 ; least, ·2 ; height, ·12. (Pfr.)
New Zealand.

c. Imperforate.

H. irradiata, *Gould; U.S. Ex. Ep.* xii., *p.* 34, *J.* 35, *Pfeiff.. M.II.V., I. p.* 29, & v., *p.* 51 ; *Cox, Aust. Land Shells, p.* 35. Shell imperforate, conically-globose, thin, whitish, above radiately tessellated with purple, and striated with closely set acute lines of growth, below rounded ; whorls 6, convex, the last somewhat angular ; aperture transverse, lunate ; peristome acute, incurved towards the columella, and scarcely reflexed.

Diam., ·25 ; height, ·37 inch.
The above description is taken from Gould. Pfeiffer states that it neither agrees with the figure, nor with the dimensions (Cox.)

Gould appears to have given both Australia and the Bay of Islands as the habitat in different publications. It has not been recognised since.

Sub-Genus—

Like Thalassia, but without keel. Turbinate.

H. kivi, *Gray; Dieff. Trav., vol.* 1, *p.* 262 ; *Helix Kivi, Pfr., M.II.V., vol.* 1, *p.* 192 ; *vol.* 5, *p.* 232, *No.* 1394 ; *Reeve, f.* 794 ; *Voy. Erebus and Terror, Moll. Pl.,* 1 *f.* 1. Shell imperforated, turbinated, white, thin, obliquely closely striated, adorned with short, irregular, oblique, purple-brown streaks ; spire sub-conical, obtuse ; whorls 6, flattish, the last rounded, convex at the base, white, smooth ; aperture broad, lunar; peristome simple, straight, columellar margin somewhat reflexed.

Diam., greatest, ·4 ; least, ·36 ; height, ·32. (Pfr.)
Auckland (Major Greenwood.)

H. granum, *Pfeiffer; P.Z.S.,* 1857, *p.* 107 ; *M.H.V., vol.* 4, *p.* 20; *vol.* 5, *p.* 63, *No.* 143. Shell perforated, turbinately-globose, thin, very closely and finely striately-ribbed, pale horny, irregularly variegated with reddish markings ; spire conoidal, slightly acute ; whorls 5½, convex, the last not descending, rather swollen near the aperture ; aperture slightly oblique, broadly lunar; peristome simple, straight, margins sub-converging, columellar margin slightly patulous.

Diam., greatest, ·16 ; least, ·14 ; height, ·12. (Pfr.)
New Zealand.
Wellington (F.W.H.)

H. guttula, *Pfeiffer; Zeit. f. Malak.,* 1853, *p.* 53 ; *M.II.V., vol.* 3, *p.* 626; *vol.* 5, *p.* 55, *No.* 74 ; *Reeve, Conch, Ic., f.* 1040. Shell imperforate, convexly-depressed, thin, very smooth, shining, pellucid, fuscous-horny; spire vaulted over; suture inconsiderable, sub-marginated; whorls 5, rather convex, slowly increasing, the last rounded at the periphery, impressed in the middle beneath, callous ; aperture slightly oblique, lunar ; peristome simple, straight, acute, basal margin slightly arcuate, thickish at the columella.

Diam., greatest, ·2 ; least, ·19 ; height, ·1.   (Pfr.)
New Zealand.   Nicobar Islands (Zelebor.)
Preservation Inlet (F.W.H.)

Genus, LAOMA—Gray.

Shell scarcely perforated, turretedly-conical, smooth, shining, pellucid ; whorls 7, flat, the last carinated, flat at the base ; aperture depressedly-quadrangular, lamellated ; peristome simple, straight.
New Zealand only.

L. leimonias, *Gray ; P.Z.S.,* 1849, *p.* 167; *Helix Leimonias, Pfr., M.H.V., vol.* 3, *p.* 144 ; *vol.* 5, *p.* 221, *No.* 1321 ; *Reeve, f.* 820. Shell sub-imperforated, turretedly-conical, rather solid, smooth, shining, pellucid, pale horny, reddish spotted ; spire turreted, rather acute ; whorls 7, flat, the last acutely keeled, flat beneath ; aperture sub-vertical, depressly quadrangular, crowded with three strong white lamellæ, one on the wall of the aperture, two on the right margin ; peristome simple, straight.

Diam., ·09 ; height, ·1.   (Pfr.)
New Zealand (Strange).
Auckland (Major Greenwood).

FAMILY—STENOPIDÆ.

Teeth numerous, nearly uniform, on a very broad lingual band. Body spiral, distinct from the foot.   Eye penduncles, and tentacles retractile under the skin.   Mantle produced into lobes at the fore part ; respiratory orifice on the right side.   Foot long and narrow, abruptly truncated behind, and furnished with a distinct mucous, caudal gland.

Genus, PARYPHANTA—Albers.

Shell widely umbilicated, depressed, covered with a thick, shining epidermis involving the peristome ; spire flat, whorls few, the last tumid, anteriorly deflexed ; umbilicus perspective ; aperture oblique, lunately oval ; peristome simple, inflexed.
Australia and S. America.

P. busbyi, *Gray ; Ann. Nat. Hist., vol.* 6, *p.* 317 ; *Pfr., M.H.V., vol.* 1, *p.* 109 ; *vol.* 5, *p.* 48, *No.* 1 ; *Reeve, f.* 380 ; *Voy. Erebus and Terror, pl.* 1, *f.* 4 ; *Chenu, fig.* 3492. Shell broadly umbilicated, depressed, sub-discoidal, opaque, white, covered with a thick, glabrous, shining, deep green coloured epidermis, which overhangs the peristome; spire flat, sub-rugose ; whorls 4½, slightly convex, the last smooth, deflexed anteriorily, depressed ; umbilicus broad, perspective ; aperture

D

obliquely lunate-oval, within shining-blue; peristome simple, inflexed
throughout.
Diam., greatest, 2·6; least. 2·1 : height, 1·14. (Pfr.)
Northern part of the North Island. Wanganui (?.)
Allied to *P. atramentaria*, from Victoria.

P. hochstetteri, *Pfeiffer; M.H.V., vol.* 5, *p.* 48, *No.* 2. Shell
umbilicated, depressed, slightly solid, irregularly plaited, and somewhat
granulated by impressed, close, oblique lines, viscidly shining, fulvous,
ornamented above with thickly-set, undulating, chestnut-coloured lines ;
spire scarcely elevated, with the crown thin, obtuse ; whorls 5½, slightly
convex, the last depressedly-rotundate, sub-angulated at the periphery,
irregularly hollowed beneath, more shining, bound with broader chestnut-coloured bands ; umbilicus moderate, oblique, not pervious; aperture very oblique, lunar; peristome somewhat inflexed, straight, anteriorly
sub-membranaceous, margins joined by a white callus.
Diam., greatest, 2·55; least, 2·2 ; height, 1·1. (Pfr.)
Limestone Mountains, New Zealand (Hochstetter.)
Picton.
The structure of this shell evidently resembles that of P. Busbyi,
from which, however, it differs in the depressed form,--in the whorls
slowly increasing --in the markings and in the colour; and also in the
umbilicus. It is figured in Hochstetter's New Zealand, page 169.

P. urnula, *Pfeiffer; Helix urnula, Pfr., P.Z.S.,* 1854, *p.* 49 ;
Reeve, Conch. Icon., No. 1306, *pl.* 187 ; *Pfr., M.H.V., vol.* 4, *p.* 8 ; *vol.*
5, *p.* 48, *No.* 4. Shell perforated, the perforation covered, helicophan-
toidal, thin, sub-membranaceous, irregularly obliquely furrowed and
malleated, a little shining, pellucid, green fuscous; spire minute,
conoidal, obtuse, pale ; suture rather deep ; whorls 3, convex, very
rapidly increasing, the last large, sub-compressed from behind, somewhat
excavated at the base ; aperture oblique, truncatedly-oval, within very
shining ; peristome simple, obtuse, sub-inflexed, margins approximating,
columellar margin from above, reflexed, adnate.
Diam., greatest, ·63 ; least, ·5 ; height, ·35. (Pfr.)
Wellington. Clutha. (F.W.H.)
Egg calcareous, white, opake, length, ·2. (F.W.H.)

Sub-Genus, Amphidoxa—Albers.

Shell perforate, depressed, thin, pellucid, whorls rather convex,
rapidly increasing ; aperture very oblique, ample ; peristome simple,
acute, the margins united by a thin callus.

a. Shell imperforate.

P. phlogophora, *Pfeiffer: P.Z.S.,* 1849, *p.* 127 ; *M.H.V., vol.*
3, *p.* 34 ; *vol.* 5, *p.* 54, *No.* 65 ; *Reeve, Conch. Ic., f.* 790 ; *Helix multi-
limbata, Jacq. et Homb., Voy. au Pole Sud., pl.* 6, *figs,* 5-8 ; *Helix flam-
migera, Pfr.,* 1852. Shell imperforate, depressed, very thin, finely
striated, shining, pellucid, fulvous-yellow, adorned with angular flame-
like markings, and rufous serrations, closely set together ; spire some-

what convex, scarcely elevated; whorls 3½, convex, rapidly increasing, the last not descending, depressed, flattish beneath, impressed in the middle; aperture diagonal, rotundly-oval; peristome simple, straight, columellar margin arcuated, ascending.

Diam., greatest, ·28; least, ·24; height, ·14. (Pfr.)

New Zealand.

b. Umbilicus narrow.

P. glabriuscula, *Pfeiffer; P.Z.S.,* 1851; *M.H.V., vol.* 3, *p.* 51; *vol.* 5, *p.* 71, *No.* 193; *Reeve, f.* 822. Shell perforate, conoidly-semi-globose, thin, smooth, pellucid, shining, pale yellow, angularly lined with rufous; spire convexly-conoidal, slightly acute; whorls 5½, slightly convex, the last not descending, flattish beneath; aperture oblique, sub-depressed, lunar; peristome simple, straight, columellar margin bent downwards, slightly reflexed above.

Diam., greatest, ·14; least, ·12; height, ·08. (Pfr.)

New Zealand (Strange.)

P. epsilon, *Pfeiffer: P.Z.S.,* 1851; *M.H.V., vol.* 3, *p.* 97: *vol.* 5, *p.* 153, *No.* 763; *H. caput spinulæ; Reeve, f.* 818. Shell umbilicated, depressed, thin, obliquely and closely plaited above, pale horny; spire rather convex; whorls 3½, rather convex, the last not descending, somewhat smooth at the base; umbilicus narrow, pervious; aperture a little oblique, rotundately-lunar; peristome simple, straight, margins converging.

Diam., greatest, ·07; least, ·06; height, ·02. (Pfr.)

New Zealand.

P. chiron, *Gray; · P.Z.S,.* 1849, *p.* 166; *Helix chiron, Pfr., M.H.V., vol.,* 3, *p.* 94; *vol.* 5, *p.* 152, *No.* 742; *Reeve, f.* 797. Shell umbilicated, depressed, arcuately and rather distantly plaited, covered with a shining, fuscous-olive epidermis; spire rather convex; whorls 3½, rather convex, the last sub-depressed, rounded at the margin, convex at the base; umbilicus narrow, pervious; aperture a little oblique, sub-lunately-rotund; peristome thin, the right margin some-what bent backwards, separated from the last whorl by a slight incision, columellar margin above rather widely-opened out.

Diam., greatest, ·24; least, ·2; height, ·12, (Pfr.)

Auckland (Greenwood.)

The upper surface resembles a minature *P. busbyi,* but the under surface is very different.

P. rapida, *Pfeiffer; Zeitschr. f. Malak,* 1853, *p.* 54, *M.H.V., vol.* 3, *p.* 633; *vol.* 5, *p.* 175, *No.* 935; *Reeve, f.* 1038. Shell unbilicated, depressed, discoidal, thin, under the lens spirally striatulated, shining, pellucid, chestnut, variegated with luteous streaks and dots; spire flat, sub-immersed; suture sub-caniculated; whorls 3½, rather convex, rapidly increasing, the last broad, depressed, rounded at the periphery, not descending anteriorly, a little convex at the base, gradually ascend-ing into a moderate umbilicus; aperture a little oblique, lunately-

rotundate; peristome simple, straight, acute, margins somewhat closely united.
Diam., greatest, ·3; least, ·26; height, ·12. (Pfr.)
New Zealand.
Variety B, Larger, luteous, adorned at the suture with a broad, articulated, chestnut-coloured band.
Diam., greatest, ·38; least, ·28; height, ·15.
Solomon Islands.
Dr. Cox states (Australian Land Shells, p. 20) that this species comes from Cape York, N. Australia. The New Zealand habitat is probably a mistake.

c. Umbilicus broad.

P. crebriflammis, *Pfeiffer; P.Z.S.*, 1851; *M.H.V., vol.* 3, *p.* 91; *vol.* 5, *p.* 149, *No.* 717; *Reeve*, 805. Shell umbilicated, depressed, thin, finely striated, shining, pellucid, luteous, adorned with thickly-set flame-like markings; spire slightly elevated, rather convex; whorls 3½, somewhat convex, the last not descending, sub-depressed, more convex at the base; umbilicus rather broad, pervious; aperture slightly oblique, lunately-oval; peristome simple, straight, right margin arcuated in front, columellar margin slightly reflexed.
Diam., greatest, ·28; least, ·22; height, nearly ·12. (Pfr.)
New Zealand (Strange.)

P. jeffreysiana, *Pfeiffer; P.Z.S.*, 1851; *M.H.V., vol.* 3, *p.* 105; *vol.* 5, *p.* 169, *No.* 878; *Reeve, f.* 788 (?). Shell umbilicated, depressed, thin, distinctly striated, pellucid, luteous, adorned with lively-coloured chestnut streaks, disposed in bundles; spire flat; suture impressed, irregularly finely plaited; whorls 4, rather convex, the last sub-depressed, rounded, not descending; umbilicus broad, opened, aperture slightly oblique, lunately-oval; peristome straight, simple, margins nearly uniting.
Diam., greatest, ·28; least, ·23; height, ·12. (Pfr.)
New Zealand (Strange.)   Auckland.
According to Reeve this shell is "transparent, horny, and shining," without colour.   He appears to have mistaken introduced specimens of *Zonites cellaria* for it.

P. coresia, *Gray; P.Z.S.*, 1849, *p.* 166; *Helix coresia, Pfr.*, *M.H.V., vol.* 3, *p.* 92; *vol.* 5, *p.* 149, *No.* 718; *Reeve, f.* 807. Shell broadly umbilicated, depressed, olive-horny, fuscous streaked, covered with a thick, shining, sub-striated epidermis; spire slightly elevated, rather convex; whorls 3, rather convex, rapidly increasing, the last sub-depressed, not descending anteriorly, dilated; aperture diagonal, sub-lunately rotund; peristome simple, thin, margins approaching, epidermis inflexed.
Diam., greatest, ·16; least, ·13; height, ·06. (Pfr.)
Auckland (Major Greenwood.)
This shell is exactly like a very minute specimen of *P. busbyi*. It differs from *P. chiron* in being smaller, more depressed, and in the

umbilicus being much wider, showing the front side of the upper whorls, which appear rather transverse. (Gray.)

Genus, NANINA—Gray.

Mantle with the front edge produced and divided into two moveable lobes, which partly cover the shell. Foot truncate, and glandular at the end; sole as wide as the foot. Shell perforate, depressed, thin, polished, granular or corrugately striated above, smooth and polished beneath; aperture lunate; peristome the thickness of the shell, straight, the columellar margin short, reflexed, often covering the umbilicus.

S. Asia and Polynesia.

N. mariæ, *Gray; Dieff., N.Z.,* ii., 262 ; *H. Mariæ Reeve, Conch, Ic.,f.* 804; *Smith, Erebus and Terror, Moll., pl.* 1, *f.* 2; *H. umbraculum, Pfr., P.Z.S.,* 1851. Shell imperforate, nearly lenticular, rather thin, slightly striate, shining, greenish horn colored, indistinctly marked with narrow, oblique, brownish stripes; spire conoidal, with the outlines convex, and the apex acuminate; suture bordered; whorls 5½, rather flat, acutely carinate, the last one not descending, rather convex beneath, and obsoletely spotted with brown; aperture oblique, depressed, nearly triangular; peristome simple, sharp, straight, with the basal margin very slightly arcuate, and shortly reflexed at the columella.

Height, ·15; greatest breadth, ·3; least breadth, ·27. (Pfr,)
Auckland (Major Greenwood.)

FAMILY—LIMACIDÆ.

Rachis teeth tricuspid,· the laterals simple, aculeate, Animal elongated, body united to the foot. Head retractile; eye-peduncles moderate; tentacles short, club-shaped. Mantle small, shield-like, joined to the back; pulmonary opening on the right side, at the lower part of the mantle. Excretory and reproductive apertures on the right side. Foot simple posteriorly.

Genus, LIMAX—Linnæus.

Body elongated, tapering behind, hinder part only keeled. Back with elongate rugosities, separated by anastomosing grooves. Mantle anterior, enclosing internally an oblong shell, front edge free, produced. Pulmonary cavity under the mantle. Genital opening just behind the base of the right tentacle.

World wide.

L. molestus, *Hutton; Trans. N.Z. Inst.,* xi., *p.* 331. Mantle short, and flatly rounded behind; smooth and sub-concentrically wrinkled. Pulmonary opening in the posterior third of the mantle. Colour variable; greyish or reddish-brown, variously marbled with dusky; sometimes quite black. Tentacles of the same colour as the back. Foot yellowish-white. Radula with 33 rows of rachis teeth, and about 20 on each side of lateral teeth. Transverse rows straight.

Dunedin. Wellington.

Genus, MILAX—Pfeiffer.

Back keeled to the shield; dorsal shield granulated or shagreened, truncated, with two small pores on its hinder edge; shell convex.

M. antipodum, *Pfeiffer; Cat. Pul. Brit. Mus.,* 177. Ovate, attenuated, rugose (in spirits), brown, back sharply keeled to the shield; back with parallel grooves diverging from the shield, with short straight branches passing across from one to the other; shield short, oblong, rounded behind, smooth, with netted grooves; breathing hole rather behind the middle of the right side; foot in three bands, the central band rather the broadest, with series of grooves on each side from a a zig-zag central groove, the side bands with close parallel straight cross grooves. (Pfr.)
Wellington and Dunedin.

M. emarginatus, *Hutton; Trans. N.Z. Institute,* xi., *p.* 331. Mantle slightly shagreened, short and emarginate behind. Pulmonary opening a little behind the centre. A depressed line circling the mantle in front from the pulmonary opening. Colour dark grey or olive above; foot and lower sides of the body yellowish-white. Shell small, nearly flat. Radula with 27 rows of rachis teeth, and about 25 on each side of lateral teeth. Transverse rows curved.
Dunedin.

FAMILY—ARIONIDÆ.

Lingual teeth numerous, uniform, close together. Animal elongate; body not distinct from the foot. Eye peduncles and tentacles retractile under the skin. Mantle shield-like on the fore part of the back; pulmonary opening on the right side. Jaw horny, lunate. A mucous gland on the upper side of the extremity of the tail.

Genus, ARION—Ferussac.

Animal elongate. Tentacles and eye-peduncles moderate, Reproductive aperture immediately below the pulmonary opening. Shell rudimentary.

A. incommodus, *Hutton; Trans. N.Z. Inst.,* xi., *p.* 331. Mantle rugose, short and rounded behind. Pulmonary opening in front of the middle. Back rounded, not pointed posteriorly. Dark lead grey; a lateral stripe on the mantle, and a longitudinal band on each side, black. Sometimes the whole upper part of the body greyish black. Foot yellow. Radula with 21 rows of rachis teeth, and about 22 on each side of lateral teeth. Transverse rows slightly curved.
Dunedin.

FAMILY—JANELLIDÆ.

Body elongated, slug-like. Tentacles none. Mantle rudimentary or absent. Pulmonary opening on the right side, close to the centre of the back. Foot not keeled, tapering, without any caudal gland. Reproductive orifice on the right side, anterior to the pulmonary opening. Shell rudimentary or present. Mouth with a horny jaw.

* New Zealand and the New Hebrides only.

Genus, JANELLA—Gray.

Mantle absent. Shell rudimentary. Back with a longitudinal groove extending along the middle of the whole length of the animal, and giving off oblique branches from each side. Eye penduncles short, cylindrical. Foot divided from the body by a broad lateral groove. Teeth numerous, similar; the plates short and serrated. New Zealand only.

J. bitentaculata, *Quoy and Gaimard ; Voy. Astrol.* ii., *p.* 149 ; *t.* 13, *f.* 1-3 ; *Adams, Gen. Moll., pl.* 80, *f.* 5 ; *Chenu., f.* 3498 ; *J. antipodarum; Gray, A. Nat. Hist.,* 2-12-414 ; *Knight, Trans. Linn. Soc.,* xxii., *p.* 381. Head distinct ; mouth oval ; tentacles rather short, clubbed at the end ; eyes very small, terminal. Back with a deep longitudinal groove extending the whole length, commencing from the head, divided rather to the left to surround the pulmonary aperture, which is placed on the back, and with oblique striæ diverging from each side of this groove. Foot scarcely distinct from the rest of the body; yellowish white. The back is dirty yellow, with pale brown spots. It has no appearance of any shield containing a horny shell (Quoy.) Teeth about 300, in a transverse row ; transverse rows forming an obtuse angle.

Tasman Bay. Wellington. Dunedin.

J. papillata, *Hutton; Trans. N. Z. Inst.,* xi., *p.* 332. Like *J. bitentaculata,* but with small papillæ on the back between the oblique grooves.

Wellington. Dunedin.

Genus, KONOPHORA—Hutton.

Back with a longitudinal central groove, giving off oblique branches on each side. Eye peduncles short conical. Foot not divided from the body by a groove.

K. marmorea, *Hutton; Trans. N. Z. Inst.,* xi., *p.* 332. Body smooth, rounded above, scarcely distinct from the foot ; tail rounded. Back with a central groove with lateral branches sloping obliquely backward. Colour blackish, marbled with pale brown on the back ; an indistinct black lateral line ; region round the pulmonary opening yellowish.

Dunedin.

---

* For remarks on the anatomy of this family, see Dr. Macdonald, A.N.H., 2nd series, vol 18, p. 38 ; and Dr. Gray, A.N.H., 3rd series, vol 6, p. 195.

FAMILY—ONCHIDIIDÆ.

Marine. Animal slug-like. Lingual membrane broad; teeth uniform, similar, in numerous straight· transverse rows. Mouth with a buccal veil, but no horny jaw. Eyes at the end of non-retractile cylindrical peduncles; tentacles none. Mantle coriaceous, large, shield-like, entirely covering the back. Respiratory orifice posterior, at the right side, under the margin of the mantle. Vent posterior, separate from the respiratory orifice. Sexes united; male organ under the right tentacle, female orifice at the posterior extremity of the body.

Genus, ONCHIDELLA—Gray.

Eye peduncle short; buccal appendages lobate. Mantle smooth or granular, without tufts or radiating proccesses on the dorsal surface.

O. patelloides, *Quoy and Gaimard; Voy. Ast.,* ii., *p.* 212, *t.* 15, *f.* 21-23. Body orbicular, somewhat conical above; mantle covered with pale yellowish-green granules; margin of the mantle perforated by sixteen white pores. Below yellowish white; tentacles brownish.
Length about an inch. (Quoy.)
Tasman's Bay. Auckland Islands.

O. nigricans, *Quoy and Gaimard: Voy. Ast.,* ii., *p.* 214, *t.* 15, *f.* 24-26; *Chenu, f.* 3506. Small, oval; back slightly elevated, broadly keeled and black above. Tentacles black, thick and short, rounded into a button at their extremity.
Length, 3 lines. (Quoy.)
Auckland to Dunedin.
In some individuals the black color passes into greenish.
The plate shews that the mantle of this species is granulated as in the last. The only difference between the two appears to be the size of the swollen extremity of the tentacles.

O. irrorata, *Gould (Peronia); U. S. Ex., Ep.* xii., *p.* 291, *f.* 383. Elongated oval, back arched, margins expanded, mottled olive and yellow, finely covered with minute, sub-equal granulations, with eight or ten elevated, radiating folds or ridges at the margin on each side, which extend a little beyond the margin, and give it a dentate appearance. Head scarcely protruding beyond the body, dilated at the exterior angles; tentacles short, slender, blue, knobbed, and with an eye-spot at the tip. Head above sky-blue, and also the mantle surrounding the foot; margin beneath ochreous. Foot a little more than one-third the width of the body.
Length, 1 inch; breadth, ½ inch; height, ¼ inch. (Gould.)
Bay of Islands.
According to Gould, this species differs from *O. patelloides* in colour, and in the form, and number of the marginal projections. It is probable that all three are but varieties of one species.

Sub-Order—Basommatophora.

Eyes sessile. Operculum absent, or present. Aquatic.

FAMILY—LIMNÆIDÆ.

Radula with numerous quadrate teeth, in transverse rows, the central minute, the laterals uncinated. Head with a broad short muzzle, dilated at the end; mouth with a horny upper jaw; tentacles flattened or filiform, with the eyes sessile at their inner bases. Mantle margin variously modified ; respiratory orifice at the right side. Foot flattened, lanceolate, or ovate. Excretory orifices on the left side of the neck. Shell varied, thin, horn-coloured ; no operculum. Animal fluviatile, living in the water, but coming to the surface to respire air.

Sub-Family—Ancylinæ.

Shell non-spiral, limpet-like.

Genus, LATIA—Gray.

Shell semi-ovate, spiral of one or more rapidly enlarging whorls; spire short, posteriorly reclined ; basal margin with a thin, narrow, flat, horizontal lamina, occupying the hind half of the left side, the left hinder edge bent down, and produced into a broad expansion on the right side. Eyes on the outer bases of the tentacles.

New Zealand only.

L. neritoides, *Gray, P.Z.S.,* 1849, *p.* 168 ; *Reeve, Conch, Ic. f.* 34 ; *Chenu fig.* 3573. Pale brown, spirally striated, internal laminæ white, transparent (Gray).' Shell ovate, smooth, vertex rather swollen, produced, olive horny (Reeve.)

Length, ·25 inch.

Auckland (Sinclair and Greenwood.)

The vertex is said to be more swollen and produced in proportion to the size of the shell in this species than in the next.

L. lateralis, *Gould, U. S. Ex. Ep.* xii., *p.* 153 ; *Reeve, Conch, Ic., f.* 35. Shell somewhat squarely ovate, rather depressed, obscurely grooved at the side ; greenish-horny (Reeve.)

Length, ·4 inch.

Sub-Family—Limnæinæ.

Shell spiral, more or less elongated, the last whorl large ; aperture oblong.

Genus, PHYSA—Draparnaud.

Tentacles slender, setaceous. Mantle covering part of the shell, the margin fringed or digitate. Foot long, acuminate behind. Shell sinistral, oblong, thin, polished ; spire acute ; aperture oval, rounded anteriorly, not dilated ; inner lip spread over the last whorl, simple in front ; outer lip acute.

P. wilsoni, *Tyron, Am. Jour. of Conch.* ii., *p.* 109, *pl.* 2, *f.* 17.

E

(Limnæa.) Sinistral, sub-fusiform, thin, spire elongated, acute ; suture deeply impressed ; whorls 6, convex, oblique, rapidly increasing in size, the last narrowly oval ; aperture sub-ovate, half the total length, narrow ; columella a little twisted and reflected, leaving a narrow, deep umbilicus. Light amber colour. L. 1·05, B. ·4. (Tyron.) An elongated shell, distinguished by its impressed suture and umbilicus.

P. antipodea, *Sowerby* ; *in Reeves, Conch, Ic. fig.* 37 *P. variabilis, Gray, in part.* Shell fusiform, inflated, ferruginous brown, opaque, slightly striated ; spire elevated, whorls convex ; last whorl ovate, swelled in the middle ; aperture ovate ; columellar fold elevated, a little obliquely twisted (Sow) ; L. ·9, B. ·5 (from the figure.)
Lake Wakatipu, Otago. Lake Takapuna, Auckland.

P. gibbosa, *Gould, U.S. Ex. Ep. ; Reeves, Conch, Ic. f.* 27. Shell shortly sub-cylindrical, pale straw, very smooth ; spire short, conical, accuminated, last whorl gibbous, or roundly-angular above ; anteriorly somewhat attenuated ; aperture elongated, outer lip rather straight ; columella plait short, tortuous (Sowerby.) L. ·55, B. ·33.

P. guyonensis, *Woods, Pro. Linn. Soc. of N.S. Wales,* iii., *p.* 138. *pl.* 13, *f.* 4. Shell sub-umbilicate, ovate, slightly striate, with the lines of growth only, somewhat shining, opaque, corroded above, yellowish-horn or olive, more or less sordidly clouded with black ; four whorls rapidly decreasing, and very much sloping ; last much larger than the rest, and broadly flattened in the middle, with two obsolete keels in the midst, short, acute ; aperture broadly ovate. Peristome acute, rounded, lip reflected, columella rather thick.
Length, ·51 ; breadth, ·3 ; aperture, length, ·36, breadth, ·2 ; length of spire, ·16 inch. (Woods.)
Lake Guyon, Nelson.
According to Mr. Woods, this species is distinguished from the last by its colour, and by the double angle on the whorls above and below the flattened portion. Specimens from the same locality have been determined by Dr. Dohrn as *P. hochstetteri,* Dunker, of which I have seen no description.

P. novæ zealandiæ, *Sowerby ; Reeves, Conch, Ic. f.* 29. Shell turbinated, solid, chestnut, smooth ; spire conical, whorls roundly-angular ; last whorl inversely conical, anteriorly somewhat accuminated ; aperture rather golden ; inner lip strong ; columella fold a little gibbous at the top (Sow.) L. ·8, B. ·48.
A distinct species, of which I have seen no specimens. Distinguished by the breadth of the body whorl posteriorly.

P. tabulata, *Gould, U.S. Ex. Ep.* xii., *p.* 116, *f.* 130 ; *Reeve, Conch, Ic.,* f. 17. Shell inflated, solid, short, greenish-brown ; spire obtuse, rather short, whorls rather square, flattened near the suture ; last whorl large, roundly angular ; aperture wide, pale within, slightly acuminated within ; inner lip strong, columellar fold thick, tortuous.
Remarkable for the flatness of the whorls above the angle (Sowerby.) L. ·9, B. ·6.
Bay of Islands. (Gould.)

Sub-Genus, *Ameria—Adams.*

Whorls flattened and angulated or carinated at the posterior part. Spire short and depressed.

Found in Australia and New Zealand only.

P. variabilis, *Gray; Dieff, New Zealand,* ii., *p.* 248. Shell ovate, spire conical, apex often eroded, whorls ventricose, swollen, and often flattened and keeled behind.

Length, ¼ to ¾ inch.

The young shells have an acute spire. Very variable in shape. (Gray.)

P. mœsta, *Adams; P.Z.S.,* 1861, *p.* 144; *Reeve, Conch, Ic. f.* 32. Shell obliquely ovate, thin, olive-brown; spire moderate; whorls 5, carinated and flattened posteriorly; aperture oval, columella plait distinct.

Long., 7; diam, 5½ lines. (Adams.)

Found in all parts of New Zealand.

Sowerby remarks that it "has very close relations with *P. tabulata* (Gould.) The chief difference consists in the rounded angles of the whorls in the latter, and the distinct square angles in the former." But he describes *P. tabulata* as remarkable for the flatness of the whorls above the angle.

P. lirata, *Woods; Pro. Lin. Soc. of N. S. Wales,* iii., *p.* 138, *plate* 13, *f.* 6. Shell small, imperforate, elongately ovate, shining, sub-diaphanous, yellowish horn, covered more or less with a sooty periostraca; whorls 4, slopingly spirally and regularly punctately lirate (liræ somewhat distant), carinate above, lines of growth close and very fine; spire exsert. acute; aperture elliptic; peristome sharp, very thin; lip not reflected but twisted, exactly defined and anteriorly produced.

Length, ·38; breadth, ·2; aperture, length, ·2; breadth, ·12; length of spire, ·12 inch. (Woods.)

Taieri River.

Not so long nor so inflated as the last. (Woods.)

The proportions given make this a longer shell than either the last or the next. (F. W. H.)

P. cumingii, *Adams; P.Z.S.,* 1861, *p.* 144. Shell ovate, thin, light-brown; spire short; whorls 4, angulated and flattened at the posterior part; aperture sub-ovate, peritreme continuous; columella plait moderate.

Long, 8; daim., 5¼ line. (Adams.)

N. Australia and New Zealand. (Cuming.)

Sub-Family—*Planorbinæ.*

Shell spiral, discoidal or depressed, many whorled; aperture crescentic.

Genus, PLANORBIS--Guettard.

Tentacles slender, filiform. Foot short, ovate. Shell dextral, discoidal; spire depressed; whorls numerous, visible on both sides;

aperture crescentic or transversely oval; peristome thin, incomplete, the upper margin produced.

P. corinna, *Gray: P.Z.S.*, 1849, *p. 167; Reeve, Conch, Ic., f. 122.* Shell depressed, white, above flat, beneath rather concave; whorls convex rounded. Like *P. albus* of Europe, but not spirally striated (Gray.)

Auckland. Lake Wakatipu.

FAMILY—AURICULIDÆ.

Radula broad and long; teeth numerous, in slightly bent cross series; central tooth narrow, tricuspid, laterals diminishing outwards. Head ending in a snout; mouth with a horny upper jaw, and with two dilated buccal lobes, united above, separate below; tentacles sub-cylindrical, contractile; eyes sessile at the inner sides of their bases. Mantle closed, with a thickened margin; respiratory orifice posterior, on the right side. Sexes united. Shell spiral, covered with a horny epidermis; aperture elongate, with strong folds on the inner lip; outer lip often dentate. No operculum. Animal lacrustine, usually frequenting salt marshes.

Sub-Genus—Melampinæ.

Amphibious, or living in brackish water. Tentacles developed; eyes at their inner bases. Shell with the inner lip plicate; outer straight and acute.

Genus, MELAMPUS—Montfort.

Foot bifid, posteriorly. Shell ovate-conoidal, solid, spire rather short; aperture elongated, narrow; columella distinctly plaited; body of last whorl smooth, or furnished with from one to five folds or teeth; peristome straight; right margin acute, furnished with transverse ridges.*

Australia. Indian Archipelago. Philippines. Ceylon. Mauritius. South Africa. Madeira. West Indies. North and South America. Polynesia.

M. commodus, *Adams; Proc. Zool. Soc.,* 1854, *p. 12; Pfeiffer, Cat. Auric. Brit. Mus., p. 10.* Shell rimate, oblong-ovate, rather solid, slightly shining; chestnut; spire conic, apex pointed; suture bordered; whorls 9, flat, the upper radiately ribbed, the last forming nearly two-thirds of the total length, rather smooth, somewhat turgid above, attenuated at its base; slightly gibbous and striated; aperture nearly perpendicular, acuminately semi-ovate; no plait on penultimate whorl; columella plait short, oblique, somewhat twisted, forming an indistinct angle with the peristome, which is simple, straight,; right margin scarcely arcuate, slightly sinuate, furnished within with three transverse ridges; columella margin callous, shining.

---

* Pfeiffer gives New Zealand as the habitat of *Melampus sulcatus* Adams; but Adams gives no locality; Cox gives it from Port Jackson.

Length, ·44 ; breath, ·2.—*(Pfeiffer.)*
New Zealand (Cuming.)

M. zealandicus, *Adams; l.c., p.* 12 ; *Pfeiffer, l.c., p.* 17. Shell rimate, conoidally ovate, rather solid, irregularly striated, slightly shining, horn coloured brownish : spire conoidal, acutely mucronate ; suture linear ; whorls nine, flat, the last forming, about two-thirds of the total length, rather swollen above, somewhat lessened towards the base, with a swollen tubercule ; aperture perpendicular, narrowly semi-ovate, rounded in front ; one middle-sized, rather transverse plait on the last whorl ; columella plait obliquely produced to the margin ; peristome acute, bordered with brown ; right margin furnished with a white callus, which sends off eight or nine short ridges ; columella margin slighty thickened.

Length, ·35 ; breadth, ·2—*(Pfeiffer.)*
New Zealand (Cuming.) Auckland.

Genus, TRALIA—Gray.

Foot posteriorly acute, entire. Shell ovate, smooth ; spire elevated ; aperture narrow, dilated anteriorly ; inner lip usually with three oblique plaits ; outer lip acute, sinuated posteriorly ; internally with one or more transverse elevated ridges.

T. costellaris, *Adams, l.c., p.* 12 ; *Pfeiffer, l.c., p.* 39 ; *Auricula zealandiæ, Hector, Cat. Col. Mus.,* 1870, *p.* 98 *(name only.)* Shell rimate, ovato-conic, solid, ribbed longitudinally, brown, with irregular pale streaks ; spire conic, blunt ; suture irregularly impressed ; whorls five or six, the upper ones flat or rather excavated, the last forming about four-sevenths of the total length, very obsoletely angled, and girdled with a pale line at its upper circumference, somewhat tuberculate at the base ; aperture nearly perpendicular, sinuately ovate ; parietal plait one, strong, deep, rather transverse ; columella plait a little smaller, produced externally ; peristome blunt ; right margin sinuated above, then thickened by an internal deposit ; columellar margin dilated, rather adnate.

Length, ·47 ; breadth, ·26.—*(Pfeiffer.)*
New Zealand (Strange.) Auckland.

T. adamsianus, *Pfeiffer, Cat. Auric., Brit. Mus. p.* 17. Shell sub-rimate, ovato-oblong, rather solid, smooth, blackish green ; spire convexly conical, pointed ; suture linear ; whorls nine, flat, the upper ones somewhat plaited, the last forming two-thirds of the total length, indistinctly angled above, marked near the suture with one larger and several narrow pale bands, irregularly sculptured with striæ of growth, rounded in front ; aperture nearly perpendicular, narrowly semi-ovate ; one middle-sized, compressed, transverse plait on the last whorl ; columella plait oblique, produced outwards ; peristome straight, bordered with white ; right margin sinuate above, furnished within with six or seven short white ridges ; columella margin callous, slightly dilated.

Length, ·4 ; breadth, ·2.—*(Pfeiffer.)*
New Zealand (Cuming.)　N. Australia and New Caledonia (Brazier Chevert Expedition).

Genus, OPHICARDELUS—Beck.

Shell ovato-oblong, umbilicated, smooth ; spire elevated, sub-conic ; aperture oval ; inner lip anteriorly dilated and reflexed, with two plaits at the fore part, the posterior spiral forming an elevated ridge round the umbilical region ; outer lip thin, simple.
Australia and New Zealand.

O. australis, *Quoy and Gaimard, Voy. Ast.* ii., *p.* 169, *pl.* 13, *f.* 34-38. Shell imperforate, ovate-conic, rather solid, almost smooth, greenish horn-colored, generally with brownish bands ; spire elongated, conic, pointed, often eroded ; suture linear ; whorls 9, flat, sculptured with slight arcuate striæ near the suture, the last forming about three-fifths of the total length ; convex, attenuated at the base ; aperture rather oblique, semi-ovate ; parietal plait one, horizontal, produced externally into an obtuse keel surrounding the umbilical region ; columellar plait oblique, reaching the margin of the aperture ; peristome sharp ; right margin smooth, dilated above in front ; basal margin rather expanded.
Length, ·6 ; breadth, ·3. (Pfr).
Auckland.　Australia and Tasmania.

Genus, MARINULA—King.

Foot simple inferiorly, without a transverse groove. Shell ovato-oblong, imperforate, solid, smooth ; spire short, acute ; aperture obovate ; inner lip broad, excavated, with three plaits, the posterior the largest ; outer lip posteriorily sinuated, internally simple, the margin acute.

M. filholi, *Hutton ; Jour. de Conch* xxvi, *p.* 42. Ovato-oblong, smooth, spire short ; inner lip with three plaits, the posterior of which is much the largest, and the anterior the smallest. Outer lip without plaits. Pale purplish brown, plaits white.
Length, ·35 ; breadth, ·2.
Auckland and Massacre Bay.

Genus, LEUCONIA—Gray.

Foot divided inferiorly by a transverse groove. Shell ovate oblong, imperforate, smooth ; spire conical ; aperture elongate, oval ; inner lip with two plaits anteriorly ; outer lip smooth internally, the margin simple, acute.

L. obsoleta, *Hutton ; Jour. de Conch* xxvi., *p.* 42. Small, thin, semi-transparent. White, with a thin brownish epidermis. Whorls 4, very finely spirally striated in young shells. Columella rather flattened, anterior plait of the inner lip almost obsolete.
Length, ·1.
Auckland.

FAMILY—AMPHIBOLIDÆ.

Radula tongue shaped, teeth in curved transverse lines. Central tooth cuspidate at the sides, lateral uncinated. Pulmonary opening on the right side. Sexes united. . Tentacles two, small, flattened, triangular. Eyes sessile at the base of the tentacles. Shell with a horny operculum.

Genus, AMPHIBOLA—Schumacher.

Shell sub-globose, solid, rugose, umbilicated; spire depressed; aperture semicircular; columella flattened and reflected, outer lip with a posterior sinus.

Australia. Polynesia.

A. avellana, *Chemnitz; Gray, Dieff. N.Z.,* ii., *p.* 248; *Wood-ward's Manual of the Mollusca, pl.* 9, *f.* 33; *Chenu, f.* 3575. Sub-orbicular, rather thick; whorls angled and flattened behind, transversely rugosely plicate; spire very short. Yellowish or reddish brown, generally more or less purple on the spire and keel; interior brownish purple; mouth white.

Axis, ·8; breadth, ·95.

Auckland to Dunedin. New Caledonia (Cox. Exchange list, p. 37). Quoy makes two varieties. A larger, 1 inch 9 lines in diameter with the spire less pointed, striæ shallower, and the interior a deep purple, passing after death into brown; and a smaller, 11 lines in diameter, rougher, spire more pointed, and yellowish in color. For the anatomy of this species see Hutton A. N. H., 1879, series 5, vol. 3, page 181.

A. quoyana, *Potiez et Michaud Galerie des Mollusques,* 1838, *p.* 288, *pl.* 1, 28, *f.* 17-18. This species resembles *A fragilis,* Q. and G., but is smaller, smoother, and painted with zig-zag brown lines. Its length is 8 lines. It is common in S. Australia, and is found all up the east coast of Australia as far as Brisbane (see MacGillivray, Voy. Rattle-snake, ii., p. 362.) Tenison-Woods also quotes it from Tasmania. The New Zealand habitat must, I think, be an error. For a drawing of *A. fragilis,* see Chenu, f. 3576.

FAMILY—SIPHONARIIDÆ.

Radula broad, rather long; teeth numerous, equal, in slightly arched transverse lines; central tooth narrow, elongated, with a small rhombic apex; lateral teeth larger, diverging, gradually diminishing in size outwards. Head with a large frontal disc, bi-lobed in front, and formed by the expanded tentacles; eyes sessile on the outer side of the disc. Respiratory orifice covered by a large fleshy lobe of the mantle; a gill in the pulmonary cavity. Shell conical, patelliform, with an internal groove on the right side. No operculum. Marine.

Genus, SIPHONARIA—Blainville.

Apex sub-central, posterior; muscular impression horse-shoe shaped, divided on the right side by a deep siphonal groove, which produces a slight projection on the margin.

South Africa. India. Phillipines. Australia. West Coast of South America, Pacific Islands.

S. obliquata, *Sowerby; Reeve, Conch, Ic., f.* 12 ; *S. scutellum, Deshayes.* Shell ovately oblong, rather depressed, radiately crookedly ridged, vertex uncinate. Ash-brown (Reeve.)
Dunedin. Chatham Islands.
This is a large species flattened on the left side. The vertex is rarely uncinate.

S. sipho, *Sowerby: Reeve: Conch., Ic., No.* 9 ; *S. exigua, Sow. ; S. crebricostata Nuttall; S. albicans, zealandica, acuta, punctata, and plicata, Quoy and Gaimard; S. inculta, Gould.* Shell somewhat acutely conical, balanus-shaped, variously radiately ribbed and ridged ; ribs and ridges opaque white ; interstices purple brown. (Reeve.)
Philippine Islands. Indian Archipelago. Mauritius. Tonga. Chatham Islands. Auckland to Dunedin.
This common species is very variable in its form and colour. Probably the next is identical with it.

S. cancer, *Reeve ; Conch, Ic., f.* 7. Shell somewhat oblong-ovate, convexly depressed, very irregular, radiately ribbed ; ribs strong. rude, sub-corrugate, the three next the siphon distant. Dull purple brown.—(Reeve.)
Cuming says that this species is from Formosa (P.Z.S., 1865, p. 197.)

S. australis, *Quoy, l.c.,* ii., *p.* 329, *pl.* 25, *f.* 32-34. Elongato-ovate, rather convex, with about thirty radiating ribs, apex posterior ; ribs unequal, undulating, yellowish white ; the grooves reddish brown ; interior fluivous, marked with white and reddish brown on the margin.
Length, 7 lines ; breadth, 5 lines ; height, 3 lines. (Quoy.)
Cooks Strait, on sea-weed.

S. spinosa, *Reeve; Conch., Ic., f.* 32. Shell ovate, rather depressed, apex laterally uncinate, radiately ribbed, ribs rather narrow, profusely squamately spined. Yellowish white.—*(Reeve.)*

S. redimiculum, *Reeve; Conch., Ic., fig.* 24 ? Shell rather depressed, oblong ; apex posterior, twisted to the left. With small, rather distant and somewhat undulating, radiating ribs, crossed by fine concentric striæ. Interior dark purple ; exterior covered by a brown horny epidermis.
Length, ·9 ; breadth, ·65.
Auckland Islands.
The apex is not quite so much twisted as in Reeve's figure. and the ribbing is of a different character, but these may be errors of the artist.

FAMILY—GADINIIDÆ.

Head distinct, flattened ; tentacles expanded, funnel-shaped. Pulmonary cavity with a single gill placed obliquely across the back of the neck. Foot flat, thin, simple.

Genus, GADINIA—Gray.

Shell conical, muscular impression horse-shoe shaped, the right side shortest, terminating at the siphonal groove, which is in front of the right side of the muscular scar. Apex sub-central.

G. nivea, *Hutton; Jour. de Conch,* xxvi, *p.* 36. Irregularly oval, white; with about forty sharp radiating ridges, crossed by concentric lines of growth.

Length, ·8 ; breadth, ·7.

Otago.

The animal of this species has not yet been examined.

ORDER—BRANCHIATA.

Respiration, aerial or aquatic ; larva with a conspicuous velum ; intestine with a hæmal flexure or straight.

Sub-Order—Prosobranchiata..

Shelled gasteropoda, with the gills in front of the heart. Diœcious.

DIVISION—NEUROBRANCHIATA.

Terrestrial or aquatic, diœcious, operculigerous, breathing air by a vascular net-work on the roof of the mantle cavity, which is open in front ; tentacles two, non-retractile, behind, or at the base of which, are the eyes ; penis anterior.

FAMILY—CYCLOPHORIDÆ.

Eyes on the side of the head, at the outer bases of the tentacles. Foot elongate. Radula narrow, with seven rows of recurved, hooked teeth. Head, probosidiform ; tentacles subulate. Operculum distinctly spiral, horny.

Genus, CYCLOPHORUS---Montfort.

Shell globosely turbinated, depressed or discoidal, usually widely umbilicated ; aperture circular ; peristome continuous, straight or ex-panded. Operculum orbicular, of many gradually enlarging whorls ; nucleus central.

C. lignarius, *Pfeiffer; P.Z.S.,* 1857, *p.* 112; *Cyclophorus lignarius, Pfr., M. Pn. V., Suppl.* 1, *p.* 44; *Suppl.* 2, *p.* 64, *No.* 24; *Reeve, f.* 94. Shell narrowly umbilicated, turbinated, rather thin, obliquely irregularly striated, rufous, covered with an opaque woody epidermis ; spire conical, rather acute ; whorls 5–5½, convex, the last flatter at the base ; aperture diagonal, ovately-rotund ; peristome double ; the outer one membran-aceous, narrowly expanded, excised at the adjoining whorl. Operc. (?) (Pfr.)

Diam., greatest, ·2 ; least, ·15 ; height, ·16. Aperture, length, ·1.

C. cytora, *Gray; P.Z.S.,* 1849, *p.* 67 ; *Cat. Cycloph., p.* 23. *No.* 38; *Pfr.; M. Pn. V., vol.* 1, *p.* 86; *Suppl.* 2, *p.* 71, *No.* 121. Shell

F

minute, trochiform, rather solid, brown, closely and uniformly spirally
striated, crossed by slight wrinkles; spire conical, nearly as high as
broad, with the apex sub-acute; whorls ·5½, moderately convex, the
last rounded and convex in front; aperture diagonal, nearly circular;
peristome simple, straight, thickened internally, with the margins approximate, united by a thin callus. Operculum horny, of a few rapidly
enlarging whorls.

Height, 0·08; breadth, 0·1 inch. (Pfr.)
Auckland (Greenwood).

Genus, PAXILLUS—Adams.

Shell pupiform, rimate, smooth; spire accuminated; aperture semi-
ovate, ascending on the body whorl; inner lip adnate, spreading, flexuous,
with a prominent tooth like fold in the middle; outer lip double,
emarginate anteriorly; umbilical region with a spiral elevated ridge
ending in a notch at the fore part of the aperture. Operculum orbicular,
of many gradually enlarging whorls; nucleus central.
Borneo.

P. peregrina, *Gould; Pro. Bost. Soc.*, 1848; *Ex. Ep.,fig.* 105;
Pfr., M.H.V., vol. 3, *p.* 583; *vol.* 6, *p.* 395, *No.* 11. Shell small, sinistral, elongated, sub-fusiform, solid, opaque, rufous-cinerous, hardly
striated, perforated; spire mamillated at the apex; whorls 8, flattened,
sub-tabulated; suture linear, deep; aperture sub-quadrate; peristome
entire, equal, slightly reflexed.

Length, ⅜; diam., 1-10th of an inch. (Pfr.)
New Zealand.

Genus, DIPLOMMANTINA—Benson.

Tentacles long and filiform; eyes sessile on their posterior part at
the base. Foot short. Operculum thin, shelly; whorls few, with thin
prominent lamellæ on their external edges. Shell thin, sub-ovate;
whorls convex, the last sub-ascendent; aperture sub-circular; inner lip
with a spiral fold; peristome double; outer lip expanded.
India. Australia.

D. chordata, *Pfeiffer; P.Z.S.,* 1855, *p.* 105; *M. Pn. V., Suppl.* 1,
p. 12; *Suppl.* 2, *p.* 11, *No.* 13. Shell sinistral, deeply rimated, sub-
fusiform, thin, smooth, strengthened with somewhat distant cord-shaped
ribs, diaphanous, waxy-whitish; spire ovately-conical, apex acute;
whorls 7, convex, the last attenuated, ascending anteriorly; aperture
slightly oblique, sub-circular; peristome double; the inner one continuous, shortly adnate, otherwise rather expanded; the outer one
shortly spread out.

Length, ·16; diam. ·08; aperture, length, ·06. (Pfr.)
New Zealand (Strange.) Variety, Lord Howe's Island (Mac-
Gillivray.)

Genus, REALIA—Gray.

Shell perforated, turreted, thin, rather smooth; aperture ovate; peristome continuous, double.

R. hochstetteri, *Pfeiffer; Malak. Bl.*, viii., 1861, *p.* 149; *M. Pn. V., Suppl.* 2, *p.* 170, *No.* 1. Shell perforated, ovately-turreted, rather solid, somewhat closely plaited, fuscous; spire convexly turreted, rather acute at the crown: suture inconsiderable, bound with a thread-like margin; whorls 7½, slightly convex, the last nearly equalling one-third of the length of the shell, below the middle sub-acutely carinated with a thread-like carination, strengthened about the perforation with another small keel; aperture vertical, ovately-rotund, sub-angulated above; peristome double; the inner one scarcely porrected; the outer one broadly expanded, concentrically striated, narrow and adnate at the contiguous whorl.

Length, ·36; diam., ·16; aperture, length, ·1. (Pfr.)
Bay of Islands (Hochstetter.)

R. egea, *Gray; P.Z.S.*, 1849, *p.* 167; *Cat. Cycloph, p.* 64, *No.* 9; *Pfr., M. Pn. V., Suppl.* 1, *p.* 153; *Suppl.* 2, *p.* 170, *No.* 2. Sub-perforate, turreted, rather solid, covered with a distantly folded fuscous scarcely shining periostraca; apex rather pointed; suture middle, folded; whorls 6½, moderately convex, last obtusely keeled, painted below the keel with a dark chestnut-coloured band; aperture somewhat oblique, ovate; inner edge of peristome continuous, slightly expanded, angled above; outer edge somewhat interrupted, dilated, bell-shaped, incurved.

Length, ·35; breadth, ·16 inch. (Pfr.)
Auckland (Greenwood.)

R. turriculata, *Pfeiffer; P.Z.S.*, 1854, *p.* 304; *M. Pn. V., Suppl.* 1, *p.* 153; *Suppl.* 2, *p.* 170, *No.* 3. Shell sub-perforated, slender, turreted, rather solid, finely striated, a little shining, blackish, marked with a pale band at the basal portion, or ornamented with angular alternating black-chestnut and yellowish white streaks, becoming blackish towards the base; spire elongate, rather obtuse at the apex; whorls 7-7½, moderately convex, the last nearly equalling one-third the length of the shell, obscurely sub-angulated beneath; apex vertical, angularly-oval; peristome continuous, double; the inner one shortly porrected; the outer one narrowly expanded, inflexed.

Length, ·36; diam., ·14; aperture, length, ·12 (Pfr.)
New Zealand.

R. carinella, *Pfeiffer; Malak. Bl.*, viii., 1861, *p.* 150; *M. Pn. V., Suppl.* 2, *p.* 170, *No.* 4. Shell perforated, turreted, rather solid, obliquely striated with small plait-like striæ, brown, faintly-marbled; spire elongated, apex somewhat obtuse; suture margined with a thread-like edging; whorls 7, slightly convex, the last scarcely exceeding one-third of the entire length of shell, carinated and strengthened about the perforation with a compressed crest-like appendage; aperture vertical, oval, angulated above; peristome fuscuous, double; the internal one continuous; the external narrowed at the penultimate whorl, in other respects, opened, slightly reflexed.

Length, ·27 ; diam., ·13 ; aperture, length, ·o8. (Pfr.)
Drury. Taupiri (Hochstetter.)

Genus, OMPHALOTROPIS—Pfeiffer.

Operculum thin, horny, few whorled. Shell perforated, or narrowly umbilicated, turreted, or globosely-turbinated, keeled around the perforation; aperture oval; peristome disconnected, straight or expanded.

O. vestita, *Pfeiffer; P.Z.S.,* 1855, *p.* 106; *M. Pn. V., Suppl.* 1, *p.* 166 ; *Omphalotropis vestita, Pfr., M. Pn. V., Suppl.* 2, *p.* 179, *No.* 30. Shell perforated, oblongly-conical, thin, striated and spirally closely ridged, covered with a somewhat fuscuous epidermis ; spire pyramidical, rather acute ; whorls 6, flat, the last armed below the middle with an acute keel, and about the perforation with a second ; aperture hardly oblique, sub-angularly oval ; peristome simple, straight, margins converging. Operculum fuscous.

Length ·2 ; diam., ·12 ; aperture, length, ·o8. (Pfr.)
New Zealand.

FAMILY—ASSIMINIIDÆ.

Foot moderate, flat. Lingual teeth 7-5 cusped, the first and second uncini dentated, the third rounded. Head rostrate, produced and emarginate anteriorly; eyes on the middle of the tentacles, near the tip. Shell covered with a horny epidermis. Operculum horny, sub-spiral.

Genus, ASSIMINEA—Leach

Tentacles short, obtuse, with the eyes near the ends. Operculum horny of few rapidly increasing whorls. Shell ovato-conical, with the spire more or less produced ; whorls flattened ; axis not perforate, or slightly rimate ; aperture ovate, entire, columellar lip thickened, outer lip acute.

Europe. India. Tasmania. Polynesia.

In this genus the body is small, and the head produced into a ringed muzzle. The foot is large, broad in front, short and rather obtuse behind. Amphibious, generally in brackish water.

A. purchasi, *Pfeiffer; P.Z.S.,* 1861, *p.* 150; *M. Pn. V., Suppl.* 2, *p.* 172, *No.* 13 *(Hydrocena.)* Shell sub-perforated, turriculated, somewhat smooth, translucid, horny-fuscous ; spire conical, rather obtuse ; whorls 5, convex, the last slightly exceeding one-third of the entire length of shell ; aperture a little oblique, sub-circular ; peristome simple, straight, very shortly interrupted at the contiguous whorl, left margin slightly reflexed.

Length, ·o8 ; diam., ·04. (Pfr.)

Bay of Islands. New Zealand. (Purchas, Hochstetter).

The animal belonging to this shell has not yet been examined, and it is therefore impossible to say whether it is an *Assiminea* or a *Hydrocena* which belongs to the last family. For a figure of the dentition of *Assiminea*, see Ann. Nat. Hist., 3rd series, iii., pl. 3, f. 12.

DIVISION—CTENOBRANCHIATA.

Gills two, one generally rudimentary, pectinate, in the mantle cavity; penis present; never ripidoglossal; upper wall of respiratory cavity generally produced into a siphon.

SECTION—SIPHONOSTOMATA.

Peritreme notched or produced anteriorly into a canal corresponding to the siphon of the mantle. Carnivorous.

Sub-Section—Toxoglossa.

Radula 1.0.1, no rachis teeth, but an intermediate and a lateral row.

FAMILY—CONIDÆ.

Head with a produced tubular veil; tentacles subulate; eyes on bulgings or slight truncatures on the outer side of the tentacles. Mantle enclosed, with an elongated siphon at the fore part. Foot simple, undivided, oblong, with a conspicuous aquiferous pore on the middle of the under surface. Teeth subulate, in two series, on a tubular prolongation of the retractile proboscis, and with a bundle of sharp subulate teeth at the extremity.

Genus, CONUS—Linnæus.

Shell conical, tapering regularly; spire short or depressed; aperture long and narrow, emarginate anteriorly. Operculum minute, nucleus apical.

C. zealandicus, *Hutton; C.M.M. p. 23.* Shell turbinate, spire short, conical; body whorl with distant spiral striæ, which at the anterior end are elevated; spire whorls spirally grooved. Pale cinnamon brown, the spiral striæ darker; posterior edge of body whorl white with chestnut spots, anterior portion of body whorl varied with white, forming an irregular spiral band before the middle; spire whorls with small chestnut spots.

Length, ·6; breadth, ·3; angle of spire, 83°.

Allied to *C. anemone*, Lamark, from Australia.

A single specimen from the Bay of Islands, is in the Wellington Museum.

FAMILY—TEREBRIDÆ.

Radula rudimentary. Tentacles very small or wanting; eyes on the tips of the tentacles or wanting. Mantle enclosed with an elongated siphon. Operculum ovate, pointed, nucleus apical. Shell dense solid turreted; aperture with an oblique notch in front; outer lip thin not variced.

Genus, ACUS—Humphrey.

Eyes on the tips of the short tentacles. Shell subulate, whorls numerous, simple; aperture elongate, emarginate anteriorly, not produced into a canal ; columella simple, incurved, not tortuous ; outer lip simple, acute, without a sinus at the fore part.

A. kirki, *Hutton, C.M.M., p.* 27 *(Cerithium).* Whorls flatish, smooth, polished, transversely plicated ; body whorl small ; mouth oval, columella smooth, straight ; canal short, slightly bent to the left. Greyish black, greyish, or yellowish white, spirally banded near the mouth with purplish brown.
Length, ·8 ; breadth, ·22 ; angle of spire, 18°.
Auckland to Dunedin.
Dr. v Martens thinks that this may be identical with *T. caliginosa,* Desh (Reeve, Conch Ic. f. 100) from the Philippine Islands.

FAMILY—PLEUROTOMIDÆ.

Teeth elongate, subulate. Mantle with a slit in the hinder part of the right side ; siphon straight. Shell turreted, sub-fusiform ; aperture with the fore part channelled, straight, and often much produced ; outer lip detached at the hind part from the body whorl, forming a sinus, or with the margin fissured near the last whorl.

Genus, PLEUROTOMA—Montf.

Tentacles wide apart ; eyes at their outer bases. Shell turreted, fusiform ; spire elevated, aperture oval ; canal long and straight ; columella smooth ; outer lip notched anteriorly, and with a deep slit near the suture. Operculum ovate, acute, nucleus apical.

P. buchanani, *Hutton; Cat. Ter. Moll. of N.Z., p.* 4. Shell fusiform, elongated ; spire acute ; whorls carinated, with fine spiral lines, and obliquely plicated anteriorly ; posterior part smooth, concave, with a slight ridge at the suture ; aperture oval ; canal produced ; body whorl longer than the spire.
Axis, ·85 ; breadth, ·27 ; angle of spire, 30°.
Auckland.

P. trailli, *Hutton; C.M.M. p.* 11. Spire acute, with broad, shallow, spiral grooves, and prominent transverse ribs on the central and anterior portions of the whorls ; posterior margin, near the suture, flat ; aperture oval, canal short. Yellowish brown ; body whorl shorter than the spire.
Length, 1·1 ; breadth, ·4 ; angle of spire, 28°.
Stewart Island, 24 fathoms.
I once thought that this was the same as *P. bætica,* Reeve, but I now doubt it.

P. zeálandica, *Smith, Ann. Nat. Hist.,* 1877, *p.* 492. Shell strong ovato-turreted, flesh-white ; spire acuminate, tapering gradually, apex brownish ; whorls 10, first 2½ polished, vitreous, convex, the rest slightly convex, keeled above with the slope level (the tabulations strongly radiately striated), impressed with 2—3 sulci (the upper large, obliquely strongly striated). Body whorls large somewhat inflated, contracted towards the base ; ornamented with about twelve strong sulci, longitudinally striated ; aperture dusky, large ; columella darkish, arched in the middle, oblique below, the lip forming a slightly recurved, short canal ; caudal keel small, set round with dusky ; slit rather broad, not deep, situated slightly above the middle of the lip. (Smith).

Length ·9 ; diameter, ·36 inch.

Remarkable for the tabulated whorls, the tabulations being very strongly radiately striated, and sometimes furnished with a spiral liration, and the conspicuous sulcations encircling the body-whorl. The slit in the labrum is situated just below the broad furrow which grooves the upper parts of the whorls.

P. antipodum, *Smith ; Ann. Nat. Hist., 4th ser.,* xix, *p.* 491. Shell small, fusiform, pale flesh-brown, with transverse white keels, and between the keels very finely longitudinally lirated ; whorls 7½, the first 2½ polished, smooth, the following four above at the suture doubly keeled, and slightly below the middle another, distant, larger one. Body whorl large, contracted towards the base, with about nine principal and about six smaller keels ; aperture oblong contracted below, smooth inside, about half the entire length ; lip thin, margin hardly crenulated, above the keel a broad but shallow incision ; columella tortuous, callous, shining ; canal short, re-curved.

Length, ·4 ; diam., ·16 inch. (Smith.)

Perhaps the same as the next species.

P. albula, *Hutton. C.M.M. p.* 12. Spire acute ; whorls spirally grooved, and with a central prominent spiral rib ; smooth ; aperture oblong, canal very short ; body whorl as long as the spire. Ochraceous white ; apex and columella white.

Length, ·35 ; breadth, ·15 ; angle of spire, 30°.

Stewart Island to Auckland.

In this species there are 7½ whorls, and the grooves are finely transversely striated.

Genus, DRILLIA—Gray.

Tentacles approximated ; eyes at their outer side, near the tip. Shell turreted, spire raised ; aperture oval ; canal short, re-curved ; inner lip thickened ; outer lip inflexed, with a deep posterior sinus, and a small sinus at the fore part ; operculum ovate, acute ; nucleus apical.

D. novæ zealandiæ, *Reeve ; Conch., Ic., f.* 143 ; *P. rosea, Quoy, l.c.,* ii., *p.* 524. *pl.* 35, *f.* 10-11 ; *not of Sowerby.* Spire acute ; whorls flattened, spirallystriated, those of the spire transversely finely ribbed ; ribs interrupted in the middle, those on the anterior part of the whorls oblique ; body whorl finely spirally and transversely striated ; sub-nodulose near the suture ; aperture oblong, canal short ; body whorl rather longer than the spire. Pale rosy white.

Length, 1·12 ; breadth, ·4 ; angle of spire, 25°.

Omaha to Stewart Island.

D. lævis, *Hutton, C.M.M., p.* 12. Spire acute ; whorls smooth, with median transverse ribs, which are flatter on the body whorl ; aperture oblong, fissure deep, close to the suture ; canal very short ; body whorl shorter than the spire ; pale yellow brown, with a broad spiral band of pink down the centre of the whorls, across the ribs ; mouth and columella white, shading off into pink.

Length, ·75 ; breadth, ·28 ; angle of spire, 30°.

Stewart Island.

D. maorum, *Smith; Ann. Nat. His., 4th series,* xix., (1877), *p.* 497. Shell fusiform, turreted, pale rose colour, between the ribs especially about the middle some brown strigæ; whorls 8½, the first 1½ convex, smooth, afterwards but slightly convex, spirally lirated, the others concavely excavated above, margined near the suture, then rather convex, with crowded obsolete ribs, rather oblique above at the excavation (sixteen in the last whorl, vanishing near the middle), spiral liræ seven, three about the middle smaller than the others; last whorl with about fifteen liræ; the middle ones rather distant, produced below into a somewhat elongated canal ; aperture elongated, its length scarcely exceeding three-sevenths of the total ; canal sub-elongated, narrow ; sinus moderate, situated in the excavation. (Smith.)

Length, ·83 ; diam., ·26 inch.

Differs from *D. novæ-zealandiæ* in the form of the whorls, the elongate canal, and different position of the sinus.

D. æmula, *Angas; P.Z.S., 1877, p.* 36, *pl.* 5, *f.* 9 *(variety from New Zealand.)* Shell elongately ovately-fusiform, purplish brown ; whorls 10, strongly carinated a little below the sutures, and sharply angulated in the middle, below which descend irregular longitudinal ribs, nodulose at the angle, strongly transversely ridged below the angle, and more finely above ; the upper space between the angle and the suture being crossed with delicate crescent-shaped descending striæ ; spire sharp ; aperture elongately ovate ; outer lip simple, a little con-tracted below ; posterior sinus moderate ; canal short. scarcely re-curved. (Angas.)

Length, 1 inch ; breadth, 4 lines (New South Wales.)

Two specimens from New Zealand have the ribs and nodulous sculpture more prominent than in the type. There are also (in the British Museum) two examples of a variety of a uniform dull yellow colour. (G. F. A.)

D. cheesemani, *Hutton ; Jour. de Conch.,* 1878, *p.* 16. Ovato-fusiform ; spire acute, of 9 whorls. Whorls rather angled, suture well marked ; spire whorls smooth in front, obliquely striated behind ; body whorl equal to or rather longer than the spire ; a smooth band at the sinus, behind which it is obliquely striated, and in front spirally ribbed ; the interstices finely transversely striated ; nine or ten ribs on the outer lip in front of the smooth band ; canal very short ; pale brown.

Length, ·75 ; breadth, ·35.

Auckland.

Genus, LACHESIS—Risso.

Shell strong, turreted, many whorled, the last whorl not very large ; surface crossed by longitudinal ribs and transverse striæ ; apex of spire mammilated ; aperture oval ; canal very short, straight, not recurved ; outer lip slightly thickened externally, crenated internally ; operculum ovate, acute, nucleus apical.

L. sulcata, *Hutton ; C.M.M., p.* 12. Body whorl about as long as the spire ; whorls rather flattened, deeply distantly spirally grooved, about eight on the body whorl ; outer lip thickened ; reddish brown, sometimes variegated with white.

Length, ·35 ; breadth, ·15.

Stewart Island.

Genus, DEFRANCHIA—Millet.

Shell turreted fusiform ; spire elevated, whorls cancellated ; aperture oval ; canal short ; outer lip with a slight emargination, or sinus at its junction with the body whorl ; operculum none.

D. luteo-fasciata, *Reeve ; P.Z.S.* 1845, *p.* 114 ; *Conch. Ic. f.* 239. Spire acute, as long as the body whorl ; transversely ribbed, and finely spirally striated ; columella smooth ; pale brown or purplish brown, with a spiral pale band.

Length, ·43 ; breadth, ·17.

Stewart Island to Auckland. Chatham Islands.

Genus, DAPHNELLA—Hinds.

Shell fusiform, thin, fragile, surface usually striated ; spire elevated, last whorl elongated ; aperture oblong-oval, slightly channelled in front ; columella simple ; outer lip acute, separated from the last whorl so as to leave a sinus.

D. cancellata, *Hutton ; Jour. de Conch.,* 1878, *p.* 18. Fusiform, thin, finely cancellated ; spire acute; aperture oblong, slightly channelled in front ; and with a slight posterior sinus ; yellowish-white, slightly blotched with brown.

Length, ·5 ; breadth. ·2.

Auckland.

FAMILY—CANCELLARIIDÆ.

Radula obsolete. Rostrum very short ; tentacles wide apart with the eyes on the outer sides near their bases ; foot small. triangular. Mantle enclosed, with a rudimentary siphonal fold ; operculum none.

Genus, CANCELLARIA—Lamark..

Shell oval, cancellated, ribbed, or reticulated, last whorl ventricose ; aperture oblong, channelled in front ; canal short, sometimes recurved ; columella with several strong oblique plaits.

C. trailli, *Hutton : C.M.M., p.* 26. Shell small, thin, oval ; spire short, whorls angled ; the entire shell very finely cancellated ; columella with three oblique folds ; outer lip slightly crenate ; white.
Length, ·25 : breadth, ·17 : angle of spire, 70°.
Stewart Island.

C. ampullacera, *Lesson ; Ann. d. Sci. Nat., series* 2, *vol.* 16, *p.* 253. Shell sub-elongated, globosly keeled ; spire acute, thickish, suture depressed, excavated ; whorls 5, the last larger, three keeled, all with regular eminences ; shell grey, umbilicus cylindrical ; aperture white, lip acute, columella broad, with two folds ; canal inflexed.
Height, 16 lines ; breadth, 15 lines.
New Zealand (?) (Lesson.)
Locality doubtful ; brought to France by the frigate Thetis, from the South Seas.

Sub-Section—Hamiglossa.

Teeth, 1.1.1., with rachis plates, and one row of lateral teeth ; head small with an elongated retractile proboscis ; tentacles close together at the base, or united by a veil over the base of the proboscis ; eyes sessile, on the outer bases of the tentacles.

FAMILY—MURICIDÆ.

Rachis teeth broad ; laterals versatile, flat with a bent up process at the end, more or less at right angles with the base ; mantle enclosed, the margins producing varices at intervals across the shell, and extending in front forming a straight more or less elongated siphon ; foot broad, simple in front ; shell spiral, often turreted, more or less extended at the fore part into a straight siphonal canal.

Sub-Family—Muricinæ.

Operculum ovate, nucleus sub-apical, within the apex ; shell with the spire usually as long as the aperture, the surface rough, or with the varices well developed.

Genus, MUREX—Linnæus.

Shell ovate ; spire rather short, with three or more rounded or spinose varices on each whorl ; aperture ovate, often small ; canal elongate, straight or bent, tubular, generally spinose ; operculum horny.

M. zealandicus, *Quoy, Voy. Astrolabe,* ii. *p.* 529, *pl.* 36, *f.* 5.7 ; *Gray, Dieff. N.Z.,* ii. *p.* 229 ; *Reeve, Conch. Ic. f.* 177. Shell globose, rather thin ; whorls angulated ; varices on the spire whorls with a single spine, those on the body whorl with five or six half-closed hollow spines, the posterior one being considerably the longest ; these spines are bent slightly backwards, and more strongly to the left ; spire produced, acute ; aperture ovate ; canal produced, half-closed, bent backwards ; spinose with the remains of the old beaks ; yellowish or pinkish white ; interior white.

Length, 2 inches ; breadth, 1·0 inch ; angle of spire, 53°.

North Island, as far south as Wellington.

Animal yellowish white, tentacles reticulated with white. (Quoy.)

M. octogonus, *Quoy, l.c.* ii., *p.* 531, *pl.* 36, *f.* 8-9 ; *Reeve, Conch. Ic. f.* 134 ; *Gray, l.c., p.* 229. Whorls spirally grooved ; varices eight or nine, each carrying two or three spines on the spire whorls, and seven to thirteen on the body whorl ; spines strongly recurved ; spire produced ; aperture ovate ; outer lip grooved ; canal produced, nearly closed, slightly recurved, spinose with the remains of the old beaks ; reddish white, ribs reddish brown, often stained olivaceous brown, interior white, tinted with violet.

Length, 2·25 ; breadth, 1 ; angle of spire, 45°.

Omaha to Cook Strait.

Mantle reddish ; foot white below, yellow on the sides with delicate reddish striæ, which are also on the head and tentacles. (Quoy.)

M. angasi, *Crosse, (Typhis) ; Jour. Conch.,* xi., *p.* 86, *pl.* 1, *f.* 2 ; *M. cos. Hutton, C.M.M.* Small ; whorls six, with a sub-nodular keel ; body whorl with shallow spiral grooves ; varices three, forming continuous wings, crisped on the inside, and with an obsolete posterior spine on each whorl ; aperture ovate ; canal rather short, straight, half closed ; bright yellowish pink, paler inside.

Length, 1 ; breadth, 0·4 ; angle of spire, 42°.

Tasmania. Australia.

Two specimens were found at the Bay of Islands by Mr. C. Traill. This species belongs to the sub-genus *Pteronotus.*

M. candida, *H. and A. Adams ; P.Z.S.,* 1863, *p.* 430. Shell ovate, solid, white, spire elevated ; whorls convex, sub-angled behind, varices thin, produced at the angles (in the last whorl often obsolete), interstices transversely lirated ; aperture oval, hardly caniculated behind, produced in front into a recurved scarcely closed canal ; lip thick, callous ; inner lip sulcated, the magin denticulated. (Adams.)

Length, 1·4 ; breadth, ·7 inch.

New Zealand (Cuming).

Perhaps the same as *Trophon ambiguus.*

Genus, TYPHIS—Montfort.

Mantle margin prolonged into the last tubular spine between the varices. Shell ovate or oblong, with projecting hollow tubes between the spinose varices, the last open, occupied by the excurrent canal ; aperture orbicular, prolonged in front into a closed siphonal canal.

T. cleryi, *Petit.; Revue, Zoologique,* 1846 ; *Reeve, Conch., Ic., f.* 11. Shell fusiform, pale fulvous, obscurely banded with brown ; whorls rounded above, attenuated below; varices fingered, fingers uncinated; tubes intermediate, distinct; canal elongated, re-curved. (Reeve.)

Genus, TROPHON—Montfort.

Shell fusiform, varices numerous, lamelliform or laciniated; spire prominent; aperture ovate; canal open, usually turning to the left; columella smooth, arcuated.

T. ambiguus, *Hombr. and Jacq. ; Voy. Pole Sud. Moll., p.* 109, *pl.* 25, *f.* 13-14. Fusiform, rather thick; spire whorls with two, and body whorl with many, spiral ridges, crossed by varices; between the spiral ridges on the body whorl there are one, two, or three smaller raised lines; aperture ovate; outer lip finely crenulated; canal produced, bent to the left and re-curved; white or yellowish white, inside pinkish brown; in the young the mouth is internally banded with pale purple.

Length, 2·4; breadth, 1·2; angle of spire, 50°.

Variable, the varices being sometimes wanting on the body whorl.

Stewart Island to Auckland.

T. stangeri, *Gray ; Dieff. N.Z.,* ii., *p.* 230. Shell small, ovate, fusiform; brown, regularly and closely centrically striated; spire acute, rather shorter than the body whorl; the upper whorl with two, and the body whorl with eight continued distant spiral ribs, the hinder ones farthest apart, and most raised; the mouth dark brown; the canal short, open; axis three quarters of an inch (Gray.)

Dunedin to Auckland.

Probably a variety of the last, in which case Dr. Gray's name will stand. *Fusus cretaceus,* Reeve (l.c., f. 48) seems hardly different.

T. incisus, *Gould; U. S. Ex. Ep.,* xii., *p.* 233. *F. plebeius,* *Hutton, C.M.M., not Fusus incisus, Martyn.* Small, fusiform; whorls convex, spirally grooved, and finely transversely plaited; aperture oval, slightly angled; outer lip grooved in the adult; canal short, slightly bent to the left; purplish, the reliefs darker and browner; inside brownish purple.

Length, ·8; breadth, ·4; angle of spire, 32°.

Dunedin to Auckland.

I am rather doubtful of this identification. For Gould's description, see Trans. N.Z. Inst., x., p. 293.

T. inferus, *Hutton, C.M.M., p.* 9. Small, ovato-fusiform; whorls spirally grooved and transversely plicated; aperture broadly ovate, angled posteriorly; outer lip crenulated; canal very short, bent to the left; aperture large, outer lip angled; canal produced; yellowish, minutely and closely spirally striped with reddish brown.

Length, 5·25; breadth, 2.35; angle of spire, 50°.

Wellington to Dunedin.

Dr. v. Martens refers this to *F. corrugatus,* Reeve, but I cannot agree with him.

T. dubius, *Hutton; Jour. de. Conch.*, 1878, *p.* 13. Ovato-fusiform, thick ; whorls 7, convex, rudely spirally ribbed, those of the spire whorls transversely ribbed ; aperture oval ; canal very short, not bent, and rounded anteriorly ; covered with a greenish-brown persistent epidermis ; interior dark purple ; canal and anterior portion of columella whitish.

Length, ·7 ; breadth, ·4.

Auckland.

Differs from *T. inferus* by its straight canal and outer lip rounded anteriorly. From *T. paivæ* it is distinguished by its greater breadth, shorter canal, and by the absence of transverse ribs on the body whorl.

T. paivæ, *Crosse ; Jour. de Conch.,* xii., *p.* 11, *f.* 7 ; *F. corticatus, Hutton, C.M.M.* Small, fusiform, thick ; whorls finely spirally grooved, and strongly transversely ribbed, about eleven ribs in the body whorl ; aperture oval ; outer lip grooved in the adult ; canal short, slightly bent to the left ; yellowish white, with thin spiral stripes of purplish black, but the colours always obscured by a thick coralline growth ; interior white, banded on the outer lip.

Length, ·75 ; breadth, ·37 ; angle of spire, 45°.

Auckland to Stewart Island. N.S. Wales.

T. duodecimus, *Gray ; Dieff., N.Z.,* ii., *p.* 230. Shell ovate, fusiform, pale yellow, longitudinally costate ; spire conical, acute ; whorls rather rounded, last whorl about half the length of the shell, with twelve concentric rounded ribs and a central white band, with some spiral ridges in front, crossing the varices, and closer over the short open canal. (Gray.)

New Zealand (Dr. Sinclair.)

T. spiratum, *H. and A. Adams ; P.Z.S.,* 1863, *p.* 429. Shell ovato-fusiform, rather thin, grey, spire lofty ; whorls angled behind, cancellated with many thin longitudinal and strong, rather crowded transverse liræ ; aperture ovate, ending in a short, open, scarcely re-curved canal ; lip thin, sulcated within ; margin angulated posteriorly. (Adams.)

Length, 1·8 ; breadth, ·9 inch.

New Zealand (Cuming.)

T. coronatum, *H. and A. Adams ; P.Z.S.,* 1863, *p.* 429. Shell ovato-fusiform, thin, chalky, white, spire moderate ; whorls angled behind, varices laciniate, distant, produced at the angle into a series of scale-like spines, the interstices smooth ; last whorl swollen, ending in a long straight beak, which is re-curved at the extremity ; aperture ovate, longer than the spire ; lip smooth, simple, canal open. (Adams.)

Length, 1·4 ; breadth, ·67 inch.

New Zealand (Cuming.)

Sub-Family—Fusinæ.

Operculum ovate, acute, nucleus apical. Shell more or less spindle-shaped, varices rudimentary or wanting.

Genus, FUSUS—Klein.

Shell fusiform, spire generally long, many whorled; aperture oval; canal long and straight; columella smooth.

F. spiralis, *Adams; P.Z.S.,* 1855, *p.* 221; *F. pensum, Hutton, C.M.M.* Fusiform, thin, white, spire elevated; spire whorls convex, contracted at the suture, transversely lirated, angulated in the middle; keel tuberculated, the lower one sub-simple; aperture oval, inner lip smooth; throat sulcated; canal long, straight. (Adams.)
New Zealand (Cuming.) Cook Strait, rare.

Genus, NEPTUNÆA—Bolten.

Shell fusiform, ventricose; spire elevated; whorls rounded, covered with a horny epidermis; apex papillary; aperture oval; canal short; inner lip simple, smooth.

N. zealandica, *Quoy; l.c.,* ii., 500, *pl.* 34, *f.* 5-4; *F. mandarinus, Reeve; Conch., Ic., f.* 8. Fusiform, elongated; whorls rounded, deeply spirally grooved, each of the grooves generally with a single elevated line, sometimes with two lines in a groove; upper whorls only of spire transversely ribbed; outer lip crenulated; canal produced; reddish brown, the reliefs darker.
Length, 5; breadth, 2·25; angle of spire, 45°.
Auckland to Bank's Peninsula; animal brown, with reddish reliefs. (Quoy.)

N. caudata, *Quoy and Gaimard; l.c.,* ii., *p.* 503, *pl.* 34, *f.* 20-21. Fusiform, elongated; whorls rounded, spirally grooved; each of the grooves with one or two elevated lines; spire whorls slightly, and body whorl strongly, transversely ribbed; outer lip crenulated; canal rather produced. Pale brownish, reliefs darker.
Length, 3·25; breadth, 1·55; angle of spire, 48°.
Cook Strait; probably a variety of the last.

N. dilatata, *Quoy, l.c.,* ii., *p.* 498, *pl.* 34, *f.* 15-16; *Reeve, Conch., Ic., f.* 49; *Chenu, f.* 602. Ovato-fusiform; whorls carinated, spirally striated, with a row of tubercles on the keel; aperture large, outer lip angled; canal produced; yellowish, minutely and closely spirally striped with reddish brown.
Length, 5.25; breadth, 2·35; angle of spire, 50°.
Common in the North Island. S. Australia. Tasmania.
Animal marbled reddish brown on yellow (Quoy.)

N. nodosa, *Martyn; Buccinum raphanus, Quoy, l.c.,* ii., *p.* 428, *pl.* 31, *f.* 5-6; *F. raphanus, Lamark, l.c.,* ix., *p.* 454; *Reeve, Conch., Ic., f.* 61. Fusiform, ventricose; whorls spirally striated, those of the spire carinated, and crossed by low transverse ribs; keel nodulose; body whorl bicarinated, each keel with a row of nodules, sometimes obsolete on the anterior one; aperture oval, angled behind; outer lip slightly crenulated; canal short, bent to the left, slightly notched anteriorly;

from yellowish white, longitudinally streaked with brownish purple, to brownish purple ; interior white.

Length, 1·65 ; breadth, 1·0 ; angle of spire, 55°.

Cook Strait.

Abundant in the North Island. Not found south of Bank's Peninsula.

Var. B.—Body whorl with twelve nodular transverse ribs, which do not reach to the suture, small.

Var. C.—Body whorl rounded ; nodules nearly obsolete. Animal reddish, with points of the same colour (Quoy.)

N. traversi, *Hutton*, *C.M.M.*, *p. 9.* Ovato-fusiform ; spire whorl and posterior portion of the body whorl longitudinally ribbed, ten ribs in a whorl ; aperture oval ; canal short, bent slightly to the left ; lips smooth ; white, with thin brown spiral stripes, ten or twelve on the body whorl ; interior white, with two brown interrupted bands on the outer lip.

Length, 1·1 ; breadth, ·58 ; angle of spire, 50°.

Chatham Islands only.

The young shell is white and semi translucent.

Genus, EUTHRIA—Gray.

Shell fusiform, smooth ; aperture oval, produced anteriorly into a long re-curved canal ; inner lip simple ; outer lip posteriorly sinuated.

E. lineata, *Chemnitz ; Buccinum linea, Martyn, Univ. Conch., pl.* 48 ; *Fusus linea, Deshayes, Anim. sans vert.*, ix., *p.* 476 ; *Fusus lineatus, Q. & G.* 11, *p.* 501, *pl.* 34, *f.* 6-8 ; *Reeve, Conch.. Ic., f.* 31 ; *Chenu, f.* 600 ; *Pollia lineolata, Gray, Dieff. N.Z.*, ii., *p.* 230. Fusiform, smooth, sometimes ribbed ; whorls flattened ; aperture oval ; outer lip grooved ; canal short, slightly bent to the left ; purplish or pale reddish brown, spiraly banded with purplish black or reddish brown.

Length, 1·4 ; breadth ; ·65 ; angle of spire, 48°.

Common. Chatham Islands. Auckland Islands.

This very variable species can be divided into the following four varieties :—

A.—White with distant dark purple bands. Transverse ribs absent on body whorl. Auckland and Auckland Islands.

B.—Like the last, but the body whorl with transverse ribs. Stewart Island.

C.—Purple, with close bands of dark purple. Common. Dunedin to Auckland. Chatham Islands.

D.—Pale orange, with dark yellowish orange bands. Dunedin. This last variety is so distinct that it almost merits a specific name.

E. vittata, *Quoy, l.c.*, ii., *p.* 504, *pl.* 34, *f.* 18-19. Shell small, fusiform, thick ; apex acute, nodulose ; base short, obscurely trans-versely striated ; yellowish brown, encircled with a band of violet ;

aperture oval, narrow; right lip sulcated; a tooth in the posterior
angle (Quoy.)
Length, ·9; diam., 4 lines.
Bay of Islands.
Foot and head yellowish white, with elongated touches of reddish-
brown; two on the top of the head, and a third surrounding each
tentacle above the eyes (Quoy.)

E. bicincta, *Hutton, C·M·M., p.* 10. Fusiform, smooth : slightly
transversely ribbed at the apex only; whorls rather flattened, faintly
transversely striated ; aperture oval ; outer lip smooth ; canal very
short, bent slightly to the left; white, with a band of purple on the
anterior portion of the spire whorls extending to the sutures, and two
similar bands on the body whorl.
Length, 1·1 ; breadth, ·55 ; angle of spire. 37°.
Chatham Islands. Auckland Islands.

E. littorinoides, *Reeve, Conch., Ic. (Buccinum,) f.* 94 ; *Chenu, f.*
631. Shell fusiform, a little re-curved at the base, smooth ; lip simple ;
olive-brown, obscurely lineated ; interior of the aperture pale flesh-
colour (Reeve.)
Perhaps a variety of *E. lineata.*

E. martensiana, *Hutton : Jour. de Conch.,* 1878, *p.* 16. Small,
fusiform, spire produced, acute ; whorls rather distantly spirally striated,
with several very fine striæ between ; spire whorls transversely ribbed ;
aperture oval, outer lip slightly grooved, with a thin margin ; canal
short, nearly straight ; purplish brown, or pale brown.
Length, ·7 : breadth, ·3 ; angle of spire, 36°.
Common in the North Island.
Smaller than the last, much narrower, and the spire whorls more
distinctly ribbed.

E. antarctica, *Reeve ; Conch., Ic. (Buccinum). f.* 30. Shell
ovately fusiform, truncated at the base ; whorls strongly plicately ribbed
towards the apex ; ribs of the last whorl fading away; exterior covered
with a thick olive epidermis; interior purple brown ; columella and
inner edge of the lip white (Reeve.)
Falkland Islands. Auckland Islands.
Var. A.—Body whorl smooth. Campbell Island and Lyttelton.

FAMILY—BUCCINIDÆ.

Teeth as in Muricidæ; head truncated; tentacles moderate ;
mantle enclosed ; siphon recurved ; foot simple ; shell usually with
an oblique fissure or notch at the fore part of the aperture ; aperture
sometimes more or less produced and recurved anteriorly.

Sub-Family—Nassinæ.

Operculum ovate, acute ; nucleus apical, the margin entire or
serrated.

In some of the genera the eyes are near the base of the tentacles; in others near their middle, and are sometimes wanting.

Genus, COMINELLA—Gray.

Shell bucciniform, marked or spotted, covered with an epidermis; spire short, acute; last whorl large, ventricose, with a posterior depressed groove at the suture, producing a contraction at the hind part of the lip.

C. maculata, *Martyn; Reeve, Conch, I.c., f.* 16; *Purpura turgida, Gray, Dieff., N.Z.,* ii., *p.* 234; *B. zealandicum, Reeve, Conch., Ic., f.* 28. Shell ovate, turgid.; spire short; whorls convex, transversely plicated; smooth; aperture ovate, callous above; outer lip thin, sinuated, smooth; pale greyish-yellow, with transverse reddish-purple spots, arranged in spiral rows; interior and columella yellow.
Length, 2; breadth, 1·3; angle of spire, 60°.
Common in the North Island. Chatham Islands. Auckland Islands.
Var. B.—Spire shorter, hinder part of the body whorl swollen; body whorl with shallow spiral grooves.

C. testudinea, *Chemnitz; Quoy, l.c.,* ii., *p.* 415, *pl.* 30, *f.* 8-11; *Reeve, Conch., Ic., f.* 66; *Purpura maculosa, Gray, Dieff. N.Z.,* ii., *p.* 233. Shell conical; whorls flattened, smooth; columella smooth; outer lip thin, crenulated; canal short. Spirally tesselated with yellowish-white and purplish-brown; sometimes purplish-brown with spiral rows of white spots; inside dark purple.
Length, 1·65; breadth, ·9; angle of spire, 47°.
Common in the North Island, and found as far south as Banks' Peninsula. Chatham Islands.
The teeth of the male and female are alike, those of the female perhaps rather the larger (Gray Guide to Mollusca, p. 15), see also Hogg, Trans. Ray Micros. Soc., 1868, pl. x. , f. 33.
Foot greenish, marked with brown; tips of the tentacles and siphon black (Quoy.)

C. nassoides, *Reeve, Conch., Ic., f.* 12. Shell thick; whorls flattened, six or seven in the spire; spirally striated and transversely plicated; a broader and deeper groove round the posterior portion of the whorls near the suture; outer lip grooved internally; columella slightly plaited anteriorly; pinkish-yellow; inside brownish; lip and columella yellow.
Length, 1·6; breadth, ·85; angle of spire, 45°.
Steward Island to Cook Strait.
Orange brown; nodules and ridges whitish (Reeve.)

C. lineolata, *Lamark; Q. & G.* 11, *p.* 419, *pl.* 30, *f.* 14-16; *Reeve, Conch., Ic. (Buccinum), f.* 36; *C. virgata, Adams, Gen. Moll., pl.* 2, *f.* 6. Shell smooth; whorls flattened, those of the spire sub-costate; inner lip smooth; outer rather thin, slightly grooved in the interior;

H

canal short ; greyish brown, with narrow spiral lines, not very close, of brownish black; columella and canal orange ; inner lip banded with brownish-purple and purplish-white.

Length, 1·15 ; breadth, ·52 ; angle of spire, 45°.
North Island to Lyttelton.

C. lurida, *Philippi, Zeits, f. Malak,* 1848; *B. costatum, var. Q. & G.* 11, *p.* 418, *pl.* 30, *f.* 19-20. Small, spire acute ; whorls finely spirally striated, and transversely ribbed ; columella smooth ; outer lip grooved inside, not angled ; canal short ; brown or purplish ; interior paler.

Length, ·7 ; breadth, ·3 ; angle of spire, 36°.
Auckland.

C. huttoni, *Kobelt, Catalog der Gattung Cominella, p.* 233; *C. quoyana, A. Adams; P.Z.S.,* 1854, *p.* 313 ; *not C. quoyi Kiener.* Shell fusiform ; spire acuminate, white, spotted with reddish-brown; whorls 8, longitudinally obliquely plicated, the folds sub-nodulose above, transversely sulcated ; aperture oval ; columella uniplicate in front ; inner lip lirate (Adams.)

New Zealand. (Mus. Cuming.)

Possibly a variety of *C. costatum,* Q. and G., which appears to be a very variable species ; it has, however, well-marked characters of its own (Adams.) The Rev. J. Tenison-Woods considers that both this species and *C. lactea* are but varieties of *C. alveolata* (Kiener), a common shell of Tasmania and South Australia (Pro. Royal Society of Tasmania, 1877.)

C. melo, *Lesson; Ann. d. Sci. Nat., series* 2, *vol.* 16, *p.* 254 (*Buccinum.*) Shell globulosely ovate, swollen, rugosely striated, reddish-brown ; whorls 6, five sub-depressed, the last ventricose, dilated, grooved ; spire short, dilated at the base; lip simple ; aperture orange.

Height, 26 lines ; breadth, 18 lines (Lesson.)

Brought from New Zealand by the frigate Venus; apparently a variety of *C. maculata.*

C. funerea, *Gould; U.S. Ex. Ep.,* xii., *p.* 253; *B. glandiforme, Reeve, Conch., Ic., f.* 109; *B. zealandicum, Hombron and Jacquinot, Voy. au Pole Sud. Moll., p.* 24, *pl.* 21, *f.* 3-6. Shell rather thin ; whorls spirally striated, and transversely ribbed ; columella smooth ; outer lip smooth, slightly angled posteriorly ; canal short ; dark brown ; inside dark purplish-brown.

Length, ·8 ; breadth, ·48 ; angle of spire, 42°.
Common from Stewart Island to Bay of Islands.

C. quoyi, *Kiener; Icon. Coq. Viv., p.* 16, *pl.* 5, *f.* 13 ; *Reeve, Conch., Ic. (Buccinum), f.* 107. Shell ovately oblong, fulvous, transversely, very numerously and finely longitudinally striated ; spire sharp ; columella prominent ; aperture oval, reddish ; lip arched, striated internally (Reeve.)

Length, 1·5 ; breadth, ·85.
Perhaps a variety of *C. maculata,* but the spire is more pointed.

C. lactea, *Reeve; Conch., Ic. (Buccinum), f.* 117. Shell oblong ovate ; spire sharp ; whorls concavely impressed round the upper part ; columella arched ; interior of the aperture radiately ridged ; milky blue, marked with obscure black lines ; interior of the aperture yellow, stained with purple-brown, radiating ridges white (Reeve.)

This species comes from Tasmania and Australia, according to Tenison-Woods, Brazier, and Bednall. Dr. Cox's specimens probably came from Tasmania.

Genus, NASSA—Martini.

Eyes on the middle of the tentacles ; lingual teeth arched, pectinated ; uncini with a basal tooth ; foot large, expanded, bifurcate at its posterior extremity ; operculum ovate, the margin serrated or entire.

Shell-like Cominella ; columella lip callous, expanded, forming a tooth-like projection near the anterior canal.

I have seen no species of Nassa from New Zealand, and think that there must be some mistake in the localities.

N. rutilans, *Reeve, Conch., Ic., f.* 147. Shell accuminately ovate, smooth, shining, variegated longitudinally with ash, olive, and grey ; spire exserted, thinly plaited at the apex ; columella arched, but little callous ; lip thickly varicose, smooth (Reeve.)

New Zealand. (Cuming.) Torres Strait. (Brazier, P.L.S. of N.S.W., i., *p.* 180.)

N. nigella, *Reeve, Conch., Ic., f.* 173. Shell accuminately ovate, transversely grooved, longitudinally granosely ribbed ; swarthy brown within and without ; columella rather expanded, shining ; lip simple, margined without (Reeve.)

New Zealand. (Cuming.)

N. novæ zealandiæ, *Reeve, Conch, Ic., f.* 186. Shell accuminately conical, mottled black and brown ; spire sharp, with the suture impressed ; whorls slightly angled at the upper part, transversely linearly grooved, longitudinally strongly grain-ribbed ; columella twisted, white ; lip thin, varicose (Reeve.)

New Zealand. (Cuming.)

N. corticata, *Adams; P.Z.S.,* 1851, *p.* 98 ; *Reeve, Conch., Ic., f.* 189. Shell ovately conic, produced at the spire, covered with a greenish brown epidermis ; whorls nodose at the upper part, last whorl ornamented in front with a sub-nodose belt, posteriorly coronated with nodules ; columella but little callous, two-plaited in front ; lip margined outwardly, ridged within (Reeve.)

New Zealand. (Cuming.)

Sub-Family—Purpurinæ.

Operculum oblong, nucleus elongate, forming the long outer edge. Eye usually near the tips of the tentacles ; siphon short ; foot moderate. Shell generally oval with a short spire, and the inner lip broad and more or less flattened.

Genus, PURPURA—Aldrovandus.

Shell oblong-oval, the last whorl large ; spire short ; aperture ovate large, with an oblique channel or groove at the fore part ; columella flattened ; outer lip simple.

P. haustrum, *Martyn; Quoy, l.c.,* ii. *p.* 554, *pl.* 37, *f.* 4-8 ; *Reeve, Conch. Ic. f.* 6. Ovato-oblong, ventricose, spire depressed, rugose, spirally striated ; outer lip thin, wrinkled ; columella hollowed, canal large ; brown, interior greyish white, with a broad band of brownish-purple on the right lip, and generally a spot of the same at the posterior end of the columella.

Length, 3 ; breadth, 2 ; angle of spire, 90°.

Auckland to Dunedin, more common in the south. Chatham Islands. There is a variety in which the whole of the interior is yellow.

For the dentition of this species see *Troschel,* "Gebiss der Schnecken," pl. 12, f. 20.

Genus, POLYTROPA—Swainson.

Spire acuminate, whorls foliated or tuberculose ; inner lip flattened ; canal small, oblique ; aperture narrowed at the fore part.

P. textiliosa, *Lamark, l.c.,* x., *p.* 77 ; *Reeve, Conch. Ic., f.* 66. Shell ventricose, broadly spirally grooved, each groove with from one to four smaller raised ridges, the main ridges also with one or two small grooves ; finely transversely striated ; outer lip crenulated and grooved internally, margin thin ; yellowish-white ; columella white ; inside yellow, with a white band round the margin of the outer lip.

Length, 2·9 ; breadth, 1·8 ; angle of spire, 73° to 95°.

Auckland to Cook Strait. S. Australia. Tasmania.

P. succincta, *Lamark; Reeve, Conch. Ic. f.* 23. Probably a variety of the last but the grooves much deeper, and without any smaller raised ridges.

Blind Bay (F.W.H). N.S. Wales.

P. striata, *Martyn. P. rugosa, Lamark. P. succincta var., Reeve. P. rupestris, H. and J. Voy. au Pole Sud., p.* 89, *pl.* 22, *f.* 23. Shell ventricose, deeply and broadly spirally grooved, the grooves crossed by thin, rather distant, transverse lamellæ, which do not reach as high as the tops of the ridges ; ridges smooth ; outer lip crenulated and grooved, margin rather thick ; white or yellowish-white ; inside white, nacrous.

Length, 2·3 ; breadth, 1·5 ; angle of spire, 68°.

Chatham Islands. Auckland to Stewart Island. Auckland Islands. Kerguelen's Land. S. Australia.

P. squamata, *Hutton; Jour. de Conch.,* 1878, *p.* 19. Ovato-acute, spire produced ; whorls narrowly, rather distantly, spirally grooved, rough with numerous thin imbricating transverse foliations ; outer lip crenulated and grooved ; columella with one fold ; brownish-white ; interior purple, columella and a band round the mouth white or yellowish.

Length, ·75; breadth, ·45; angle of spire, 54.°
Dunedin.

P. retiaria, *Hutton; Jour. de Conch.*, 1878, *p.* 20. Ovato-fusiform; whorls keeled, spirally ribbed; four or five ribs on the body whorl in front of the keel, and one small rib behind it; ribs crossed at regular intervals by transverse plications, dividing the surface of the shell into squares; the whole shell covered by delicate transverse foliations; aperture oval; columella rounded; canal short, slightly bent; greyish-white; interior purple.
Length, ·9; breadth, ·5.
Auckland.

P. quoyi, *Reeve; Conch, Ic., f.* 71 ; *P. rugosa*, *Quoy and Gaimard,* ii., *p.* 569, *pl.* 38, *f.* 19-21. Shell somewhat fusiform, produced at each end ; whorls concavely depressed round the upper part, logitudinally very finely laminated, encircled with rough and scabrous ribs and ridges ; columella excavated; aperture small ; lip crenated within ; whitish or light brown ; interior of the aperture purple-brown. (Reeve.)
Common in the North Island, not common in the South.
A very variable species, probably a variety of the next.
Animal green with yellowish-white spots ; tentacles and siphon whitish (Quoy.)

P. scobina, *Quoy and Gaimard; Voy. Astrol. Zool.,* ii., *p.* 567, *pl.* 38, *f.* 12-13 ; *Reeve, Conch. Ic., f.* 72 (bad ;) *P. tristis, Dunker, Reise der Novara Moll., pl.* 1., *f.* 4. Shell ovato-oblong, transversely ribbed, rough ; yellowish-brown ; interstices with imbricating lamellæ ; aperture oval, small, dark ; lip undulated, tuberculated within, sulcated ; spire conical, thick, subacute. (Quoy.)
Auckland to Dunedin, abundant.
A very variable species.

P. patens, *Hombron and Jacquinot; Voy. au Pole Sud. Moll., p.* 85, *pl.* 22, *f.* 1-2. Shell reddish-grey : spire of fine whorls, of which the four first are very small ; the last three times as large as the others taken together ; whorls ornamented with transverse threads, with regular intervals ; mouth reddish, broad, oval, the left lip turned back, and with granulations corresponding to the transverse threads ; canal rather short, inclined to the right ; right lip very flat, diminishing towards the spire, and terminated by a reddish patch. (H. and J.)
Length (from the figure), ·85 inch.

P. biconica, *Hutton; Jour. de Conch.*, 1878, *p.* 20. Small, broadly fusiform ; spire short, acute ; body whorl inflated posteriorly, and narrowed anteriorly ; spirally ribbed, and slightly transversely plicated ; whitish, tessellated with dark brown on the ribs ; interior dark purplish-brown, toothed with white on the right lip.
Length, ·4 ; breadth, ·28.
North Island.

P. tesselliata, *Lesson; Rev. Zool. Dec.,* 1840: *Ann. d. Sci. Nat., Series* 2, *Vol.* 16, *p.* 255 *(Purpura.)* Shell ovately-elongate, covered with longitudinal flexuous lines, and transversely striated; grooves deep, with numerous regular quadrate perforations; shell reddish; spire elongated, obtuse; whorls flat, tessellated, the last ventricose, depressed at the suture; lip toothed, interior reddish, ornamented with four spots.

Height, 12 lines; breadth, 9 lines. (Lesson.)
New Zealand.
This may be the same as either *P. retiaria* or *P. quoyi*.

Genus, RICINULA—Lamark.

Shell ovate, solid; spire short; whorls tuberculated or spinous; aperture linear, narrow, contracted by callous projections, with an oblique emarginate canal in front; inner lip wrinkled; outer lip internally with plait-like teeth, often digitate.

R. iodostoma, *Lesson; Magasin de Zoologie,* 1842, *Moll. pl.* 58; *Deshayes, Anim. Sans. Vert.,* x., *p.* 54; *Reeve, Conch., Ic., f.* 4. Shell ovate, thick, ponderous, rather depressed; spire very short; transversely striated, and oboletely-ribbed; ribs more prominent at the margin; aperture strongly toothed, thickened at the upper part; whitish; ribs brownish black; intermediate striæ brown; aperture bright pinkish-purple.

Length, 1·4; breadth, 1·2.—*(Reeve.)*
New Zealand (Lesson.)   Straits of Macassar (Rohr.)
Mr. Kirk mentions a species of *Ricinula* as occurring at Great Omaha (Trans. N.Z. Inst., v., p. 369.)

FAMILY—ANCILLIDÆ.

Mantle enclosed, the siphon re-curved; foot voluminous, usually reflexed over the sides of the shell, bifid behind; shield grooved on the upper surface; side lobes not much produced; head concealed; eyes none; tentacles rudimentary; operculum small, ovate, acute, sometimes entirely wanting.

Genus, Ancillaria—Lamark.

Shell oblong, sub-cylindrical, polished; spire short; suture filled up with enamel; columella callous, anteriorly, twisted; outer lip thin, simple, acute.

A. australis, *Sow.; Reeve, Conch., Ic., f.* 7; *Chenu, f.* 893; *Quoy, l.c.,* iii., *p.* 20, *pl.* 49, *f.* 13-17; *A. albisulcata, Quoy, l.c.,* iii., *p.* 19. *pl.* 49, *f.* 5-12. Shell ob-ovate; spire accuminate, callously obtuse in old shells; columella constrictedly twisted; an obsolete tooth near the anterior end of the outer lip; leaden-blue or brownish-purple in the centre, often margined with white, both ends generally tinged with chestnut; interior brownish-purple.

Length, 1·75; breadth, ·8.
Common in the North Island.   Chalky Inlet.

A. pyramidalis, *Reeve; Conch., Ic., f.* 11. Shell ovate, rather thin, ventricose, purplish-fawn colour, callosity fuscous; spire pyramidally accuminated, callous throughout; columella arcuately twisted (Reeve.)
Nelson.
Scarcely distinct from the last. *A. Novæ-zealandiæ*, Sow., f. 41, is no doubt the young of one or the other.

FAMILY—LAMELLARIIDÆ.

Lingual teeth in three or seven series, the central broad, the lateral versatile; lateral teeth simple, curved; tentacles separated at their bases, and bearing the sessile eyes at their origin externally; mantle included, lining the shell; foot oblong, obtusely quadrate in front, rounded behind; hind or operculigerous lobe greatly developed, entirely covering and concealing the shell; operculum none. Shell thin, spiral, covered by the hind lobe of the foot.

Genus, CORIOCELLA—Blainville.

(?) Mantle deeply fissured and bilobed in front, the surface depressed and covered with numerous hexagonal tubercules. Shell spiral, calcareous, ear-shaped, thin, sub-opaque; spire short; whorls rounded, last whorl large; aperture patulous.

C. ophione, *Gray; P.Z.S.*, 1849, *p.* 169. Shell oblong, elongate, pellucid, white; spire very short, conical; whorls convex, last whorl very large, convex, rather iridescent; aperture ovate; pillar lip curved, slightly reflexed (Gray.)
Auckland. (Major Greenwood.)
I do not know on what evidence Adams refers this species to *Coriocella*, for the shell only appears to have been described. An animal found near Dunedin by Mr. G. M. Thompson, and which I take to be Gray's *Lamellaria ophione*, belongs perhaps to the genus *Cryptocella* (H. and A. Adams.)' The mantle is smooth but much wrinkled, resembling the convolutions of the brain; it is considerably expanded and waved laterally, but is not produced nor bi-lobed anteriorly, nor is it fissured on the back; the colour of the whole animal is yellow. The eyes are sessile on the external side of the tentacles, near the base, as in *Lamellaria*. The shell resembles that of *Cryptocella*.

FAMILY—FASCIOLARIIDÆ.

Lingual teeth in three series (1. 1. 1.) the central re-curved, toothed at the tip, the lateral not versatile (*Odontoglossate;*) lateral teeth very broad, linear, with many equal teeth; central tooth narrow, small; mantle enclosed, with a straight siphon : operculum ovate-acute, nucleus apical.

Genus, LATIRUS—Montfort.

Shell turreted, fusiform, umbilicated; spire produced; whorls nodulous; aperture oval-oblong; outer lip thin, crenulated; columella straight, with two or three small oblique plaits in front; animal of a dull red-colour.

L. decoratus, *Adams;* *P.Z.S.,* 1854, *p.* 316. Shell ovato-fusiform, white varied with chestnut, longitudinally plicated, transversely lirated, the liræ alternately larger and smaller, two near the suture moniliform; aperture oval; canal short; columella with three plicæ; inner lip sulcated (Adams.)

New Zealand. (Mus. Cuming.) Andaman Islands. (Smith P.Z.S. 1878, p. 812.)

FAMILY—MITRIDÆ

Teeth in three series (1. 1. 1.) the laterals fixed, not versatile *(Odontoglossate;)* head small and narrow; tentacles close together at the base; eyes above the base or towards the outer middle of the tentacles; mantle enclosed; siphon simple at the base; foot small, triangular; operculum none or rudimentary. Shell with the columella more or less plicate; apex of spire acute.

Sub-Family—Mitrinæ.

Head moderate; eyes usually near the outer middle or tip of the tentacles; foot truncate in front. Shell for the most part destitute of epidermis; columella distinctly plicate.

Genus, MITRA—Lamark.

Shell fusiform, thick; spire elevated, acute; aperture small, notched in front; columella obliquely plaited; operculum small.

M. obscura, *Hutton,* *C.M.M., p.* 19. Shell ovato-conical; spire acute; whorls sub-carinate, those of the spire transversely plicate; body whorl very finely longitudinally striated; beak spirally striated behind; aperture narrow; columella with four plaits, the anterior one small; outer lip angled, deeply notched in front; blackish-brown, spotted with white, especially on the spire; interior purplish; beak brown.

Length, ·64; breath, ·33; angle of spire, 60°.

Bay of Islands. A single dead specimen in the Colonial Museum, Wellington.

M. rubiginosa, *Hutton;* *C.M.M., p.* 20 *(Columbella.)* Fusiform, smooth; whorls transversely plicated; spire elevated, acute; aperture rather broad; outer lip thin; not swollen; columella with four oblique teeth; pink or brownish-pink.

Length, ·3; breadth, ·15.

Auckland to Lyttelton. Chatham Islands.

Sub-Family—Columbellinæ.

Head elongated; eyes near the outer bases of the tentacles; foot anteriorly produced. Shell usually covered with an epidermis; inner lip anteriorly toothed or tuberculed; outer lip gibbous in the middle or at the hind part.

Genus, COLUMBELLA--Lamark.

Shell ovato-oblong, triangular or fusiform; spire acute at the apex; aperture long narrow, contracted in the middle; inner lip curved, crenulated or denticulated; outer lip dentate, gibbous, thickened in the middle.

C. zebra, *Gray; Reeve, Conch., Ic., f. 72.* Shell oblong, somewhat pyramidal, smooth, fulvous, conspicuously striped longitudinally with chestnut; aperture rather broad, lip slightly thickened within, faintly denticulated (Reeve.)

C. choava. *Reeve; Conch., Ic., f. 239; Pyrene flexuosa, Hutton, Jour. de Conch.,* 1878, *p.* 23. Shell ovate, smooth, yellowish, freckled with chestnut brown; spire obtuse; whorls convex; aperture small; lip simple, faintly notched at the upper part (Reeve.)

A small olive-brown shell, mottled with somewhat obscure waved marks of chestnut-brown (Reeve.) Auckland.

A black variety appears to be nearly as common as the type. The teeth on the outer lip are often obsolete, thus bringing it into the genus *Pyrene.*

Sub-Section—Rhachiglossa.

Radula with rachis plates only; head as in *Hamiglossa.*

FAMILY—VOLUTIDÆ.

Lingual teeth in a single central series, often toothed; head large, with the eyes sessile on the sides below the base of the tentacles; tentacles far apart, united by a broad veil over the head; mantle sometimes greatly developed, covering the sides of the shell; siphon re-curved, short, with auricles on each side of the base; foot very large, partly hiding the shell; operculum none. Shell with distinct plaits on the columella; apex of spire mamillated.

Sub-Family— Volutinæ

Teeth linear, with a single conical apex, the base angularly diverging; mantle margin included, not covering the sides of the shell.

Genus, VOLUTA—Linnæus.

Shell oval or fusiform; spire more or less produced; aperture large, without a canal.

V. pacifica, *Lamark, l.c.,* x., 399; *Q. & G.,* ii., *p.* 625, *pl.* 44, *f.* 6; *V. arabica, Gml.; Chenu, f.* 971. Shell ovato-fusiform; whorls rather flattened in the adult, with a row of tubercles increasing in size anteriorly; shell rather thin; aperture large, widening anteriorly; columella with four or five plaits; fulvous with dark brown or blackish, angular, flexuous, anastomosing, transverse markings, which being thicker

I

and darker in certain places, form three or four more or less distinct spiral bands on the body whorl : sometimes entirely covered with a dark reddish-brown coating.

Length, 7·5 ; breadth, 3 ; angle of spire, 40° to 48 .

Var B.—*V. elongata, Swainson).* Pale fulvous, without any markings ; whorls smooth ; columella with five or six plaits ; sometimes covered over with a dark reddish-brown coating, like the typical form.

Auckland to Stewart Island.

Animal wine-purple, dusted with yellow : hood bordered with reddish. (Quoy.)

V. gracilis, *Swainson ; Exotic., Conch., pl. 42 ; Reeve, Conch., Ic., f. 40 ; V. fusus, Quoy and Gaimard, Voy. Astrol., ii., p. 627. pl. 44, f. 7, 8.* Shell small, thick, elongato-oval ; spire whorls flattened, plicate ; body whorl smooth or sub-plicate posteriorly ; aperture elongate, rather narrow ; columella with four plaits ; outer lip thickened ; fulvous with chestnut-brown, angular, flexuous, anastomosing, transverse markings, not forming bands ; sometimes covered with a dark reddish-brown coating.

Length, 2·15 ; breadth, ·78 ; angle of spire, 36° to 40°.

Rare. Auckland.

Animal yellow, finely dotted with red-brown. (Quoy.)

V. kirki, *Hutton, C.M.M., p.* 18. Broadly ovate ; spire depressed ; a few blunt tubercles on the body whorl : columella with four very deep plaits ; aperture large ; inner lip with a thin callus ; yellowish-brown.

Length, 1·75 ; breadth, 1·57 ; angle of spire, 80°.

A single specimen is in the Auckland Museum.

FAMILY—MARGINELLIDÆ.

Lingual teeth broad and lunate, with many conical, rather distant dentations ; tentacles close together at the base ; eyes above the base or near the middle of the tentacles ; mantle with expanded side lobes covering the shell ; siphon elongate, simple at the base ; foot large, truncate in front, produced behind ; operculum none. Shell porcellanous, polished, with distinct plaits on the columella : outer lip with the margin thickened, or with a marginal callus.

Genus, MARGINELLA—Lamark.

Shell smooth, bright ; spire short or concealed ; aperture truncated in front ; columella plaited ; outer lip (of adult) with a thickened margin.

M. albescens, *Hutton, C.M.M., p.* 19. Shell small, oval, translucent ; spire short ; aperture narrow ; columella with four plaits ; white, with indications of two yellow spiral bands.

Length, ·2 ; breadth, ·1.

Stewart Island. Chatham Islands.

M. vittata, *Hutton, C.M.M., p.* 19. Sub-cylindrical, rather flattened below ; spire concealed ; columella with four or five plaits near the anterior end ; outer lip not thickened (young? ;) yellowish-white, with thin interrupted spiral bands of brown ; columella white.
Length, ·35 ; breadth, ·2.
Two specimens in the Colonial Museum, Wellington, locality uncertain.

Genus, ERATO—Risso.

Shell smooth ; spire distinct, conical ; aperture narrow ; outer lip thickened towards the middle ; columella with distinct plaits at the fore part.

E. lactea, *Hutton, sp. nov.* Shell smooth, white, or tinted with pale brown ; spire of four whorls ; right lip margined, slightly swollen in the middle, smooth within ; columella with four plaits, the two anterior more oblique than the other two ; the posterior the largest.
Length, ·5 ; breadth, ·3 inch.
Auckland to Cook Strait.

Sub-Section—Tænioglossa..

One row of rachis teeth, and three lateral plates on each side (3. 1. 3.)

Series————Proboscidifera.

Head small ; proboscis retractile under the base of the tentacles.

FAMILY—TRITONIIDÆ.

Lingual teeth in seven rows (3. 1. 3.) central generally toothed ; lateral in three series, converging, the inner often broad, the two outer subulate, versatile ; mantle enclosed ; siphon straight ; foot small ; operculum ovate, annular, nucleus sub-apical. Shell with varices on the whorls ; aperture with a straight canal in front.

Genus, TRITONIUM—Link.

Shell oblong ; spire prominent ; whorls with a few remote and non-continuous varices ; columella rough or smooth ; canal re-curved, short or long ; outer lip internally crenated or denticulated.

T. australis, *Lamark, l.c.,* ix., *p.* 625 ; *Reeve, Conch., Ic., f.* 12 ; *Chenu, f.* 686. Spire produced ; whorls flattened, spirally grooved, both the grooves and the ridges sub-grooved ; some of the ridges sub-nodular ; columella callous, with a tooth at the posterior end, and generally with some wrinkles at the anterior end ; outer lip expanded, nodular, the nodules generally arranged in groups of two or three ; brownish-pink, variegated with brown, inside pinkish-white ; columella ochraceous; outer lip white with brown transverse bands from the nodules to the edge.

Length, 7; breadth, 4; angle of spire, 50°.

North Island. Chatham Islands. N.S. Wales.

T. spengleri, *Chemnitz; Lamark, l.c.,* ix., *p.* 627 ; *Reeve, Conch. Ic. f.* 36 ; *Chenu. f.* 691. Shell thick, ponderous, spire produced; whorls flattened, spirally grooved, with a row of nodules, which are sometimes obsolete on the body whorl; varices few; columella with a small rounded tooth at the posterior end, and sometimes a few wrinkles in the centre; outer lip much expanded and plicated; canal short, subperforate; yellowish white, covered with a pale brown transparent epidermis.

Length, 5·5; breadth, 3; angle of spire, 40°.

Auckland to Stewart Island. Chatham Islands. N.S. Wales. Tasmania.

T. olearium, L., *Reeve, Conch. Ic. f.* 32 ; *T. acclivis, Hutton C.M.M., p.* 13. Shell thick; spire rather depressed, bent slightly backwards, and to the right; whorls broadly spirally channelled, the posterior ridges with blunt nodules; varices few (one only); columella wrinkled; outer lip grooved; canal slightly produced; pale brown; columella dark chocolate brown; outer lip and varices banded with the same colour and white.

Length, 2·75; breadth, 1·6; angle of spire, 70°.

Auckland. Australia.

T. fusiformis, *Kiener, Ic. Coq.* iv. *p.* 36, *pl.* 5, *f.* 2 ; *Reeve, Conch. Ic. f.* 6. Shell abbreviately fusiform, solid, with eight varices; spire accuminated, apex sharp; whorls irregularly convoluted, rather angular at the upper part, transversely striated, striæ alternately tessellated with blunt oblong granules, interstices between the striæ very finely crisped, middle of the whorls armed with an oblique or slanting row of large prominent tubercules; yellowish-bay colour, transverse striæ light brown upon the solid varices, then articulated with bright brown and bay; columella smooth, armed at the upper part with a small callosity; aperture round, interior milk-white, lip slightly denticulated within; canal rather short, curved backward. (Reeve.)

Auckland and Sydney at 12 and 15 fathoms (Frauenfeld). Sydney (Angas).

Genus, RANELLA—Lamark,

Shell ovate, compressed; varices two on each whorl, rounded, forming a border to the shell.

R. leucostoma, *Lamark, l.c.,* ix., *p.* 542 ; *Reeve, Conch. Ic. f.* 4. Oval; whorls spirally striated; varices nearly continuous, with several elongated tubercles between them; columella with a prominent posterior tooth and a few anterior wrinkles; outer lip thickened, toothed; canal short; reddish brown, varices banded with white and blackish-purple; inside white; covered with a brown hairy epidermis.

Length, 2·5 ; breadth, 1·5 ; angle of spire, 50°.
North Island. Martin's Bay. Australia.

R. vexillum, *Sowerby; R. argus, Dieff., N.Z.,* ii., *p.* 229*; Reeve, Conch. Ic., f.* 13 ; *Chenu, f.* 713 ; *R. tumida, Dunker.* Oval, obliquely compressed ; whorls spirally striated, some of the ridges sub-nodulose ; varices flattened, not continuous ; columella with a thick posterior tooth, and a few median wrinkles ; outer lip dentate, teeth in pairs ; canal short ; chestnut-brown, ridges sometimes purplish ; varices coloured similarly to the rest of the shell ; inside white ; covered with a brown hairy epidermis.

Length, 4 ; breadth, 2·4 ; angle of spire, 62°.
Tasmania. Auckland to Stewart Island. Chatham Islands.

In *R. argus* the columella is smooth, and the body whorl transversely plicately noduled. In *R. vexillum* the columella is wrinkled, and the body whorl is not transversely plicated. Our species varies, sometimes running into one, sometimes into the other.

FAMILY—DOLIIDÆ.

Lingual teeth in seven rows (3. 1. 3.,) central generally toothed, lateral in three series, converging, the inner often broad, the two outer subulate, versatile. Mantle enclosed, the siphon re-curved ; foot small ; operculum none. Shell thin, ventricose ; whorls with transverse ribs ; aperture with an oblique notch in front.

Genus, DOLIUM—Browne.

Shell ventricose, spirally grooved ; last whorl very large ; outer lip waved.

D. variegatum, *Lamark, l.c.,* x., *p.* 143 ; *Reeve, Conch. Ic., f.* 7. Grooves simple, without any elevated line ; columella smooth, perforated ; suture excavated ; yellowish brown, varied longitudinally with darker and irregularly spotted with purplish-brown on the ribs ; interior yellowish-brown ; columella white.

Length, 4·75 ; breadth, 4 ; angle of spire, 120°.
Smaller and not so much spotted as Australian specimens.
From the North Cape to Tauranga. Australia.

FAMILY—CASSIDIDÆ.

Radula short, broad, triangular, with many rows of similar, lancet-shaped teeth, and a single small dentated tooth in the central series. Mantle enclosed, with a re-curved siphon ; foot large, dilated ; operculum annular ; nucleus in the middle of the straight inner edge. Shell ventricose, su'·-globose ; whorls often variced.

Genus, CASSIS—Browne.

Last whorl large ; aperture linear, long, with a short sharply re-curved sinistral canal in front ; inner lip forming a large transversely wrinkled plate ; outer lip thickened, reflected, plicate or toothed.

C. pyrum, *Lamark, l.c., x., p.* 33 ; *Reeve, Conch. Ic., f.* 29 ; *Chenu, f.* 1130 ; *C. striatus, Hutton, Cat. Tert. Moll., p.* 8 *(young.)* Shell ovate, ventricose ; whorls obtusely angled, nodulose on the angles ; upper whorls finely striated ; aperture dilated ; columella smooth, with a large plait at the anterior end ; outer lip reflexed, smooth ; pinkish-white, with bands of chestnut-brown wavy spots ; outer edge of lip banded with purplish-brown.
Length, 3·25 ; breadth, 2·25 ; angle of spire, 102°.
North Island. Martin's Bay. Tasmania. Australia.
The young shell is distantly spirally striated.

C. achatina, *Lamark, l.c., x., p.* 33 ; *Reeve, Conch, Ic., f.* 28. Ovato-acute, ventricose ; whorls flattened, smooth ; aperture moderate ; columella smooth, with a few plaits at the anterior end ; outer lip smooth ; purplish brown, spirally variegated with lighter and darker ; interior pale purple.
Length, 1·5 ; breadth, 1 ; angle of spire, 85°.
Omaha. Australia. Cape of Good Hope.

SERIES.—ROSTRIFERA.

Head produced into a rostrum, with the tentacles on the side of its base.

FAMILY—CYPRÆIDÆ.

Radula rather long, with seven series of teeth (3. 1. 3.,) each row composed of one broad, quadrate, uncinated, axile tooth, flanked on each side by three uncinated hooked laterals ; outer lateral teeth conical, entire or toothed. Head broad ; rostrum short ; tentacles long and subulate, with the eyes on swellings at their external bases. Mantle furnished with a siphon, and with large expanded side lobes covering the shell ; branchial plumes single ; foot simple ; operculum none. Shell usually polished ; the last whorl large, convolute, wholly or partially concealing the others ; outer lip greatly inflexed and toothed ; inner lip dentate or corrugated.

Genus, CYPRÆA—Linnæus.

Shell ovate, smooth ; inner lip with a fold in front.

C. punctata, *Linnæus ; Reeve, Conch. Ic., f.* 101. Shell ovato-oblong, small, thin, polished ; spire mamillate ; inner lip sparingly toothed, smooth in the middle ; white.
Length, ·55 ; breadth, ·37.
Doubtfully identified ; the typical form inhabits the Philippines, and

is sparingly spotted with red. A single specimen is in the Colonial Museum, Wellington, from the Bay of Islands.

Genus, TRIVIA--Gray.

Shell ovate, transversely ribbed, no distinct fold on the inner lip.

T. australis, *Lamark, l.c.,* x., *p.* 545 ; *Reeve, Conch. Ic., f.* 138 ; *Chenu, f.* 1734. Transverse striæ interrupted by an impressed median line ; spire visible ; white, with one or two flesh-coloured spots on the back, and the two extremities of the same colour.

Length, ·4 ; breadth, ·32.

Hauraki Gulf, in various places. Australia and Tasmania.

T. coccinella, *Lamark, l.c.,* x., *p.* 544 ; *Reeve, Conch. Ic., f.* 129 ; *Chenu, f.* 1732. Transverse striæ deep, not interrupted on the back ; spire hidden ; above pale pink, with a few obscure spots of brown, below white.

Length, ·4 ; breadth, ·25.

Bay of Islands. (Mr. C. Traill.)

Reeve considers this to be the same as *T. europæa.* I have no New Zealand specimens for comparison. It does not appear to be known in Australia.

FAMILY—APORRHAIDÆ.

Radula with seven series of teeth (3. 1. 3.,) the median hooked, denticulated, the first lateral uncinate, the second and third claw-shaped. Rostrum elongate, tapering ; tentacles subulate, bearing the eyes on slight prominences at their external bases ; mantle with the outer margin expanded or lobed, and with a rudimentary siphon in front, bent to the right ; foot small, oblong, simple ; operculum annular, ovate or pointed, the nucleus small apical. Shell with the canal bent to the right ; outer lip sinuous, lobed, or digitate.

Genus, STRUTHIOLARIA—Lamark.

Mantle with the outer edge simple ; operculum unguiculate, with the nucleus apical. Shell oblong-oval ; spire accuminated ; apex obtuse ; aperture with a short canal in front; columella thickened, polished, truncate anteriorly ; outer lip thickened and sinuous.

New Zealand, Australia and Kerguelen's Land only.

Tentacles subulate, lateral ; eyes small on outer side of the base ; lingual membrane thin ; teeth (3. 1. 3.,) central sub-ovate ; apex truncated, reflexed, entire ; lateral slender, subulate, curved ; apex acute, entire ; inner largest ; foot small, oblong. (Gray.)

S. papulosa, *Martyn : Chenu. f.* 1649 *and* 1652 ; *Murex stramineus, Gml.; Woodward's Manual of the Mollusca, pl.* 4, *f.* 6 ; *S. nodulosa, Lamark ; S. papulosa and S. vermis : Reeve, Conch. Ic., f.* 3 *and* 4.

Shell ovato-acute; whorls angled, with a row of nodules on the ridge; spirally striated; whorls seven or eight; yellowish, with close longitudinal waved stripes of purple; interior purple; mouth yellow, or white in old shells.

Length, 3·5; breadth, 1·9; angle of spire, 55°.

Var. B.—Dark reddish-brown, covered with a white chalky epiderdis; mouth greyish-white, stained with black on the outer edges.

Var. C.—*S. gigas, Sowerby; Chenu, f.* 1651; *S. vermis, Reeve:* whorls rounded, sub-nodulose.

North Island, common. Stewart Island, rare.

S. australis, *Gml.; Buccinum vermis, Martyn; Adams' Gen. of Shells, pl.* 27, *f.* 6; *S. crenulata, Lamark; Quoy and Gaimard, l.c.,* ii., *p.* 430, *pl.* 31, *f.* 7-9; *S. australis, Reeve; Conch. Ic., f.* 1; *Chenu, f.* 1653. Shell ovato-acute; whorls 6, angled, sub-noduse, finely spirally striated; body whorl flattened in the centre; columella very oblique; reddish-brown, with longitudinal undulating streaks of darker; mouth yellowish-brown; interior pale violet.

Length, 1·75; breadth, 1; angle of spire, 55°.

Not found south of Cook Strait. Animal yellowish-white, with fine reddish striæ. (Quoy.) Quoy and Gaimard figure the animal, and give a short account of its anatomy.

S. inermis, *Sowerby; Thes.* i., *f.* 12. Shell ovato-acute; whorls 6, rounded; widely spirally striated; body whorl slightly flattened in the centre; sutures deeply excavated; pale brownish, longitudinally streaked with reddish-brown.

Length, 1·6; breadth, 1·1; angle of spire, 62°.

Very rare south of Cook Strait, not uncommon in the north.

S. tricarinata, *Lesson; Ann. d. Sc. Nat., Series* 2, *Vol.* 16, *p.* 256. Shell ovato-oblong, very finely transversely striated, yellowish-brown, without marks; whorls 6, large, depressed in the middle, girdled in the depression with two grooves; the first keel salient, with a row of small nodules; lip thick, white and brown.

Height, ·87 inch; breadth, ·55 inch.

The suture is not deep. (Lesson.)

South Island of New Zealand.

Lesson considers this as quite distinct from *S. nodulosa* and·from *S. crenulata.*

FAMILY—TRICHOTROPIDÆ.

Lingual teeth in seven series (3.1.3); the central hamate and denticulated, the lateral curved, the inner denticulated, the two outer simple. Rostrum broad and short; tentacles wide apart, bearing the eyes on swellings at the extremities of their lower halves. Mantle enclosed, with a rudimentary siphonal fold. Foot small simple. Operculum subannular, ovate, horny, with a sub-lateral nucleus. Shell spiral, more or less turbinate; whorls covered with an epidermis; aperture sub-emarginate anteriorly; columella not plicate.

Genus, TRICHOTROPIS—Broderip.

Shell turbinated, thin, whorls keeled ; mouth large, columella obliquely truncated.

T. inornata, *Hutton, C.M.M. p.* 26 ; *T. clathrata, Sow. Conch. Ic. f.* 10 ; *Voy. Erebus and Terror, Moll. pl.* 1, *f.* 21. Small, cancellated, spire produced, without fringes ; a short anterior canal ; pale brown or white.

Length, ·43 ; breadth, ·25 ; angle of spire, 40°.
Auckland to Stewart Island. Chatham Islands.

The following is Sowerby's description :—Shell fusiform, covered with a thin pale epidermis, cancellated with slightly beaded spiral ribs, and interstitial regular small concentric ribs ; spire accuminated, whorls angular, carinated above ; aperture sub-trigonal, anteriorly acuminated ; umbilicus narrow.

SECTION—HOLOSTOMATA.

Peritreme entire, no siphon.   Herbivorous.

Sub-Section—Ptenoglossa.

Rachis teeth none, laterals numerous (∞.0.∞ .)

FAMILY—SCALARIDÆ.

Lateral teeth simple, unguicular.   Tentacles subulate, with the eyes on the outer side of their bases.   Mantle enclosed, with a rudimentary siphonal fold.   Foot obtusely triangular, grooved below, furnished in front with a fold or mentum.   Operculum horny, spiral, of few whorls. Shell spiral, turreted, variced ; aperture entire, without any notch or canal.

Genus, SCALARIA—Lamark.

Shell solid, lustrous ; whorls convex, sometimes separated, ornamented with numerous longitudinal ribs ; aperture round, peritreme continuous, thickened.

S. zelebori, *Frauenfeld, Reise der Novara, Moll. pl.* 1, *f.* 6.   Shell pyramidal, accuminate, imperforate, white ; whorls about ten, rounded, transversely obsoletely grooved, suture deeply disjoined ; varices numerous, rather thick, erect, rather turned back, undulately crenated, subangular near the suture ; last costula distinctly spirally marked ; aperture sub-rotund.

Length, ·95 ; breadth, ·32 inch.   (Frauenfeld.)
Auckland.

Frauenfeld refers this species, with doubt, to Adams' sub-genus *Opalia,* in which the shell is turreted, and imperforate, the whorls not disunited, the last with a conspicuous spiral ridge round the umbilical region.

K

S. lyra, *Sowerby, Thes. Conch., No.* 4, *Sp.* 27 ; *Reeve's Conch. Ic. f.* 23 ; *S. lineolata, C.M.M., not of Keiner.* Shell accuminate, imperforate or sub-perforate ; whorls five to seven, rounded ; varices numerous, about twenty in the body whorl, thin ; mouth oval ; white, with a pale brown band on the anterior part of the body whorl.

Length, ·45 ; breadth, ·2 ; angle of spire, 32°.

Auckland. Philippine Islands.

FAMILY—SOLARIIDÆ.

Tentacles folded, with the suture below ; eyes sessile on the surface of their bases ; mantle included ; gill cavity divided by a longitudinal fold ; foot moderate, formed for walking ; operculum horny, spiral, ovate or circular. Shell trochiform ; axis widely perforated ; aperture not pearly within ; the tongue is unarmed (Gray.)

Genus, PHILIPPIA—Gray.

Operculum flat, orbicular, many whorled. Shell discoidal, sub-conic, smooth ; aperture sub-quadrate, not pearly within ; umbilicus wide ; the margin crenulated.

P. lutea, *Lamark, Anim. Sans. Vert.,* ix., *p.* 100 ; *Reeve, Conch. Ic. (Solarium,) f.* 14 ; *Adams, Gen. Moll., p.* 25, *f.* 8 ; *Solarium luteum, Chenu, f.* 1355. Shell rather obtusely conoid, yellow ; whorls slopingly convex, smooth, decussately malleated, encircled at the periphery, with two white red-beaded keels ; umbilicus small, but little crenated (Reeve.)

Mediterranean. Australia. Hauraki Gulf. (Mr. C. Mathews.)

According to M. Philippi, the animal resembles *Trochus,* and possibly the genus should be united to *Monilea.*

FAMILY—JANTHINIDÆ.

Lateral teeth numerous, uniform, simple, slender ; head proboscidi-form ; tentacles short and obtuse, with pointed eye pedicels at their base ; eyes none ; gills plumose, partially exserted ; foot small, flat, rudimentary, furnished with a vesicular appendage on the hinder part ; sexes separate (?) : eggs cohering into a raft ; no operculum. Shell thin, translucent, spiral, more or less turbinate, with a sinistral nucleus (Pelagic.)

Genus, JANTHINA—Bolten.

Shell sub-globose, violet, spiral ; spire short ; whorls slightly angula-ted ; aperture large, quadrangular ; inner lip reflexed ; columella tortu-ous ; outer lip thin, notched or sinuated near the middle.

The swimming raft is regarded by some naturalists as a modified operculum. The ovarian capsules are fixed to its under surface. *

For a description of the animal, see A. Adams in the Ann. Nat. Hist., 3rd Series, x., p. 417, and Dr. Lacaze Duthiers, in the same periodical, 3rd Series, xvii., p. 278.

J. communis, *Lamark, Anim. Sans. Vert.,* ix., *p.* 4 ; *Reeve, Conch. Ic., f.* 5 ; *Chenu, f.* 517 (bad,) 518 ; *Helix ianthina, L.* Whorls four, convex, finely obliquely striated ; spire depressed ; mouth large ; columella rather short, twisted to the right ; violet, getting whitish on the spire.

Length, ·65 ; breadth, ·82 ; angle of spire, 107°.
North Island. N.S. Wales.

J. iricolor, *Reeve, Conch. Ic., f.* 23. Shell somewhat globose, very thin ; spire obtusely conical, more or less immersed ; whorls rather narrow, rounded concentrically irregularly plicately striated ; striæ sinuated in the middle, purple violet, transparently iridescent ; columella scarcely reflected, rather twisted ; aperture open, slightly channelled at the base (Reeve.)
North Island.

J. exigua, *Lamark, Anim. Sans. Vert.,* ix., *p* 5 ; *Reeve, Conch. Ic., f.* 21 ; *Chenu, f.* 519. Whorls four, convex, rather deeply obliquely striated ; mouth large ; columella straight, long ; outer lip deeply notched ; violet, with a whitish spiral band on the posterior margin of the whorls.

Length, ·4 ; breadth, ·4 ; angle of spire, 85°.
Abundant on exposed sandy coasts.
North and South Islands. Chatham Islands. N.S. Wales and S. Australia.

Sub-Section—Tænioglossa.

One row of rachis plates, and three lateral plates on each side (3.1.3.)

SERIES—PROBOSCIDIFERA.

Head small ; proboscis retractile under the base of the tentacles.

FAMILY—NATICIDÆ.

Animal bulky. Radula short. Tentacles lanceolate, wide apart, united by a veil ; eyes usually absent, or very minute, and placed beneath the tentacular veil. Mantle enclosed. Foot very large and expanded, rounded at both ends, much produced in front, where it is furnished with a fold which covers the head and tentacles ; operculigerous lobe very ample, reflected upon and partially concealing the sides and back of the shell. Operculum spiral, few whorled. Shell spiral, usually smooth or polished, more or less globular ; aperture semi-lunar, sometimes very large.

Genus, NATICA—Adanson.

Animal entirely retractile within the shell. Operculum horny, with a calcareous outer layer. Shell sub-globose ; spire rather elevated ; columella adherent to, and spirally contorted in, the umbilicus.

N. zealandica, *Quoy, Voy. Astrolabe,* ii., *p.* 237, *pl,* 66, *f.* 11-12 ; *Reeve, Conch. Ic., f.* 90. Shell smooth, perforate, pillar visible in the umbilicus ; very finely transversely striate ; inner lip callous ; operculum shelly ; yellowish or reddish brown, with about six interrupted spiral chestnut brown bands ; the spots generally lunate ; interior pale brown ; columella, mouth, and interior portion of body whorl, white.

Length, 1·1 ; breadth, 1·05.

Omaha to Stewart Island ; common in the north, rare in the south. Chatham Islands.

Genus, LUNATIA—Lamark.

Animal entirely retractile within the shell. Operculum simple, cartilaginous. Shell sub-globose ; spire rather elevated ; inner lip thin, or with a moderate callus ; umbilicus wide, pervious, not funiculate.

L. australis, *Hutton ; Jour. de Conch.,* 1878, *p.* 23. Globose, smooth, whorls 3½ ; suture well marked, but not excavated ; umbilicus rather narrow, without any groove ; inner lip with a callus ; brown or grey.

Length, ·3 ; breadth, ·3.
Auckland.
I have not seen the operculum.

L. vitrea, *Hutton, C.M.M. p.* 21. Shell polished, smooth, white ; perforated, pillar not visible in the umbilicus ; operculum horny.

Length, ·35 ; breadth, ·34.
Stewart Island and Chatham Islands.

FAMILY—PYRAMIDELLIDÆ.

Teeth rudimentary. Tentacles broad, folded, ear-shaped, connate at their base, bearing the eyes immersed at their inner sides ; mantle enclosed, with a rudimentary siphonal fold ; foot produced and truncate anteriorly, with a fold or mentum in front ; operculum horny, subspiral, with the columella margin sinuated. Shell turreted ; aperture entire, or not produced into a canal in front ; columella plaited. Marine.

Genus, OBELISCUS—Humphrey.

Turreted, smooth ; aperture semi-oval, entire, rounded anteriorly ; columella straight, with more or less numerous folds.

O. roseus, *Hutton, C.M.M., p.* 22. Whorls flattened, smooth ; white or pinkish, spirally banded with dark-pink.

Length, ·2 ; breadth, ·1.
Stewart Island.

Genus, CHEMNITZIA—D'Orbigny.

Shell slender, elongated ; whorls plaited ; apex sinistral ; aperture simple, ovate ; peristome incomplete.

C. zealandica, *Hutton. C.M.M., p.* 22. Turreted ; whorls transversely plaited, smooth ; white.

Length, ·23 ; breadth, ·1.
Stewart Island to Auckland.
Very like *Turbonilla nitida*, Angas, Proc. Zool. Soc., 1867, p. 112.

Genus, ODOSTOMIA—Fleming.

Shell subulate or ovate, smooth ; apex sinistral; aperture ovate ; peristome not continuous ; columella with one fold ; lip thin ; operculum indented on one side.

O. lactea, *Angas; Proc. Zool. Soc.*, 1867, *p.* 112, *pl.* 13, *f.* 11. Shell turreted ; whorls flattened, very finely transversely striate ; white, sometimes slightly tinged with pink ; sub-diaphanous.
Length, ·3 ; breadth, ·14.
Stewart Island to Auckland. Australia.

FAMILY—EULIMIDÆ.

Teeth rudimentary. Tentacles simple, subulate ; eyes sessile at their outer bases ; mantle enclosed, with a rudimentary siphonal fold ; foot linguiform, produced in front, with a bi-lobed mentum or fold above the front margin ; operculigerous lobe developed at the sides into even-edged, unequal expansions or lobes ; operculum horny, ovate, sub-spiral. Shell white, smooth, polished, turreted ; aperture entire in front; columella simple.

Genus, EULIMA—Risso.

Spire frequently with an interrupted varix on one side; apex acute ; aperture oval, pointed behind ; inner lip reflected over the pillar ; axis imperforate ; outer lip thickened internally.

E. chathamensis, *Hutton, C.M.M., p.* 23. Turreted ; apex blunt ; spire whorls obsoletely transversely plaited ; white.
Length, ·23 ; breadth, ·13.
Chatham Islands. Auckland.

SERIES—ROSTRIFERA.

Head produced into a rostrum, with the tentacles on the sides of its base.

FAMILY—CERITHIIDÆ.

Radula long and linear ; laterals hooked, multicuspid ; outer laterals conical, curved. Rostrum broad and short ; tentacles wide-apart, subulate ; eyes on short pedicels united to the outer sides of the tentacles ; mantle-margin with a rudimentary siphonal fold in front ; gill composed of a single series of plates; foot broad and short, angulated in front ; operculum horny, spiral or sub-spiral. Shell spiral, many whorled ; aperture more or less channelled in front ; outer lip often expanded in the adult.

Sub-Family—Potamidinæ.

Operculum circular, of many whorls. Shell usually covered with a brown epidermis ; the fore-part of the aperture more or less channelled not produced into a beak.

Genus, CERITHIDEA—Swainson.

Eye pedicels, very long and thick, connate with the tentacles nearly to their tips. Shell turreted ; apex of spire more or less decollated ; aperture rounded, slightly emarginate anteriorly, with a dilated thickened margin.*

C. alternata, *Hutton, C.M.M., p. 26, not Cerithium alteratum, Sow.* Whorls deeply spirally grooved, with a small ridge in the bottom of each groove, and transversely plicated ; outer lip expanded ; yellowish-brown ; interior white, with spiral bands of purplish-black.
Length, ·95 ; breadth, ·38 ; angle of spire, 23°.
Tauranga. A single specimen only in the Colonial Museum, Wellington.

C. bicarinata, *Gray; Dieff. N.Z.* ii., *p.* 241 ; *Voy. Erebus and Terror, Moll., pl.* 1, *f.* 20 ; *Reeve, Conch. Ic. (Cerithidea) f.* 27 ; *C. lutulentum, Kein Mon. Cerith, pl.* 23, *f.* 1 ; Whorls rather convex, obsoletely spirally striated, and transversely plicated ; the body whorl with two spiral ridges on the anterior end, separated by a concave groove ; blackish-purple, generally with a rough brown or reddish-brown coating.
Length, 1·12 ; breadth, ·38 ; angle of spire, 23°.
Common in the North Island, not found south of Banks Peninsula.

C. nigra, *Hombron and Jacquinot Voy. Pole Sud., pl.* 24, *f.* 34-36 ; *C. subcarina, Sowerby; Reeve, Conch. Ic. (Cerithidea) f.* 28 ; *C. australis, Gray, Dieff. N.Z.,* ii., *p.* 241 ; *nec. Lamark.* Whorls nearly flat, slightly transversely plicated ; body whorl with two spiral grooves at the anterior end ; brownish-black, often with a brown coating ; interior dark purple, with one or two lighter bands.
Length, ·45 ; breadth, ·17 ; angle of spire, 28°.
Auckland to Dunedin. Chatham Islands.

Genus, BITTIUM—Leach.

Operculigerous lobe with rudimentary expansions on each side, and furnished with a roundish, lanceolate cirrus (Lovén). Operculum subcircular, of four volutions. Shell turreted, granular, often with irregular varices ; aperture with a slight canal in front, not produced nor recurved ; inner lip simple ; outer lip acute, not reflexed, nor expanded.

B. terebelloides, *v. Martens, Critical list of the Moll. of N.Z., p.* 26 ; *C. cinctum, Hutton, C.M.M., p.* 27. Conical, turreted, yellowish on the upper three whorls ; body whorl with four smooth spiral keels of

---

* *Crithium bicolor* and *C. striatum* of Hombron and Jacquinot, are quite unlike any shell found in New Zealand, and are probably Polynesian or Australian species.

nearly equal size, the interstices between them with faint perpendicular striæ ; at the base of the body whorl there is a blunt angle, and beneath it a fifth keel ; aperture deeply notched at the base, without any protruding canal ; the specimens, which are imperfect at the top, have a length of ·33 inch, and a breadth of ·1. They show ten whorls. (Martens.) Auckland to Stewart Island.

B. exilis, *Hutton, C.M.M., p. 27.* Whorls flat, deeply spirally grooved, and transversely plicated ; sulcus deep ; aperture rounded ; canal moderate ; light brown.
Length ·21 ; breadth, ·07.
Stewart Island, 30 fathoms.
This species sometimes has two nodular ridges on the spire whorls.

Genus, TRIPHORIS—Deshayes.

Tentacles clavate at the tips, united at their bases by a sinuated veil. Operculum orbicular, few whorled. Shell turreted, sinistral ; aperture round, produced anteriorly into a closed tubular canal, sometimes with a posterior closed canal.

T. angasi, *Crosse, Jour. de Conch.* 1865, *pl.* 1, *f.* 12-13 ; *C. minimus, Hutton, C.M.M., p. 27.* Whorls flat, sinistral, spirally grooved and transversely plicated : aperture rounded : anterior canal short, recurved, posterior canal very short, open ; pale brown.
Length, ·25 ; breadth, ·7.
Stewart Island, 30 fathoms. Bay of Islands. Australia.
I am indebted to Dr. v. Martens for this identification.

T. gemmulatus, *Adams and Reeve, Voy. Samarang, Moll., p.* 46.
Dr. v. Martens says that he has received this species from New Zealand. I have not been able to obtain a description of it.

FAMILY—MELANIIDÆ.

Radula long and linear ; lateral teeth uncinate, multicuspid ; rostrum broad, annulated ; tentacles subulate. with the eyes on bulgings at their outer sides ; mantle margin fringed, with a rudimentary siphonal fold in front ; gill composed of rigid cylindrical plates ; foot broad and short, angulated in front ; operculum horny, ovate, sub-spiral. Shell turreted, covered with a thick dark-colored epidermis ; aperture often channelled or emarginate in front ; outer lip simple ; fluviatile, sometimes viviparous.*

Sub-Family—Melanopsinæ.

Operculum ovate, sub-spiral. Shell covered with an epidermis ; aperture with a distinct notch in front.

---

* *Melania mirifica,* Adams (P.Z.S., 1853, p. 99), is said by Reeve to come from New Zealand, but Adams gives New Ireland as the habitat.

Genus, MELANOPSIS—Ferussac.

Shell ovate ; last whorl elongated, smooth, or longitudinally plicate ; spire short, acute ; aperture oblong, distinctly notched in front ; inner lip thick, with a callus posteriorly ; outer lip simple, acute.

M. trifasciata, *Gray ; Dieff., N.Z.,* ii., *p.* 263 ; *Voyage Erebus and Terror, Moll., pl.* 1, *f.* 18-22 ; *M. zealandica, Gould, U.S. Ex. Ep.,* xii., *p.* 130 ; *Reeve, Conch. Ic., f.* 2. Shell ovate, thin, dark olive ; spire short, conical, about ⅓ the length of the body whorl ; the last whorl with three equi-distant chestnut bands ; the callosity of the inner lip yellow (Gray.)
Dunedin.

M. strangei, *Reeve, Conch. Ic., f.* 3. Shell somewhat globosely ovate, rather thick, olive ; whorls very few, slopingly ventricose, longitudinally wrinkled and malleated, partially obsoletely noduled ; aperture ovate, slightly effused at the lower part ; columella callous at the upper part, then excavated, concavely twisted at the base, but little reflected (Reeve.)

According to Reeve this has a different contour, and a less twisted columella than the last species. It is no doubt the same as fig. 18 of the Voyage of the Erebus and Terror. I have not seen it from the South Island.

FAMILY—LITTORINIDÆ.

Radula long ; rachis teeth broad and hooked ; laterals hooked and oblong ; outer laterals conical, curved. Rostrum moderate, entire ; eyes sessile on the outer side of the tentacles ; no neck lobes nor lateral cirri ; mantle with a rudimentary siphonal fold in front ; gills 2, one very large, occupying nearly the whole surface of the branchial cavity, and formed of flat, free plaits ; foot with a linear duplication in front, and a groove along the under surface ; operculum horny, spiral, of few whorls. Shell spiral, turbinated or depressed ; aperture simple in front, never pearly within.

Genus, LITTORINA—Ferussac.

Eyes sessile near the outer bases of the tentacles. Shell turbinate, solid, of few whorls ; axis imperforate ; spire short ; aperture sub-circular, entire ; columella lip rather flattened ; outer lip simple, acute.
On rocks above low water mark ; semi-amphibious.

L. cincta, *Quoy, l.c.,* ii., *p.* 481, *pl.* 33, *f.* 20-21 ; *Reeve, Conch. Ic., f.* 53. Ovato-conical ; spire acute ; body whorl spirally striated ; aperture oval ; columella flattened ; bluish black, with fine spiral bluish-white lines ; generally covered with a brown epidermis ; interior deep violet ; columella dark chestnut-brown.
Length, ·85 ; breadth, ·5 ; angle of spire, 46°.
Abundant in the South Island, rare in the North. Chatham Islands.
The operculum is many whorled (Tenison-Woods, P.L.S. of N.S. Wales, iii., p. 67.)

L. cærulescens, *Lamark; Anim. Sans Vert.,* ix., *p.* 217 ; *L. diemenensis, Quoy, l.c.,* ii., *p.* 479, *pl.* 33, *f.* 8-11 *; Reeve, Conch. Ic., f.* 94. Ovato-conical ; spire acute ; body whorl lightly spirally striated, sub-carinated in large specimens ; columella flattened ; bluish-white, with a broad spiral band of blackish-blue on the body whorl ; interior violet with a white band round the mouth.

Length, ·45 ; breadth, ·26 ; angle of spire, 43°.
Auckland to the Bluff, but smaller in the South. Chatham Islands. Australia. Tasmania.

L. luctuosa, *Reeve, Conch. Ic., f.* 65. Shell accuminately ovate, imperforated ; whorls slantingly convex; longitudinally plicately striated, spirally grooved towards the lower part ; livid brown ; aperture rather small, chestnut ; columella purplish (Reeve.)
New Zealand. (Cuming.)

L. novæ zealandiæ, *Reeve, Conch. Ic. , f.* 74. Shell somewhat globosely turbinated ; spire rather short, very sharp ; whorls rounded, spirally irregularly linearly grooved ; opaque white, obscurely very faintly red-flamed ; aperture nearly rounded ; chestnut-brown in the interior ; columella very broadly excavated, livid chestnut (Reeve.)
New Zealand. (Cuming.)

Genus, RISELLA—Gray.

Eyes situated on the tentacles ; operculum ovate, sub-spiral. Shell trochiform, with a flat or concave base ; axis imperforate ; whorls flattened, the last angulated, often acutely keeled ; aperture depressed, oblique, rhombic, dark or variegated internally ; outer lip acute, simple.

R. melanostoma, *Gml.; Adams' Gen. Moll., pl.* 23, *f.* 5*a, b.; Chenu, f.* 2127 ; *R. kielmanseggi, Frauenfeld, Voy. der Novara, Moll., f.* 1. Shell conical, bluish-brown ; whorls plicato-nodulose, rugose, marked with numerous oblique points ; body whorl acutely angled ; base flattish, spirally grooved ; throat yellowish-white.
Length, ·53 ; breadth, ·64.
Auckland.
For the difference between the male and female of this species, see the Rev. J. Tenison-Woods, P.L.S. of N.S. Wales, i., p. 242.

Genus, FOSSARINA—Adams and Angas.

Shell turbinated, depressed, broadly unbilicated ; whorls spirally ribbed ; aperture circular, large, not pearly within ; lip arcuate, simple ; operculum horny, sub-spiral.

F. varius, *Hutton, C.M.M., p.* 35 *(Adeorbis.)* Spirally grooved, smooth ; brown, irregularly varied with darker and white ; interior purple, varied with white.
Length, ·17 ; breadth, ·3.
Stewart Island to Auckland. Chatham Islands

L

FAMILY—RISSOIDÆ.

Inner lateral teeth very broad ; the apices incurved, lobed ; outer laterals dissimilar, all with denticulated apices. Rostrum more or less adnate below to the fore-part of the foot ; tentacles setaceous, with the eyes on bulgings at their outer bases ; neck lobes none ; foot angulated in front, acuminate behind ; operculigerous lobe with developed lateral expansions, and usually furnished with a caudal tentacular filament ; operculum horny, sub-spiral. Shell generally white, spiral, more or less turreted ; aperture usually simple in front.

Genus, RISSOINA—D'Orbigny.

Operculum semi-lunar, sub-spiral ; muscular impression longitudinal, with an elongated process before it. Shell turreted, ribbed or cancellated ; many whorled ; spire acuminate ; aperture ovate, effuse anteriorly, slightly channelled in front ; outer lip anteriorly dilated, thickened internally.

R. plicata, *Hutton, C.M.M., p.* 29. Elongated ; whorls 6 ; spire whorls with two, body whorl with about five, spiral ribs ; spire and posterior part of body whorl transversely plicated ; mouth round ; white.
Length, ·15 ; breadth, ·05.
Stewart Island.

R. rugulosa, *Hutton, C.M.M., p.* 28. Elongated ; whorls seven, smooth, obscurely transversely ribbed ; aperture ovate ; white or yellowish-white.
Length, 3 ; breadth, ·12.
Stewart Island. Chatham Islands.

R. purpurea, *Hutton, C.M.M., p.* 29. Elongated ; whorls 6, flat, not polished ; sutures obscure ; aperture round ; spire purple or purplish-red, with a posterior spiral white band ; body whorl yellowish, also with a posterior white band at the suture.
Length, ·1 ; breadth, ·05.
Stewart Island.

R. subfusca, *Hutton, C.M.M., p.* 28. Whorls 5, flattened, smooth, but not polished ; aperture round ; pale brown.
Length, ·12 ; breadth, ·05.
Stewart Island.

R. fasciata, *Adams, P.Z.S.,* 1851, *p.* 264 ; *Reeve, Conch. Ic., f.* 119. Shell subulately-turreted, solid, dirty white, banded with reddish-brown ; whorls 8, rather convex, transversely finely striated, longitudinally plicated ; plicæ oblique, equal, rather distant ; aperture semi-ovate, sub-channelled in front ; lip sub-dilated (Adams.)
New Zealand. (Sowerby.) Sydney. (Strange.)

Genus, BARLEEIA—Clark.

Operculigerous lobe simple; foot slightly emarginate posteriorly; operculum testaceous, sub-annular, under surface with a raised rib and a long, pointed, testaceous apophysis proceeding from the nucleus. Shell turbinately conical; whorls tumid, smooth or transversely striated; aperture oval, entire, contracted behind, rounded in front; outer lip acute, simple.

B. flamulata, *Hutton: Jour. de Conch.*, 1878, *p.* 28. Smooth; red, generally with oblique white rays; whorls 6 or 6½.
Length, ·25.
Auckland.

B. rosea, *Hutton, C.M.M., p.* 29. Ovate; whorls 4, rather flat, smooth, polished; mouth round; white or bright-pink.
Length, ·07; breadth, ·05.
Stewart Island.

B. nana, *Hutton, C.M.M., p.* 28. Whorls 5, swollen, finely transversely ribbed; aperture ovate; white.
Length, ·1; breadth, ·05.

B. impolita, *Hutton, C.M.M., p.* 29. Ovate; whorls 4, rounded, finely spirally striated; mouth ovate; white, not polished.
Length, ·1; breadth, ·06.
Stewart Island.

Genus, BYTHINELLA—Moguin-Tandon.

Operculigerous lobe simple; operculum sub-spiral. Shell elongately conical, thin, smooth, covered with an olivaceous epidermis; axis imperforate; aperture oval; peritreme continuous; outer lip acute, simple.*
Fresh water.

B. antipoda, *Gray; Dieff., N.Z.,* ii., *p.* 241; *Voy. Erebus and Terror, Moll., pl.* 1, *f.* 19. Shell ovate, acute, sub-perforated, (generally covered with a brown earthy coat); whorls rather rounded; mouth ovate; axis three lines; operculum horny and sub-spiral (Gray.)
Var.—Spire rather longer; whorls more rounded. (Gray.)
Auckland. Dunedin.

B. zealandiæ, *Gray; Dieff., N.Z.,* ii., *p.* 241; *Voy. Erebus and Terror, Moll., pl.* 1, *f.* 19 (below). Shell ovate, turreted, imperforated, pellucid, greenish, generally covered with a brown earthy coat; whorls

---

* I follow the Rev. J. Tension-Woods in putting these shells into the genus *Bythinella*, but they are very different in form from *Bythinella nuclea* (Lea) from California. Mons. Fischer considers that *Hydrobia* should be restricted to marine shells only; Dr. Paladilhe, on the contrary, restricts it to fresh water forms (Ann. d Sci. Nat., vi-i., p. 7.)

convex; mouth roundish, ovate, rather reflexed; axis three lines; operculum horny, sub-spiral.
Like the former, but smaller and more tapering. (Gray.)
Lake Guyon.

B, egena, *Gould, Pro. Bost. Soc.,* iii., *p.* 75 ; *A gracilis, Gould, U.S. Ex. Ep., p.* 127, *f.* 131. Shell minute, elongate, turreted, delicate, smooth, or with faint striæ of growth, covered with a thin, pale green epidermis; spire acute; whorls 5, convex, the last one half the length of the shell, and partially perforate; aperture ovate, one-third the length of the shell ; peristome entire, acute, rising before an indistinct umbilical chink, one-third the length of the shell, somewhat evasive (Gould.)
Length of axis, ⅛ inch ; breadth, ¹⁄₁₀ inch.
Bank's Peninsula.
Probably *B. antipoda, zealandiæ,* and *egena* are identical.

B. spelæa, *Frauenfeld ; Verhandl de k.k. Zoologisch, Botanischen, Gesellsch in Wien.,* 1863, xiii. ; *Band, p.* 1022. Shell conical, solid, bone-colored, sub-transparent, faintly shining. Five whorls slightly convex; suture a little excavated ; aperture oval ; margin dark, dilated, free above, connected below with the mouth, where it covers the narrow fissure-like umbilicus.
Length, ·1 inch ; breadth, ·05 inch. (Frauenfeld.)
Probably small specimens of *B. antipodum.*

B. fischeri, *Dunker; Mal. Blatt,* viii., 1862, *p.* 152. Shell oblong-conic, sub-turrited, rimate, sub-solid, horny or reddish ; whorls 6 or 7, rounded, obsoletely striated ; suture deep; last whorl half the length of the shell ; aperture ovate ; peristome thickened, continuous ; operculum sub-spiral, thin.
Length, ·28 ; breadth, ·15. (Dunker.)
Lake Rotoiti and Auckland.
Distinguished by its convex whorls and deep suture. Dr. Dunker agrees with Dr. v. Martens that it may possibly be *P. corolla* without spines; but this is very doubtful, as I have never found *P. corolla* near Dunedin, while *B. fischeri* is common.

B. badia, *Gould, U.S. Ex. Ep.,* xii., *p.* 126, *f.* 150. Shell minute, elongate, ovate-turreted, rather solid, of a Spanish-brown colour; spire of five or more whorls, forming an acute spire, eroded at tip; whorls moderately convex, shouldered above, the last indistinctly angular at periphery ; imperforate ; aperture one-third the length of the shell ; peristome complete ; edge black, thick ; operculum sub-circular, eccentric ; surface smooth.
Length, ⅛ inch ; breadth, ¹⁄₁₂ inch. (Gould.)
Bank's Peninsula.

B. reevei, *Frauenfeld, l.c., p.* 1024. Shell small, acute, conical, solid, dull-whitish, sub-transparent ; whorls 5½, angulated, nearly flat and perpendicular, step-like ; occasionally the whorls are more convex, and angles less step-like, although always distinct ; aperture moderate, oval ;

margin sharp, close to the columella, so that the visible umbilicus is reduced to a fissure; keel sometimes with a brown margin, and sometimes irregularly granulated.

Length, ·15 ; breadth, ·08. (Frauenfeld.)
Probably the same as the last. I have a specimen from Auckland.

Genus, POTAMOPYRGUS—Stimpson.

Shell ornamented with spines; rhachidian tooth not strongly trilobate below; basal denticles of each tooth minute and close to the lateral margins; denticles of intermediate tooth numerous and equal in size.

P. corolla, *Gould, U.S., Ex., Ep.,* xii., *p.* 129, *f.* 149; *Reeve, Conch. Ic. (Melania,) f.* 366; *Paludestrina cumingiana and P. salleana; Fischer, Jour de Conch.,* viii., *p.* 208-209; *H. crossei, Frauenfeld, l.c., p.* 595; *A. ciliata (Gould,) Frauenfeld, l.c., p.* 1025. Shell ovate, thin, transparent, pale olive; whorls 5 to 6, broadly angled round the upper part, spined at the angle; aperture somewhat squarely ovate (Reeve.)
Common in the North Island.

P. Cumingiana is said, by its author, to be distinguished by its globular ventricose form; absence of spines on the first 3½ whorls, their greater number (17-20) on the last whorl; their length and obliquity (curving toward the spire;) the obsolete keel on the last whorl corresponding to the spines; and the peristome being slightly thickened and entire. *P. salleana* is more conical, less globular, shorter spines, and, on the last four whorls, keels lirate but below the spines; the last whorl is proportionately less swollen. (Tenison-Woods.)

FAMILY—TURRITELLIDÆ.

Radula minute, very short; teeth in seven series (3. 1. 3.,) each series consisting of a sub-quadrate median tooth, with an incurved, denticulated apex, and of three similar ligulate uncini on each side, all with hamate, serrulated summits. Rostrum short, broad; tentacles long and subulate; the eyes slightly prominent on their external bases; mantle with a fringed margin, obscurely siphonated at the right side; branchial plume single, very long; foot very short, truncate in front, rounded behind, grooved beneath; operculigerous lobe simple; operculum horny, circular, multi-spiral; edge of the whorls fimbriated. Shell spiral, many whorled; aperture simple in front.

Genus, TURRITELLA—Lamark.

(Sub-Genus, *Haustator.*) Aperture sub-quadrangular; whorls with a broad groove in the middle; outer lip sinuated.

T. rosea, *Quoy, l.c.,* iii., *p.* 136, *pl.* 55, *f.* 24-26; *Reeve, Conch. Ic., f.* 41. Whorls flattened, spirally striated, the ribs of unequal sizes, generally several small ones between bigger ones, at irregular distances; sutures deep in the anterior whorls only; mouth sub-quadrate; reddish-brown or yellowish; finely spirally banded with purplish-brown.

Length, 3·5; breadth, ·95; angle of spire, 20°.

Common in the North, rare in the South.   Chatham Islands.

Animal : foot greenish or yellowish, spotted with brown; mantle with whitish lunules, regularly disposed; tentacles white.   (Quoy.)

T. vittata, *Hutton, C.M.M., p. 29.*   Whorls flattened, sutures generally scarcely showing; finely spirally striated; mouth sub-quadrate; yellowish-white with distant spiral brown bands, about four on the base.

Length, 1·8; breadth, ·5; angle of spire, 15°.

North Island.

T. fulminata, *Hutton, C.M.M.., p. 29.*   Whorls flattened in the centre, sutures deep; finely spirally striated throughout; mouth sub-quadrate; white with longitudinal undulating markings of pinkish-brown.

Length, 1·2; breadth, ·3; angle of spire, 18°.

Great Barrier Island and Auckland.

T. pagoda, *Reeve, Conch. Ic., f. 60.*   Shell somewhat pyramidally turreted; whorls 14 or 15 in number, spirally sharply-ridged, conspicuously encircled with a single sharp rib towards the base; first few whorls two ribbed, the upper one quickly disappearing; whitish, obscurely flamed with light fulvous colour (Reeve.)

Great Barrier Island.

Closely related to *T. conspersa* from China.

Genus, EGLISIA—Gray.

Shell elongately turreted; whorls numerous, rounded, with obsolete longitudinal varices, suture depressed; aperture orbicular, small; inner lip flattened, incrassated, angulated at the fore-part, not reflexed anteriorly; outer lip thickened internally; animal unknown.

E. symmetrica, *Hutton, C.M.M., p. 30.*   Whorls rounded, with three equal and equally distant spiral ribs; sutures deep; mouth roundish; white.

Length, ·67; breadth, ·22; angle of spire, 23°.

Stewart Island.

FAMILY—VERMETIDÆ.

Dentition (?)   Rostrum produced; tentacles short, triangular, eyes small, at their external bases.   Mantle with the margin entire, embracing the neck; gills enclosed in a line on the left side of the mantle cavity. Foot cylindrical, not serving for locomotion, dilated, sub-clavate, or truncated in front.   Operculum horny, circular, many-whorled or wanting. Shell irregularly twisted, tubular, attached, often regularly spiral when young ; aperture round.*

* *Vernetus cariniferus*, Gray, Dieff., N.Z., ii., p. 242, and Zoology of the Voyage of the Erebus and Terror, Moll., pl. 1, f. 23, is an Annelid.

Genus, SIPHONIUM—Browne.

Operculum large, smooth, circular, concave ; scar central, rugose. Shell usually fixed, tubular, whorls often carinated, irregular and tortuous ; aperture round, peritreme acute, continuous.

S. lamellosum, *Hutton; C.M.M., p.* 30. Shell thick, irregularly twisted, with numerous imbricating transverse ridges, which are often reflexed ; mouth round, operculum hemispherical ; white, sometimes tinged with pale violet. Diameter of mouth, ·2.

Forms large masses not attached to other bodies. Deep water.

Genus, CLADOPODA—Gray.

Foot elongate, front end simple, hinder extremity oblong, clavate, or sub-truncate. Operculum none. Shell tubular, irregularly sub-spirally twisted, whorls disunited ; aperture round, peritreme acute, continuous.

C. zealandica, *Quoy, l.c.,* iii., *p.* 293, *pl.* 67, *f.* 16-17*; Morch, P.Z.S.,* 1862, *p.* 82. Shell white or brownish, lightly longitudinally striated ; animal, with the head blackish with red spots ; margin pale yellow ; foot spotted with red ; the head is yellowish behind, brown and dotted with red in front ; the foot yellowish with red spots ; the mantle is broadly bordered with bright orange. (Quoy).

Bay of Islands.

Genus, STEPHOPOMA—Morch.

Shell fixed in the adult, contorted, solitary or agglomerated ; aperture lightly inflexed above, obsoletely effuse below ; lines of growth bi-arcuate, bent back ; operculum closely spiral, below convex, above concave, setæ long, multifid, protected ; animal viviparous.

S. roseum, *Quoy, l.c.,* iii., *p.* 300, *pl.* 67, *f.* 20-24, *Morch, P.Z.S.,* 1861, *p.* 150. Shell small, spirally extended, cylindrical, rugose, pink. (Quoy).

Length, 6 to 8 lines.

Foot long and cylindrical. Body black, with yellowish tints. (Quoy).

FAMILY—SILIQUARIIDÆ.

Like *Vermetidæ*, but the mantle and shell with a longitudinal slit ; operculum many-whorled.

Genus, SILIQUARIA—Brug.

Operculum fringed ; foot end truncate, circular; shell glassy internally.

S. Australis, *Quoy, l.c.,* iii., *p.* 302; *Chenu, fig.* 2310. Shell irregularly spiral, sub-cylindrical, transversly rugose ; longitudinally finely striated ; white, reddish behind. (Quoy.)

Length, 4 inches 2 lines ; diameter of tube at the base, 8 lines. Australia.

A small *Siliquaria*, found in the Hauraki Gulf, may perhaps belong to this species.

FAMILY—CALYPTRIDÆ.

Rhachis teeth small and broad, with the apex hooked, the lateral teeth ⌐long and hamate. Head large, transverse ; muzzle slightly produced, furnished anteriorly with buccal appendages ; tentacles short, subulate, eyes small, on bulgings at their external bases ; mantle considerably developed, lining the shell, simple edged in front ; branchial plume single, placed obliquely across the mantle cavity ; foot flat, expanded ; operculum none. Shell patelliform ; apex more or less spiral ; aperture wide, with an internal shelly appendage. The eggs are carried and hatched under the neck, in front of the foot.

Genus, TROCHITA—Schumacher.

Foot transversely-oblong, bilobed in the middle in front. Shell orbicular, trochiform, more or less spiral ; apex central or sub-central ; whorls convex, radiately rugosely plicate ; axis imperforate ; aperture wide, with an oblique transverse, sub-spiral lamina, simple on the columella margin.

T. scutum, *Lesson; Voy. Coquille, Zool.,* ii., *p.* 395 ; *T. tenuis, Gray, P.Z.S.,* 1867, *p.* 735. Depressed ; spire conical, salient, almost median ; surface with concentric striæ, covered with a yellowish epidermis ; aperture entire, rounded, thin ; interior pearly, very smooth ; columella short, a little dilated at its base, and continued as a thin horizontal lamina, striated and convex above, indented in front and connected with the edge on the left side ; umbilicus none (Lesson.)

Length, 11 lines ; breadth, 9 lines ; height, 4 lines. Auckland to Dunedin.

T. novæ zealandiæ, *Lesson, l.c.,* ii., *p.* 395 ; *T. maculata, Quoy, and Gaimard, l.c.,* iv., *p.* 422, *pl.* 72, *f.* 6-9 ; *Reeve, Conch. Ic., f.* 15. Shell rounded, convex ; spire small, conic, salient, lateral, posterior, covered with a thick epidermis, lamellate, and with three elevated rays ; interior concave, pearly ; aperture entire, thin ; columella lateral, dilated at its insertion and furnished with a triangular lamina which partly hides the wide umbilicus ; the columella is continued into a transverse lamina, indented on its free border, and attached to the left margin ; this lamina is pearly, slightly convex, smooth ; epidermis deep greenish-yellow ; interior white ; a spot of purple in the centre (Lesson.)

Length, 10 lines ; breadth, 8 lines ; height, 3½ lines. Auckland to Dunedin.

Tentacles, mantle, and foot yellow; rest of the animal white. (Quoy.)

Genus, CRYPTA—Humphrey.

Head large, transverse, depressed; foot rounded, slightly truncate in front. Shell ovate, oblong; apex posterior, oblique, sub-marginal; aperture elongated, polished within, the posterior half covered by a horizontal shelly lamina; edge of lamina rather straight.

C. costata, *Deshayes; Anim. Sans Vert.,* vii., *p.* 644; *Q. & G., l.c.,* iii., *p.* 414, *pl.* 72, *f.* 10-12; *Chenu, f.* 2353; *Reeve, Conch. Ic., (Crepidula,) f.* 21. Shell ovate, radiately ribbed, ribs distant, flexuous, prickly tubercled, interstices striated; brownish-white, stained and lineated towards the margin with purple; margin flexuous; internal appendage rather large; opal white, concave (Reeve.)
North Island.
Carpenter considers this species the same as *C. aculeata,* Gml. (Cat. Mazatlan Shells, in the British Museum, p. 268.)
Tentacles black at their external base; extremity of the head, tentacles, and contour of the foot yellow, the margin of the mantle marked with the same colour; remainder of the animal white (Quoy.)

C. monoxyla, *Lesson; Voy. Coquille, Zool.,* ii., *p.* 391; *C. contorta, Quoy and Gaimard, l.c.,* iii., *p.* 418, *pl.* 72, *f.* 15-16. Shell oblong, elongated, slightly spiral, convex above, concave below, the right margin arched, excavated in the middle, contracted in front, the left margin rounded; keel convex and dorsal, slightly spiral; apex posterior, terminal; internal lamina slightly sunk, the free margin straight, nearly flat and slightly striated above; greenish-white; interior white and pearly, with a greenish tint in the centre (Lesson.)
Length, 7 lines; breadth, 4½ lines; height, 3 lines.
Bay of Islands to Auckland. Only found in the North.
Animal yellow. (Quoy.)

C. unguiformis, *Lamark; Anim. Sans Vert.,* vii., *p.* 642; *Reeve, Conch. Ic. (Crepidula,) f.* 1; *Chenu, f.* 2360. Shell oval or oblong, flat or concave, often twisted, smooth, externally concentrically striated, sometimes covered towards the margin with a yellowish hairy epidermis, internally shining white; appendage rather largely septum-shaped, slightly notched at the side (Reeve.)
Extremely variable in form, according to its place of attachment, but always thin and white.
Auckland to Dunedin.
For a figure of the teeth, see Gray's "Guide to the Mollusca," p. 115.

FAMILY—CAPULIDÆ.

Tongue membrane winged on each side in front; teeth as in *Calyptridæ.* Rostrum lengthened; tentacles subulate, with the eyes on bulgings at their outer bases; mantle simple in front; gill forming a

M

single plume placed obliquely across the mantle cavity, laminæ elongate,
linear, partly exposed; foot folded on itself, the sides simple, anteriorly
thin and strap-shaped, posteriorly thick, orbicular and concave; operculum none. Shell limpet-like; apex sub-spiral, in the young regularly
spiral; interior simple; muscular impression horse-shoe shaped.

Genus, HIPPONYX—Blainville.

Shell thick, obliquely conical; apex posterior; base shelly, with a
horse-shoe shaped impression.

H. australis, *Lam. an. s.v.*, vi., *p.* 335; *Quoy and Gaimard, l.c.,*
iii., *p.* 434; *pl.* 72, *f.* 25-34. Shell thick, obovate, gibbous, obliquely
conical, reddish; longitudinal striæ thick and undulating; apex acute,
inflexed; margin denticulated; interior white, centre yellow (Lamark.)
     New Zealand and Chatham Islands. Australia.
     Animal probably yellow, with the mouth and tentacles black.
(Quoy.)

FAMILY—ACMÆADÆ.

Radula long, with two central, and two hooked lateral teeth on each
side in an oblique line, the inner often the larger. Head with a short
muzzle; mouth with cartilaginous jaws; tentacles subulate; eyes on
bulgings at their outer bases; mantle margin simple or fringed; gill
forming a single pectinated plume on the side of the back of the neck;
foot large, ovate, with a simple impressed groove; operculum none.
Shell depressed, conical, or cup-shaped; aperture wide, with a cresentic
muscular impression, interrupted in the region of the head.

Genus, ACMÆA—Eschscholtz.

Mantle margin fringed; foot oval, flat. Shell patelliform, regular,
depressedly conical, surface smooth or with radiating striæ; apex anterior,
sub-central; aperture very wide, muscular impression non-symmetrical, the
anterior part under the right side.

A. pileopsis, *Quoy and Gaimard, l.c.,* iii., *p.* 359, *pl.* 71, *f.* 25-27.
Shell ovato-convex, very finely longitudinally striated; blackish, spotted
or reticulated with white; interior bluish; margin black; apex re-curved
near the margin (Q. & G.)
     Length, 9 lines; breadth, 7 lines; height, 4 lines.
     Bay of Islands and the French Pass to Dunedin. Auckland Islands.

A. cantharus, *Reeve, Conch. Ic. (Patella,) f.* 131. Shell ovate,
rather thin, convex; apex very anterior, sharp, hooked, smooth; black,
irregularly blotched with white; interior blackish-chestnut (Reeve.)
     Differs from the last only in the larger white blotches. Tenison-
Woods says that it comes from Tasmania.

A. fragilis, *Chemnitz; Quoy, l.c.,* iii., *p.* 351, *pl.* 71, *f.* 28-30;

Lottia fragilis, Gray, *Dieff. N.Z.,* ii., *p.* 240; *P. unguis-almæ,* Lesson, *Voy.* *Coquille, Zool.,* ii., *p.* 420. Ovate, depressed, membranaceous, pellucid, concentrically striated; apex re-curved, marginal; green, with sub-concentric brown bands; interior with a green ring round the muscular impression.

Auckland to Dunedin.

Animal uniformly clear orpiment yellow; tentacles black (Quoy.)

A. corticata, *sp. nov.* Oval, conical, with fourteen to twenty-two rounded, roughened ribs; apex sub-central; brownish or purplish-white; interior white, sometimes with a black margin; above the muscular impression white or brown, sometimes faintly radiately streaked with black.

Height, ·35; length, ·55; breadth, ·5.

Dunedin.

This small species much resembles *P. puncturata,* Lamark, from Honduras, but it has no red marks. The animal is bluish-white, irregularly spotted with dark-purple. The shell is very variable, but easily recognised by its rugose ribs, looking as if it was covered with a coralline growth.

DIVISION—ASPIDOBRANCHIATA.

Herbivorous; upper wall of respiratory cavity not prolonged into a siphon; radula with one rachis row, 4—6 intermediate, and many small lateral rows (rhipidoglossal.) Foot large; gills two, generally nearly equal; penis none. Shell conical, spiral, or flat. These are the *Scutibranchs* of Cuvier.

FAMILY—NERITIDÆ.

Lingual dentition, very similar to that of the *Trochidæ,* the central teeth few, the laterals very numerous. Head with a short broad muzzle; tentacles slender and subulate, with the eyes on stout peduncles at their outer bases; no head lobes or neck lappets; foot oblong, triangular, the sides simple, without filaments or lateral membranes. Operculum articulated, shelly, sub-spiral. Shell depressed or oval, not umbilicated; spire very short; cavity simple, from the absorption of the interal portions of the whorls; aperture semi-ovate, not pearly within.

Genus, NERITA—Linnæus.

Animal with the mantle-margin festooned. Shell smooth or spirally grooved; epidermis horny; outer lip thickened and sometimes denticulated within; columella with its inner edge straight and toothed.

N. atrata, *Lamark, l.c.,* viii., *p.* 603; *Reeve, Conch. Ic., f.* 16; *N. nigra,* Gray, *Dieff. N.Z.,* ii., *p.* 240. Shell spirally striate, blue-black, white and chalky when eroded; interior grey; columella and near the mouth white; mouth and outer edge of columella blue-black; operculum papillose outside, pale purple, with two spiral bands of blackish-purple.

Length, ·7 ; breadth, 1.
Common in the North, not found south of Wellington. Australia and Tasmania.

Genus, NERITINA--Lamark.

Operculum shelly, the outer surface smooth, with two apophyses, the upper shorter, sometimes dilated and crested, the lateral in the form of an arched rib. Shell globose, oval, thin, covered with a horny epidermis ; aperture semi-lunar ; inner lip straight, flattened, the margin smooth or denticulated ; outer lip simple internally.
Generally fresh water, but sometimes brackish or salt water.

N. zealandica, *Recluz, P.Z.S.,* 1845, *p.* 120. Shell ovato-oblong, ventricose, thin ; whorls 3—4, upper often eroded, the last horizontally compressed near the suture ; black, thickly painted with grey longitudinal angled lines, sometimes yellowish above, and broadly fasciated below ; columella sub-compressed, saffron-yellow, margin denticulated and scarcely arched in the middle ; outer lip thin, dirty reddish, interior milky, and slightly thickened (Recluz.)
Height, ·8 ; breadth, ·3 inch.
" New Zealand ; on stones in mountain streams."
The locality is probably erroneous, but I have re-produced the description, as it has been overlooked in former lists.

FAMILY—TROCHIDÆ.

Radula elongate, rachis teeth broad, laterals five, denticulated, uncini very numerous, slender, with hooked points. Head proboscidiform ; tentacles subulate, sometimes ciliated ; eyes on free peduncles at their outer bases ; two more or less developed head lobes between the tentacles ; gill single, long, and linear ; sides of the foot with a large neck lappet near the eye peduncle, continuous with a conspicuous sidemembrane bearing on its free margin from three to five tapering filaments ; operculigerous lobe often ornamented with cirri ; operculum horny, spiral, often with a solid convex calcareous coat ; rarely wanting. Shell pyramidal, turbinate or ear-shaped ; aperture pearly within.

Sub-Family—Turbininæ.

Operculum orbicular, horny, with a solid, convex, calcareous coat. Shell turbinate, the last whorl rounded and ventricose ; aperture subcircular ; inner lip smooth, simple.

Genus, TURBO—Linnæus.

Turbinated, solid ; whorls convex ; aperture large, rounded, slightly produced in front ; operculum shelly and solid, callous outside, internally horny and pauci-spiral.

T. smaragdus, *Martyn ; Lamark, l.c.,* ix., *p.* 194 ; *Q. & G., l.c.,* iii., *p.* 219, *pl.* 60, *f.* 6-8 ; *Adams' Gen. of Moll. pl.* 43, *f.* 1 ; *Chenu, f.* 2532. Sub-globose, imperforate ; smooth, or slightly roughened with oblique transverse striæ ; columella flattened ; blackish green, covered with a brown epidermis (old worn dead shells are sometimes pink ;) inside white, slightly iridescent ; mouth dark-green.

Length, 2·25 ; breadth, 2·4 ; angle of spire, 85° to 103°.

Var. B.—Spire whorls with one, and body whorl with three, spiral rounded·ribs ; columella generally dilated and flattened anteriorly.

In the young the spire whorls are sometimes sub-spinose.

Common.   Auckland to Dunedin.

T. granosus, *Martyn ; T. rubicundus, Reeve, Conch. Ic., f.* 11 ; *Chenu, f.* 2552 ; *Hogg. Trans. Micros. Soc.,* 1866, *pl.* xi., *f.* 51 (teeth.) Sub-globose, imperforate, with spiral moniliform ribs ; whorls 4 ; columella with a sinistral depression ; reddish-purple, varied with white ; interior white, slightly iridescent.

Length, 2·15 ; breadth, 2·35 ; angle of spire, 85°.

Chatham Islands.   Auckland to Dunedin.   Auckland Islands.

The operculum has a convex, sub-central, granular rib, and a sharp-edged sub-marginal keel, and forms the genus *Modelia* of Gray.

T. shandi, *Hutton, C.M.M., p.* 35.   Spire depressed ; whorls flattened, with several moniliform spiral ribs, the marginal rib of the body whorl larger than the others ; white or pinkish-white, varied with brown and purplish-brown ; interior white, slightly pearly.

Length, ·3 ; breadth, ·5.

Chatham Islands only.

The generic position of this shell is at present doubtful, as the operculum is not known.

T. lajonkairii, *Deshayes, Mag. de Zool.,* 1839; *Reeve, Conch. Ic., f.* 5.   Shell ovate, umbilicated ; whorls obscurely undulately irregularly ribbed and ridged, two angled in the middle, scaled at both angles ; scales somewhat laciniated and frondose, gradually fading towards the apex ; whitish, banded with green at the angles ; pearly within (Reeve.)

New Zealand. (Deshayes.)   Keeling Island. (Darwin.)

A large species, distinguished by the vivid green bands on the angles of the whorls.   I do not think that it really belongs to New Zealand.

T. undulatus, *Chemnitz, Conch. Cab.,* x., *pl.* 169, *f.* 1640-1 ; *Reeve, Conch. Ic., f.* 3.   Shell orbicular, broadly and deeply umbilicated ; whorls sometimes grooved, sometimes smooth ; bluish-green, longitudinally marked with white zig-zag streaks (Reeve.)

New Zealand (Earl.)   Australia.

Sub-Family—Astraliinæ.

Operculum oblong or ovate, with an external, solid calcareous coat. Shell trochiform, flat or concave at the base ; whorls rugose or spinose, the last often stellate or keeled ; aperture usually sub-quadrate.

Genus, CALCAR—Montfort.

Trochiform, thick, with a flat or concave base ; whorls keeled or stellated ; aperture angled outside ; operculum shelly, concave outside, with a spiral rib.

C. cookii, *Lamark, l.c.,* ix., *p.* 131 ; *Q. & G., l.c.,* iii., *p.* 224, *pl.* 60, *f.* 19-23 ; *Cookia sulcata, Adams, Gen. Moll., pl.* 45 *f.* 3 ; *Chenu, f.* 2581. Conical, body whorl rather ventricose ; whorls rounded, obliquely plaited and crossed by oblique rough imbricating laminæ sloping the opposite way to the plaits ; central part of base smooth, hollowed in the middle ; pinkish-brown ; pearly inside.

Length, 2·25 ; breadth, 3·5 ; angle of spire, 86° to 92°.

Common in the North Island, very rare in the South. Chatham Islands.

C. davisii, *Stowe, Trans. N.Z. Inst.,* iv., *p.* 218. Conical ; body whorl sharply angled and keeled ; whorls slightly rounded, obliquely plaited and crossed by oblique rough imbricating laminæ sloping the opposite way to the plaits ; central part of the base smooth, scarcely hollowed in the middle ; pinkish-brown ; pearly inside.

Length, 3·65 ; breadth, 3·3 ; angle of spire, 57° to 60°.

Cook Strait and Blind Bay.

The spire is much more acute than the last, but perhaps it is only a variety.

C. imperialis, *Lamark, l.c.,* ix., *p.* 122 ; *Q. & G., l.c.,* iii., *p.* 226, *pl.* 61, *f.* 1-4 ; *Woodward's Manual of the Mollusca, pl.* 10, *f.* 4 ; *Hogg, Trans. Micros. Soc.,* 1866, *pl.* 11, *f.* 46 (teeth.) Conic, obtuse ; whorls convex, with spiral scaly ribs, and a spinose radiate margin ; spines curved to the left and backwards ; perforation funnel-shaped, extending to the apex ; above purplish or reddish-purple ; base nearly white ; interior iridescent.

Length, 1·8 ; breadth, 3·5 ; angle of spire, 110°.

From Hauraki Gulf to Stewart Island. Chatham Islands.

In the young shell the marginal spines are fewer and longer than in older ones. As the animal gets older the upper spines break off to the base, and get so covered with coralline growth that they are difficult to distinguish.

Sub-Family—Rotellinæ

Rostrum rudimentary ; frontal lobes greatly developed ; operculum horny, thin, of many gradually enlarging whorls finely ciliated on the outer edge. Shell orbicular, depressed, polished, porcellanous ; umbilical region often covered with a large callus.

Genus, ROTELLA—Lamark.

Orbicular, depressed, imperforate, polished ; base convex and callous ; mouth sub-rotund ; inner lip ending in a simple point.

R. zealandica, *Hombron and Jacquinot, Voy. Pole Sud. Moll., p.* 53, *pl.* 14, *f.* 5-6 ; *Reeve, Conch. Ic., f.* 11 ; *Umbonium zealandicum, Adams, P.Z.S.,* 1853, *p.* 189 ; *Chenu, f.* 2604-6. Body whorl rather angled, more or less sulcated along the keel ; colour variable ; generally yellowish-white, with radiating chestnut rays ; rays often purple or pink ; sometimes entirely brownish-pink, with an iridescent play of colours; columella white, with a circular band of purple.

Length, ·5 ; breadth, ·85 ; angle of spire, 92° to 111°.

Common. Auckland to Dunedin.

Although this shell is very common on sandy beaches, I have never obtained one alive.

Sub-Family—Trochinæ.

Operculum horny, orbicular, composed of numerous narrow whorls, with the nucleus central. Shell conoidal or pyramidal, the last whorl more or less angulated at the circumferance, and usually flattened beneath ; aperture more or less transverse, wider than long.

A.—Shell subulately conical ; porcellanous ; aperture
      not pearly within -   -   -   -   - *Bankivia.*

B.—Shell conical, with a flat base.
    a.—Umbilicated.
        Margin of umbilicus smooth -   -   - *Anthora.*
        ,,   ,,   ,,   crenated -   -   - *Clanculus.*
    b.—Imperforate.
        Aperture quadrangular -   -   -   - *Zizyphinus.*

C.—Shell elevately conoidal ; imperforate.
    a.—Columella, more or less toothed.
        Whorls granulated or ribbed -   -   - *Thalotia.*
        Whorls smooth or polished -   -   - *Elenchus.*
    b.—Columella not toothed.
        Outer lip thin -   -   -   -   - *Cantharidus.*

D.—Shell conoidal.
    a.—Umbilicated.
        1.—Aperture subrhomboidal.
            Columella simple -   -   -   - *Gibbula.*
            A spiral ridge encircling the umbilicus - *Chlorostoma.*
        2.—Aperture circular.
            Whorls with granular ribs · -   - *Euchelus.*
            Whorls smooth or striated- -   - *Margarita.*
    b.—Imperforate.
        Columella forming a ridge on the outer lip- *Diloma.*
        ,,   ending in a small tubercule - *Trochocochlea.*

E.—Shell depressed.
        Umbilicus wide, callous -   -   -   - *Monilea.*

Genus, ANTHORA—Gray.

Shell conoidal ; whorls compressed, sub-quadrate, flat in front ; aperture contracted, quadrangular ; pillar lip twisted, simple ; axial cavity moderate, narrow, with several opaque sub-spiral ridges.

A. tuberculata, *Gray, Dieff. N.Z.,* ii., *p.* 239 ; *Voy. Erebus* *and Terror, Moll., pl.* 1, *f.* 6 ; *T. acinosus, Gould.* Shell conical, rather produced, whitish ; whorls flat, with four series of large rounded tubercles ; the front of the last whorl flat, with rather close spiral ridges, the inner ones the largest, and the outer ones very small ; umbilicus conical, with three spiral ridges ; opaque-white (Gray.)

Auckland to Dunedin. Chatham Islands.

A. tritonis, *A. Adams, P.Z.S.,* 1854, *p.* 132. Shell elevatly-conical, pseudo-umbilicated, green variegated with white ; upper whorls rather gibbous, ornamented with transverse rows of granules ; last whorl angulated, the base concave, white, concentrically striated, umbilical region funnel-shaped ; columella tortuous above, the margin tuberculated (Adams.)

New Zealand. (Cuming.)

Perhaps the same as the last.

A. viridis, *Gmelin ; Reeve, Conch. Ic.* (*Trochus*), *f.* 79 ; *T. fulvolabris, Homb. and Jacq., Voy. Pole Sud., p.* 56, *pl.* 14, *f.* 14-16. Shell excavately umbilicated, conical, green ; whorls seriately plicately grained ; grains sometimes small and obtuse, sometimes larger, fewer, and somewhat spinous ; base flatly concave, circularly striated (Reeve.)

Perhaps the same as *A. tuberculata.*

A. chathamensis, *Hutton, C.M.M., p.* 36. Whorls flat, with an elevated upper edge, and, together with the base, spirally striated ; columella with a slight posterior fold, anterior portion nearly smooth ; axial cavity small, smooth ; white with pink or brownish-purple markings ; base white, with interrupted pink spiral lines.

Length, ·3 ; breadth, ·35 ; angle of spire, 70°.

Chatham Islands only.

A. tiarata, *Quoy, and Gaim., l.c.,* iii., *p.* 256, *pl.* 64, *f.* 6-11 ; *P. elegans, Gray, Dieff. N.Z.,* ii., *p.* 238. Whorls slightly convex, often with an elevated upper edge, and six or seven spiral rows of beads ; columella with a slight posterior fold, anterior portion toothed or smooth ; axial cavity deep, smooth, conical ; white with brownish-purple dots both on the upper surface and on the base ; axial cavity white.

Length, ·45 ; breadth, ·6 ; angle of spire, 75°.

Common in the North, rare in the South Island. Dunedin. A very variable shell.

Animal : Tentacles and filaments white ; foot white, with a brown, border below, and a broad black band on the sides ; mouth black (Quoy.)

For an account of an abnormal form of operculum in this species, see Gray, Ann. Nat. Hist., series 2, vol. 18, p. 468.

Genus, CLANCULUS—Montfort.

Shell conoidal ; axis imperforate ; whorls almost always granulated, the last rounded at the periphery ; aperture usually narrowed ; columella spirally twisted above, forming a false umbilicus, with a crenate margin;

end of columella with numerous, strong, tooth-like plaits; outer lip often strongly dentate internally.

C. variegatus, *Adams, P.Z.S.,* 1851, *p.* 160. Shell depressed, conical, pale, variegated with brownish-red ; whorls swollen above, ornamented with rings of granules ; body whorl acutely angled, base flat ; umbilicus crenulated ; columella tortuous above, margin reflexed, crenulated, base terminated by a biplicate tooth (Adams.)
Auckland (?) Common in S. Australia.

Genus, EUCHELUS—Philippi.

Turbinated, sub-globose ; whorls with granulated spiral ribs; often perforated ; columella with a small tooth in front ; outer lip thick, internally crenated ; operculum sub-circular, of few rapidly enlarging whorls.

E. bellus, *Hutton, C.M.M., p.* 37. Small, imperforate, anterior end of columella with a deep notch ; pinkish-white varied with darker ; inside white, pearly.
Length, ·25 ; breadth, ·25.
Chatham Islands. Auckland.

Genus, DILOMA—Philippi.

Shell conoidal, smooth, imperforate, umbilical region covered with a thin porcellanous expansion of the columella ; columella margin produced anteriorly, forming an elevated ridge round the inner margin of the outer lip.

D. æthiops, *Gmelin ; T. zealandicus, Quoy, l.c.,* iii., *p.* 257, *pl.* 64, *f.* 12-15 ; *Monodonta reticularis, Gray, Dieff. N.Z.,* ii., *p.* 238. Sub-globose ; whorls spirally distantly grooved and obliquely striated ; rough when not worn ; purplish black or purple, spirally tessellated with white ; mouth purplish black, ouside of columella brownish ; when not rubbed, brownish-purple.
Length, 1 ; breadth, 1·2.
Very common ; variable in shape, the spire being sometimes much depressed.
Auckland to Dunedin. Auckland Islands. Chatham Islands.
Animal : Foot yellow below, with a brown stripe round the contour, black on the sides, with touches of yellowish-white behind ; filaments greenish ; mouth yellowish (Quoy.)

D. hectori, *Hutton, C.M.M., p.* 37. Sub-globose, conical, roughish ; purplish black ; the spire when eroded dark-green ; anterior portion of body whorl yellow ; mouth yellow, with a thin purple ring inside.
Length, ·75 ; breadth, ·8.
West Coast of the South Island. Dunedin.
More conical than the next species, and differently coloured, but perhaps a variety of it.

N

D. undulosa, *Adams, P.Z.S.,* 1851, *p.* 182 : *Voy. Erebus and Terror, Moll., pl.* 1, *f.* 15 : *Trochus attritus, Hombron and Jacquinot, Voy. Pole Sud., p.* 57, *pl.* 14, *f.* 19-20. Shell globoso-conical, imperforate ; spire depressed, greenish, ornamented with longitudinal undulating lines of purplish-black, longitudinally substriated ; inner lip smooth ; margin of the columella sub-tuberculated ; outer lip sulcated within; margin brownish-yellow, articulated with purplish-black (Adams.) Dunedin.

D. nigerrima, *Chemnitz,* v. *pl.* 185, *f.* 1848 ; *Adams' Gen. Moll., pl.* 47, *f.* 7 ; *Chenu, f.* 2658 ; *Turbo nigerrimus, Gml. ; Turbo quoyi, Kien : Turbo araucanus, D'Orb ; Labio melanoloma, Menke.* Purplish-black, lightly spirally striated, interior white, iridescent.
Length, ·55 ; breadth, ·85.
Auckland to Dunedin. Chatham Islands. Auckland Islands.

D. corrosa, *Adams, P.Z.S.,* 1851, *p.* 180. Shell turbinated, imperforate ; spire slightly elevated ; whorls rounded, rugose, dirty-blue ; body whorl sub-angulated ; inner lip smooth ; columella simple ; outer lip margined with yellow (Adams.)
New Zealand. (Hart.) Dunedin.

D. (?) concolor, *Adams, P.Z.S.,* 1851, *p.* 180. Shell turbinately-conical, imperforate ; spire acute, brownish, longitudinally obliquely striated, transversely sub-lirate ; inner lip smooth ; umbilical region impressed ; columella arcuate, terminated in front by a tubercle ; outer lip margined with brownish-black (Adams.)
New Zealand. (Hart.)

D. gaimardi, *Philippi ; T. cingulatus, Quoy, l.c.,* iii., *p.* 259, *pl.* 64. *f.* 16-20 *(not of Brocchi ;) Monodonta angulatum, Gray, Dieff. N.Z.,* ii., *p.* 238. Depressed, conical, with spiral granular ribs ; black, the ribs with a few yellowish spots ; aperture white.
Length, ·3 ; breadth, ·5.
Auckland to Dunedin.
Animal black above, smoky below. (Quoy.)

Genus, TROCHOCOCHLEA---Klein.

Shell solid, conoidal, imperforate in the adult ; whorls smooth or transversely lirate, the last rounded at the periphery ; aperture nearly rhomboidal ; columella thick and rounded, ending anteriorly in a slightly prominent tubercle.

T. subrostrata, *Gray, Dieff. N.Z.,* ii., *p.* 238 ; *Smith, Voy. Erebus and Terror, Moll., pl.* 1, *f.* 14. Shell conical, sub-orbicular; solid, black, with close wavy longitudinal yellow lines ; spire short , whorls 5 ; last large, rounded, hinder part with three to six spiral keels ; axis imperforated ; throat smooth and silvery (Gray.)
Auckland to Dunedin.

T. mimetica, *Hutton, Jour. de Conch.,* 1878, *p.* 32. Perforated;

inner lip thin, slightly expanded over the always open umbilicus; purple, with oblique slightly waved white lines; columella more or less stained with green.

Length, ·5 ; breadth, ·6.

Auckland.

T. excavata, *Adams and Angas, P.Z.S.*, 1864. *p.* 37 ; *T. constricta, Hutton; Jour. de Conch.*, 1878, *p.* 33 *(not of Lamark.)* Shell depressedly conoidal, imperforate, greenish, cinerous. ornamented with close undulating longitudinal purplish-black spots; whorls convex, transversely sulcated ; the last large, acutely angled at the periphery ; base flat ; aperture sub-quadrate, very oblique ; lip white, excavated ; inner lip smooth (A. & A.)

Length, 3 lines ; breadth, 4 lines.

New Zealand. (Angas.)

A depressed species, with a concave base, and with the inner lip excavated.

Genus, CHLOROSTOMA—Swainson.

Shell conoidal, usually deeply umbilicated, or with the umbilical region covered with a callus ; whorls smooth or longitudinally corrugated ; the last generally keeled at the periphery ; aperture oblique ; inner lip with an acute tubercle at the fore part, continuous with a spiral ridge which encircles the umbilicus; outer lip angular at the base, usually with one or two tubercles.

C. niger, *Chemnitz*, v. *pl* , *f.* 1647 ; *Trochus nigerrimus, Gml.; C. corrugatum, A. Adams, P.Z.S.*, 1851, *p.* 182. Shell orbicular-conoidal, deeply umbilicated ; spire sub-acute, longitudinally corrugately plicated and obliquely striated ; last whorl sub-rotund ; base flat, convex ; umbilical region white, sub-callous; columella with two tubercles, the upper large (Adams.)

I do not know on whose authority this shell has been put down to New Zealand.

Genus, THALOTIA—Gray.

Conical, turreted, solid, granulated, imperforate ; mouth longer than wide ; columella sub-truncate, tubercular ; outer lip thickened and crenulated within ; operculum multi-spiral.

T. conica, *Gray, in King's Voyage, Appendix* ii., *p.* 479 ; *Adams' Gen. Moll., pl.* 48, *f.* 1 ; *Chenu, f.* 2620. Whorls 7, ornamented with spiral moniliform lines, of which there are six on the spire whorls, and about eight on the body whorl in front of the mouth ; columella ending abruptly in a rounded tooth ; body whorl dark-purple, with oblique, more or less zig-zag pale lines ; spire whorls paler, the beading spotted with brown and dark purple ; often pale purple, with the beading dark-purple.

Length, ·75 inch.

Auckland (?) Australia. Tasmania.

Genus, ZIZYPHINUS—Leach.

Trochiform, conical, imperforate; body whorl angular; mouth quadrangular; columella simple, sometimes terminated by a tooth.

Z. punctulatus, *Martyn; Gray, Dieff. N.Z.,* ii., *p.* 237 ; *Reeve, Conch. Ic., f.* 95 ; *T. diaphanus, Quoy and Gaim, l.c.,* iii., *p.* 254, *pl.* 64, *f.* 1-5. Shell ovately conical, imperforate, rust white, dotted in rows with red and white; whorls 7, slopingly rounded ; gemmed throughout with rows of granules; narrowly canaliculately impressed at the suture ; aperture obliquely ovate, nearly circular (Reeve.)

Auckland to Dunedin.   Chatham Islands.

Z. granatum, *Chemnitz; Lamark, l.c.,* ix., *p.* 145 ; *Z. tigris, Martyn; Reeve, Conch. Ic., f.* 4. Rather solid ; body whorl ventricose, not much angled, with fine spiral moniliform lines, about eighteen to twenty-five on the body whorl in front of the mouth, from the suture to the keel ; columella with a small callosity over the umbilicus ; chestnut, more or less marbled with white.

Length, 2·13 ; breadth, 2·5 ; angle of spire, 75°.
Auckland to Cook Strait.   Chatham Islands.

Z. spectabilis, *Adams, P.Z.S.,* 1854, *p.* 37, *pl.* xxvii., *f.* 7 ; *Reeve, Conch. Ic., f.* 5. Shell regularly conoid, rather ponderous ; whorls slopingly convex, grain ridged ; ridges rather distant, grains large, interstices between the ridges smooth, excavated, flesh-colour, or yellowish ; ridges dotted with pinkish-red (Reeve.)

Axis, 1·75 to 2 inches.
New Zealand. (Cuming.)

Z. scitulus, *Adams, P.Z.S.,* 1854, *p.* 38 ; *Reeve, Conch. Ic., f.* 44. Shell umbilicated, tumidly conical, rather thin, orange fulvous, minutely articulated with crimson dots, and here and there flaked with white; whorls convexly sloping, spirally striately ridged ; ridge next the suture larger (Reeve.)

Axis, ·55 inch.
New Zealand. (Strange.)   Common in Australia.

Z. selectus, *Chemnitz; Reeve, Conch. Ic., f.* 1. Like *Z. granatum,* but the spiral moniliform lines are further apart, about ten on the body whorl in front of the mouth, from the suture to the keel, and the beading is larger ; purplish-chestnut, varied with darker, often forming a row of spots at the suture.

Length, 1·4 ; breadth, 1·5 ; angle of spire, 75°.
Cook Strait.

Z. cunninghami, *Gray; Reeve, Conch. Ic., f.* 6. Thin ; whorls flattened ; suture obscure ; body whorl much angled with fine spiral moniliform lines. about ten on the body whorl before the mouth, from the suture to the keel, beading much smaller than in the last ; columella with a large callosity over the umbilicus ; pinkish white, with reddish-purple dots on the ribs ; base nearly white.

Length, 1·35 ; breadth, 2·2 ; angle of spire, 85.°
Common in Cook Strait, not known in the South.

In the young the body whorl is less sharply angled ; there is often a row of purple spots round the suture, and the base is ornamented with interrupted pinkish-brown lines.

Genus, CANTHARIDUS—Montfort.

Ovate conical ; whorls slightly keeled ; columella with a small tooth in front ; outer lip entire ; throat smooth ; mouth sub-ovate, rather elongate ; operculum circular.

C. iris, *Gml. : Elenchus iris, Gray, Dieff. N.Z.,* ii., *p.* 239 ; *Woodward's Manual of the Mollusca, pl.* 10, *f.* 8. Whorls slightly rounded, smooth, spirally striated ; body whorl more or less keeled ; pinkish, with irregular longitudinal zig-zag red markings ; apex often transversely banded with white.

Length, 1·3 ; breadth, 1·1 ; angle of spire, 50°
Common in the North, rare in the South. Chatham Islands.

The young shell is perforated, but the perforation gets covered over by a callous expansion.

C. zealandicus, *Adams, P.Z.S.,* 1851, *p.* 169 ; *C. iris, Chenu, f.* 2669 ; *T. purpuratus, Lam.,* ix., *p.* 158. Whorls slightly rounded, smooth, spirally striated ; body whorl slightly keeled ; imperforate ; Purple, or pinkish-purple, with irregular longitudinal zig-zag reddish-purple markings.

Length, 1·8 ; breadth, 1·4 ; angle of spire, 50°.
North Island only. Chatham Islands.

C. purpuratus, *Martyn ; T. elegans, Gmelin ;* Whorls slightly rounded, rough, spirally grooved and obliquely striated ; body whorl slightly keeled ; imperforate ; rose-pink or pinkish-white, with longitudinal flexuous streaks of rose-pink.

Length, 1·1 ; breadth, ·7 ; angle of spire, 50°.
Auckland to Dunedin, rare in the South.

C. texturatus, *Gould, U.S. Ex. Ep., p.* 181, *f.* 206. Shell conical, imperforate, solid, girded with about five obtuse ribs on the upper, and nine on the lower whorls ; colour cinereous. tinted-green or roseate, generally faintly tessellated with pale rose spots on the ribs ; intercostal spaces half the breadth of the ribs ; surface having the lines of growth faintly laminated, and crossed by fine revolving lines ; when somewhat worn the prominence of the rib becomes smooth, and the cancellated sculpture appears only in the interspaces ; nacreous underneath, as appears by its roseate pearly tip ; whorls 7, scarcely convex, the basal one obtusely angular ; aperture nearly circular, somewhat effuse at the base ; columella rounded, edged with green ; outer lip bevelled within ; interior pearly, faintly greenish, scarcely iridescent ; operculum thin, horny, multi-spiral (Gould.)

Axis, 1 inch ; diameter, ·7 inch.

C. jucundus, *Gould, U.S. Ex. Ep., p.* 177, *f.* 209. Shell small, solid, low conical, composed of about six conical whorls, with a slight vertical portion at base ; the whole girdled with fine uniform beaded lines, the alternate ones being generally smaller, sometimes even not beaded, and the two basal ones surrounding the vertical portion being larger ; base a little convex, similarly sculptured with about twelve concentric lines gradually diminishing from the centre to the circumference the umbilical region colourless, not perforated, and with a groove-like impression beside the columella ; aperture rhomboidal-orbiculate ; columella arcuate, smooth ; lip simple ; colours arranged in radiating flamules, alternately white, strawberry-red, and pale flesh colour, gradually shaded into each other ; on the base the dark or light red are distributed along the granules in a somewhat articulate manner ; nacreous beneath.

Axis ⅔ inch ; diameter ¾ inch (Gould.)

C. pallidus, *Hombron and Jacquinot, Voy. Pole Sud., Moll., p.* 55, *pl.* 14, *f.* 12-13. Shell elongated, conical, encircled longitudinally by ribs which enlarge anteriorly ; colour whitish, with spots of brown placed obliquely, and corresponding in all the whorls ; mouth pearly, oval, iridescent in the interior (H. & J.)

Length, ·85 ; breadth, ·65 inch.

C. episcopus, *Homb. and Jacq., Voy. Pole Sud., Moll., p.* 55, *pl.* . Shell blackish, shining, reddish when young, burnished afterwards, and at last taking, towards the last whorls, a deeper tint ; spire long, of five whorls ; mouth rounded, trenchant, and pearly in the interior ; no umbilicus (H. & J.)

Length, 1·1 : breadth, ·8 inch.

Auckland Islands. Campbell Island.

C. huttonii, *Smith, P.L.S., Zool.,* xii. (1876,) *p.* 558 ; *Gibbula plumbea, Hutton, Jour. de Conch.,* 1878, *p.* 33. Shell shortly conical ; umbilicus covered ; bluish-black or purplish-black, at the apex worn white ; whorls 5-6, rather convex, ornamented with 7-8 spiral striæ and lines of growth ; last whorl obtusely angled at the periphery, below slightly convex, lightly impressed in the umbilical region ; aperture quadrato-circular, iridescent within, finely sulcated ; lip a little thickened, whitish, with a narrow black margin ; columella scarcely arcuate, thickened, covering the perforation.

Height, ·35-·58 ; Diameter, ·28-·42 inches. (Smith.)

Abundant from the Bay of Islands to Dunedin.

C. pupillus, *Gould, U.S. Ex. Ep., p.* 186, *f.* 208. Shell small, ovate-conic, rather solid, perforate, ash coloured, with darker greenish on the ribs, sub-surface brilliant silvery ; surface with small flattened, nearly equal and equi-distant ribs, about five on the upper whorls, separated by interspaces of the same width, and with fine crowded lamellar lines of growth by which the interspaces are distinctly barred ; spire of six convex whorls, the last obtusely angular, flattened at base and with much finer and more crowded ribs and grooves ; aperture

circular; columella somewhat arcuate, with a minute groove like umbilicus at its side; lip sharp; interior pale and opaque near the lip; minutely punctured, and with crimson iridescence within (Gould.)
Axis, ·3; diameter ·25.

C. tenebrosus, *A. Adams, P.Z.S.*, 1851, *p.* 170. Shell small, elevato-conical, imperforate, blackish, transversely sulcated, sulci whitish, smooth; whorls hardly convex, the last sub-angulated; base convex; aperture sub-rotund, interior white, pearly; lip sulcated within (Adams.)
New Zealand (British Museum.)
This shell is narrower and more coarsely sulcated than *C. huttonii.*

C. rufozona, *A. Adams, P.Z.S.*, 1851, *p.* 170. Shell conoidal, pale, ornamented with transverse red ribs, interstices smooth; last whorl rounded; lip lirated within, the margin articulated with red (Adams.)
This species is added to our list, on the authority of Mr. E. A. Smith, who says that specimens from New Zealand exist in the British Museum.

Genus, ELENCHUS—Humphrey.

Conical, imperforate; spire elevated, pointed; whorls flattened, smooth, polished; aperture oval, sub-triangular; columella with a tooth near the middle; outer lip thickened interiorly.
Australia.

E. dilatatus, *Sowerby, Proc. Zool. Soc.*, 1870, *p.* 251. Shell short, sub-cinereous, rather distantly spirally ribbed; spire short; whorls 4, the last broad; aperture dilated; greenish-blue, iridescent. Remarkable for the expansion of the last whorl (Sowerby.)
New Zealand. (Brazier.)

Genus, BANKIVIA—Beck.

Conical; spire elevated; whorls smooth; aperture sub-quadrangular, not pearly inside; columella twisted, simple.

B. varians, *Beck, in Krauss Sudafric Moll.; Woodward's Manual of the Mollusca, pl.* 10, *f.* 9; *Chenu, f.* 2674-5. Variable in colour, white, purple, rose, or black; plain or banded, sometimes with longitudinal wavy lines.
Length, ·6.
Cook Strait. Australia. Tasmania.
Neither the animal nor the operculum of this genus are known.

Genus, MONILEA—Swainson.

Orbicular, depressed, largely umbilicated; whorls spirally grooved; the body whorl rounded; umbilicus surrounded by a striated callosity; columella terminated in front by one or two tubercles.

M. egena, *Gould, U.S. Ex. Ep., p.* 196, *f.* 228 *(Solarium;) M. zealandica, Hutton, C.M.M.* Spire acute; whorls deeply spirally grooved, some of the ridges sub-granular; umbilicus transversely finely striated; brownish-white, with radiating flexuous bands of brownish-purple.

Length, ·2 ; breadth, ·3 ; angle of spire, 80°.
Auckland.

Genus, GIBBULA—Leach.

Conical, solid, generally umbilicated; aperture sub-rhomboidal, the angles rounded; columella gradually arched; operculum of many gradually enlarging whorls.

G. sanguinea, *Gray, Dieff. N.Z.,* ii., *p.* 238 ; *Smith's Voy. Erebus and Terror, pl.* 1, *f,* 12. Shell top-shaped; white, with rows of numerous blood-red spots; whorls flattened, the last obscurely keeled; the front rather convex, with sharp-edged, low, spiral keels (Gray.)
Auckland. Chatham Islands.

G. simulata, *Hutton, C.M.M., p.* 36. Whorls convex, faintly spirally striated, umbilicus generally closed : pink or pinkish-brown, generally with white markings on the spire.
Length, ·3 ; breadth, ·25.
Chatham Islands only.

G. nitida, *Adams and Angas, P.Z.S.,* 1864, *p.* 36. Shell elevately-conoidal; apex obtuse, widely umbilicated, smooth, shining, greenish-yellow, painted with longitudinal purple and red flammules, and with transverse interrupted lines of the same; whorls swollen, transversely striated, the last obtusely angled at the periphery; base convex; umbilicus angled at the margin; aperture rotundo-quadrate; interior vividly iridescent; lip simple; inner lip sulcated (A. & A.)
Length, 2½ lines; breadth, 2¼ lines.
Hokianga. (Angas.)

G. inconspicua, *Hutton, C.M.M., p.* 36. Depressed; whorls convex, faintly spirally striated; umbilicus always open; brownish-green or brown, more or less marked with purplish-brown and white.
Length, ·15 ; breadth, ·2.
Perhaps the same as the last.

G. oppressa, *Hutton, Jour. de Conch.,* 1878, *p.* 34. Whorls flattened posteriorly, and more or less keeled; closely spirally ribbed, the ribs rounded but rather rough; axis sub-perforated; aperture sub-rhomboidal; dark purplish-black.
Length, ·23 ; breadth, ·25.
Auckland.

Genus, MARGARITA—Leach.

Shell thin, usually without any colouring, globosely conoidal, umbilicated; whorls rounded, smooth or transversely striated; aperture nearly circular; columella ending in a simple point.

M. antipoda, *Hombron and Jacquinot, Voy. au Pole Sud.,* iv., *p.* 58, *pl.* 14, *f.* 26-28. Shell small; spire of three whorls, the two first extremely small; iridescent above and below, with transverse bands of greenish on the upper part; aperture large and round; left lip sharp, the right flattened; umbilicus just indicated, and almost stopped up by the right lip; operculum horny, regularly multi-spiral. (H. & J.)
Length, ·35; breadth, ·35 inch.
Auckland Islands.

M. fulminata, *Hutton, C.M.M., p.* 36. Whorls convex, smooth, umbilicus generally open; colour various, generally pink, with white radiating markings round the sulcus, but sometimes white zig-zag markings extend over the whole shell; sometimes olivaceous, with or without white markings.
Length, ·3; breadth, ·3.
Chatham Islands only.

M. rosea, *Hutton, C.M.M., p.* 36. Depressed; whorls convex, smooth, faintly transversely striated; pinkish-white, with three or four narrow pink spiral bands, and some purplish spots on the body whorl near the suture.
Length, 1·5; breadth, ·23.
Stewart Island. Campbell Island.

M. zealandica, *Sowerby, in Reeve's Conch. Ic., f.* 17. Shell depressed, conical, spirally grooved, spotted with red; last whorl flattened beneath; umbilicus broad, keeled; aperture small; columella strong, slightly cuneate below (Sowerby.)
Dunedin (F.W.H.)

Sub-Family—Stomatellinæ.

Foot often very thick, fleshy, developed posteriorly; operculum thin, horny, ovate, of few rapidly increasing whorls, often entirely wanting. Shell more or less ear-shaped, of few whorls; aperture very wide.

Genus, SCISSURELLA—D'Orbigny.

Animal like *Margarita;* tentacles long, pectinated, with the eyes at their base; foot with two pointed lappets and two long slender pectinated cirri on each side. Operculum thin, horny, sub-spiral. Shell minute, spiral, heliciform, depressed, widely umbilicated; spire short; aperture sub-orbicular, not pearly within; outer lip with a narrow fissure or slit in the adult.

S. mantelli, *Woodward, P.Z.S.,* 1859, *p.* 202, *pl.* 46. Like *S. elegans,* but rather larger, more depressed, more strongly ornamented, and a longer scissural band (Woodward.)
New Zealand (W. Mantell,) among iron-sand. For a figure of *S. elegans,* see Chenu, f. 2717, p. 364.

o

FAMILY—HALIOTIDÆ.

Radula with a small median tooth, flanked by two beam-like laterals and numerous uncini with denticulated hooks, the four inner being very large. Head with a short broad muzzle; tentacles subulate, with the eyes on stout cylindrical peduncles at their outer bases, and with a fimbriated lobe, or an emarginate veil between them. Mantle margin fissured in front, the left lobe elongated into an anal siphon, occupying the anterior perforation of the shell ; gills two, unequal. Foot thick and fleshy, the sides with a double membrane, furnished with serrated lobes and filaments on the edges, and continued anteriorly in a free crest under the head. Operculum none. Shell ear-shaped ; aperture large, nacreous and iridescent internally, perforated with a series of holes.

Genus, HALIOTIS—Linnæus.

Ear-shaped, with a small flat spire ; aperture very wide, iridescent, exterior striated, dull ; outer angle perforated by a series of holes, those of the spire progressively closed; muscular impression horse shoe-shaped, the left branch greatly dilated in front.

H. iris, *Martyn ; Lamark, l.c.,* ix., *p.* 23 ; *Reeve, Conch. Ic., f.* 37. Spire small, obtuse ; outer lip continuous and produced beyond the body whorl ; columella slightly concave, the posterior end not curved into a spiral; outside rugose, plicated ; outside pale brownish-white ; interior dark metallic-blue and green, with yellow reflexions and an iridescent play of colours ; paler in the young.
Breadth, about 6-5 inches.
Common. Chatham Islands. Auckland Islands. Auckland to Dunedin.

H. rugoso-plicata, *Chemnitz ; Reeve, Conch. Ic., f.* 7 ; *Chenu, f.* 2734 ; *H. australis, Lamark, l.c.,* ix., *p.* 25. Spire large, obtuse, body whorl with obliquely longitudinal plications crossed by fine transverse rough striæ ; posterior portion of outer lip not projecting beyond the body whorl ; posterior end of columella produced into a broad spiral ; outside pinkish-brown ; interior pale, highly iridescent.
Breadth, about 3·75.
Omaha to Dunedin. Chatham Islands. Auckland Islands. South Australia.

H. gibba, *Philippi, Abbild und Besch, Conch. Haliotis, pl.* ix., *f.* 2 ; *Reeve, Conch. Ic., f.* 42 ; *Voy. Erebus and Terror, pl.* 1, *f.* 16. Spire moderate, obtuse ; body whorl longitudinally grooved, and irregularly transversely plicated ; posterior portion of outer lip not projecting beyond the body whorl ; posterior part of columella much curved, but hardly spiral ; outside variegated with green. brown, and white ; interior pale, highly iridescent.
Breadth, about 2·5.
Not so common as the others.
Omaha to Dunedin. Chatham Islands. Campbell Islands.

H. zealandica, *Reeve, P.Z.S.,* 1846, *p.* 57 ; *Conch. Ic., f.* 64. Shell oblong, rather depressed, spirally irregularly grooved; intermediate ridges obtuse, now broad, now narrow ; six holes open ; exteriorly peculiarly marbled with reddish-chestnut and red-tinged white (Reeve.) New Zealand. (Cuming.)

H. cruenta, *Reeve, P.Z.S.,* 1846, *p.* 59 ; *Conch. Ic., f.* 56. Shell ovate, a little attenuated anteriorly ; spire rather elevated, spirally peculiarly striated in a waved and wrinkled manner ; perforations somewhat approximated ; eight open ; beautifully variegated with white dotted scarlet, and scarlet dotted white (Reeve.) New Zealand. (Cuming.) Perhaps the same as *II. rugosso-plicata.*

H. stomatiæformis, *Reeve, P.Z.S.,* 1846, *p.* 57 ; *Conch. Ic., f.* 74. Shell oblong, ovate, very convex, spirally striated, radiately finely plicated ; spire nearly terminal, elevated ; five perforations open ; marbled with olive-green (Reeve.) New Zealand. (Cuming.)

FAMILY—FISSURELLIDÆ.

Radula with a central median tooth, five denticulated uncini, and numerous slender hooked laterals. Body broad and conical. Head with a short wide muzzle ; tentacles subulate, with the eyes on slightly elevated tubercles at their external bases. Mantle margin fissured in front, the free edges forming an anal siphon occupying the anterior fissure or perforation in the apex of the shell ; gills two, symmetrical on the back of the neck. Foot dilated, sides with the upper part furnished with a series of .short cirri, or rudimentary filaments. Operculum none. Shell, in the adult, conical, symmetrical, not spiral, either pierced at the apex, or more or less grooved or fissured anteriorly ; aperture wide, not pearly within, muscular impression crescentic, open in front.

Genus, FISSURELLA.—Bruguiere.

Mantle margin fringed with cirri ; anal siphon short, truncate membranous, projecting from the perforation in the shell. Shell conical, radiately ribbed ; apex sub-anterior, or central ; anal perforation oblong, sub-apical.

F. squamosa, *Hutton, C.M.M., p.* 42. Solid, oblong, with strong radiating, more or less squamose, ribs ; anal perforation small, apical margin crenated ; brownish ; interior white. Height, ·25 ; length, ·9 ; breadth, ·6 ; anal perforation, ·08.

Genus, LUCAPINA—Gray.

Mantle margin fimbriated, reflexed more or less over the edges of the shell. Shell small, depressed, cancellated, with a large sub-central perforation, bordered internally by a callosity.

L. monilifera, *Hutton, C.M.M., p.* 42. Ovate, white, radiated with moniliform ribs and obscurely cancellated; border smooth or crenated.

Height, ·2 ; length, ·6 ; breadth, ·45.

Stewart Island, 15 fathoms.

Genus, EMARGINULA—Lamark.

Mantle margin simple, reflexed over the edges of the shell; anal siphon with prominent membranous margins projecting from the fissure in the shell; foot with a rudimentary operculigerous lobe. Shell oval, conical, elevated, the apex recurved; surface cancellated; anterior margin notched; muscular impression with recurved points.

E. striatula, *Quoy and Gaimard, l.c.,* iii., *p.* 332, *pl.* 68, *f.* 21-22 ; *Reeve, Conch. Ic., f.* 47. Shell ovato-conic, fragile, granulose, longitudinally and transversely finely ribbed; apex obliquely recurved; margin crenulated; fissure very deep; greenish-gray (Q. & G.)

Length, 5 lines; breadth, 3½ lines; height, 3½ lines.

Wellington. Dunedin.

E. australis, *Quoy and Gaimard, l.c.,* iii., *p.* 328, *pl.* 68, *f.* 11-12 ; *Reeve, Conch. Ic., f.* 19. Shell ovate, conical, inflated, white; longitudinal ribs alternately thick, rough and small; apex median, obtuse, recurved; margin undulated (Q. & G.)

Length, 1 inch 1 line; breadth, 10 lines; height, 9 lines.

Lyttelton. Australia.

Genus, TUGALIA—Gray.

Shell oblong, narrowed in front; back elevated, cancellated; apex posterior, recurved; aperture crenulated on the edge, sinuated in front.

T. parmophoidea, *Quoy and Gaimard, l.c.* iii., *p.* 325, *pl.* 5, *f.* 15-16 ; *Reeve, Conch. Ic., f.* 4 ; *Chenu, f.* 2798-9 ; *T. elegans, Gray, Dieff. N.Z.,* ii., *p.* 240. Shell ovato-oblong, convex and arcuate; margin denticulated; greenish yellow; cancellated with very thin rough and close striæ; apex obtuse; fissure almost none (Q. & G.)

Auckland to Dunedin. Chatham Islands. S. Australia.

Genus, PARMOPHORUS—Blainville.

Mantle margin simple, permanently more or less produced and covering the sides of the shell; foot moderate, smooth, with a series of short lateral cirri. Shell elongato-oblong, depressed; apex posterior; margin sinuated in front; smooth and white.

P. unguis, *Linnæus; Reeve, Conch. Ic. (Scutus,) f.* 5; *P. australis, Lam., A.s.V.,* vii., *p.* 579 ; *Woodward's Manual of the Mollusca, pl.* 11, *f.* 9 ; *Chenu, f.* 2801. Shell rather short, straight, broad, rather flattened, smooth, concentrically continuously striated; sides straight;

anterior margin widely truncated, very slightly sinuated; anterior area broad, smooth (Reeve.)
Auckland to Dunedin.
For the dentition of this species, see Hogg, Trans. Royal Micros. Soc., 1866 (in the Quart. Jour. of Micros. Science,) pl. 12, f. 57. Reeve considers that *P. australis* is the same as *P. elongatus*, Blainville, from Australia.

DIVISION—CYCLOBRANCHIATA.

Gill lamellar, on the inner surface of the mantle, forming a more or less complete ring just beneath the margin. Radula with no middle plate, and ridged lateral and intermediate plates. Side of foot with a sunken groove. Shell conical, symmetrical.

FAMILY—PATELLIDÆ.

Mouth with horny jaws; radula very long; teeth in numerous transverse rows (2. 4. 2.,) central two pairs; lateral two on each side, the inner one larger and lower down; uncini three. Head with a short muzzle; tentacles subulate, with the eyes on the outer side of the swollen base. Mantle margin fringed. Operculum none. Shell simple, conical; muscular impression crescentic, interrupted in front.

Genus, PATELLA—Linnæus.

Mouth emarginate below; gills extending round the body, interrupted on one side near the neck. Shell orbicular or oval; apex subcentral, inclined anteriorly; aperture wide, the margin entire or spinose, simple within.

P. magellanica, *Martyn, Reeve, Conch. Ic., f.* 19. Shell ovate, pyramidally concave, very high, radiately ribbed; ribs rather broad, rude, absoletely bluntly tubercled; ash-brown, ribs darker, blotched with black; interior ash-tinged (Reeve.)
Length, 2¾ inches.
Straits of Magellan. Auckland Island. Campbell Island. Kerguelen's Land. Doubtfully identified.

P. inconspicua, *Gray, Dieff. N.Z.,* ii., *p.* 244. Shell conical, oblong, with about twenty radiating ribes; the apex erect; disk white, rather greenish under the tip.
Length 1½ inches. (Gray.)
Wellington. Dunedin.
Probably a small variety of the last

P. redimiculum, *Reeve, Conch. Ic., f.* 50; *Voy. Erebus and Terror, pl.* 1, *f.* 24; *P. radians, Reeve, l.c., f.* 25; *P. pottsi. Hutton, C.M.M., p.* 44. Shell ovate, moderately convex; apex very much inclined anteriorly, radiately ribbed; ribs rounded, rather distant, obsoletely nodose, front ribs very short; olive-ash; ribs more or less black; interstices blotched with black and white; interior dull ash; nucleus fulvous (Reeve.)

Auckland Islands. Otago. Banks' Peninsula.

This species passes into *P. magellanica*; but the typical state is distinguished by its more depressed form, and more anterior position of the apex.

P. reevei, *Hutton; P. imbricata, Reeve, Conch. Ic., f.* 93 *(nec Linnæus.)* Shell ovate, tumidly convex; apex anterior, obtuse, radiately many ridged; ribs close set, scarcely raised, everywhere densely, sharply imbricated; dark blue-black; interior lead-blue, orange rust in the middle (Reeve.)

Wellington. Dunedin. Chatham Islands.

P. argyropsis, *Lesson; Voy. Coquille, Zool.,* ii., *p.* 419; *P. decora, Philippi; Reeve, Conch. Ic., f.* 33. Shell oval, slightly convex, much depressed; apex obtuse, short, anterior, the inferior face lightly concave; margin thin, sinuous, angulated at the termination of each of the diverging ribs which cover the upper face; ribs separated, having in the interval a median line and very fine and very close transverse lines; above greenish; below silvery, marked with purplish brown grooves which correspond to the ribs on the dorsal face (Lesson.)

Length, 15 lines; breadth, 13 lines; height, 3 lines.

Bay of Islands, on rocks. Otago.

P. affinis, *Reeve, Conch. Ic., f.* 108; *P. argentea, Quoy and Gaimard, Voy. Astrol.,* iii., *p.* 345 *(nec Linnæus;) N. carli, Hutton, C.M.M. (nec Reeve.)* Shell oblong-ovate, depressed; apex very anterior, small, rather sharp, radiately ridged and striated; ridges and striæ numerous, obtuse, slightly waved; dark olive, ornamented with obliquely blood blotched broad rays; interior sub-transparent, iridescent (Reeve.)

Otago. Cuming cites this species from Formosa (P.Z.S., 1865, p. 197.)

P. pholidota, *Lesson; Voy. Coquille, Zool.,* ii., *p.* 420; *P. floccata, Reeve, Conch. Ic., f.* 106. Shell, oval, sub-depressed, convex; apex conic, placed two-thirds anterior; margin simple, entire, regular; upper surface ornamented with very fine radiating close striæ, crossed by some concentric striæ, but little pronounced. Shell thin, pale yellow, covered with irregular and angular spots of brownish-purple and pale brown-red; interior shining silvery, speckled with purplish-brown; the tip reddish and black; in the young the interior is silvery, but covered with broad bands of golden reddish-brown (Lesson.)

Length, 17 lines; breadth, 13 lines; height, 5 lines.

Bay of Islands.

This species passes into the next.

P. radians, *Gmelin, 13th ed. Linnæus' Syst. Nat., p.* 3720; *Chenu, f.* 2847. Apex anterior; upper surface smooth or slightly ribbed; colour yellowish-white, with narrow dark brown radiating bands, which are sometimes interrupted.

Auckland to Dunedin. Auckland Islands.

P. denticulata, *Martyn; P. margaritaria, Chemnitz; Reeve, Conch. Ic., f. 74; Voy. Erebus and Terror, pl. 1, f. 26; P. ornata, Deshayes, Anim. sans vert., vii., p. 542.* Oval, conical, more or less depressed, radiately ribbed ; apex not recurved ; margin crenated ; pale greenish or reddish-yellow, with about twelve brownish-black rays spotted with white ; interior above the muscular impression purplish-black ; below silvery, rayed with pale yellow and brownish-black.
Heigth, ·4 ; length, 1 ; breadth, ·7.
Auckland to Dunedin.

P. flava, *Hutton, C.M.M., p.* 44. Ovate, conical, radiately ribbed ; apex recurved ; margin crenated ; pale-yellow, inclining to orange towards the apex ; interior, above the muscular impression, more or less orange ; below silvery.
Height, 1 ; length, 2·2 ; breadth, 1·8.
Amuri Bluff. Stonyhurst.
The young shell is more orange, and has the apex sub-anterior.

P. antipodum, *Smith ; Voy. Erebus and Terror, Moll., p.* 4, *pl.* 1, *f.* 25. Shell rotundly ovate, a little narrowed in front ; the apex much inclined anteriorly, one-fourth the length from the front margin, radiately rather finely ribbed ; ribs crossed by fine concentric lines of growth; orange-yellow, clouded with white around the middle, varied with ten or eleven black narrow rays placed at nearly equal distances, those in front being rather more approximated than the rest ; interior brilliant pearly orange-yellow, the exterior black rays especially visible at the margin, which is crenulated (Smith.)
Length, 1·1 ; width, ·85 ; height, ·37 inch.

P. tramoserica, *Martyn, pl.* 16 ; *Reeve, Conch. Ic.. f,* 27. Shell ovate, sub-conoid, radiately ribbed ; ribs close set, sometimes obscurely nodosely tubercled, rarely a little prickled ; yellowish or rose tinged, rayed with black ; rays white-spotted, or with the interstices altogether black ; interior more or less brightly coloured at the margin (Reeve.)
New Zealand (Martyn and Gould.) Common in Australia.

P. stellularia, *Quoy, l.c.,* iii., *p.* 347, *pl.* 70, *f.* 18-20 ; *Reeve, Conch. Ic., f.* 96. Oval, depressed, with small granular ribs ; reddish, with white rays at the apex, or two white lines at the posterior end ; interior white ; apex anterior.
Height, ·3 ; length, 1·4 ; breadth, 1. (Quoy.)
Cook Strait. Bank's Peninsula.

P. stellifera, *Chemnitz, Lamark, l.c.,* vii., *p.* 535. Ovate, rather depressed, with fine radiating decussate ribs ; apex not recurved ; blackish or reddish-brown, with radiating white stripes, which some-times do not reach the margin ; interior white, silvery; tip greenish-brown.
Height, ·25; length, ·95 ; breadth, ·7.
Cook Strait.

P. stella, *Lesson; Voy. Coquille, Zool.,* ii., *p.* 421. Solid, small, depressed, irregularly oval; apex sub-central, sharp, with seven radiating angular ribs, rounded above, thick, separated by wide depressions; these ribs are divergent, and number four in front and three behind. In the middle of each pair there is a smaller rib, and two on the sides in the interval which separates the four anterior from the three posterior. Shell greenish above, spotted with black in double interrupted circles; the border is stellate, with seven angles, having teeth in the intervals; the interior face is slightly hollowed, thick and granular in front; bluish-white; apex white, dotted with maroon (Lesson.)

Length, 10 lines; breadth, 9 lines; height, 3 lines.

P. earlii, *Reeve, Conch.; Ic., f.* 71. Shell rotundately ovate, slightly attenuated in front, convexly raised; apex inclined anteriorly, radiately ridged; ridges small, very few and distant, with the interstices irregularly elevately striated; pale green, broadly wave-variegated with olive-black; interior transparently iridescent; milk-white in the middle (Reeve.)

P. flexuosa, *Hutton, C.M.M., p.* 45. Ovate, depressed, not ribbed, but with fine concentric striæ; margin entire; pale yellowish, with deeply waved concentric brown lines; interior silvery.

Height, ·6; length, 1·7; breadth, 1·4.

Stonyhurst.

Perhaps a variety of the last.

P. rubiginosa, *Hutton, C.M.M., p.* 42. Conical, ovate; apex sub-anterior, thin, smooth, radiately ribbed; ribs thirteen to seventeen; outside white; interior pinkish.

Height, ·2; length, ·6; breadth, ·5.

Auckland to Bank's Peninsula. Chatham Islands. Auckland Islands.

DIVISION—POLYPLACOPHORA.

Gills in two lamellar series, one on each side of the hinder part of the body under the mantle edge. Valves eight, forming a linear imbricate series on the middle of the back. Radula long, linear; central series with many teeth, middle one unlike the rest, outer lateral one on each side, very large, with a black opaque hook; lateral teeth several, forming jointed unarmed lamellæ; one erect, hooked (4-6.2.1.2.4-6.;) monœcious; anus posterior, median.

FAMILY—CHITONIDÆ.

Head surrounded by a semi-circular veil or hood; eyes and tentacles none; mouth with cartilaginous jaws. Gills in a series of lamellæ between the mantle and the foot. Foot oblong, rounded at each end. Shell of eight imbricated valves or plates, immersed in the coriaceous mantle, which forms an expanded margin beyond them.

Sub-Family—Chitoninæ.

Mantle simple, without any pores or tufts of spines on the sides.

Genus, CHITON—Linnæus.

Mantle covered with regularly disposed, smooth, imbricate, roundish, conspicuous scales. Shell with the valves external, transverse, broad ; the hinder valve with the apex superior.

C. pellis-serpentis, *Quoy; Voy. Astrolabe*, iii., *p*. 381, *pl.* 74, *f.* 17-22 ; *Reeve, Conch. Ic., f.* 84 ; *Chenu, f.* 2850. Oval ; mantle with moderate sized scales ; valves elevated, rounded, solid, opaque ; posterior margins curved, meeting in an obtuse point on the back ; terminal areas with radiating moniliform lines ; lateral areas of intermediate valves with curved radiating ribs, concave behind, and crossed by curved longitudinal furrows, which are concave upwards ; median areas slightly longitudinally striated ; dorsal line smooth and polished on the anterior parts of the valves, but striated on the posterior parts ; mantle yellowish or greenish-white, with about twenty transverse black bands ; valves generally greenish-black, passing into yellowish on the back, and with a triangular black spot, with its apex pointing backwards, along the dorsal line of all the intermediate valves ; it is generally much eroded, but the size and colour of the scales on the mantle are always sufficient to distinguish it from other New Zealand species.
Length, 1·5 ; breadth, ·75.
Abundant on rocks between high and low watermarks.
Pitt's Island. Auckland to Dunedin.

C. sinclairi, *Gray*, *Dieff. N.Z.*, ii., *p.* 263 ; *Voy. Erebus and Terror, pl.* 1, *f.* 17 ; *Hutton, Trans. N.Z. Inst.,* iv., *p.* 177. Pale brown, polished, the terminal valves with many, and the lateral areas with few indistinct broad nodulose ridges, the central area polished, with pale longitudinal streaks, and with a few short, deep irregular longitudinal grooves on the hinder edge of the sides (Gray.)
Great Barrier Island. Tasmania (Bednall and Reeve.)
Tenison-Woods says the Tasmanian habitat is doubtful. Differs from *C. pellis-serpentis* in being polished, and in having the central plates smooth, except at the outer angles.

C. stangeri, *Reeve, Conch. Ic., f.* 150. Shell ovate, terminal valves, and lateral areas of the others, rayed with rows of closely packed square appressed granules ; central areas smooth in the middle, closely ridged on each side ; interstices rather deep ; yellow and green, tesselated with green spots ; ligament squamosely coriaceous (Reeve.)
Perhaps a variety of the last.

C. concentricus, *Reeve, Conch. Ic., f.* 95 ; *Hutton, Trans. N.Z. Inst.,* iv., *p.* 176. Shell oblong, ovate, umbones somewhat beaked, terminal valves and lateral areas of the rest concentrically grooved ; central areas longitudinally ridged ; ridges rather distant ; interstices hollowed ; posterior terminal valve umbonated and distinguished in the middle by a small smooth triangular shield ; bronzed ; mantle granuosely coriaceous ; tessellated with brown (Reeve.) ·
Australia. (Bednall.) New Zealand. (Earl.)

P

C. sulcatus, *Quoy; Voy. Astrolabe,* iii., *p.* 385, *pl.* 75, *f.* 31-36 *(not of Wood, nor of Reeve;) Hutton, l.c., p.* 178. Body elongato-oval; greenish; mantle scaly; valves sub-triangular, sulcated, the sides granulose and white; posterior valve broad, granulosely sulcated (Quoy.)

King George's Sound.   Auckland.

The mantle is narrow; the scales greenish, with a small brown spot on each.   Valves rounded; the anterior simply granulose, with eleven or twelve teeth.

C. insculptus, *A. Adams, P.Z.S.,* 1852, *p.* 91, *pl.* 16, *f.* 4. Shell oblong, much elevated, terminal valves, and the lateral areas of the others radiately ribbed; ribs granular, the granules transverse, rather crowded, obsolete at the margins; umbones keeled; anterior terminal valve umbonated; median areas longitudinally strongly lirated; liræ obsoletely rugoso-granuled; median areas red, with two blackish-brown parallel lines down the centre of the valves; mantle with brownish-yellow and brown scales; scales smooth, shining, convex (Adams.)

New Zealand, on dead shells in deep water.   (Strange.)

C. glaucus, *Gray; Spic. Zool.,* 1830, *p.* 5; *C. quoyi, Deshayes, Anim. sans vert.,* vii., *p.* 509; *Reeve, Conch. Ic., f.* 68; *C. viridis, Quoy (nec Chemnitz:) Voy. Astrolabe,* iii., *p.* 383, *pl.* 71, *f.* 23-28.   Oval; mantle with moderate sized scales; valves elevated, flattened on each side; posterior margins slightly concave, with a small central point; the anterior valve, the greater part of the posterior valve, and the lateral areas of the intermediate valves with fine radiating striæ; median areas very finely longitudinally striated; generally dark olive-green, or blackish-green when dry, but sometimes brown, or green rayed with brown, and the mantle is sometimes varied with white.

Length, 1·5; breadth, ·75.

Common under stones in pools left by the retreating tide.   Auckland to Dunedin.   Found also in Australia.

Perhaps a variety of *C. chilolensis.*

C. æreus, *Reeve, Conch. Ic., f.* 36; *Voy. Erebus and Terror, Moll., pl.* 1, *f.* 9.   Shell oblong, ovate, angularly raised in the middle; valves rudely impressly striated throughout; umbonal eminence smooth; dull green; ligament granosely coriaceous (Reeve.)

Genus, LEPIDOPLEURUS—Risso.

Mantle covered with minute, flattened, longitudinally grooved scales.   Shell with the valves external, broad; the hinder valve with the apex sub-central; the plates of insertion of the valves thin and smooth edged, those of the central valves with a single notch in some species, in others four or five lobed; laminæ of insertion of the terminal valves many lobed.

L. canaliculatus, *Quoy; Voy. Astrolabe,* iii., *p.* 394, *pl.* 75, *f.* 37-42.   Elongated, elevated, strongly keeled; valves triangular, longitudinally sulcated, crenulated posteriorly; mantle with fine scales (Quoy.)

Tasman's Bay. (Quoy.) Stewart Island. (F.W.H.)
Generally rose colour, sometimes greenish spotted with red (Quoy.)

L. contractus, *Reeve, Conch. Ic., f.* 78. Shell oblong, peculiarly contracted at the extremities, especially the anterior; terminal valves and lateral areas of the rest concentrically granulated; granules solitary; central areas very minutely and closely ridged; ridges curved and conspicuous towards the sides, finer towards the middle, and decussated with oblique striæ; light bay, flamed in the middle with brown; ligament granosely coriaceous, dark brown (Reeve.)
New Zealand. (Cuming.)

L. longicymbus, *De Blainville; Sowerby, Conch. Illus., f.* 67; *Reeve, Conch. Ic., f.* 163; *Chenu, f.* 2857. Oblong; mantle with very minute scales; valves rounded; posterior margins straight, or slightly concave; terminal areas with fine radiating moniliform lines; lateral areas with radiating ribs crossed by rather deep, curved, transverse furrows; median areas of both terminal and intermediate valves finely punctate; brown variously tinted with green, yellow, or whitish, sometimes pink on the back when rubbed; often entirely greenish-brown, minutely freckled with yellow; often brown, with a broad white stripe down the back.
Length, 1·4; breadth, ·65.
Very variable both in shape and colour.
Common under stones. Auckland to Dunedin. Pitt's Island. Auckland Islands. Campbell Island. Found also in Australia.

L. circumvallatus, *Reeve, Conch. Ic., f.* 177. Shell oblong, ovate, terminal valves and lateral areas of the rest sculptured with concentric ridges; central areas very minutely reticulated; posterior terminal valve umbonated; blackish-red, spotted with black; ligament arenaceous, tesselated (Reeve.)
Distinguished from *C. longicymbus* by the conspicuous ridge with which it is encircled.
Campbell Island.

L. empleurus, *Hutton, Trans. N.Z. Inst.,* iv., *p.* 178. Oblong; margin with very minute scales; valves rather elevated and flattened on each side, sub-carinate; posterior margins slightly concave, with a small central point; terminal and lateral areas raised above the rest; minutely punctate; median areas minutely punctate, sometimes with a row of deep longitudinal pits along the anterior edges of the raised lateral areas; uniform yellowish-pink.
Length, ·75; breadth, ·3.
Founded on two specimens in the Colonial Museum, locality not stated.

L. rudis, *Hutton, Trans. N.Z. Inst.,* iv., *p.* 179. Oblong; margin with minute scales; valves elevated, flattened on the sides, not keeled; apex of anterior valve recurved, with its posterior margin slightly convex at the sides, and deeply concave in the centre; posterior margins of intermediate valves straight; posterior valve rather small; apex posterior, pointed and emarginate ; anterior valve, and lateral areas, with radiating moniliform ribs ; posterior and median areas widely, but rather irregularly, deeply longitudinally furrowed, with narrow ridges between ; margin grey, with broad irregular reddish-brown transverse bands ; valves greyish-brown ; interior greyish-white.

Length, 1·75 ; breadth, ·75.

Founded on a specimen in the Colonial Museum, locality not stated.

Genus, TONICIA—Gray.

Margin of the mantle simple, naked, nearly smooth, or velvety ; last valve entire ; valves external, transverse, broad ; the hinder valve with the apex superior ; laminæ of insertion of the terminal valves many lobed, those of the middle bi-lobed.

T. undulata, *Quoy ; Voy. Astrolabe,* iii., *p,* 393. *pl.* 75, *f.* 19-24 ; *Adams, Gen. Moll., pl.* 54, *f.* 3. Oval ; valves rounded, polished, sub-carinate ; posterior margins straight, produced into a rather acute central point ; terminal area of anterior valve, and lateral areas of inter-mediate valves, with indistinct radiating moniliform ridges ; posterior valve, and median areas of anterior and intermediate valves, with waved transverse striæ ; mantle reddish-brown ; valves generally green, inclin-ing, more or less, to yellowish on the back, with the waved striæ brown ; sometimes the valves are greyish-green, with many of the undulating striæ white.

Length, 1·15 ; breadth, ·55.

Auckland to Dunedin. Chatham Islands. Tasmania.

Not uncommon under stones at low water.

T. rubiginosa, *Hutton, Trans. N.Z. Inst.,* iv., *p.* 180. Oblong ; margin slightly tomentose ; valves rather elevated, sub-carinate, flattened on each side ; posterior margins straight, produced into an acute central point ; lateral areas indistinct, the whole surface rather coarsely granu-lar, the granules smaller on the back ; pink, getting yellowish on the back.

Length, ·45 ; breadth, ·2.

Cook Straits. Foveaux Straits. (H. Filhol.)

T. lineolata, *Frembly ; Zool. Jour.,* iii., *p.* 204 ; *Reeve, Conch. Ic., f.* 34 ; *Chenu, f.* 2867. Shell oblong, ovate, somewhat attenuated anteriorly ; terminal valves and lateral areas of the rest very minutely granulated ; central areas smooth ; yellowish fulvous, regularly painted with reddish-chestnut concentric waved lines, and more or less blotched with the same colour ; ligament horny, transparent (Reeve.)

Dunedin. Auckland Islands. Campbell Island. Chili.

The New Zealand specimens have the valves coloured dark purple-black, as in Reeve's figure, 34 b.

T. atrata, *Sowerby, Mag. Nat. Hist.,* 1840 ; *Conch. Illus., f.* 57-58 ; *Reeve, Conch. Ic., f.* 103. Shell oblong, ovate ; valves smooth ; the ter-minal posterior truncated, and lateral areas of the rest obscurely rayed with a very few granules ; brown rayed with yellowish lines, with a dark triangular spot on the umbonal summit of each valve ; ligament horny, transparent (Reeve.)

Macquarie Island. Falkland Islands. (Sowerby.)

Our species agrees very well with Reeve's figure, but not with his description. The anterior terminal area is distantly radiately ribbed, and the lateral areas are sometimes defined by a single rib. The umbone of the posterior valve is more posterior than in the drawing, and the valves are of a uniform brown colour. The mantle is of the same colour as the valves.

Sowerby gives the Falkland Islands as the locality for this species, but Reeve doubts it and gives no habitat at all.

Genus, ACANTHOPLEURA—Guilding.

Mantle densely beset with unequal corneo-calcareous, often very long spines, or with small calcareous spicula, giving it a spinulose appearance. Shell with the valves external, broad, transverse ; the hinder valve with the apex sub-central. The plates of insertion of the terminal valves are many lobed, of the posterior sometimes somewhat obsolete, and of the middle bilobed.

A. cælatus, *Reeve, Conch. Ic., f.* 101 ; *T. zig-zag, Hutton, Trans. N.Z. Inst.,* iv., *p.* 180. Shell oblong, ovate, somewhat attenuated anteriorly, terminal valves, the posterior of which is small and slanting, and lateral areas of the rest broad-ribbed and neatly curved with close-set waved laminæ ; central· areas very minutely reticulated ; beautifully ornamented with green and pink ; mantle horny, here and there bristly (Reeve.)

I follow Adams in placing this species in *Acanthopleura,* for I presume that he has seen the type specimens ; but it appears to me to belong more properly to *Mopalia.*

Genus, CHÆTOPLEURA—Shuttleworth.

Mantle beset with horny bristles. Shell with the valves external, broad, transverse ; the hinder valve with the apex sub-central ; laminæ of insertion of the hinder valve many-lobed, those of the middle valve bi-lobed or six-lobed.

C. nobilis, *Gray, Dieff. N.Z.,* ii., *p.* 245; *Voy. Erebus and Terror, Moll., pl.* 1, *f.* 8. Mantle rugose, rough, with scattered long tapering brown bristles ; valves brown, convex. evenly rounded, with very minute dots like shagreen, the lateral area slightly marked with three or four indistinct rays ; inside white.

Length, 3. (Gray.)

Auckland. Cook Strait. Martin's Bay.

Genus, MOPALIA—Gray.

Mantle moderately wide, bristly or hairy, with a sinuosity on the hinder lower edge; valves with a small portion of the lateral areas covered by the mantle; hinder valve large, with the apex sub-central, and posteriorly slightly sinuated; plates of insertion of all the valves with a single notch on each side.

M. ciliata, *Sowerby; Reeve, Conch. Ic., f.* 124; *A. complexa, Hutton, Trans. N.Z. Inst.*, iv., *p.* 181. Shell oblong, ovate; anterior terminal valve radiately eight-ridged; interstices undately granosely striated; posterior small, retuse; lateral areas anteriorly decussately granosely striated; grains obtuse throughout; ash green, sparingly stained with yellow towards the middle; mantle horny, beset with a few bristles (Reeve.)
S. Australia. (Angas.)

Sub-Family—Cryptoplacinæ.

Mantle with a double series of pores beset with horny bristles, or a single series of pores furnished with tufts of calcareous spines.

Genus, PLAXIPHORA—Gray.

Mantle with a double series of pores beset with bifurcate bristles, one row at the insertion of the valves, the other at the external margin; mantle-margin smooth and horny, or more or less covered with setose or furfuraceous scales. Shell with the valves broad, transverse, external; the hinder valve small, with the apex posterior, and with a slight notch on the hind lower edge, its plate of insertion slightly raised, smooth, not divided into lobes at the sides; plates of insertion of the middle valves bi-lobate, those of the anterior usually about nine-lobed.

P. biramosa, *Quoy and Gaimard, Voy. Astrolabe,* iii., *p.* 378, *pl.* 74, *f.* 12-16; *T. corticata, Hutton, Trans. N.Z. Inst.*, iv., *p.* 180. Body oval, flattish, red, girdled with two series of double bristles; margin hairy; valves flattish, greenish-red or white, anteriorly transversely striated (Q. & G.)
Wellington. Campbell Island.
Reeve is quite wrong in uniting this species with *C. setiger,* King.

P. terminalis, *Smith, Voy. Erebus and Terror, Moll., p.* 4, *pl.* 1, *f.* 13. Shell elongately-ovate, rather elevated, roundly angled along the top of the valves; black or bluish-black, with a white wedge-shaped stripe, with a black one within it down the centre of the valves, forming a continuous white stripe divided by the black one along the centre of the shell; in some specimens with a few short white dashes diverging from the radiating ridges; the intermediate valves mucronated, bisected on each side by one raised radiating rib; the posterior margins sinuated and thickened by coarse concentric lamellæ; the entire surface is covered with minute striate-wrinkling, those near the ridge being coarser than the rest, and radiating from it like the webs from the shaft of a feather; the posterior terminal valve has the mucro quite terminal; the anterior valve radiately eight-ribbed with diverging oblique striations on each side of them; interior greenish-blue; valve lobes whitish, the sinus between them deep; bristles on the mantle short, few, and horny, those from the nine pores being thicker than the rest (Smith.)

Length, 1·65; breadth, ·8 inch or less.

Genus, ACANTHOCHITES—Risso.

Mantle densely spinulose, surrounded with a series of setigerous pores. Shell with the valves deeply immersed, sub-equal, externally contiguous, the exposed part moderate, cordate, as broad as long; plate of insertion of the anterior valve six-lobed, that of the middle bi-lobed, that of the posterior five-lobed.

A. zealandicus, *Quoy and Gaimard, Voy. Astrolabe,* iii., *p.* 400, *pl.* 73, *f.* 5-8; *A. hookeri, Gray, Dieff. N.Z.,* ii., *p.* 262; *Reeve, Conch. Ic., f.* 58. Oblong; mantle spiny, with nine large radiating tufts of spines on each side; valves flatly triangular, sub-carinate; posterior margins slightly convex, with an obtuse central point; terminal and lateral areas granulose; median areas smooth; lateral areas very large; mantle brown; spines pale green; valves generally greyish-black, more or less varied with yellowish; often yellowish or reddish on the dorsal line; occasionally greenish.

Length, 1; breadth, ·4.

Auckland to Dunedin. Japan.

Not uncommon on stones below low watermark.

The spines on the mantle vary from green to brown. Green is the more common colour in the north, while brown appears to be universal in Otago.

A. porphyreticus, *Reeve, Conch. Ic., f.* 56. Shell somewhat elongately ovate; valves punctured in the middle, verrucosely rough on each side, with a single ridge along the edge of the lateral areas; anterior terminal valve radiately five-ribbed; posterior small, blunt; cinerous purple, with a conspicuous yellow spot, dotted with black at the edge, and stained with bright purple in the middle, along the umbonal summit of each valve (Reeve.)

Dunedin. Cook Strait.

A. ovatus, *Hutton, Trans. N.Z. Inst.,* iv., *p.* 182. Ovate, attenuated in front; margin spiny, with nine small bundles along each side; valves flatly triangular, sub-carinate; posterior valve very narrow; apex recurved; posterior margins of the anterior plate sloping backwards into a point, those of the posterior plates nearly straight; anterior valve with ten, and lateral areas with two on each side, radiating nodulose ridges; median areas with slightly waved longitudinal ridges; dorsal line smooth; mantle pale reddish-brown; spines white; valves greenish-white; yellowish on the dorsal line.

Length, ·6; breadth, ·5.

Cook Strait. Dunedin. On seaweed.

A. **violacea,** *Quoy and Gaimard, Voy. Astrolabe, Zoologie, vol.* iii., *p.* 403, *pl.* 73, *f.* 15-20; *Reeve, Conch. Ic., f.* 41. Oval, rather convex; mantle fleshy, smooth, reddish or yellowish-brown, with nine fascicles of bristles on each side; valves close, triangular, violet, the first hexagonal; variety with the mantle yellowish-brown, sprinkled with red spots (Q. & G.)

Length, 1 inch 8 lines; breadth, 1 inch 1 line; height, 6 or 7 lines.

Tasman Bay. Auckland.

In this species the exposed parts of the valves are small, nearly cordiform, rather flattened, sharp in the middle, finely and very closely granulated throughout. The mantle is broad, horny, with nine whitish fascicles on either side (Reeve.)

Genus, CRYPTOCONCHUS—Blainville.

Mantle with a single series of pores, thick, smooth, elevated at the pores into conical tubercles. Shell with the valves sub-cordate, the exposed part very small, linear, much longer than broad; the plates of insertion of all the valves have only a single notch on each side, which is sometimes rudimentary.

Found in New Zealand only.

C. **porosus,** *Burrow; Adams, Gen. Moll., pl.* 55, *f.* 4; *C. monticularis, Quoy, Voy. Astrolabe,* iii., *p.* 406, *pl.* 73, *f.* 30-36; *Reeve, Conch. Ic., f.* 57; *Chenu, f.* 2885. Oblong; mantle smooth, covering the whole body except a small linear opening at the apex of each valve; valves depressed, rounded; posterior margins convex and emarginated; exposed portions of valves smooth; nine bundles of spines on each side, situated over the valves; dark reddish-brown when dry; inside greenish-grey.

Length, 1; breadth, .45.

Dunedin to Auckland.

When alive the mantle varies from bright orange to light brown.

Sub-Order—Heteropoda.

Diœcious, pelagic, translucent; foot compressed, fin-like; shell thin or none; viscera in a nucleus; gills pectinate or filamentary; propodium vertical, fin-like, mesopodium suctorial in the males of some, the sucker having circular and radiating fibres.

FAMILY—FIROLIDÆ.

Animal cylindrical, translucent, furnished with ventral and tail fins for swimming; gills exposed on the posterior part of the back, or covered by a small hyaline shell.

· Genus, CARINARIA—Lamark.

Animal large, translucent, granulated; ventral fin rounded; tail large, compressed; gills numerous, pinnate, projecting from beneath the shell, which is limpet-shaped, with a posterior sub-spiral apex, and a fimbriated dorsal keel; nucleus minute, dextrally spiral.

C. australis, *Quoy, Voy. Astrolabe, p.* 394, *pl.* 29, *f.* 9-16. Shell thin, hyaline, transversely sulcated; apex obliquely inclined; keel undulated; spire obtuse, on the right towards the whorls four elongated oval apertures; swimming foot extended, quadrilateral (Quoy.)

Sub-Order—Opisthobranchiata.

Gills exposed or slightly covered, behind the heart; hermaphrodite, mostly carnivorous; gelatinous, full of sea water. Shell when present enclosed in the folds of the mantle; abdomen rudimentary, not spirally developed in the adult, or protected by a shell; larva shell-bearing, and furnished with deciduous cephalic fins.

DIVISION—TECTIBRANCHIATA.

Gill forming a tuft or plume on the side, towards the hind part of the body, under a fold of the mantle, and usually protected by a shell. Both adult and larva shell-bearing. Foot elongate, formed for walking. Marine.

FAMILY—ACTÆONIDÆ.

Teeth, central none, lateral numerous, uncinated, in a diverging cross series. Head depressed, forming a quadrate disc, bi-lobed in front, with broad, posterior, tentacular lobes; eyes sessile on the middle of the head. Mantle included within the shell; branchial plume single. Foot oblong, truncate in front, obtuse behind. Operculum horny, linear, transverse. Shell solid, involute, with the columella plicate or spirally twisted.

Genus, BUCCINULUS—Plancus.

Ovate, with a conical many-whorled spire; mouth long, narrow, rounded in front; columella with two spiral folds; operculum horny, elliptical, lamellar.

B. kirki, *Hutton, C.M.M., p.* 51. Whorls six, finely and rather distantly spirally grooved, those on the centre of the whorls rather farther apart; columella with one double fold; white.
Length, ·8; breadth, ·3.
Omaha.

B. albus, *Hutton, C.M.M., p.* 51. Whorls seven, rather deeply equi-distantly spirally grooved, and lightly transversely striated; columella with a broad double anterior fold, and a smaller posterior one; white.
Length, ·35; breadth, ·15.
Auckland.

R

FAMILY—APLUSTRIDÆ.

Teeth, central none, laterals numerous, uniform. Head with the frontal disc produced into large car-like tentacular lobes folded over the back of the shell, and furnished with bifid labial appendages; eyes sessile at the inner bases of the tentacular lobes. Mantle with the inner margin thin and membranous, the outer forming a thick fleshy lobe, curving round the spire of the shell; branchial plume long and single. Foot large and membranous, auriculate in front, rounded behind. Operculum none. Shell external, involute, ornamented with coloured bands or markings; aperture more or less channelled at the fore part.

Genus, BULLINA—Ferussac.

Shell ovate, solid; axis perforated; spire rather elevated; whorls transversely grooved, with coloured markings; aperture longitudinal, broadly channelled in front; inner lip thin, adnate to the body whorl; columella arched forwards, and obliquely sub-truncate anteriorly; outer lip grooved internally, and with the margin crenulated.

The animal is not known.

B. lineata, *Wood, Ind. Test. Suppl., pl.* 3; *Reeve, Conch. Ic., f.* 2; *Chenu, f.* 2915. Shell sub-ovate, ventricose, yellowish or rosy-white, ornamented with two bright-red lines and others longitudinal, slightly waved distant, disjoined; spire obtuse, rather elevated; columella uniplicate, tortuous (Sowerby.)

Hauraki Gulf (rare). Australia.

FAMILY—CYLICHNIDÆ.

Teeth, central none, lateral 6.6, the inner large and hooked, the outer small and uniform, rarely wanting. Head with the frontal dsc depressed, sub-quadrate, truncate in front, produced behind into broad, flattened, recumbent, tentacular lobes, with the eyes immersed in the front of their bases. Mantle with a posterior thickened process or lobe. Foot shorter than the shell, truncate in front. Operculum none. Shell external, spirally convoluted, more or less cylindrical, without coloured markings.

Genus, CYLICHNA—Loven.

Tentacular lobes connate, indistinct; eyes sessile on their front bases; mantle with a thick posterior lobe partially closing the aperture of the shell; shell without spire, the apex concave; aperture straight.

C. striata, *Hutton, C.M.M., p.* 52. Small, smooth, white, longi-tudinally finely striated; aperture scarcely produced above the spire.

Length, ·1; breadth, ·05.

Auckland.

FAMILY—BULLIDÆ.

Teeth, central one, lateral numerous, uniform, in an arched series. Animal partly investing, but not entirely covering the shell. Tentacular frontal disc expanded, emarginate behind ; eyes none, or sessile on the middle of the frontal disc. Mantle with the right margin thickened, the left thin, adhering to the body whorl of the shell. Foot with the sides greatly developed, often reflexed and covering the sides of the shell, or expanded for swimming. Gizzard usually armed with horny or calcareous plates. Shell external, involute, more or less covered by the reflexed lateral lobes of the foot.

Genus, BULLA—Klein.

Eyes conspicuous, sessile on the middle of the frontal disc : mantle with the outer margin forming a thick fleshy lobe ; foot with the lateral lobes moderate, and the hind part not extending beyond the shell. Shell oval, ventricose, solid, smooth ; aperture longer than the shell.

B. oblonga, *Adams; B. australis, Gray, Dieff. N.Z.,* ii., *p.* 243 ; *Chenu,* 2940 ; *Reeve, Conch. Ic., f.* 9. Large, elongated, cylindrical, with a few spiral lines near the base ; chestnut-brown, faintly varied with grey.
Length, 2 ; breadth, 1·1.
Coasts north of Auckland. Australia. Tasmania.

B. quoyi, *Gray, Dieff. N.Z.,* ii., *p.* 243 ; *Voy. Erebus and Terror, Moll., pl.* 1, *f.* 11 ; *B. striata, Quoy, l.c.,* ii., *p.* 354, *pl.* 26, *f.* 8-9. Ovate, smooth, with a few spiral lines near the base ; olivaceous, marbled with purplish-grey, and occasionally with white dots.
Length, 1·4 ; breadth, ·9.
Auckland. Mazatlan. (Reigen.)
The specimen figured by Reeve is not *B. quoyi.*

Genus, HAMINEA—Leach.

Eyes distinct, sessile on the middle of the head ; mantle with the outer margin large, fleshy, and reflexed on the apex of the shell ; foot with the lateral lobes very much expanded, covering the sides and front of the shell, the hind part extending beyond the shell. Shell ovate, horny, thin, covered by a thin epidermis, lightly transversely striated.

H. zealandiæ, *Gray, Dieff. N.Z.,* ii., *p.* 243 ; *Voy. Erebus and Terror, pl.* 1, *f.* 10. Shell ovate, sub-globose, imperforated, thin, pellucid, very slightly concentrically striated, covered with a very thin greenish periostraca, the inner lip rather spread over the pillar in front, smooth (Gray.)
Length, about an inch.
Auckland.

H. obesa, *Sowerby; Reeve, Conch. Ic., f.* 13 (1868.) Shell short, broad, sub-globose, smooth, lightly and obliquely wrinkled above, pale

fulvous, white within, a little narrowed posteriorly; umbilicus broad; columella broad, arched; outer lip squarish above, rather straight in the middle (Sowerby.)
Length, ·8 inch.
Auckland. (Cheesman.) Tasmania. (Tenison-Woods.)
Probably the same as the last.

H. cuticulifera, *Smith, Ann. Nat. Hist.,* 4-9-350. Shell elongato-cylindrical, above and below roundly quadrate, thin, white; epidermis white, shining near the vertex and base tinted yellow, transversely sub-distantly striated with lines of growth, both above and below; aperture broad, base dilated, hardly produced above the vertex; columella short, sub-straight, reflexed, covering the umbilical region; callus very thin, scarcely shining, joined to the vertex; lip thin, thickened in the middle (Smith.)
Length, ·55; diam., ·27 inches.
New Zealand and Port Jackson.

Genus, AKERA—O. F. Muller.

Head disc elongated, entire behind; eyes none; mantle with a fimbriated edge projecting through the slit in the spire; foot with the lateral lobes greatly dilated, folded in repose over the sides of the shell. Shell convolute, ovate, or sub-cylindrical, thin; spire truncated, the whorls distinct, channelled, the last whorl disjoined from the others at the suture; aperture elongate, pyriform, rounded and entire in front; inner lip excavated; outer lip posteriorly free, angulated.

A. tumida, *Adams, in Sowerby's Thes.,* ii., *pl.* 125, *f.* 169; *Reeve, Conch. Ic., f.* 2. Shell sub-cylindrical, rather straight, with a single central band of brown; spire contracted, flat, with the last whorl tumid above; aperture rather square in front, contracted behind, with the outer lip a little produced above the centre; columella rather straight, narrow (Sowerby.)
The shores of New Zealand. (Sowerby.)

FAMILY—PHILINIDÆ.

Teeth, central none, lateral one or two, large, hooked. Cephalic disc oblong or sub-quadrate, without tentacular lobes; eyes none, or if present, sessile on the head. Mantle covering and concealing the shell. Foot not produced posteriorly; the sides dilated, thick and fleshy. Gizzard armed with calcareous plates. Shell none, or internal, enclosed in the mantle; when present, loosely involute.

Genus, PHILINE—Ascanias.

Animal investing the shell; eyes none; foot not produced posteriorly; the side lobes large and fleshy. Shell fragile, ovate, convolute; spire none; aperture very large, open.

P. angasi, *Crosse (?,) Jour. de Conch.*, 1865, *pl.* 2, *f.* 5; *Reeve, Conch. Ic., f.* 4. Shell large, ovately sub-quadrate, or acuminated, white, spirally substriated, concentrically slightly undulated; aperture wide, posteriorly sub-quadrate, elevated; penultimate whorl elongated (Sowerby.)

Auckland.

As I have not seen the animal, this identification is conjectural; the only shell I have seen was small.

FAMILY—APLYSIIDÆ.

Teeth, central one, lateral numerous, similar. Head with separate ear-like tentacles; eyes sessile on the head. Mouth armed with horny jaws, and with produced labial tentacles. Mantle with an internal calcareous plate protecting the gill. Foot with large lateral lobes, usually folded across the back. Shell rudimentary, internal, contained in the mantle. The gizzard is armed with teeth; the reproductive orifices are beneath the right tentacle; and the anus is dorsal, and is either sessile or tubular.

Genus, APLYSIA---Gmelin.

Body elongated; gills concealed; foot with the lobes dilated, and serving for swimming; anal aperture simple, sessile. Shell sub-cartilaginous, ovate; apex acute. When molested they discharge a purple fluid.

A. brunnea, *Hutton, Trans. N.Z. Inst.,* vii., *p.* 279, *pl.* xxi., *f.* .
Animal of a uniform rich dark brown, about four inches in length. Shell horny, ear-shaped, firm, the whole shell very finely concentrically striated; epidermis pale brown.

Length, ·9; breadth, ·7 inch.

Wellington and Dunedin.

A. venosa, *Hutton, Trans. N.Z. Inst.,* vii., *p.* 279, *pl.* xxi., *f.* .
Animal yellowish-brown, veined with dark brown, about six inches in length. Shell membranous; the apex rather coarsely concentrically striated, the rest of the shell smooth and polished; epidermis pale straw-colour.

Length, 1·25; breadth, 1 inch.

Wellington.

Genus, ACLESIA—Rang.

Body oval, pointed behind, covered with digitated appendages; gills included within the branchial cavity; anal orifice simple. Shell none.

A. glauca, *Cheeseman, P.Z.S.,* 1878, *p*, 277, *pl.* xv., *f.* 4. Animal 3·5 inch long; ovate, produced in front; entirely covered with numerous simple and branched appendages, the largest of which are

sometimes eight lines long; colour on the sides pale greyish-brown,
passing on the back into a dull sea-green; the whole surface with
numerous irregularly shaped black blotches that are longest on the
back. Along the back a double row of eight-twelve emerald green spots,
each surrounded with a zone of umber; dorsal tentacles three-quarter
inch long, folded so as to appear tubular; labial tentacles similar in
shape but larger; foot long and narrow, pointed behind, without side
lobes; sole pale sea-green (Cheeseman.)
Auckland.

FAMILY—PLEUROBRANCHIDÆ.

Head with auriform tentacles; eyes sessile on the head, at the bases
of the tentacles; mouth provided with an oral veil, corneous jaws, and
an armed radula. Gills composed of a double row of leaflets in the
form of a long branchial plume at the side of the body under the edge
of the mantle. Shell calcareous and external, membranous and internal,
or wanting. No upper jaw; teeth short, arranged in a quincunx.

Genus, PLEUROBRANCHUS—Cuvier.

Tentacles dorsal, ear-like; labial appendages transverse, folded and
truncate; mantle smaller than the foot, only partly covering the head,
simple behind, covering and concealing the shell. Foot very large,
extending beyond the mantle. Shell internal, thin, oval, membranaceous.

P. ornatus, *Cheeseman, P.Z.S.,* 1878, *p.* 275, *pl.* xv., *f.* 1-2. Body
three-four inches long, depressed, nearly equally rounded at both ends;
colour varying from pale buff to a clear reddish-brown, with irregular
blotches of rich dark red-brown; mantle large, extending over and
concealing both head and foot, quite smooth; margin thin, entire;
dorsal tentacles short, stout, abrubtly truncate, finely transversely
wrinkled, approximate at their origin, but diverging, reddish-brown
tipped with white; eyes black, placed a little distance behind the
tentacles; oral tentacles, united by a thin veil concealing the mouth,
and carried in advance of the foot. Shell half to three-quarter inch long,
squarish oblong, thin, and membranous, semi-transparent, slightly iridescent, closely marked with somewhat irregular concentric striæ; colour
white or brownish (Cheeseman.)

Genus, PLEUROBRANCHÆA—Meckel.

Tentacles dorsal; eyes none; labial appendages united by a narrow,
transverse oral veil; mantle indistinct, indicated by a narrow band on
the right side; anal orifice above the gill; foot narrow. Shell none.

P. novæ-zealandiæ, *Cheeseman, P.Z.S.,* 1878, *p.* 276, *pl.* xv.
f. 3; *Trans. N.Z. Inst.* xi. *p.* 375. Body oval, convex, thick and fleshy,
smooth, but the whole surface covered with minute puckers and folds;
colour light grey, with anastomosing lines of dark greyish-brown, and

sprinkled with numerous minute, almost microscopic, white dots ; mantle smooth, not nearly so long as the foot, and not concealing the branchia ; oral veil broad, semicircular in front, and with a delicate fringed margin, produced at each side into a short tentacle like lobe ; buccal plates two, large, finely and regularly reticulated ; dorsal tentacles wide apart, short and stout, projecting outward, folded down the outer side ; tips obliquely truncate ; eyes minute, black, at the inner bases of the tentacles, quite internal and not to be seen, without dissection ; foot long, extremely flexible ; sole pale ashy grey. Shell none (Cheeseman.)

Auckland. Wellington.

Division—Nudibranchiata.

Gills exposed, or contractile into cavities on the surface of the mantle. Adult animal without any shell. Larva shell bearing. Foot elongate, formed for walking. Hermaphrodite.

Section—Anthobranchiata.

Gills plumose on the hinder part of the mantle, disposed in a circle, or semi-circle, round the vent.

FAMILY—DORIDIDÆ.

Teeth many in each cross series, sub-similar, inner often smaller. Mantle edge simple. Gills surrounding the vent, on the middle of the hinder part of the back, in a common cavity, retractile ; mantle large, either entirely or almost covering and concealing the foot. Skin strengthened with spiculæ, more or less definitely arranged.

Sub-Family---Platyglossæ.

Oral tentacles free ; odontophore broad, with numerous spines in each transverse row.

Genus, DORIS -Linnæus.

Tentacles (rhinophores) dorsal, sub-clavate, laminated, retractile within a cavity. Gills arborescent, retractile; vent in the centre of the gills; surface of the mantle smooth or tubercular ; sheaths of the tentacles often crenate on their margins.

D. **punctata**, *Quoy and Gaimard, Voy. Astrol. Zool.*, ii., *p.* 262, *pl.* 18, *f.* 8-10. Body elongated, soft, flat, broad behind, reddish, marked with red spots ; anus prominent ; tentacles laciniated.

Length, 2½ inches (Q. & G.)

New Ireland. (Q. & G.) New Zealand. (Abraham.)

D. **tuberculata**, *Cuvier; Alder and Handcock, Monograph of Brit. Nudibranch, Moll., pl.* 3. Elliptical, sub-depressed, lemon-yellow or buff-orange, often variegated on the upper side with blotches of sage-green, pink and greyish-brown ; mantle thickly covered with flattish, spiculose, unequal tubercles, the smaller ones more numerous than the others; it extends considerably beyond the foot; dorsal tentacles slightly conical, yellow and strongly laminated above, smooth, transparent, and nearly colourless below; branchial plumes nine, tripinnate, recurved, large and spreading; they are transparent, obscure white, with a purple or lilac tinge at the edges; faintly freckled, and can be completely retracted within a cavity, the margins of which close over them; head rather small, with two small tubercular oral tentacles; foot broadish, rounded and grooved in front, less broadly rounded behind, and of a lemon-yellow or orange colour, with the liver appearing through the centre; two or three inches long, but occasionally reaching to four or even five inches (A. & H.)

Northern European Coasts. Western North America. New Zealand. (Abraham.)

D. granulosa, *Abraham; P.Z.S.,* 1877, *p.* 253, *pl.* xxix, *f.* 1-3. Body oblong, elliptic, not very depressed; mantle ample, presenting a granular appearance from a close covering of small, sessile, unequal rounded tubercles; rhinophores minutely laminated, rather slender, sub-conical or pyriform (in one specimen the apices are slightly enlarged and rounded;) their cavities are wide, and have the margins produced into short tuberculated and denticulated sheaths; branchiæ eight, rather short, slender and spreading, bipinnate, surrounding the short tubular anus in a circle interrupted behind; the two hindermost plumes are deeply divided; the margin of their common cavity is nearly smooth; oral tentacles small, free, flat and linear; foot oblong, truncated and transversely grooved in front, with the upper lamina deeply notched, the lower slightly so; the posterior extremity is rounded, and the border flattened; mantle spicules small, very short, and spindle-shaped; odontophore broad, with numerous lateral spines, which are comparatively large and recurved at an angle; colour (in spirit) dirty yellowish (Abraham.)

Length (in spirit) ·68; breadth, ·45 inch.

D. longula, *Abraham, P.Z.S.,* 1877, *p.* 253, *pl.* xxix, *f.* 4-5. Body oblong, rounded at both ends; mantle ample, covered with a minute sub-equal granulation; rhinophores short, broad, and aparently conical; their cavities with the apertures simple, and not produced; branchiæ twelve, small, slender, bipinnate, in a complete circle round the tubular anus; retractile in a wide cavity with minutely and irregularly denticulated margin; oral tentacles small and linear; foot oblong, rounded at the ends, transversely grooved in front, with both laminæ notched; it reaches behind to the edge of the mantle, and its border is free and flattened; colour (in spirit) a dirty cream (Abraham.)

Length (in spirit) ·73; breadth, ·27 inch.

D. muscula, *Abraham, P.Z.S.,* 1877, *p.* 256, *pl.* xxix, *f.* 6-7. Body elliptical, convex; mantle covering the head and the foot, but not laterally flattened or extended into a border; it is covered above with very small, close, equal, elongated, linear or sub-clavate tubercles; rhinophores (not visible in the specimen) retractile into cavities of which the mouths are produced into short tuberculated sheaths; branchiæ nine, small, simply pinnate, or bearing lateral laminæ, and compressed ; the margin of the cavity into which they are retractile is fringed with small elongated tubercles ; oral tentacles rather flat and linear ; foot oblong, rounded at the ends, with a deep transverse groove in front, the upper lamina being thin and mesially divided ; it does not extend behind as far as the mantle-edge ; colour (in spirits) greyish, with a yellowish tinge beneath, on the back is a band of faint reddish-brown, extending from between the rhinophores nearly as far as the branchiæ, and bordered on each side by an equally broad indistinct blue-band, shading into gray on the outer sides ; the two latter bands join together between the rhinophores and before the branchiæ ; the coloration of these bands is produced by a very minute close freckling between the small tubercles (Abraham.)

Length, ·52 ; breadth, ·36 inch.

D. lanuginata, *Abraham, P.Z.S.,* 1877, *p.* 255, *pl.* xxix., *f.* 15-17. Body ovate, rather convex ; mantle large, expanded all round, with a wavy irregular crenate border ; it is covered closely with numerous, small, soft, linear, tubercles ; rhinophores clavate, short, thick, truncated at the apices, and with numerous fine lamellæ extending far down ; they are retractile within large wide denticulated and tuberculated sheaths ; branchiæ five, short, broad, tripinnate, set deeply in a pallial cavity with raised denticulate margin ; the short tubular anus is situated almost between the two posterior plumes ; oral tentacles flat, spatulate, and longitudinally grooved above ; foot oblong, rounded at both ends, with a deep transverse slit in front, the upper lamina divided, and with a short process in the middle ; flattened, and with crenulate edge at the sides and posteriorly ; colour (in spirit) dirty greyish-brown, mottled with darker, the dark shade prevailing over the upper surface, except on the more central dorsal area ; below the tint is uniform and lighter, with the exception of a few dark brown spots ; the upper surface of the border of the foot is freckled and sparsely spotted with dark brown (Abraham.)

Length (in spirit,) 1·3 ; breadth, ·9 inch.

D. wellingtonensis, *Abraham, P.Z.S.,* 1877, *p.* 259, *pl.* xxix., *f.* 27-28 ; *O. tuberculatus, Hutton, C.M.M., p.* 54., *nec. Cuv.* Body oval, convex, swollen ; mantle thick, fleshy, not extended or flattened at the border ; covered with large rounded flat pustules, between which are scattered small opaque, whitish, tubercular spots ; rhinophores small, clavate, compressed from before backwards, each with more than twenty-six small laminæ, lying between shallow longitudinal depressions, and extending low down ; the apices are styliform, and marked with laminæ, except at the extreme rounded tip ; they are retractile through large, wide, fleshy sheaths ; branchiæ seven, ramose, tripinnate, moderate in size, surrounding the tubular anus, which is placed near, and opposite to the interval between the last two plumes ; the whole system is retractile within a large deep cavity, the margin of which is crenulate and wavy, and can be contracted completely over them ; oral tentacles short, thick, tubercular, truncated, and apparently with a central pit on

s

the apex; foot oblong, broad, fleshy, flatly rounded, and without an anterior groove; posteriorly it is obtusely accuminated; colour (in spirit) dirty white; the mantle spicules seem to be absent (Abraham.)

Length, 1·65 ; breadth, 1·2.

When living the pustules on the mantle are hemispherical ; the foot and rhinophores are bright orange; the mantle dirty yellowish orange; branchiæ paler. It is sometimes 4 or 5 inches in length.

Auckland to Dunedin.

D. carinata, *Quoy, l.c.,* ii., *p.* 254, *pl.* 16, *f.* 14-16 ; *Chenu, f.* 3052. Oval, convex, rough, keeled above; dirty-yellowish ; tentacles truncate, pediculated ; branchiæ tuberculated, covered with small rude hairs ; branchiæ of four little ciliated tubercles ; size small ; colour yellowish-white ; foot whitish (Q. & G.)

River Thames.

This species belongs to the genus *Atagema* of Gray.

Sub-Family—Leptoglossæ.

Oral tentacles united into a veil ; odontophore narrow and strap-shaped, with but few spines in each transverse row.

Genus, ACANTHODORIS—Gray.

Body convex; mantle moderate, covered with soft papillæ; oral tentacles united in a veil, with free flattened lateral ends; branchiæ united at the base, non-retractile ; odontophore narrow, with two large spines, and several rudimentary ones in each transverse row, none central ; usually a spinose buccal collar, and rudimentary under jaw.

North Atlantic and New Zealand only.

A. mollicella, *Abraham. P.Z.S.,* 1877, *p.* 262, *pl.* xxx., *f.* 1-4. Body ovate, convex, soft ; mantle covering the back and sides, but not extending over the border of the foot ; bearing above large, long, linear, or sub-conical ; soft papillæ, which are especially numerous at the sides and around the branchiæ ; rhinophores, long, slender, pointed, apparently conical, and laminated far down ; the denticulated sheath, through which each is retractile, has two of the antero-lateral divisions enlarged and produced into two long flat conical papillæ; branchiæ seven to nine, bipinnate, non retractile, their bases united, and set in a star round the short tubular anal opening ; oral veil short from before backwards, with the lateral ends free and flattened ; foot broad and oblong, truncated (or the outline curving inwards) in front, and without a transverse groove ; it is flatly rounded behind, and the border all round is flattened, crenulate, and extending beyond the mantle, particularly posteriorly ; colour (in spirit) uniform dark greyish-olive (Abraham.)

Length (in spirit) 1·1 ; breadth, ·7 inch.

Auckland Islands only.

A. globosa, *Abraham, P.Z.S.,* 1877, *p.* 262, *pl.* xxx., *f.* 5-9. Body ovate, broad, very convex and inflated ; mantle membranous on the back and sides, reaching down over the foot, except perhaps quite behind, and bearing scattered, soft, conical, pointed, tubercles, which are more numerous towards the border; the rhinophores are apparently rather short and slender, laterally flattened and retractile within sheaths, of which two of the marginal denticulations are enlarged; branchiæ seven, bi- (? tri-) pinnate, non-retractile, situated around the anus, far back and low down; oral veil short, very wavy, the sides prolonged, free, and flattened; foot broad, truncate in front, with a very indistinct transverse groove; it is rounded behind, and the margin all around is very wavy; colour (in spirit) transparent white, with a blue coloration on the back and sides; some of the lower tubercles have a reddish or brownish-tinge at the base; the rhinophores are faint-purplish, becoming lighter at the apex; the branchiæ are variegated with gray; underneath the margin of the mantle is marked with fine close, radiating reddish-brown purplish lines; the foot and oral veil are yellowish-white (Abraham.)

Length, ·8; breadth, ·5 inch.

<h3 style="text-align:center">SECTION— AIOLOBRANCHIATA.</h3>

Gills various, not arranged round the vent, but usually in rows along the sides of the body.

<h3 style="text-align:center">FAMILY—ÆOLIDIDÆ.</h3>

Tongue narrow; teeth in a single central series; jaws horny; tentacles subulate, simple, rarely ringed, contractile; gills superficial, fusiform or branched, on the sides of the back; vent lateral, on the right side.

Sub-Family—Æolidinæ.

Gills in two rows on each side; foot developed.

Genus, PHIDIANA—Gray.

Tentacles clavate, perfoliate; oral tentacles subulate; gills in cross rows along the back; branchiæ linear, crowded; caudal extremity slender and greatly extended; eyes none.

P. longicauda, *Quoy, l.c.,* ii., *p.* 288, *pl.* 21, *f.* 9-10. Elongate, graceful, very soft; apex acute; tailed; below brown; branchiæ in many series.

Length, 2 inches; of the tail, ½ an inch.

Head reddish-yellow; back brownish, also most of the branchiæ; rest of the body is white. (Q. & G.)

Cook Strait.

Class—Scaphopoda.

Head rudimentary ; a pair of horny jaws ; mouth surrounded by many filiform tentacles ; eyes none ; radula wide, of 25-30 joints, each of 5 plates, the median one toothed, the inner lateral, uncinated, the outer lateral, unarmed. Anal sinus with two openings ; foot small, consisting of a central cylindrical lobe, with two lateral wing-like epipodia ; diœcious.

FAMILY—DENTALIIDÆ.

Body elongated. Mantle circular. Gills two, symmetrical; operculum none. Shell elongate ; vertex perforated, posteriorly inclined ; aperture circular, not constricted.

Genus, DENTALIUM—Linnæus.

Shell symmetrical, tubular, tapering, recurved ; apical perforation entire.

D. zealandicum, *Sowerby, in Reeve's Conch. Ic., f.* 8 (1872.) Shell rather straight, narrow, banded with pale ferruginous brown, armed with numerous rough ribs, very little arched; aperture rather narrow (Sowerby.)

Length, 2·3 ; breadth, anterior end, ·35 ; posterior end, ·06 (from figure.)

D. pacificum, *Hutton, C.M.M., p.* 5 (1873.) Solid, tapering, slightly curved, longitudinally grooved ; grooves unequal, about thirty at the anterior end, but diminishing in number towards the apex ; white.

Length, 2·4 ; breadth, anterior end, ·3 ; posterior end, ·05.

Perhaps the same as the last.

Class—Pteropoda.

Head more or less distinct; eyes none; mouth often furnished with cup-shaped appendages; fins on the sides of the mouth or neck; body ovate or roundish, often enclosed in a thin translucent shell. Animal free, floating on the surface of the sea; hermaphrodite.

ORDER—THECOSOMATA.

Head indistinct, with two wings on the sides of the mouth. Tooth of lingual membrane hooked, with a strong hooked tooth on each side. Gills internal. Body inclosed in a shell.

FAMILY—HYALIDÆ.

Body enclosed in an elongate or globular thin shell. Head not distinct; fins two, large, united. Gills internal.

Genus, HYALEA—Lamark.

Shell globular, translucent; mouth narrower than the cavity, with a lateral slit on each side; dorsal plate produced into a hood; posterior extremity tridentate.

H. affinis, *D'Orb; Cavolina affinis, Gray, Cat. Ptr., Bril. Mus., p. 7; Reeve's Conch. Ic., f. 3 (Pteropoda.)* Shell inflated in front, flattish behind, broader than high, finely transversely striated on the upper anterior portion, almost smooth below and on the back; posteriorly three spined, the lateral ones short, the middle one slightly reflexed; dorsal lip produced, with three broad rounded ribs, which run along the back towards the median spine; brownish.
Chatham Islands.

Class—Lamellibranchiata.

No head, nor eyes. Shell composed of two valves, occasionally with supernumerary pieces ; heart with two chambers ; nervous system with three principal pairs of ganglia. Gills lamellar, two on each side. Usually diœcious.

ORDER—ISOMYA.

Adductor scars two, equal, or sub-equal on each valve.

SECTION—SINUPALLIATA.

Pallial line with a deep sinus.

Sub-Order—Pholadacea.

Mantle closed, but allowing two more or less elongated siphons to pass out, which are contiguous at the base ; the inferior with two pairs of branchiæ in it.

FAMILY—PHOLADIDÆ.

Animal symmetrical, club-shaped or worm like. Palpi elongate, linear. Mantle partly exposed, closed in front, except an aperture for the foot ; siphons large, elongated, united nearly to their ends ; orifices fringed. Gills narrow, prolonged into the branchial siphon, attached throughout, closing the branchial chamber. Foot short and truncated.

Shell gaping at both ends, thin, white, brittle ; hinge plate reflected over the umbones, and a long curved muscular process beneath each ; anterior muscular impression on the hinge plate ; pallial sinus very deep.

Boring holes in wood and rocks.

Genus, BARNEA—Risso.

Shell ovato-oblong ; gaping anteriorly ; a single lanceolate dorsal accessory piece ; hinge margin reflected. Siphons naked at their base, both branchial and anal cirrated.

B. similis, *Gray, Dieff. N.Z.,* ii., *p.* 254 ; *Reeve, Conch. Ic. (Pholas,) f.* 10. Rather elongate, acute in front, tapering behind ; with concentric laminæ, which are higher and closer together at the anterior end, where they are crossed by radiating lines ; sub-spinose at the crossings ; dorsal plate elongate, acute in front, truncated behind.

Height, 1 ; length, 2·5.
Common in the North Island. Waikouaiti.

Genus, PHOLADIDEA—Turton.

Siphons with horny or shelly pieces at their base, the branchial siphon cirrated, the anal plain at the end. Shell widely gaping in front, but closed by a callous plate ; two dorsal pieces, straight.

P. spathulata, *Sowerby, P.Z.S.,* 1849, *p.* 162 ; *Reeve, Conch. Ic. (Pholas,) f.* 45. Shell elongated, closed, obliquely divided ; anterior part radiately ribbed, sub-angulated ; posterior part concentrically lightly striated, subtruncated, protected at the margins by an integument, produced at the end into a horny cup with spathulate sides ; two equal laminæ, bilobed posteriorly, elongated anteriorly at the umboes (Sowerby.)
As far South as Waikouaiti.

P. tridens, *Gray, Dieff. N.Z.,* ii., *p.* 254; *Voy. Erebus and Terror, pl.* 2, *f.* 8 ; *Reeve, Conch. Ic., f.* 38. Ovate, with a deep central groove ; front half with close waved concentric ridges ; hinder half with distant regular concentric grooves ; front gape large, broad, ovate, at length closed up, the two hinder processes forming together a cup about as long as broad, each furnished with a sub-marginal and central rib (Gray.)
According to Sowerby, this species comes from Monte Christo.

Genus, TEREDO—Linnæus.

Animal worm-like ; siphons furnished at their extremity with two shelly styles or pallettes ; umbonal muscle covered only with a coriaceous epidermis, and not protected by shelly accessory valves. Shell globose, gaping anteriorly and behind ; valves trilobate, divided by a single transverse groove ; hinge margins inflexed anteriorly ; interior of valves furnished with a long curved process. Living at the inner extremity of a burrow, partly or entirely lined with shell.

T. antarctica, *Hutton, C.M.M., p.* 59. Shell globose, the valves tri-lobed, ear-shaped behind. lower lobe produced, acute, the interior process for attachment of the pedal muscle. dilated at the end ; anterior end deeply notched, the notch forming a right angle ; outside smooth behind, striated in front by lines parallel to the edge of the notch, the striæ on the lower and posterior part being finer than those on the upper and anterior part, and the interstices with minute cross striæ, while the interstices of the upper striæ are smooth ; tube obsolete ; pallettes elongate, slightly curved. penniform.
Auckland to Dunedin.

Sub-Order—Myacea.

Siphons long, united ; gills not extending into them. Shell gaping behind, with an inner hinge cartilage. Shell and siphons covered with periostracum.

FAMILY—GLYCIMERIDÆ.

Animal symmetrical, oblong. Mantle lobes united and thickened in front ; siphons large, elongated, often invested with a thick wrinkled epidermis, united nearly to their ends, the orifices fringed ; pedal opening small. Gills two on each side, narrow, unequal, united behind, and extending into the branchial siphon. Foot small, digitiform, inferior, furnished with a byssal groove. Shell equivalve, thick, gaping at both ends ; hinge with a rudimentary cardinal tooth ; ligament external, solid and prominent, placed upon a more or less strong callosity : pallial impression irregular, sinuated behind.

Genus, SAXICAVA—Bellevue.

Palpi small, free ; siphons large, united nearly to their ends ; orifices fringed. Shell oblong, irregular, generally equivalve, inequilateral, slightly gaping at both ends ; hinge linear, without teeth or with a rudimentary one on each valve : ligament external ; pallial line sinuated, not continuous.

S. australis, *Lamark, Anim. sans vert.*, v., *p.* 153 ; *Reeve, Conch. Ic., f.* 8 ; *S. distorta, Say ; Hiatella minuta, Gray in Dieff. N.Z.*, ii., *p.* 252. Shell oblong, very rugose, more or less distorted ; umboes large, much elevated, nearly terminal ; posterior side obliquely produced, angular, obsoletely spinose at the angle ; ventral margin sloped upwards at the end ; terminal margin opliquely truncated : dorsal margin straight, with a flattened area (Sowerby.)

Auckland to Dunedin. Australia. Tasmania. America.

This shell is said by Sowerby to be more tumid, especially towards the umboes than *S. arctica,* with which it has generally been confounded.

Genus, PANOPÆA—Menard.

Siphons large, united nearly as far as their extremities, and invested with a thick wrinkled epidermis. Shell equivalve, inequilateral, gaping at each end, thick ; ligament external on prominent ridges, one prominent tooth in each valve ; pallial impression strong, with a more or less deep sinus.

For notes on the anatomy of this genus, see Woodward in P.Z.S., 1855, p. 218.

P. zealandica, *Quoy, l.c.*, iii., *p.* 547, *pl.* 83, *f.* 7-9 ; *Reeve Conch. Ic., f.* 9. Oval, inequilateral, sub-compressed, widely gaping, longitudinally plicated ; umbones obtuse, recurved ; white.

Height, 1·11 ; length, 3·1 : breadth, 1·1. (Q. & G.)

Sowerby says this species is from Queensland.

Common in the North, rare in the South. Chatham Islands.

P. solandri, *Gray, Dieff. N.Z.*, ii., *p.* 255 ; *Reeve, Conch. Ic., f.* 6. Oblong, ventricose, rounded in front, rather narrower and truncated behind, smooth ; white ; much more ventricose than the last (Gray.)

FAMILY—CORBULIDÆ.

Body not symmetrical. Palpi, long, narrow, pectinated on both sides. Mantle closed, except anteriorly; pedal orifice small, the margins dentate; siphons short, united, the orifices fringed with cirri, the anal furnished with a tubercular, membranous, retractile valve. Gills two on each side, dependent, separate, moderately prolonged. Foot long, sub-cylindrical, furnished with a byssal groove. Shell porcellanous; valves unequal, closed posteriorly; hinge with a conical tooth and a cartilage pit in each valve. Pallial line slightly sinuated.

Genus, CORBULA--Bruguiere.

Shell inequilateral, gibbous, rounded in front and produced posteriorly; ligament internal; pallial sinus slight; pedal scars distinct from the adductors.

C. zealandica, *Quoy, l.c.*, iii., *p.* 511, *pl.* 85, *f.* 12-14; *C. callowæ, Reeve, Conch. Ic., f.* 21. Small ovato-trigonal, swollen behind, finely longitudinally striated; yellowish or pinkish white; interior brownish, margin brown.
Height, ·3; length, ·5; breadth, ·25. (Quoy.)
Common in the north. Found also in Australia.
Reeve says that his *C. callowæ* differs from *C. zealandica* in that " it is not striated, nor does the anterior side present the tellina-like flexuosity of that species."

C. erythrodon, *Lamark, ·Anim. sans vert.*, vi., *p.* 138; *Reeve, Conch. Ic., f.* 4. Shell ovate, nearly equivalve, anterior side the more produced, and angularly carinated; longitudinally grooved, pale, interior stained round the edge with red or pinkish-purple (Reeve.)
China. Japan.
Neither this species, nor the last, are found in the South Island.

C. adusta, *Hinds. P.Z.S.*, 1844, *p.* 26; *Reeve, Conch. Ic., f.* 30. Shell somewhat obliquely triangular, smooth, rather swollen, rounded posteriorly, slightly angulately accuminated anteriorly; reddish-brown, covered with a horny epidermis; umbones eroded (Reeve.)
New Zealand. (Cuming.)

C. haastiana, *Hutton, Jour de Conch*, 1871, *p.* 84. Sub-trigonal, very inequivalve, covered with a brown epidermis; rounded posteriorly, obsoletely keeled anteriorly; right valve very finely striated; the left deeply grooved; ventral margin sinuated anteriorly; yellowish-white.
Height, ·4; length, ·4.
Lyttelton.

FAMILY—ANATINIDÆ.

Mantle margins united. Siphons elongate, generally more or less separate, the orifices fringed. Mantle with a small valvular aperture under the siphons. Gills pinnate, apparently one on each side, the

T

outer laminæ prolonged dorsally beyond the point of attachment. Foot more or less linguiform. Shell with the interior nacreous, more or less gaping at the extremities ; ligament external ; cartilage internal, placed in corresponding pits and furnished with a free ossicle.

Genus, ANATINA—Lamark.

Siphons covered with a rugose epidermis. Shell oblong, ventricose, very thin, often translucent, sub-equivalve ; umbones fissured, directed backwards ; hinge with a spoon-shaped cartilage process in each valve ; pallial sinus wide and shallow.

A. tasmanica, *Reeve, Conch. Ic., f.* 20. Shell nearly equilateral, oblong, rather compressed, sub-hyaline, rather obsoletely granulated, sides rounded, but little gaping, posterior rather the narrower (Reeve.) Auckland. Collingwood. Australia and Tasmania.

Genus, LYONSIA—Turton.

Siphons short, separate at their extremities. Shell with the left valve slightly larger, thin ; cartilage plates oblique, covered by an oblong ossicle ; pallial sinus angular ; interior sub-nacreous.

L. vitrea, *Hutton, C.M.M., p.* 61. Elongately oblong, very thin, slightly gaping and truncated behind ; umbones sub-central, smooth, white, finely longitudinally striated : pallial sinus extending to the centre of the shell, rounded.
Height. ·5 : length, ·75.

Genus, THRACIA—Leach.

Siphons divergent, separate nearly their entire length, their orifices fringed. Shell oblong, slightly compressed, attenuated and gaping posteriorly ; cartilage process thick, not prominent, with a cresentic ossicle ; pallial sinus shallow.

T. novæ zealandiæ, *Reeve, Conch. Ic., f.* 19. Shell somewhat triangularly ovate, rather solid, posteriorly rather broadly angled ; left valve flat ; concentrically rudely plicately striated, especially towards the umbones ; umbones rather sharp, a little beaked, whitish, smooth (Reeve.)
Possibly a variety of *T. australica.*

Genus, NEÆRA—Gray.

Siphons short, united, the orifices of both with a few long cirri, the anal with a membranous valve. Shell thin, transparent, generally prolonged into a gaping beak behind ; hinge with a small spoon-shaped process in each valve, and a large lateral recurved tooth in the right valve.

N. trailli, *Hutton, C.M.M., p.* 62. Ovate, produced behind : white, with distant concentric laminæ, which become obsolete on the beak; beak rugose.
Height, ·2 ; length, ·4.
Stewart Island, 14 fathoms.

Genus, MYODORA, Gray.

Trigonal, rounded in front, attenuated and truncated behind ; right valve convex, left flat ; interior pearly ; cartilage narrow, triangular, between two tooth-like ridges in the left valve, with a free sickle-shaped ossicle ; pallial line sinuated.

M. striata, *Quoy, l.c.,* iii., *p.* 537, *pl.* 83, *f.* 10 ; *Reeve, Conch. Ic.,* *f.* 6 ; *Chenu, f.* 215. Ovato-trigonal, solid, longitudinally striated, anterior end rounded, posterior sub-angulated and folded ; sub-equilateral ; apex acute ; white ; interior pearly.
Height, 1·3 ; length, 1·55.
Common in the North, rare in the South. Dunedin.
The Natives call this shell " pakira."

M. plana, *Reeve, P.Z.S.,* 1844 ; *Conch. Ic., f.* 3 ; *M. brevis,* *C.M.M.* Shell triangularly oblong, slightly truncated anteriorly, very flat, concentrically striated ; striæ raised, rather distant, those of the left valve the more prominent (Reeve.)
Height, ·35 ; length, ·4.
Stewart Island. Philippines.

M. ovata, *Reeve, P.Z.S.,* 1844 ; *Conch. Ic., f.* 4 ; *Chenu, f.* 216. Shell ovate, somewhat triangular ; left valve ventricosely concave ; right valve slightly convex, concentrically striated ; striæ raised, somewhat obsolete near the anterior margin, those of the right valve numerous and close, of the left valve prominent, and rather distant ; umbones depressedly incurved (Reeve.)
Height, ·6 ; length, ·45.
Stewart Island. Australia. Tasmania. Philippines.

M. rotunda, *Sowerby, P.Z.S.,* 1875, *p.* 129, *pl.* xxiv., *f.* 8. Shell roundly sub-trigonal, very inequivalve, white, both valves concentrically strongly striated, with two slight angles on the posterior side ; dorsal margin excavated, scarcely incurved ; umbones acute, of a bluish tint ; right valve very ventricose, with two ribs from the umbones to the posterior margin ; left valves flat ; triagonal ligamentary pit rather small (Sowerby.)
Height, ·9 ; breadth, 1·0 inch.
The right valve is much deeper ; umbones more central ; dorsal margin less incurved and more sloping ; ligamentary pit much smaller, and the whole shell rounder than in *M. striata.*

Genus, CHAMOSTRÆA—Roissy.

Shell inequivalve, solid, attached by the right valve ; left valve flat.
Australia and New Zealand only.

C. albida, *Lamark*, vi., *p.* 585; *Woodward's Manual of the Mollusca, pl.* 23, *f.* 14. Right valve keeled, attached by its anterior side; umbones anterior, sub-spiral; left valve with an oblong curved ossicle.
Length, 2·5.
Auckland to Cook Strait. Chatham Islands. Australia. Tasmania.

FAMILY- MACTRIDÆ.

Labial tentacles long and pointed, pectinated on their inner sides. Mantle lobes more or less free beneath, united before and behind, the margins more or less distinctly fringed; siphons united to their extremities, which are surrounded by fringes of simple cirri. Foot lanceolate, sub-anterior. Shell equivalve. Hinge with two cardinal teeth in each valve, the hinder small, compressed, often rudimentary, the front triangular, more or less deeply notched; lateral teeth of left valve simple, of right valve double; cartilage in an internal triangular pit behind the cardinal teeth. Siphonal inflexion distinct.

Sub-Family—Mactrinœ.

Mantle lobes free. Shell sub-triangular, ovate, nearly closed behind; lateral teeth distinct, well developed, laminar.

Genus, MACTRA—Linnæus.

Hinge with the cardinal teeth moderate; lateral teeth distinct; ligament external, in an oblique, triangular groove opening into the upper edge of the cartilage pit; pallial sinus angular.

M. discors, *Gray, Mag. Nat. Hist.,* 1837, *p.* 371; *Reeve, Conch. Ic., f.* 17; *Voy. Erebus and Terror, pl.* 2. *f.* 4. Shell rotundately ovate, somewhat triangular, rather thick, equilateral, regularly convex, smooth, greyish-white, covered towards the margin with a blackish-brown epidermis; posterior side rather flattened, surrounded with a slightly keeled obtuse angle; umbones small, closely approximated; lunule and area plicately striated; sinus of the mantle very short, broad, and semicircular (Reeve.)
Auckland to Dunedin.

M. murchisoni, *Deshayes, P.Z.S.,* 1854; *Reeve, Conch. Ic., f.* 76. Shell ovate, sub-ventricose, rather solid, white, smooth, covered towards the margin with a straw-coloured epidermis, nearly equilateral, anterior side rounded, posterior rather the longer, slightly angularly produced; angle linearly keeled; lunule very large, wrinkle ridged; umbones close set (Reeve.)
Apparently a younger specimen of the last.

M. scalpellum, *Deshayes, P.Z.S.,* 1854; *Reeve, Conch. Ic., f.* 106; *D. pusilla, Hutton, C.M.M., p.* 64. Shell triangularly oblong, thin, very compressed, equilateral, smooth, shining white; extremities

rather attenuately rounded; umbones very small, close; lunule and area very narrow, indistinct, plicately striated (Reeve.)
Much like a *Tellina*.
Stewart Island.

M. æquilateralis, *Deshayes, P.Z.S.*, 1853, *p.* 17; *Reeve, Conch. Ic., f.* 14; *Voy. Erebus and Terror, pl.* 2, *f.* 10. Trigonal, nearly as high as long, solid, longitudinally striated; lunule smooth; anterior end subangulated, slightly flattened above; posterior angled and flattened above; white; umbones tipped with purplish; interior yellowish, sometimes purplish in the upper part.
Height, 1·75; length, 2·25.
Common. Auckland to Dunedin.

M. donaciformis, *Gray; Beecher's Voy. Moll. p.* 154; *Reeve. Conch. Ic., f.* 62. Shell ovately triangular, inequilateral, swollen, semi-cordate; umbones sharp, opposite. distant, transversely very finely striated; white, beneath a fulvous epidermis, anteriorly obtuse, posteriorly broadly flat and angled, accuminated at the extremity (Reeve.)
New Zealand. (Cuming.)

Sub-Family—Lutrariinæ.

Mantle lobes generally united. Shell oblong or elongate, gaping behind; lateral teeth very small, rudimentary, often obsolete, especially in the adult shell.

Genus, STANDELLA—Gray.

Shell ovate, hinder slope more or less keeled; hinge with the lateral teeth short, smooth, the anterior oblique; ligament sub-external, marginal, not separated from the cartilage.

S. ovata, *Gray, Dieff. N.Z.,* ii., *p.* 251; *Reeve, Conch. Ic. (Mactra,) f.* 30; *M. rudis, Hutton, Cat. Tert., Moll. N.Z., p.* 19; *M. deluta, Gould, U.S. Ex. Ep.* Ovate, ventricose, inequilateral, thin, slightly concentrically wrinkled; rounded in front, rather attenuated and produced behind; white, covered with a thin pale brown periostraca, much produced beyond the edge behind; inside yellow; lateral teeth short, very high and sub-triangular (Gray.)
Auckland to Dunedin.

S. elongata, *Quoy and Gaimard, l.c.,* iii., *p.* 518, *pl.* 83, *f.* 1.2, *nec., Reeve; M. inflata, Hutton, Cat. Tert., Moll. N.Z., p.* 18. Oval, anterior side shorter, rounded, its dorsal margin rather concave; posterior side rounded, its dorsal margin convex; umbones rather inflated, incurved; smooth or lightly concentrically striated.
Height, 2·3; length, 3.

S. notata, *Hutton, C.M.M., p.* 64; *M. elongata, Reeve, Conch. Ic., f.* 43, *nec., Q. & G.* Thick, solid, concentrically striated round the margin; lunule and area plicately rugose, rest smooth; anterior end shorter, attenuated; right valve with two lateral teeth on each side; left valve with the anterior hinge tooth bifid, and the anterior lateral deeply notched; cartilage pit broad and flat; pallial sinus reaching to the centre of the shell; white, with brown spots and dashes; covered with a thin brown epidermis.

Height, 2·5; length, 4.

Stewart Island, 25 fathoms.   North Island.

Genus, ZENATIA—Gray.

Equivalve, inequilateral, oblong, umbo anterior, sub-marginal, gaping at both extremities, covered by a thick and projecting epidermis; cartilage plate prominent, cardinal teeth distinct, no lateral teeth; pallial sinus deep, horizontal; hinge posterior.

Z. acinaces, *Quoy and Gaimard, l.c., p.* iii., *p.* 545, *pl.* 83. *f.* 5-6; *Reeve, Conch. Ic. (Lutraria), f.* 14; *Chenu, f.* 248; *Z. cumingiana, Deshayes, P.Z.S.* 1844: *Reeve, Conch. Ic., f.* 13. Shell thin, compressed, oval oblong, arcuate, greyish-yellow, interior emerald green, behind finely striated, outside greyish-yellow, the umbo almost white; interior white, pearly and iridescent, yellowish towards the umbo (Q. & G.)

Length, 1 inch 10 lines; height, 9 lines; thickness, 4 lines.

Auckland to Dunedin.   Australia.

The figures of Reeve, No. 14, and of Chenu, are very bad.

Z. deshayesii, *Reeve, Conch Ic. (Lutraria) f.* 1; *Z. solenoides, Desh. P.Z.S.,* 1854; *nec Lamark.* Shell elongately oblong, thinnish, rather narrow, concentrically densely striated, striæ somewhat wrinkle-like; sides equally rounded, the anterior very long, much gaping. Rust-flesh tinged, covered with a greenish olive epidermis (Reeve.)

No doubt the same as the last.

Genus, VANGANELLA—Gray.

Transversely oblong, thin, compressed, covered with a smooth epidermis, sub-equilateral, rounded in front, attenuated and sub-angular behind, with two divergent ribs in the interior; cardinal teeth of the left valve near together, those of the right valve separated; lateral teeth small, thin; ligament sub-external, marginal, cartilage-plate, elongated, not very deep.

New Zealand only.

V. taylorii, *Gray; Ann. Nat. Hist.,* 1853, xi., *p.* 476; *Voy. Erebus and Terror, pl.* 2, *f.* 5; *Chenu, f.* 249; *Adams' Gen. of Moll., pl.* 102, *f.* 2; *Lutraria lanceolata, Reeve, Conch, Ic., f.* 17. Shell rather compressed, white, smooth, covered with a pale-brownish-white polish; periostraca darker coloured on the upper part of the front edge; the upper hinder slope irregularly wrinkled with periostraca (Gray).

Cook Strait to Dunedin.

Genus, RAETA—Gray.

Shell cordiform, ventricose, thin; sub-angular and slightly gaping behind ; cardinal tooth strong, posterior lateral tooth small ; ligament sub-external, marginal, not separated from the cartilage.

R. perspicua, *Hutton, C.M.M., p. 65.* Ovate, ventricose and rounded in front, compressed and sub-angular behind ; umbones posterior, turned forwards, with broad rounded concentric corrguations that show in the interior, and crossed by fine undulating tranverse striæ. Yellowish-white.

Height, 2 ; length, 2·75.

A single dead specimen from the Bay of Islands is in the Colonial Museum, Wellington.

Genus, CÆCELLA—Gray.

Shell oblong, sub-equilateral. Hinge with the cardinal tooth of left valve broad, triangular, notched ; lateral teeth very small, close to the cardinal tooth ; cartilage pit produced into the cavity of the shell ; ligament marginal, near the cartilage.

C. zelandica, *Deshayes, P.Z.S.,* 1854, *p.* 335. Shell elongato-transverse, elliptic, rather convex, solid, inequilateral, transversely striated, covered with a yellowish epidermis, pellucid white, equally obtuse and decurrent at each side ; anterior side shorter ; inferior margin slightly arched ; cardinal tooth compressed, triangular, accuminate, prominent ; pit narrow, deep, oblique, accuminate at the base ; lateral teeth narrow, unequal, anterior short ; pallial sinus deep, broad, sub-trigonal, apex obtuse (Deshayes).

New Zealand (Cuming).

Sub-Order--Tellinacea.

Siphons long, fully separate ; mantle wide open in front ; outer gill lamellar, often rudimental ; foot large.

FAMILY—TELLINIDÆ.

Palpi large and triangular. Mantle widely open anteriorly and with the margins usually fringed or furnished with short filaments, siphons very long, slender, diverging ; gills unequal, united beneath. Foot compressed, broad, geniculate and linguiform. Shell generally with two cardinal teeth in each valve, occasionally with lateral teeth ; shell compressed, usually closed and equivalve ; muscular impressions rounded, pallial sinus very large ; ligament on the shortest side of the shell, external, strong ; cartilage none.

Genus, PSAMMOBIA—Lamark.

Oval-oblong, equivalve. sub-equilateral, slightly gaping at each end ; hinge straight, teeth ?, sometimes bifid. no laterals : muscular impressions large, equally distant from the hinge.

P. stangeri, *Gray, Dieff. N.Z.,* ii., *p.* 253 ; *Reeve, Conch. Ic., f.* 12. Oblong, solid, rounded in front and rather obliquely truncated behind,

concentrically striated.   Purplish white, obscurely rayed with darker :
interior pinkish-purple.
Height, 1·5 ; length, 2·5.
Common.   Auckland to Otago.
The Natives call this shell " wahawaha."

P. lineolata, *Gray, Dieff. N.Z.,* ii., *p.* 253 *: Voy. Erebus and
Terror, Moll. pl.* 2, *f.* 11 *; Reeve, Conch. Ic., f.* 58.   Elongato-oblong,
compressed, rounded in front and slightly angled behind ; purplish-pink,
with darker concentric bands, and radiating rays of lighter : interior
reddish-purple.
Height, 1·5 ; length, 3.
Common.   Auckland to Dunedin.   Chatham Islands.

P. zealandica, *Deshayes. P.Z.S.,* 1854, *p.* 319 ; *P. zonalis, C.M.
M., non. Lam.*   Shell ovate, transverse. equilateral, rather short, rounded
on both sides, compressed, transversely obsoletely and irregularly striated ;
white, ornamented with interrupted rays or spots of purplish-red, interior
white, rays paler ; pallial sinus large, broad, deep, elliptic (Deshays).
New Zealand (Cuming).

P. affinis, *Reeve, Conch. Ic., f.* 22.   Shell ovately transverse, equilateral, transversely rudely striated, striæ almost obsolete in the middle,
distinct anteriorly, slightly plicated posteriorly ; yellowish white, pro-
miscuously rayed towards the margin with flesh-rose, sides rounded, the
posterior but little truncated (Reeve).
New Zealand, and the Philippine Islands.

Genus, SOLETELLINA—Blainville.

Shell, oval-oblong, compressed, equivalve, sub-equilateral, umbones
slightly posterior, rounded in front, more attenuated and sub-carinate
behind ; hinge straight ; teeth $\frac{2}{2}$.

S. nitida, *Gray, Dieff. N.Z.,* ii., *p.* 253 *: Smith, Voy. Erebus and
Terror, Moll. pl.* 2, *f.* 9 ; *nec. Reeve, f.* 6.   Shell oval, oblong, thin, pellucid, porous, rounded in front and rather tapering behind, covered with
a hard polished horn-colored periostraca : inner surface purplish white,
or purple ; hinge teeth small (Gray).
Auckland to West Coast Sounds and Dunedin.
The following is Reeves' description of the specimen figured under
this name : Shell rather compressed, nearly equilateral, purplish-white,
covered with a smooth, shining, transparent, horny epidermis, anterior
side rounded, posterior shorter, slopingly acuminated, and concentrically wrinkled.
New Zealand.   (Strange.)

S. siliqua, *Reeve, Conch. Ic., f.* 10.   Shell narrowly transverse,
thin, equilateral, smooth, flesh-white, covered with a shining transparent
olive horny epidermis, faintly two-rayed on the posterior side, anterior
side rounded, posteriorly obliquely acuminately rounded (Reeve.)
New Zealand.   (Hart.)

Probably the same as the last.

S. incerta, *Reeve. Conch. Ic., f.* 13; *Deshayes, M.S.S.* Shell oblong, transverse. broader posteriorly, thin, inequilateral, smooth, covered with a thin horny epidermis, obscurely two-rayed posteriorly, anterior side rounded, posterior obliquely truncated (Reeve.)

New Zealand. (Strange.)

S. nitens, *Tryon, American Journal of Conchology,* v. (1870,) *p.* 171, *pl.* 16, *f.* 9. Shell ovately transverse, somewhat inequilateral, conversely flattened over the umboes, sides and ventral margin well rounded, thin, purple, with a very thin shining horn-coloured epidermis, purple within.

Length, 1·98; height, ·1 inch.

New Zealand. (T. B. Wilson.)

Like *S. nitida,* Gray, but more swollen, and not angled and acuminated posteriorly. (Tryon.)

Genus, TELLINA—Linnæus.

Slightly inequivalve, compressed, rounded in front and slightly folded behind; umbones sub-central; teeth $\frac{2}{2}$; laterals $\frac{1}{1}$, most distinct in the right valve; pallial sinus very wide and deep; ligament external, prominent.

T. alba, *Quoy and Gaimard, l.c.,* iii., *p.* 500, *pl.* 81, *f.* 1-3; *Reeve, Conch. Ic., f.* 180. Oblong, very thin, pellucid, white, very finely concentrically striated; anterior end rounded and obsoletely plicated above; posterior end produced, sub-angular, slightly folded; lateral teeth obsolete.

Height, 1·4; length, 2·2.

Auckland to Catlin River.

The Natives call this shell "hohe-hohe." It is not the same as *T. albinella,* Lam. which is found in Australia. I doubt whether it is the same as *T. alba,* Chemnitz.

T. deltoidalis, *Lamark,* vi., *p.* 206; *Reeve, Conch. Ic., f.* 29; *T. lactea, Quoy and Gaimard. l.c.,* iii., *p.* 501. *pl.* 81. *f.* 14-16 *(not of L.nnæus.)* Ovate, thinnish, white, very finely concentrically striated; anterior end rounded; posterior rather produced, sub-angular, strongly folded; right valve with two cardinal teeth, the posterior bifid, and a small lateral tooth on each side; left valve with one bifid cardinal tooth

Height, ·14; length, 1·75.

Auckland to Stewart Island.

T. disculus, *Desh. P.Z.S.,* 1854, *p.* 360; *Reeve. Conch. Ic., f.* 306; *T. sublenticularis. Sow.. Conch. Ic.. f.* 255; *T. lactea, Gray, l.c.,* ii., *p.* 254. Sub-orbicular. rather thick, strongly concentrically striated; anterior end rounded; posterior end shorter, very obtusely sub-angular, slightly folded; right valve with two slight cardinal and one strong lateral tooth on each side; left with two cardinal teeth, and a notch on the hinge plate near the posterior end of the ligament; yellowish-white;

L

umbones yellow, interior white round the margin and bright-yellow between the muscular impressions and up to the umbones.

Height, 1·5; length, 1·5.

North Island only. Chatham Islands.

Very close to *T. lenticularis*, Sowerby, from Japan. Reeve gives the Philippines as the habitat of *T. disculus*.

T. subovata, *Sowerby; Reeve, Conch. Ic., f.* 160; *T. lintea, Hutton, C.M.M., p.* 67. Shell snow white, half pellucid, equally compressed, rather squarely ovate, smooth, not flexuous; posterior side rather short, with the dorsal margin sloping, truncated at the end; posterior angle nearly obsolete; ventral margin rather straight; anterior side oblong, dorsal margin sloping, excavated near the umbones, very obtusely angular at the end; cardinal teeth small, no lateral teeth; ligament partly imbedded (Reeve.)

Stewart Island.

T. ticaonica, *Deshayes, P.Z.S.,* 1854, *p.* 358; *Reeve, Conch. Ic., f.* 304. Shell small, elongato-ovate, transverse, compressed, hyaline, very thin, inequilateral, shining, polished, the whole pale rose colour; anterior side longer, obtuse, rather convex above, inferior margin parallel; posterior side short, truncated, sub-angular below; ligament short, prominent; hinge very narrow; double tooth small, bifid in the right valve; pallial sinus large, deep, above much angled, ascending under the umbones (Deshayes.)

Stewart Island. Philippines (Cuming.) Australia.

T. strangei, *Deshayes, P.Z.S.,* 1854, *p.* 362. Shell ovato-subtrigonal, rather convex, thin, pellucid, inequilateral, pale yellow, transversely very finely lamellated, and regularly decussated with longitudinal striæ; lamellæ regular, equidistant, short; anterior side longer, above scarcely declining, obtuse; posterior a little attenuated, obtuse, hardly flexed, inferior margin regularly convex; umbones small, hardly prominent, lunule small, scarcely excavated, lanceolate, smooth; lateral teeth large, sub-equal, equi-distant (Deshayes.)

New Zealand (Cuming.)

T. glabrella, *Deshayes, P.Z.S.,* 1854, *f.* 366; *Reeve, Conch. Ic., f.* 296; *Smith, Voy. Erebus and Terror, pl. 2, f. 7.* Shell ovato-trigonal, transverse, compressed, thin sub-equilateral, chalk-white, epidermis pale yellowish, unequally obsoletely transversely striated; anterior side longer semi-elliptical, obtuse, convex above and below; posterior side attenuated, trigonal, above straight and declining; inferior margin straight in the middle, arched at the ends; umbones acute; flexure narrow, scarcely visible; hinge narrow, bidentate, teeth unequal, small, laterals none; pallial sinus deep, gibbons above, then declining (Deshayes).

New Zealand (Cuming).

Genus, CAPSELLA Gray.

Shell ovate oblong, transverse, rounded at both ends, covered with a greenish epidermis; ligament short, external; margin of valves entire.

C. radiata, *Deshays, P.Z.S.,* 1854, *p.* 348. Oblong, rounded in front and rather obliquely truncated behind, with fine concentric striæ, which are slightly waved at the posterior end ; teeth strong; bright salmon colour, paler towards the margin, and with fine waved interrupted radiating striæ of darker.

Height, ·5; length, ·9.
Stewart Island. Philippines (Coll. Cuming).

FAMILY—PAPHIIDÆ.

Animal as in *Tellinidæ*, siphons thick, diverging, separate from the base. Foot tongue like. Shell equivalve, closed, with a cartilage in an internal pit, and with a simple compressed primary tooth, and a rudimentary process in the place of the second tooth ; pallial sinus small.

Genus, MESODESMA—Deshayes.

Oval or sub-trigonal, thick, compressed, closed ; ligament internal, in a deep central pit ; a minute anterior hinge tooth and ¦ lateral teeth in each valve ; muscular scars deep, pallial sinus small.

M. novæ-zealandiæ, *Chemnitz ; Reeve, Conch. Ic. f.* 21 ; *P. roissyana, Lesson. Voy. Coquille, Zool.* i., *p.* 424, *pl.* 15, *f.* 4 ; *M. chemnitzii, Deshayes ; Quoy and Gaimard, l.c.* iii., *p.* 505, *pl.* 82, *f.* 9-11. Shell oblong-ovate, transverse, rather solid, nearly equilateral, sides rounded, anterior a little the shorter ; whitish, irregularly striated, covered with a thin fulvous white shining horny epidermis (Reeve).

Height, 1·5 ; length, 2·25.
All over New Zealand, but more common in the North. Auckland Islands.

The Natives call this shell " kokota." or " pipi."

M. ovalis, *Deshayes, P.Z.S.,* 1854, *p.* 336 ; *Reeve, Conch. Ic., f.* 7, Shell oblong oval, rather thin, compressed towards the margin, nearly equilateral, posterior side a little the narrower ; shining white ; rather obscurely striated ; partially covered with a blackish epidermis (Reeve).

Probably the young of the last.

M. ventricosa, *Gray, Dieff. N.Z.,* ii., *p.* 252 ; *Voy. Erebus and Terror, Moll., pl.* 3, *f.* 6. Ovate, wedge-shaped, truncated behind, thin. ventricose, opaque white, smooth. slightly concentrically striated ; covered with a thin nearly transparent horn-coloured epidermis ; edge thin ; lateral teeth short, smooth, compressed, close to the cartilage pit, the front one of the left valve the largest ; pallial sinus not quite reaching to the centre of the disc (Gray).

North Shore. Cook Strait. (Dieffenbach).

Differs from *M. lata* in having the pallial sinus deeper, in being more inequilateral, and in having two obsolete keels radiating from the unibones to the margin down the anterior end of the valves, whereas in *lata* there is but a single obsolete angulation. It is very close to *M. donacia,* Lam., from Chili.

M. lata, *Deshayes; Reeve, Conch. Ic., f. 4.* Shell triangularly ovate, broad, compressed, concentrically densely irregularly striated, striæ more grooved at the sides; posterior side rounded, anterior much shorter, angularly truncated ; umbones rather flattened ; whitish, covered with a pale yellow horny epidermis (Reeve).
Dunedin.

M. spissa, *Reeve, Conch. Ic.. f. 18.* Shell triangularly oblong, thick ; anteriorly rather sharply angled and truncated ; posteriorly rounded : compressed at the umbones ; posterior area rather broad, sub-concave ; light fuscous white, irregularly striated (Reeve.)
Abundant. Chatham Islands. Auckland to Dunedin, more common in the south.
The Natives call this shell "tuatua."
This is probably the same as *M. sub-triangulata,* Gray, Ann. Phil. (see Dieff.. N.Z., ii., p. 252,) of which I have not been able to find a description. It is not the same as *M. cuneata,* Lam., which is found in South Australia.

Sub-Order— Veneracea.

Siphons moderate : mantle wide, open in front ; foot large, pointed ; gills four.

FAMILY--VENERIDÆ.

Labial palps small, triangular, acute. Mantle with a somewhat large pedal opening ; siphons short, unequal, united for the greater part of their length ; gills large, sub-quadrangular, united behind. Foot large, compressed, linguiform, sometimes furnished with a byssal groove. Shell regular, free, or perforating, closed or somewhat gaping. Hinge usually composed of three diverging primary or cardinal teeth in each valve ; ligament external, marginal. Muscular impressions smooth, oval ; pallial sine sinuated.

Sub-Family— Venerinæ.

Siphons free at their extremities. Foot lanceolate, without a byssal groove. Shell ovate, sub-trigonal ; hinge with the cardinal teeth triangular, and with an anterior lateral tooth.

Genus, VENUS—Linnæus.

Mantle margins fringed or furbelowed ; siphons unequal, separate, diverging, the branchial with a double row of cirri, the inner one long and simple, the outer shorter, furcate or stellate ; anal siphon conical, crowned with short cirri. Shell oval, thick, inequilateral, swollen ; hinge with three cardinal teeth, simple or bifid, in each valve, and a small anterior lateral tooth ; transversely grooved or lamellate, margin finely crenulated ; pallial line short and sinuous, always oblique.

V. nodosa, *Dunker: Reeve, Conch. Ic., f.* 57 ; *V. tuberosa, Deshayes, Cat. Conch., Brit. Mus., p.* 99. Cordato-globose, inequilateral, thick, solid, chaffy, with regular, concentric, thick, convex, broad, tuberculous ribs ; tubercules unequal, the posterior ones larger, obliquely diverging, median obsolete ; umbones large, swollen, cordate, longitudinally striated ; lunule brown, broadly cordate, flat, impressed, finely striated ; ligamental area excavated, elongato-lanceolate ; marked with large transverse spots (Deshayes.)

New Zealand (British Museum.)

Reeve states that this shell comes from West Africa, which is probably correct.

V. oblonga, *Hanley: Reeve. Conch. Ic., f.* 1 ; *Smith, Voy. Erebus and Terror, pl.* 2, *f.* 1 ; *V. zealandica, Gray, Dieff., N.Z.,* ii., *p.* 249 *(not of Quoy and Gaimard.)* Ovato-cordate, ventricose, solid, with close, regular, slightly elevated, concentric laminæ, which are higher at each end ; lunule large, ovato-cordate ; margin finely crenulated ; brown or brownish-white ; interior white.

Height, 1·8 ; length, 2·3.

Auckland to Dunedin. Auckland Islands.

V. crebra, *Hutton, C.M.M., p.* 70. Ovato-cordiform, sub-trigonal, very thick, swollen, with rather close concentric striæ, which are crenulated at the anterior end by fine transverse striæ ; posterior end truncate ; umbones large, much curved forwards ; lunule cordate, pallial sinus short, broad, trigonal, deeply margined ; brown ; interior white.

Height, 1·75 ; length, 1·9.

North Island.

Genus, CHIONE--Muhlfeldt.

Mantle margins plicato-dentate ; siphons short, broad, unequal and united at the base, the branchial with two rows of cirri, the anal ciliated. Shell oval, sub-trigonal ; hinge with two or three cardinal teeth in each valve, but no anterior lateral tooth ; pallial sinus short, broad, triangular.

C. lamellata, *Lamark. Anim. sans vert.,* vi., *p.* 349; *Reeve, Conch. Ic., f.* 78; *Chenu, f.* 368. Oval, angled in front, with distant transverse lamellæ which are striated on the outside, and recurved and fringed in the adult ; white.

Height, 1·5 ; length, 2·25.

Auckland (Cheeseman). S. Australia and Tasmania.

C. yatei, *Gray, Dieff. N.Z.,* ii., *p.* 250 ; *Reeve, Conch., Ic., f.* 84, *Voy. Erebus and Terror, pl.* 3, *f.* 11 ; *V. lucasii, Homb. and Jacqu. ; V. calcarea, Gould. U.S. Ex. Ep.* Ovate, sub quadrate, compressed, inequilateral ; anterior end short, sub-angulated ; posterior truncated ; with thin, concentric, erect, distant lamellæ, which are much higher and

dentate at the posterior end ; lunule lanceolate, imbricatostriate ; pale
yellowish or brown, purplish at the umbones.
Height, 1·8 ; length, 2·1.
Common on the coasts of the North Island, and Massacre Bay ;
Dunedin rare.
The Natives call this shell " pukauri."

C. stuchburyi, *Gray, Dieff. N.Z.,* ii., *p.* 250; *Reeve, Conch. Ic.,*
f. 59 ; *Smith, Voy. Erebus and Terror. pl.* 3, *f.* 4 ; *V. dieffenbachii, Gray,*
Dieff. N.Z., ii., *p.* 250 ; *V. zealandica, Quoy. l.c.,* iii., *p.* 522, *pl.* 84, *f.* 5-6.
Ovato-cordiform, sub-trigonal, swollen, thick, radiately ribbed, and with
distant concentric lamellæ, which are higher on the anterior end ; pos-
terior end smooth, both the ribs and the lamellæ obsolete ; pallial sinus
short, broad, trigonal ; hinge plate curved and strongly sinuated ; lunule
not margined ; reddish-brown, paler behind, interior bluish-white, with
more or less dark purple on the posterior end.
Height, 1·75 ; length, 2.
Common, Auckland to Dunedin ; Auckland Islands ; Chatham
Islands.
The Natives call this shell " huai " or " pipi."
V. dieffenbachii, Gray, is the young of this species.

C. costata, *Quoy, l.c.,* iii., *p.* 521, *pl.* 84, *f.* 1-2 ; *V. crassicostata,*
Reeve, Conch. Ic., f. 42.   Oval, swollen, inequilateral, rugose, truncated
behind ; with thick radiating ribs crossed by concentric striæ ; white,
sometimes yellowish on the umbones ; interior white, with the apex, and
generally the posterior end, purple.
Height, 1·2 ; length, 1·55.
Common in the South.
The Natives call this shell " kaikai-kororo."

C. lima, *Sowerby ; Deshayes, l.c., p.* 137 ; *Reeve, Conch. Ic., f.* 2.
Oval, sub-quadrate, pale, sparingly variegated with brown, radiately ribbed ; ribs rounded, serrated, concentrically ridged, ridges on the ribs
acuminate ; dorsal margin lined with brown, slightly declining, in front
greatly declining ; lunule impressed, fulvous ; ventral margin rounded.
(Deshayes.)
New Zealand (Cumming).

C. mesodesma, *Quoy ; Venus mesodesma et crassa et denticulata*
et violacea, Quoy, l.c., pl. 84 ; *V. spissa, Deshayes, Anim. sans vert.* vi., *p.*
373 ; *V. spurca, Sowerby ; Reeve, Conch. Ic., f.* 90.   Ovate, sub-trigonal,
rather compressed, sub-equilateral, longitudinally grooved ; lunule lanceolate ; white or brown, with radiating bands or zig-zag lines of brown
or purplish-brown ; interior white in the centre with more or less violet
round the margins ; very variable in colour.
Height, ·7 ; length, 1·1.
Common.   Philippines and Valparaiso.

C. gibbosa, *Hutton, C.M.M., p.* 71.   Ovato-trigonal, gibbous,
sub-equilateral, longitudinally grooved, lunule cordate ; yellowish-white ;

interior white in the centre, with more or less brownish-purple round the margin.

Height, ·55 ; length, ·65.

A single right valve only, but common as a fossil at Wanganui.

C. paupercula, *Chemnitz; Deshayes, Cat. Conch., Brit. Mus., p.* 158; *Wood Ind. Test., pl.* 7, *f.* 31. Sub-cordate, smooth, sparingly marked with reddish spots and veins on a brownish ground.

New Zealand (British Museum). Australia (?).

Chemnitz gives this shell from Coromandel; it is not mentioned by Reeve.

Genus—CALLISTA—Poli.

Mantle margins plicate, with filaments above the base of the respiratory siphon ; siphons united to their ends, crowned with simple cirri. Shell ovato-oblong ; a small, anterior, lateral tooth ; pallial sinus broad, oblong, profound, horizontal : margin entire : three cardinal teeth in each valve.

C. multistriata, *Sow.: Thes. Conch. I., p.* 628, *pl.* 136, *f.* 177 : *Reeve, Conch. Ic., f.* 60 *(Dione :) Deshayes, l.c., p.* 64. Oval, sub-elongate, finely concentrically striated ; anterior end shorter ; posterior sub-acuminate ; lunule ovate, reddish ; variegated and interruptedly radiated with brown, fulvous, or pink : pallial sinus broad.

Height. ·55 ; length, ·85.

Wellington (F. W. H.)

I cannot agree with Mr. Tenison-Woods in considering C. *diemanensis,* Hanley, as a synonym of this species.

C. disrupta, *Sow.; Thes. Conch. I., p.* 743, *pl.* 163, *f.* 208 : *Deshayes. l.c., p.* 69. Oval, sub-compressed, finely concentrically striated : anterior end rather short : posterior sub-acuminate ; lunule excavated, dorsal margin arched, variegated with large brownish-purple spots ; yellowish-white, spotted and interruptedly rayed with yellowish-brown, or purple : pallial sinus narrow.

Height. ·9 ; length, 1·05.

New Zealand. (British Museum.) Australia. (Angas.)

Dr. v. Martens considers both this species and the last as synonyms of C. *planatella,* Lamark.

Sub-Family – Artemiinæ.

Siphons united ; foot sub-quadrangular, without a byssal groove. Shell orbicular ; pallial sinus oblique, triangular.

Genus, ARTEMIS—Poli.

Mantle margin plicate. Shell orbicular, compressed ; pallial sinus oblique, triangular ; hinge large, with three cardinal teeth in each valve, and an anterior lateral tooth. Shell ornamented with concentric striæ.

A. australis, *Gray, Dieff. N.Z.,* ii., *p.* 249 (1843 ;) *D. anus, Phil. Zeits, für Mal.,* 1848, *p.* 132 ; *Reeve. Conch. Ic., pl.* 2, *f.* 10 ; *Deshayes, Cat. Conch. in British Museum, part* 1, *p.* 23. Orbicular, longer than high, with close elevated concentric laminæ, decreasing in number towards each extremity, where they are higher and reflexed towards the umbones ; lunule cordate, deeply impressed, lamellate ; margin of tooth plate much sinuated ; anterior cardinal tooth striated ; pallial sinus horizontal, the angle pointing below the anterior adductor impression ; pale pinkish-brown ; interior white, getting violet round the margin.

Height, 2·45 ; length, 2·6.

Common in the North Island, not found South of Oamaru.

As *Venus australis* (Q. & G.) has been identified with *A. variegata,* Gray (1838,) from the Philippine Islands, Dr. Gray's name may be allowed to stand for our shell, especially as Philippi's name is highly objectionable.

A. subrosea, *Gray, Dieff. N.Z.,* ii., *p.* 249 ; *Reeve. Conch. Ic., f.* 19 ; *Smith, Voy. Erebus and Terror, Moll., pl.* 3, *f.* 2. Orbicular, rather longer than high, closely concentrically striated, the striæ, decreasing in number and getting rather higher at each end ; lunule cordate, deeply impressed, striate ; margin of tooth plate very slightly sinuated ; anterior cardinal tooth slightly striated or smooth ; pallial sinus ascending, the angle pointing at the anterior adductor impression : pale pinkish-white, sometimes pinker at the umbones.

Height, 1·9 ; length, 1·95.

Common in the North Island ; Dunedin rare. Chatham Islands.

The Natives call this shell, and also *Tapes intermedia,* "hakari."

A. lambata, *Gould, U.S. Ex. Ep.,* xii., *p.* 422, *f.* 536. Orbicular, rather compressed, very finely concentrically striated, the striæ more distant and more elevated towards the posterior end, thin ; umbones small, uncinate ; lunule cordate, impressed, margined ; ligament sub-enclosed ; posterior tooth of the right valve large, deeply bifid ; white.

Height, 1 ; length, 1.

North Island only.

A. carpenteri, *Römer, Monogr., pl.* 10, *f.* 2 (1862.) Cordato-orbicular, thin, sub-compressed, rounded anteriorly, perpendicularly sub-truncated behind, very inequilateral, with dense, regular, rounded, concentric liræ, towards the extremities, especially behind, generally confluent, the rest sub-lamellar, and terminating in small turned-over foliæ ; radiating striæ obsolete in the middle ; pale ferruginous ; umbones rather swollen, much re-curved ; anterior ventral margin rounded, strongly ascending, the posterior rather straight, directed upward ; anterior dorsal margin very short, concave ; lunule cordate, impressed, clearly margined ; area lanceolate, excised, surrounded with an acute margin : ligament deeply immersed ; pallial sinus large, lingulate : apex very broad, rounded.

Length, 1·29 ; Height, 1·23 ; thickness, ·57 inch.

New Zealand (Baron v. Mueller.)

I doubt the correctness of this locality.

A. grayi, *Zittel, Reise der Novara, Palæ., p.* 45, *pl.* xv., *f.* 11. Orbicular, solid, swollen, with distant, thin, concentric laminæ, hardly elevated on the sides ; umbones swollen, incurved, acute ; anterior side arched ; posterior rounded ; lunule large, oblongo-cordiform, somewhat impressed, striated, margined ; pallial sinus triangular, ascending, the angle acute (pointing above the anterior adductor impression.)

Height, 1·4 ; length, 1·4 ; breadth, ·9 (Zittel.)

A single valve, of a recent specimen from the Chatham Islands, is in the Otago Museum.

Sub-Family—Tapesinæ.

Siphons free at their extremities ; foot lanceolate, byssiferous. Shell oblong, transverse ; hinge with the cardinal teeth compressed ; lateral teeth single or none.

Genus, TAPES—Muhlfeldt.

Siphons united as far as the middle, diverging at their ends ; branchial siphon crowned with arborescent tentacles ; anal siphon ending in simple, cylindrical tentacles ; mantle margin simple. Shell ovato-oblong, inequilateral, margin entire ; three cardinal teeth in each valve, simple or bifid ; pallial sinus deep, oblong, horizontal.

T. intermedia, *Quoy, l.c.,* iii., *p.* 526, *pl.* 84, *f.* 9-10 ; *Reeve, Conch. Ic., f.* 59. Ovate, transverse, sub-truncated posteriorly, concentrically striated, decussated by very fine ridiating striæ ; lunule lanceolate, broad ; hinge three-toothed, two of which are bifid ; brownish or yellowish-white ; interior white, or grey, more or less marked with violet at the posterior end.

Height, 1·75 ; length, 2·25.

Common. Auckland Islands.

The young shell is yellowish, more or less marked with fine purplish brown waved lines. The Natives call this shell, and also *Artemis subrosea,* " hakari."

T. fabagella, *Deshayes, Proc. Zool. Soc.,* 1853, *p.* 10 ; *Reeve, Conch. Ic., f.* 66. Ovate, inequilateral, rather compressed, thin, fragile ; anterior end shorter, obtuse ; posterior broader, obliquely truncated ; dorsal margin straight, ventral arched ; finely concentrically striated, much fewer and lamellate at the posterior end ; front and middle finely radiately striated ; umbones small, quite smooth ; pallial sinus deep, trigonal, base broad ; white both inside and outside.

Height, ·5 ; length, ·75. (Desh.)

New Zealand. (Cuming.)

T. galactites, *Lamark, l.c.,* vi., *p.* 359 ; *Deshayes, Cat. Veneridæ, Brit. Mus. p.* 183 ; *Reeve, Conch. Ic., f.* 65. Shell rather elongately oblong, anteriorly obtusely angled, white, smoothly decussated throughout, both sides rounded (Reeve.)

Height, 1·25 ; length, 2·2.

New Zealand. (Reeve.) Australia and Tasmania.

v

Genus, VENERUPIS—Lamark.

Siphons long, unequal, united as far as the middle; the respiratory siphon fringed at the orifice with a double series of cirri; foot small, conical, linguiform, and byssiferous. Shell irregular in shape, inequilateral, gaping behind, three teeth in one valve and two or three in the other, pallial sinus deep and broad.

V. reflexa, *Gray, Dieff. N.Z.,* ii.. *p.* 250 ; *Voy. Erebus and Terror, Moll., pl.* 2, *f.* 3. Shell oblong, very irregular, rounded in front and truncated behind ; surface with thin sharp-edged, reflexed, concentric ridges, which are highest and most bent over and back at the hinder edge, and they generally have two or three lower concentric ridges between them ; hinge teeth 3.3 ; inside yellowish, hinder half blackish-purple, with a yellow edge (Gray.)
Auckland to Dunedin, rare in the south.

V. paupercula, *Deshayes, P.Z.S.,* 1853, *p.* 5; *Reeve, Conch. Ic., f.* 28. Shell ovate, compressed, transverse, inequilateral, irregularly contorted, anterior obtuse, posterior perpendicularly truncated, dirty reddish-white, transversely irregularly rugose and striated ; interior white, behind marked with violet : pallial sinus broad, deep, apex very obtuse, horizontal (Desh.)
New Zealand. (Cuming.)
Probably the same as *V. brevis,* Quoy and Gaimard, from Tasmania. Sowerby says that this species is from Mazatlan.

V. siliqua, *Desh., P.Z.S.,* 1853, *p.* 5, *pl.* xviii., *f.* 1 ; *Reeve, Conch. Ic., f.* 20. Shell elongate, transverse, rather swollen, inequilateral, yellowish-white, anterior obtuse, posterior obtusely angled, truncated. transversely, unequally sulcato-striated, sulca and striæ irregular. numerous, appressed, some sensibly larger behind, forming short regular, erect, laminæ ; umbones small, swollen ; lunule scarcely distinct, prominent in the middle ; pallial sinus narrow, elongated ; apex obtuse (Deshayes.)
New Zealand. (Cuming.)

V. elegans, *Deshayes, P.Z.S.,* 1853, *p.* 5, *pl.* xviii., *f.* 2 ; *Voy. Erebus and Terror, pl* 2, *f.* 6. Shell elongated, transverse, narrow, inequilateral, inflato-cylindrical, front attenuated short, behind broader, obtusely truncated, posterior side obtusely angled, longitudinally very finely and elegantly granular-striate, transversely multi-lamellate ; lamellæ unequal, obtuse in front, crenulated, behind finer and broader, minutely crisped ; lunule ovato-elongate, prominent in the middle, rimate ; area narrow, deep, canaliculated ; interior of valves white, the margin finely crenulated ; pallial line submarginal, the sinus short, angled, base broad (Deshayes.)
New Zealand. (Cuming.)

V. insignis, *Deshayes. P.Z.S.,* 1853, *p.* 6, *pl.* xviii., *f.* 4 ; *Reeve, Conch. Ic., f.* 2. Shell ovato-transverse, sub-quadrate, very unequal, more or less inflated and irregular, yellow, margins reddish. longitudinally frequently and finely lirate; liræ at the posterior side deeply angled or divaricate, and joining one another; anterior side very short, posterior slightly broader, obliquely truncated; superior and inferior margins parallel; umbones oblique, swollen, approximate; interior of valves reddish-saffron, towards the periphery violet; pallial sinus narrow, deep, apex acuminate, ascending (Deshayes.)

New Zealand. (Cuming.)

FAMILY—PETRICOLIDÆ.

Shell ovate, thin, swollen, inequilateral, equivalve, gaping at both ends; teeth two in each valve, unequal, the larger bifid; pallial line remote from the margin in front, broad and deeply sinuated behind.

Genus, PETRICOLA—Lamark.

Ovate, transverse, thin, hinge broad.

P. serrata, *Deshayes*, *Cat. Veneridæ*, *Brit. Mus.*, *p.* 212; *Sowerby*, *in Reeve's Conch. Ic.*, *f.* 1. Elongate, very narrow, cylindrical; dirty reddish; extremities obtuse, gaping; longitudinally ridged, the ridges larger and denticulated at the anterior end, thin in the middle, and more numerous and undulating at the posterior end; valves thin; interior dirty white; pallial sinus elongate; apex obtuse; base broader (Deshayes.)

New Zealand. (Cuming.)

SECTION—INTEGROPALLIATA.

Pallial sinus small or none. Shell regular, rarely gaping ventrally, with hinge teeth.

Sub-Order—Cyprinacea.

Gills, two on each side, unequal; foot large.

FAMILY—CARDIIDÆ.

Palpi slender, acuminate; mantle freely open in front; siphons distinct, but very short, and nearly sessile, their bases and sides furnished with tentacular filaments; gills two on each side, thick, united together behind the body. Foot very long and geniculate. Shell cordate, swollen, equivalve; cardinal teeth irregular; laterals remote, or none; pallial line simple; ligament external; generally radiately ribbed, rarely smooth; posterior differently sculptured to the front and sides.

Genus, CARDIUM—Linnæus.

Ventricose; umbones prominent; margins crenulated; pallial line more or less sinuated; umbones sub-central.

C. striatulum, *Sowerby*; *Reeve*, *Conch. Ic.*, *f.* 60; *C. pulchellum*, *Gray*, *Dieff. N.Z.*, ii., *p.* 252, *nec Reeve*. Sub-cordate, rather ventricose, thin, rosy-white varied with red; umbones generally white;

interior white, varied with red, finely radiately ribbed, those on the hinder margin spinulose.

Height, ·75; length, ·87.

Auckland to Stewart Island, 15 fathoms; rare in the south.

FAMILY—CYRENIDÆ.

Labial palps lanceolate. Mantle open in front, the margins simple ; siphons short, plain-edged, produced, either partially separated, or completely united to their extremities ; gills two on each side, large, unequal, united behind. Foot large, tongue-shaped. Shell more or less tumid, sub-orbicular, closed, covered with a hard, olive, brittle, often polished epidermis ; beaks frequently eroded ; surface of valves concentrically striated or furrowed. Hinge composed of three, or sometimes two diverging cardinal teeth ; lateral teeth compressed ; ligament external. Pallial line simple, or with a slight siphonal inflexion. Fresh water.

Genus, SPHÆRIUM—Scopoli.

Siphons separate, diverging into two nearly equal tubes. Shell equivalve, thin, oblong, cordate, equilateral, more or less inflated, smooth or concentrically striated ; hinge with two moderately diverging cardinal teeth in each valve, the front of right valve, and the hinder of left valve smallest ; lateral teeth elongate, compressed, smooth, of right valve double, of left simple.

S. novæ-zelandiæ, *Deshayes, Cat. Conchif., Brit. Mus., p.* 272, *P.Z.S,,* 1854, *p.* 342 ; *Reeve, Conch. Ic., f.* 37. Shell ovato-transverse, equilateral, compressed, shining, pellucid, bluish-grey, abundantly irregularly transversely banded ; anterior side obtuse, slightly declining ; posterior side broader, rounded, inferior margin convex ; umbones small, obtuse, scarcely prominent ; ligament small, inconspicuous ; hinge very narrow, bidentate ; teeth small ; laterals small, the anterior rather larger (Deshayes.)

New Zealand and Australia. (British Museum.)

S. lenticula, *Dunker, Mal. Blatt.,* viii., 1861, *p.* 153. Shell, small, sub-orbicular, nearly equilateral, rather compressed, very thin pale horn-colour, or sub-straw-colour, pellucid, concentrically and delicately striated ; umbones rather obtuse.

Length, ·16 inch. (Dunker.)

Lakes Rotoiti and Taupo. (Hochstetter.) Lake Guyon. (F. W. H.)

This may be the same as *S. lenticularis,* Sowerby, in Reeves' Conchologia Iconica, fig. 6, for which no locality is given.

Genus, PISIDIUM—Pfeiffer.

Siphons united as far as the extremities. Shell equivalve, thin, usually tumid, sub-oval, inequilateral, smooth, or concentrically striated; hinge with two moderately diverging teeth in each valve, the front of right, and the hinder of left valve the smaller; lateral teeth elongate, smooth, compressed, of right valve double, of left valve simple; ligament external.

P. novæ-zealandiæ, *Prime, P.Z.S.,* 1862, *p.* 3; *P. novo-zealandicum, Prime, Ann. Lyceum of Nat. Hist., New York,* 1867, *p.* 91. Shell minute, transverse, oval, sub-oblique, very inequilateral, rather compressed, thin; the anterior side produced, elongated and rounded, the posterior sub-truncated; umbones small and obtuse; epidermis yellowish-horn colour and polished (Prime.)
Length, ·16; height, ·12; thickness, ·08 inch.
New Zealand. (Cuming.)

Sub-Order—Lucinacea.

Mantle lobes free beneath, united posteriorly, forming a separate siphonal opening; gills one on each side; foot cylindrical, elongate, inferior*; anterior adductor muscle usually elongate.

FAMILY—LUCINIDÆ.

Labial palps small and rudimentary. Mantle lobes free beneath, furnished behind with one or two sessile siphonal apertures; gills one on each side, large, oval, thick. Foot cylindrical, elongate, inferior, usually hollow throughout its entire length, the tube opening into the spaces of the visceral cavity. Shell orbicular, free, closed; hinge teeth one or two, laterals ½ or obsolete; pallial line simple; muscular impressions elongated, rugose; interior dull, obliquely furrowed.

Genus, LUCINA—Bruguiere.

Siphonal orifices simple, without a prolonged anal tube; white; umbones depressed; lunule distinct; ligament semi-internal; anterior muscular impression elongated within the pallial line; posterior oblong.

L. divaricata, *Lamark, Anim. sans vert.,* vi., *p.* 226; *Reeve, Conch. Ic., f.* 47*a*; *Chenu, f.* 572. Orbicular, sub-globose, with thin undulating bifarious striae, margin even, no lateral teeth.
Heigth, 1·12; length, 1·25.
Auckland to Chalky Sound. Chatham Islands. Tasmania.

FAMILY—UNGULINIDÆ.

Mouth with four foliaceous, membranous palps. Mantle margins united, with the exception of a large inferior pedal opening, and a small sessile anal aperture. Gills two pairs on each side, united behind. Foot vermiform, ending in an erectile gland, channelled throughout its length. Sub-orbicular, closed; hinge of two diverging bifid cardinal teeth, without laterals; ligament marginal.

L. lactea, *A. Adams, P.Z.S.,* 1855, *p.* 225, (*nec Lamark*). Shell thick, orbicular, sub-ventricose, milk-white, concentrically lamellated;

lamellæ distant, regular, the interstices decussated with elevated radiating striæ, and transverse lines; umbones nearly median, rather prominent; anterior side rounded, sub-truncate, and sub-angulated ; posterior side rounded ; anterior cardinal tooth broad and prominent ; interior thickened white, ventral margin crenulated (Adams).

Australia and New Zealand. (Strange).

Genus, DIPLODONTA—Bronn.

Mantle-margins nearly plain ; pedal and anal apertures wide apart. Shell equivalve ; two unequal cardinal teeth in each valve ; the anterior of the left and the posterior of the right bifid ; ligament external.

D. **zealandica,** *Gray, Dieff., N.Z.,* ii., *p.* 256 ; *Smith, Voy. Erebus and Terror, pl.* 3, *f.* 8 ; *L. inculta, Gould, U.S. Ex. Ep.* xii., *p.* 417 ; *Atlas, f.* 524. Shell sub-orbicular, rather compressed, rather solid, opaque white, smooth, very slightly concentrically striated, and covered with a thin smooth periostraca (Gray).   Rather compressed, smooth, very slightly concentrically striated, rather solid ; opaque white.

Height, ·75 ; length, ·75.

Auckland.

D. **globularis,** *Lamark, l.c.,* vi·, *p.* 231 ; *Reeve, Conch. Ic. (Lucina,) f.* 53. Orbicular, inflated, umbones rather prominent ; very finely concentrically striated, thin, pellucid ; horny white.

Height, 1 ; length, 1·12.

Auckland to Stewart Island, 14 fathoms.   Australia.

D. **striata,** *Hutton, Jour. de Conch.,* 1878, *p.* 51 ; *L. novæ-zealandiæ, Reeve, Conch. Ic. (Lucina,) pl.* ix., *f.* 14 *(not of Gray.)*   Shell somewhat globose, inequilateral, swollen posteriorly, concentrically rudely, irregulary striated ; no lunule ; hinge with two central teeth in each valve, one of which is erect and bifid ; whitish, covered with a light brown epidermis (Reeve).

Height, ·4 ; length, ·4.

New Zealand.   (Cuming).   Kapiti, Cook Strait.

FAMILY—LASEIDÆ.

Mantle with only one siphonal opening, the anal, which is sometimes sessile, sometimes produced into a tube ; the mantle folded anteriorly into a canal or tube.   Foot ligulate, grooved, with a byssiferous organ, and capable of being used as a creeping disk.   Shell thin, often transparent, and sometimes gaping.   Hinge straight, with one or two cardinal teeth ; lateral teeth compressed or none.

Genus, KELLIA—Turton.

A very short posterior anal siphon ; anterior tube undivided, entire below.   Shell sub-orbicular, sub-equilateral, closed, smooth or concentrically striated ; one valve with two cardinal teeth near together and a distant lateral tooth ; the other with a single concave cardinal and a distant lateral tooth ; ligament internal or sub-marginal.

K. cycladiformis, *Deshayes, Trait élém., pl.* 11. *ff.* 6-9, *P.Z.S.,* 1855, *p.* 181 *(Erycina.)* Shell ovato-sub-rotund, swollen, inequilateral, smooth, shining, clothed with a thin glaucous grey epidermis, iridescent, transversely finely and irregularly striated ; anterior side shortly obtuse ; valves thin, translucent ; hinge very narrow, cardinal teeth two in the left valve, minute, disjoined at the base, unequal ; lateral teeth remote ; anterior muscular impression very small, circular, the posterior oval, continuous with the pallial impression (Desh.)

North Australia. (Jukes.) New Zealand. (Quoy.)

Genus, PYTHINA—Hinds.

Equivalve, equilateral ; umbones small ; left valve with two small unequal teeth and two strong lateral teeth ; right valve with a small central tooth, and two bifid lateral teeth ; two ligaments.

P. stowei, *Hutton, C.M.M., p.* 76. Transversely oval, thin, white, pellucid, with rather strong ribs divaricating from the centre and crossed towards the margin by a few distant concentric grooves ; interstices slightly rugose ; margin crenulated at each end.

Height, ·3 ; length, ·5.

Islet Reef, Cook Strait, two left valves only. Auckland. (Cheeseman.)

FAMILY—SOLEMYIDÆ.

Palpi very small and slender. Mantle closed, except at a large opening with cirrated edges, anteriorly, for the passage of the foot, and at a small opening at the posterior extremity, also cirrated. Gills forming a very thick lobe on each side, situated far posteriorly, and having a longitudinal sulcus in the middle of each. Foot large, truncated and excavated at its extremity, which has fimbriated edges. Shell elongated, equivalve, very inequilateral, gaping, invested in a thick epidermis.

Genus, SOLEMYA—Lamark.

Shell cylindrical, ligament concealed, pallial line obscure ; umbones posterior ; one compressed very oblique cardinal tooth in each valve ; epidermis dark and horny, extending beyond the margin.

S. parkinsoni, *Smith, Voy. Erebus and Terror, Moll., p.* 6, *pl.* 3, *f.* 1 ; *Reeve, Conch. Ic., f.* 4. Dark brown, rayed with paler, interior greyish.

Height, ·7 ; length, 1·9.

Stewart Island to Auckland.

Dental callosity moderately broad, and prdouced acutely towards the shorter or posterior side of the valve (not truncated as in *S. australis ;)* the extension of it within the valve is thin, nearly separated from it at the base by a depression ; the transverse expansion of the ligament is elongate and narrow; the posterior muscular scar is narrower than in the Australian species (Smith.)

FAMILY—ASTARTIDÆ.

Labial palps plicate, short, triangular. Lobes of mantle disunited in their entire length, the branchial margin bearded; gills two pairs, rounded in front, tapering and free behind the body. Foot conical, compressed, rather angulated behind. Shell thick, triangular or cordiform, oblong, generally covered with a brown epidermis; often ornamented with concentric striæ; hinge thick, large, and solid.

Genus, CRASSATELLA—Lamark.

Mantle entirely open, with the inhalent margins cirrated; palpi triangular; foot compressed, triangular and grooved. Shell solid, closed, equivalve, attenuated behind, lunule distinct; hinge composed of two sub-diverging, striated primary teeth placed in front of a cartilage pit : lateral teeth usually one in each valve; ligament internal, inserted in a pit in each valve.

C. obesa, *Adams, P.Z.S.,* 1852, *p.* 90. Shell equivalve, inequilateral, thick, gibbous, covered with brownish-red, silky epidermis, transversely strongly plicated, folds prominent, vanishing towards the ventral margin; lunule impressed. lanceolate; posterior side sub-produced, angled, margin truncated; anterior side gibbous, margin rounded (Adams).
New Zealand, deep water. (Mr. Strange).

C. bellula, *Adams, P.Z.S.,* 1852, *p.* 95; *Gouldia isabella, Hutton, C.M.M., p.* 76. Shell ovato-trigonal, sub-equilateral, yellowish-pink, immaculate, transversely concentrically plicated, folds obtuse, rather crowded, regular, in front undulating and getting smaller (under the lens rugulose); posterior side rounded, anterior scarcely truncated : umbones acute, small, approximated (Adams).
Cook Strait.

Genus, CARDITA—Lamark.

Foot sickle-shaped, not byssiferous. Shell equivalve, inequilateral, sub-orbicular, generally with radiating ribs; cardinal teeth oblique, directed to the same side.

C. australis, *Lamark, Anim. sans vert.* vi., *p.* 383; *Quoy and Gaimard, l.c.,* iii., *p.* 480, *pl.* 78, *f.* 11-14; *C. tridentata, Reeve, Conch. Ic., f.* 22. Sub-orbicular, inequilateral, swollen, with about twenty-two nodulose radiating ribs, the nodules on the hinder side sub-spinose; lunule cordate, umbones oblique. recurved; margin plicated; pale brownish-white; interior white, more or less marked with rosy or purple.
Height, 1·5; length, 1·75.
Common. Chatham Islands. Stewart Island.

The young shell is slightly marked with reddish-brown, and all the ribs are sometimes sub-spinose. The Natives call this shell "purimu."

C. zealandica, *Potiez and Michaud, Gall. des Moll.*, 1838, *p.* 166. Shell sub-orbicular, inequilateral, swollen, greyish-white, internally spotted with blackish-purple, polished ; cancellated with numerous longitudinal striæ and transverse sub-lamellæ ; umbones oblique, recurved, hinge two-toothed ; margin finely plicated (P. & M.).

C. lutea, *Hutton ; C. zealandica, Deshayes, P.Z.S.*, 1852, *p.* 101, *not of P. & M.* Shell small, orbiculato-subtrigonal, depressed, longitudinally 14-ribbed, sub-equilateral, pale brownish ; ribs regular, for a time sub-squamose, equal to the interstices ; umbones small, acute, sub-opposite ; lunule not very deep, brown, lanceolate (Deshayes).
Auckland.

C. bimaculata, *Deshayes, P.Z.S.*, 1852, *p.* 102, *pl.* xvii., *f.* 4-5. Shell ovato-subtrigonal, inequilateral, depressed, both sides obtuse, under the rough brown epidermis greyish-white, radiately ribbed ; ribs 17-19, narrow, equal, not larger than the interstices, with regular erect sharp scales, narrower behind ; apices acute ; lunule deep, ovato lanceolate ; interior of the valves white with a brown spot on either side (Deshayes).
New Zealand. (Cuming).

C. amabilis, *Deshayes, P.Z.S.*, 1852, *p.* 102, *pl.* xvii., *f.* 8-9. Shell sub-orbicular, laterally compressed, sub-equilateral, radiately finely ribbed, yellowish-white, irregularly spotted with pale brown ; umbones small opposite ; lunule flat, scarcely excavated, smooth, ovate ; ribs 28, regularly crenato-noduled ; hinge thicked, in the right valve unidentate, in the left bidentate, teeth of right valve triangular large ; interior of valves white (Deshayes).
New Zealand. (Cuming.) Tasmania. (Tenison-Woods.)

C. difficilis, *Deshayes, P.Z.S.*, 1852, *p.* 103, *pl.* xvii. *f.* 16, 17. Shell ovato-transverse, inequilateral, swollen, solid, convex at the margins, white, epidermis rough brownish, unspotted ; radiately ribbed ; umbones oblique, opposite ; lunule very small, deep, smooth, flat ; ribs sub-angled, crenato-scaly, sharp, especially at the umbones and the posterior side ; interstices sub-equal to the ribs ; interior of valves very white ; hinge narrow (Deshayes).
New Zealand. (Cuming).

C. purpurata, *Deshayes, P.Z.S.*, 1852, *p.* 100, *pl.* xvii., *f.* 12, 13. Shell ovato-transverse, sub-trigonal, inequilateral, anterior shorter, obtuse, depressed, radiately sulcated, yellowish-white, reddish behind ; umbones oblique, prominent ; lunule small, deep, flat, smooth ; transverse ribs shortly scaled, 26, narrower behind, roughish, one more prominent than the others ; interior of valves pale purple, at the margin vividly radiated with purple (Deshayes).
New Zealand. (Cuming).

w

Genus, MYTILICARDIA—Blainville.

Foot rounded, grooved, byssiferous. Shell elongated, very inequilateral, with projecting squamose ribs ; anterior cardinal tooth triangular and diverging, posterior cardinal double in the left valve, no anterior laterals.

M. excavata, *Deshayes, P.Z.S.*, 1852, *p.* 100, *pl.* xvii., *f.* 1, 2, 3. Shell elongato-transverse, very inequilateral, anterior very short, subtruncated, posterior dilated, sinuated and gaping below, longitudinally and radiately ribbed, white, posterior ribs yellowish-pink or dirty brown; umbones small, compressed, approximated, very oblique, lunule narrow, very deep ; ribs unequal, the first on the anterior side narrower, the rest perceptibly broader, and thicker, armed with long scales (Deshayes).

New Zealand from Auckland to Dunedin and the Chatham Islands. Australia and Tasmania.

Sub-Order—Unionacea.

Mantle margins free, teeth absent or present. Shell covered with a thick epidermis ; embryos with at first only one adductor ; fresh water.

FAMILY—UNIONIDÆ.

Labial palps wider than long, usually united as far as the middle of their hind margins. Mantle lobes entirely disunited, not produced into siphonal tubes, the branchial region fringed with cirri, the anal plain. Foot large, thick, tongue shaped, somewhat produced anteriorly, not provided with a byssal groove. Shell equivalve, covered externally with an epidermis ; pearly in the inside ; hinge variable.

Genus, UNIO—Retzius.

Outer gill united to the mantle as far as its extremity, inner gill not united to the foot; foot moderate. Shell equivalve, inequilateral, variable in shape, covered with an olivaceous epidermis ; beaks usually eroded ; hinge with primary teeth, and with elongated laterals ; ligament external, more or less elongated ; pallial impression simple ; muscular scars conspicuous.

U. menziesii, *Gray, Dieff. N.Z.,* ii., 257 ; *Reeve, Conch. Ic., f.* 152. Shell oblong, high, compressed, thin, obliquely truncated behind; covered with a thin olive periostraca, and much excoriated near the umbo ; the hinder lateral teeth elongated, only elevated on their hinder extremity, where they are crowded ; the inner anterior tooth of the right valve large, thick, ovate, rugose ; the rest small, compressed ; the disc of the shell brown, varied (Gray.)

Rather smooth, compressed, and thin. Distinguished from other New Zealand species by its being more winged posteriorly. I have not found the inner anterior tooth of the right valve so thick and rugose as Dr. Gray's description would lead one to except.

Length, 2·5 ; height, 1·45 inch (from Reeve's figure.)
Rivers in the North Island and Lake Taupo. (Dieffenbach.)
Ashburton River and Hutt River. (F. W. H.)

U. aucklandica, *Gray, Dieff. N.Z.,* ii., *p.* 257 ; *Reeve, Conch. Ic., f.* 156. Shell oblong and rather thick, rounded in front, and rather obliquely truncated behind, covered with a thick olive periostraca ; umbo black, decorticated, cardinal teeth low, blunt, oblique, hinder lateral teeth laminar, far off ; the inner surface pearly, purplish near the umbo, greenish on the hinder edge (Gray.) Shell oblong-ovate, thin, compressed, concentrically densely thread striated ; umboes radiately wrinkle-ridged ; sides rounded ; anterior very short ; posterior obscurely convexely angled (Reeve.)
Length, 2·2 ; height, 1·15 inch (from Reeve's figure.)
Bay of Islands and Auckland (Dr. Sinclair.) Lake Takapuna, Auckland. (F. W. H.)

U. zelebori, *Dunker, Reise der Novara, Moll., p.* 2, *f.* 28. Shell oval-oblong, rather thin, sub-ventricose, rather compressed towards the base ; anterior end shortly rounded ; posterior linguiform, finely concentrically striated ; epidermis thin, pale olive, sub-horny ; umboes swollen, turned forward, inclined and rugosely angled ; upper margin arched, sub-excavate in front ; lower margin straight, sub-sinuated in the middle ; cardinal teeth compressed, acute, crenated, laterals sub-straight, the superior in each valve smaller as usual ; anterior muscular impressions deep, unequal, the smaller sub-reniform ; interior iridescent below the umbones, faint and yellowish (Dunker.)
Length, 2 ; height, 1 ; thick, ·64 inch.
Hardly distinguishable from the last in shape, but the dorsal margin does not ascend from the umbo, but runs parallel to the ventral margin.
River Wairarapa. (F. W. H.)

U. hochstetteri, *Dunker, Mal. Blatt.* viii., 1861, *p.* 153 ; *Reeve, Conch. Ic., f.* 463. Shell thickish, depressed, very inequilateral, narrow and very short in front, broadly biangular, and somewhat winged behind, of a uniform blackish olive, very indistinctly sub-verrucose in the middle, elsewhere unsculptured ; ligamental edge curved and rising; hinder area concave, no lunule ; nacre bluish white, variegated with olive ; primary teeth somewhat transverse ; lateral teeth elongated, much raised, and obliquely truncated at their extremities (Reeve.)
Length, 2·1 ; height, 1·5 inch (from Reeve's figure.)
Distinguished by its great height, and the posterior end being truncated almost perpendicularly.
Lake Taupo and River Waikato. (Hochstetter.)
I have never seen this species.

U. lutulentus, *Gould, U.S. Ex. Ep.,* xii., *p.* 428, *f.* 542 ; *Reeve, Conch. Ic., f.* 122 *and f.* 386. Shell somewhat squarely oblong, very compressed, anterior side moderately rounded, posterior slopingly expanded, then truncated, concentrically rudely plicately striated; black (Reeve, species 122.)

Length, 3·3; Height, 1·6 inch (from Reeve's figure.)

Shell thin, much compressed, of a yellowish-olive green, not rayed, nearly smooth, with a few distant obscure, short, divergent corrugations on the broad umbonal slope; hinder dorsal edge somewhat curved and elevated; ventral margin scarcely retuse; beaks not prominent; nacre dirty white; cardinal teeth laminar (Reeve's species 386.)

Length, 2·15; height, 1·2 inch (from Reeve's figure.)

River Clutha. (F. W. H.)   Auckland. (Dr. Sinclair.)

Both these shells can hardly belong to the same species, but I am not able to refer to the original description. What I take to be *U. lutulentus*, is distinguished by its tolerably uniform longitudinal grooving, and somewhat resembles Reeve's figure, No. 122. I cannot say which of Reeve's references is correct.

Sub-Order—Arcacea.

Mantle edges free all round; foot large; hinge teeth many, symmetrical.

FAMILY—ARCIDÆ.

Animal oblong. Mantle freely open, simple or fringed. Mouth surrounded by labia formed out of the extremities of the branchiæ; no true palps. Foot oblong, bent, grooved throughout its length so as to form a disc with plain or slightly crimped margins. Shell not pearly within, closed, or gaping inferiorly. Hinge of numerous teeth disposed in a straight or curved line; equivalve.

Sub-Family—Arcinæ.

Gills sub-pinnate, separate from each other behind; a byssal groove at the base of the foot. Shell with the hinge margin straight; cartilage in small marginal pits.

Genus, BARBATIA—Gray.

Oblong or sub-quadrangular, covered with a rough but perishable epidermis; hinge of numerous teeth, of which the central ones are the smallest; the lateral ones increasing in size and getting more oblique.

B. decussata, *Sow*, *P.Z.S.*, 1833, *p.* 18; *Reeve, Conch. Ic., f.* 81. Oval-elongate, margin sinuated, smooth or sometimes crenulated in the young, covered with a brown hairy epidermis; surface with fine radiating ribs, decussated by longitudinal striæ; brown or yellowish; interior white, varied with brownish purple.

Height, 1·25; length, 2·5.

Auckland to Stewart Island. Australia. Pacific Ocean.

B. pusilla, *Sowerby, Proc. Zool. Soc.*, 1833, *p.* 18; *(? A. donaciformis, Reeve, Conch. Ic, f.* 104.*)* Ovato sub-rhomboidal, white, concentrically ridged and decussated at both ends by radiating striæ, these striæ being absent from a small portion of the anterior central area ; anterior end short, rounded ; posterior longer ; dorsal margin angled behind ; hinge slightly curved.

Height, ·35 ; length, ·7.

Dead shells only have been found in New Zealand.

Australia. Peru.

Sub-Family—Pectunculinæ.

Gills dependent ; foot securiform, simple, without any byssal groove at the base. Shell orbicular, with the hinge-margin semi-circular ; cartilage in small marginal pits.

Genus, PECTUNCULUS—Lamark.

Orbicular, nearly equilateral, smooth or radiately striated ; umbones central, divided by a striated ligamental area ; hinge semicircular ; adductors sub-equal ; pallial line simple ; margins crenated inside.

P. laticostatus, *Quoy, l.c.,* iii., *p.* 466, *et P. ovatus, Quoy, l.c.* iii., *p.* 467 ; *P. laticostatus, Reeve, Conch. Ic., f.* 8. Orbicular, convex, thick, equilateral, with broad rounded radiating ribs, which become obsolete towards the margin in old individuals ; finely concentrically striated ; six or eight teeth on each side, with a broad smooth area between them ; reddish-brown, interior white or brownish ; old shells are more or less truncated behind, and the young are often varied with white.

Height, 3 ; length, 3.

Auckland to Stewart Island. Chatham Islands.

Found fossil in Australia, but not recent. The concentric striæ soon wear off, and the shell often becomes quite smooth.

P. flammeus, *Reeve, Conch. Ic., f.* 7 ; *P. grayanus, Dunker, P. Z.S.,* 1856, *p.* 357. Shell rather triangular, white, vividly painted with reddish-brown, flaming triangular lines ; teeth comparatively minute ; area of the ligament small (Reeve).

Auckland. N.S. Wales. (Angas).

P. striatularis, *Lamark,* vi., *p.* 493 ; *Reeve, Conch. Ic., f.* 27, *Chenu, f.* 881. Orbicular, convex, thick, sub-equilateral, umbones curved slightly forwards ; finely radiately striate, and still more finely concentrically striate ; teeth, seven to twelve on each side, not divided by a smooth space ; yellowish brown, more or less irregularly marked with reddish ; interior varied with brown.

Height, 1 ; length, 1.

Omaha. Stewart Island.

FAMILY—NUCULIDÆ.

Lips broad, triangular, large, striated internally, one in each pair of labial palps, long, curled, linear, and fimbriated at its margins, the other short and filiform. Mantle freely open, the edges simple, without siphonal tubes ; gills small, pinnate, united behind. Foot compressed, deeply grooved, forming when expanded an ovate disc with serrated edges. Shell covered with an epidermis, pearly within. Hinge with a great number of comb-like teeth, interrupted in the middle by the ligamental impression.

Genus, NUCULA—Lamark.

Trigonal, with the umbones turned to the short posterior side ; epidermis olive, margins crenulated ; hinge with an internal prominent cartilage pit, and a series of sharp teeth on each side.

N. nitidula, *A. Adams, P.Z.S.*, 1856, *p.* 51; *Reeve, Conch. Ic., f.* 27. Shell very oblique, gibbose, anterior end obliquely sub-truncated, posterior rounded, produced ; shining, obscurely sulcated ; umbones sub-acute ; pale brown, margins of the valves finely crenulated (Adams). Under a lens it is seen to be radiately striated.
Auckland to Stewart Island.

N. strangei, *A. Adams, P.Z.S.*, 1856, *p.* 52 ; *Reeve, Conch. Ic., f.* 15, *Voy. Erebus and Terror, Moll., pl.* 2, *f.* 14. Shell obliquely ovate, inæquilateral, sub-compressed ; covered with a shining golden green epidermis ; anterior end shorter, excavated at the lunule ; posterior longer, rounded ; areæ lanceolate, elevated, superficially oscurely concentrically sulcated (Adams.)
Wellington. N.S. Wales. (Angas.)

N. sulcata, *A. Adams, P.Z.S.*, 1856, *p.* 53 *(nec Philippi;) Reeve, Conch. Ic., f.* 10. Shell very convex, obliquely ovate ; umbones prominent ; anterior end shortly rounded ; pale olive strongly concentrically sulcated, radiately striated ; striæ stronger near the margins ; margins crenulated (Adams.)
Auckland to Wellington.

N. castanea, *A. Adams, P.Z.S.*, 1856, *p.* 53 ; *Reeve, Conch. Ic., f.* 19. Shell oval, very oblique, sub-compressed, chestnut, anterior end shortly truncated, middle of the lunule prominent ; posterior end sloping, rounded ; hardly smooth, obsoletely concentrically striated, obscurely radiately striated ; margin of valves closely crenulated (Adams.)
New Zealand. (Cuming.)

N. striolata, *A. Adams, P.Z.S.*, 1856 ; *Reeve, Conch. Ic., f.* 9. Shell oblique, sub-ovate, thick, ventricose, sculptured concentrically with flexuous, undulated sulci ; posterior side sub-trigonal ; dorsal margin sloped ; anterior side rather short ; lunule small ; umboes prominent, oblique, full (Sow.)
Sowerby says that the specimens in the British Museum, obtained from Mr. Cuming, came from New Zealand ; but Adams, when describing the same specimens, said that they came from the China Seas. Adams is probably right.

N. grayi, *D'Orbigny, Am. Merid, p.* 53; *Sowerby, in Reeve's Conch. Ic., f.* 13. Shell ovate, very transverse, slightly accuminated at both ends, thin, rather inflated, very smooth, olive; posterior side produced; dorsal area compressed, elevated, sub-aliform, end acuminated; anterior side a little produced, cuneated; lunule short, defined (Sow.)
New Zealand. (Cuming.) South America. (D'Orb.)

FAMILY—LEDIDÆ.

Labial palps appendiculate, convoluted, very long. Mantle freely open, the margins fringed and usually furnished with ventral lobes; siphonal tubes united, long, slender, and completely retractile. Gills narrow, plume-like, attached throughout their length. Foot compressed, slightly geniculate, deeply grooved, forming an oval disc with crenate edges. Shell oblong, thin, pearly within. Hinge as in *Nuculidæ;* ligament internal or external.

Genus, LEDA—Schumacher.

Shell oblong, rounded in front, produced and pointed behind; hinge like *Nucula*; margin even; pallial line with a small sinus; interior pearly.

L. concinna, *A. Adams, P.Z.S.,* 1856, *p.* 48; *Reeve, Conch. Ic., f.* 15. Shell very thin, compressed, sides gaping, pale brown, concentrically lirate; liræ narrow, regular, rather distant; anterior side short and rounded; posterior longer and beaked; beak produced, thin, sub-recurved, truncate; area lanceolate, narrow, bordered on each side by a crenate rib (Adams.)
Cook Strait to Stewart Island.

L. fastidiosa, *A. Adams, P.Z.S.,* 1856, *p.* 49; *Reeve, Conch. Ic., f.* 31 (?.) Shell transversely ovate, yellowish-brown, concentrically lirate with brown; shining, concentrically finely and regularly sulcated; anterior side sub-produced and rounded; posterior angulated and beaked; beak acuminate; ventral margin behind, sub-sinuous, and sub-produced in the middle (Adams). A shining, pale fuscous, ventricose species, very gibbous in the middle, and beautifully grooved transversely, the beak slender, pointed, and recurved (Adams.)
Reeve says that this species is smooth and straw-coloured; his figure does not agree with Adams' description.
New Zealand. (Cuming.)

L. micans, *A. Adams, in Thesaurus Conchyliorum; Sow. in Reeve's Conch. Ic., f.* 39. Shell acuminately ovate; pale fulvous, sculptured with fine oblique sulci, interrupted posteriorly in two rays; anterior side rather long; posterior side rather short, acuminate, radiately angulated, dorsal area depressed, narrow (Sowerby.)
New Zealand. (British Museum.)

Genus, SOLENELLA—Sowerby.

Shell oval, gaping and truncated behind; valves concentrically striated and covered with a brownish-green epidermis; hinge line straight, with small comb-like teeth.
South America. New Zealand and Kerguelen's Land only.

S. australis, *Quoy and Gaimard, l.c.,* iii., *p.* 471, *pl.* 78, *f.* 5-10 ; *Reeve, Conch. Ic., f.* 4 ; *Voy. Erebus and Terror, Moll., pl.* 2, *f.* 13 ; *Neilo cumingii, A. Adams, P.Z.S.,* 1852, *p.* 93 ; *Chenu, f.* 914. Transversely oblong, rounded in front ; produced and waved behind ; posterior dorsal margin slightly concave ; posterior end truncated, emarginated ; ventral margin straight ; valves with rather distant (about forty to an inch) concentric, rather elevated striæ ; pale olive-green, interior greyish-white.
Height, ·5 ; length, 1·1.
Wellington Harbour. Stewart Island.
The specimen from Stewart Island has the posterior margin less sinuated.

ORDER—HETEROMYA.

Muscular scars double, unequal, sometimes becoming monomyary in the adult. Shells generally equivalve, ligament external, no lateral teeth.

FAMILY—MYTILIDÆ.

Labial palps elongate, pointed, free. Mantle margins free, or united behind to form a more or less complete anal tube. Gills two on each side, nearly equal, elongated, dependent, united behind to each other and to the mantle. Foot narrow, strap-shaped, furnished with a byssal groove. Shell equivalve, oval or elongated, closed ; umbones anterior ; epidermis thick and dark, often filamentose ; ligament internal, submarginal, very long ; hinge edentulous ; pallial line simple ; anterior muscular impression small and narrow ; posterior large, obscure.

Sub-Family—Mytilinæ.

Hinder part of mantle only slightly produced ; anterior adductor muscle small.

Genus, MYTILUS—Linnæus.

Mantle freely open ; ventral margin simple ; branchial furnished with pinnated fringes ; anal opening plain and sessile. Shell wedge-shaped, rounded behind ; umbones terminal, pointed ; hinge teeth minute or obsolete ; pedal impressions two in each valve, small, simple, close to the adductors.

M. magellanicus, *Lamark, l.c.,* vii., *p.* 37 ; *Reeve, Conch. Ic., f.* 22 ; *Chenu, f.* 746. Oblong, sub-trigonal, angled, uncinate, with thick longitudinal undulating granulose ribs; bluish or reddish-purple; interior violet; a single small tooth in the right valve.

Height, 1·65; length, 3.

Common from Cook Strait southward. Chatham Islands. South America. Auckland Islands. Campbell Island. Kerguelen's Land.

M. polyodontes, *Quoy, l.c.,* iii., *p.* 462, *pl.* 78, *f.* 15-16. Similar to the last, but with eight or ten nearly equal teeth at the extremity of the hinge. Founded, I think, upon an erroneous observation.

M. latus, *Chemnitz (not of Lamark ;) Reeve, Conch. Ic., f.* 12 *and f.* 24; *M. smaragdinus, C.M.M.; M. canaliculatus. Martyn ?* Oblong, beak obtuse, swollen, smooth, margin even; covered with an olivaceous brown epidermis, under which it is green varied with chestnut-brown; margin green; inside purplish-white, iridescent; hinge with one or two small teeth.

Height, 3; length, 8·75.

A very variable shell; sometimes small specimens are bright-green, and sometimes pale yellow.

Common throughout New Zealand. Tasmania.

The young can hardly be distinguished from *M. smaragdinus* of China.

M. edulis, *L. Reeve, Conch. Ic., f.* 33; *M. dunkeri. Reeve, l.c., f.* 17? Oblong, oval, dilated and compressed behind; umbones slightly uncinate; covered with a dark olive-brown epidermis, below which it is blue; inside bluish-white, muscular impressions and a band round the margin blackish-blue; three or four small teeth in the left valve and one in the right.

Height, 1·6; length, 3.

Common in the South, not so common in the North. Great Barrier Island. Auckland Islands. Campbell Island.

This may be the *M. canaliculus,* of Hanley, which is also found in Kerguelen's Land; and perhaps *M. ungulatus,* Chemnitz.

M. ater, *Frauenfeld, Reise der Novara, Moll., pl.* 2, *ff.* 29-30. Small, oblong, inflated, black, obsoletely concentrically striated, covered with a shining coriaceous epidermis; narrow and obtuse in front, rounded behind; umbones tumid; dorsal margin declining in front, straight behind, near the base sub-parallel; ventral margin sub-sinuated, pearly, sub-fuscous or livid, slightly iridescent (Frauenfeld.)

Height, ·5; length, 1.

Common. Auckland to Dunedin.

Sub-Family—Crenellinæ.

Hinder part of the mantle produced, forming false siphons.

Genus, CRENELLA—Brown.

Mantle closed anteriorly; anal tube perfect and produced. Shell short and tumid; centre smooth and both ends ornamented with radia-

x

ting striæ; hinge margin crenulated behind the ligament; interior brilliantly nacreous.

C. impacta, *Hermann; Reeve, Conch. Ic (Modiola,) f.* 64; *C. discois, Lamark.* vii., *p.* 23; *Chenu, f.* 753. Oval, sub-diaphanous, the extremities radiately ribbed, and the middle finely longitudinally striated; brown, with sometimes a mixture of green near the edge; inside highly iridescent.

Height, ·85; length, 1·3.

Common. Auckland to Dunedin. Chatham Islands. Europe. North America.

Genus, MODIOLA—Lamark.

Margin of mantle simple, open; anal tube short, more or less perfect. Shell oblong, inflated in front; umbones anterior, obtuse; hinge toothless; pedal impressions three in each valve, the central elongated; epidermis often produced into long beard-like fringes.

M. australis, *Gray; Sowerby in Conch. Ic., f.* 21. Shell ovately fan-shaped; posterior side very short; anterior broadly dilated, convex in the middle, concentrically striated; yellowish chestnut, sparingly bearded towards the margin (Sowerby.)

Stewart Island. Australia.

M. areolata, *Gould, U.S., Ex. Ep.,* xii., *p.* 452, *f.* 562. Smooth, swollen; covered with chestnut-brown hairy epidermis, under which it is pinkish; inside yellowish-white, getting purplish behind.

Height, 1·15; length, 2.

Common. Chatham Islands. Auckland Islands.

The Natives call this shell "purewha."

Probably identical with the last.

M. fluviatilis, *Hutton, Jour. de Conch.,* 1866, *p.* 53. Smooth, finely concentrically striated; epidermis smooth, brownish-black, under which it is purple; inside bluish-white, purplish round the margin.

Height, ·5; length, 1.

Great Lagoon, Chatham Islands. Dunedin. In brackish water.

Sub-Family—Lithodominæ.

Hinder part of mantle more or less produced; anterior adductor muscle moderate.

Genus, LITHODOMUS—Cuvier.

Shell oblong, cylindrical, extremities rounded, covered with a thick epidermis; hinge linear without teeth; ligament marginal, internal; interior nacreous; boring in stones.

L. truncatus, *Gray, Dieff. N.Z.,* ii., *p.* 259. *Reeve, Conch. Ic., f.* 3; *Voy. Erebus and Terror, Moll., pl.* 2, *f.* 12. Shell oblong, sub-cylin-

drical, thin, short, and roundly truncated in front, contracted in the middle, and rather produced and tapering behind, covered with a dark brown periostraca; umbones rather prominent, inflexed; inner side purplish, rather pearly (Gray).
Auckland; rare in the south.

L. gruneri, *Reeve, Conch. Ic.,* f. 12. Shell acutely elongated, peculiarly angularly gibbous about the umbones, attenuated anteriorly; dark chestnut, obliquely flexuosely furrowed throughout (Reeve).
New Zealand. (Cuming.)
Carpenter says that this species is from Western America.

FAMILY—AVICULIDÆ.

Mantle freely open, margins cirrated; no siphons. Palps large. Foot small, cylindric, furnished with a byssal grove. Adductor muscles very unequal, the posterior much the larger. Shell sub-inequivalve, oblique, resting on the smaller or right valve, and attached by a byssus; interior nacreous; often eared, hinge line straight, cartilage in one or several grooves.

Genus, PINNA—Linnæus.

Mouth with foliaceous lips; anus with a long ligulate valve. Shell equivalve, wedge-shaped; umbones quite anterior; posterior end truncated and gaping; ligament groove linear, elongated.

P. zealandiæ, *Gray, Dieff. N.Z.,* ii., *p.* 259; *Reeve, Conch. Ic., f.* 13; *Voy. Erebus and Terror Moll., pl.* 3, *f.* 7; *P. senticosa, Gould, U.S. Ex. Ep., p.* 448. Triangular, elongate; brown; inside purplish; valves convex, with rather close obsolete longitudinal ribs, armed with close short semi-cylindrical hollow spines.
Height, 4; length, 9·5.
Auckland to Dunedin. Found also in Australia.

Genus, AVICULA—Klein.

Shell oblique inequivalve, fragile, rather smooth; right valve most convex; a sinus in the left for the passage of the byssus; hinge line straight, the extremities produced, the anterior coudiform or beaked; a single cardinal tooth in each valve under the beak.
I have not seen either of the two following species, and doubt the correctness of the locality.

A. glabra, *Gould, U.S. Ex. Ep., p.* 442, *f.* 552. Shell thin, semi-elliptical, slightly oblique, surface generally smooth and shining; color pale greenish, with opake white radations; dorsal edge long and straight, slightly produced into a queue, from which the posterior edge, after a slight inflexion, descends directly at right angles; back broadly rounded; anterior edge a little oblique; ear triangular, closely and loosely striated;

re-entering angle obtuse ; nacre silvery white, margin pale greenish or
ochreous; no perceptible cardinal tubercle, and with a short lateral
ridge simulating a tooth (Gould).

Length and height, 2¼ inches.

A. fucata, *Gould, U.S. Ex. Ep., p.* 441, *f.* 551. Shell obliquely
ovate, surface with short loose laminæ ; color radiated yellowish and
rose-red, shining ; dorsal edge produced into a short acute wing, externally forming a right angle, then sweeping backwards ; anterior forming
an acute angle and sweeping forwards forms the obliquely ovate outline ;
auricle long, triangular, finely and loosely laminated ; re-entering angle
a right angle, edge sharp and simple ; nacre silvery white, becoming
violaceous at the edge ; cardinal tooth of left valve very strongly
developed, inflexed ; lateral tooth short, delicate, bifurcate in right valve.

Length, 2½ inches ; height, 2¼ inches. (Gould.)

In his " Expedition Shells " Gould says that this species comes from
Fiji, but in the U.S. Ex. Ep. he says it comes from New Zealand.

ORDER—MONOMYA.

One adductor only ; ligament nearly internal; mantle unifoial ; hinge
nearly or quite toothless, with one circumpallial nerve ; no pallial sinus,
nor siphon. Shell generally inequivalve.

FAMILY—PECTINIDÆ.

Mouth surrounded by foliaceous leaflets ; labial palps truncated,
smooth externally, pectinated within. Mantle freely open, the margins
double, the inner pendent, bearing fringes of tentacular filaments, and at
its base a row of ocelli ; branchial leaflets equal, each pair partially
doubled on itself. Foot small, cylindrical, with a byssal grove. Sexes
united. Shell free or adhering, eared, ligament internal. Adductor
muscles united.

Genus, PECTEN—Linnæus.

Shell oblong or sub-orbicular, regular, equivalve, close ; valves
generally with scaly rays ; ears unequal, the posterior with a sinus for
the byssus ; hermaphrodite.

P. zealandiæ, *Gray, Dieff. N.Z.,* ii., *p.* 260 ; *Voy. Erebus and
Terror Moll., pl.* 3, *f.* 7 ; *P. dieffenbachii, Reeve, Conch. Ic., f.* 88. Sub-
orbicular, valves sub-equal, inflated, with about forty radiating sub-equal
rough ribs, sometimes ornamented with scales ; ears very unequal, margin
rather undulated ; variable in colour : yellow, red, purple, or brown.

Height, 1·65 ; breadth, 1·6.

Great Barrier Island to Stewart Island. Chatham Islands.

P. gemmulatus, *Reeve, Conch. Ic., f.* 111. Shell somewhat triangularly orbicular, thin compressed, equilateral, nearly equivalve, radiately
densely ridged, ridges here and there larger ; very beautifully, minutely,

prickly serrated throughout; whitish, stained with flesh rose ; ears very unequal (Reeve).
This appears to be the same as the last species.

P. multicostatus, *Reeve, Conch. Ic., f.* 173. Shell ovate, rather thin, gibbous, equilateral, equivalve; valves rayed by thirty rather distant, narrow, obscurely noduled ribs, finely scaled at the sides ; deep vermilion, unspotted, marbled with white at the umbones ; ears very unequal (Reeve).
Apparently the same as *P. zealandiæ.*

P. pica, *Reeve, Conch, Ic., f.* 173. Shell orbicular, compressed, equilateral, nearly equivalve, valves rayed with twenty-one narrow ribs, interstices excavated ; white variegated with grey and brown-black ; ears large, nearly equal (Reeve).
Distinguished by the ears being nearly equal.
New Zealand.   (Cuming.)

P. australis, *Sowerby, Thes. Conch.* 1. *p.* 76 ; *Reeve, Conch. Ic., f.* 103. Shell orbicular, sometimes rather ventricose, scarcely equilateral, equivalve, valves ranged with twenty-four ribs, which are peculiarly three divided, and densely finely serrated ; blackish violet or orange rose, unspotted ; ears unequal (Reeve).
Foveaux Straits.   Australia and Tasmania.
Mr. Tenison-Woods gives this as a variety of *P. asperimus.* Lamark.

P. radiatus, *Hutton, C.M.M., p.* 82. Orbicular, equivalve, compressed, with about eighty equal rough radiating striæ; ears unequal ; thin ; margin crenulated ; red, ochraceous, or brownish-purple.
Height, 1·8 ; breadth, 1·7.
Stewart Island, 13 fathoms.

P. (Dentipecten) vellicatus, *Hutton, C.M.M., p.* 82. Irregularly orbicular, sub-equivalve, produced in front, longitudinally irregularly five-plaited, and with small radiating ribs, crossed by fine concentric striæ ; ears unequal ; hinge line obscurely striated ; margin undulating. Reddish, purplish, or white spotted with pink.
Height, 1·6 ; breadth, 1·6.
Cook Strait to Stewart Island.
Possibly the same as *P. convexus* of Quoy and Gaimard, or *P. roseopunctatus,* Reeve, Conch. Ic., f. 84.

Genus, VOLA—Klein.

Shell sub-orbicular ; inequivalve ; superior valve flattened ; rayed ; ears nearly equal.

V. laticostatus, *Gray, Dieff, N.Z.,* ii., *p.* 260 ; *Pecten novæ zealandiæ, Reeve, Conch. Ic., f.* 36. Thick, with fourteen to eighteen smooth radiating ribs, the larger ones sometimes depressed, with one or two interrupted longitudinal grooves ; flat valve with the ribs distant and narrower ; reddish brown to purplish-white; interior white or brownish.
Height, 5·5 ; length, 6.

Common in the North, very rare in the South. South Australia. (Angas.) Chatham Islands.

Mr. Tenison-Woods regards this as identical with *Pecten fumatus, L.*

FAMILY—RADULIDÆ.

Body produced, in part linguiform. Mouth surrounded by tentacular filaments. Mantle without any ocelli on the edge, the margin fringed with tentacular filaments ; anal tubes cylindric, visible externally. Foot compressed, not byssiferous. Shell gaping at the sides, usually white. Hinge edentulous.

Genus, LIMA—Brug.

Shell equivalve, compressed, obliquely oval ; anterior side straight, gaping ; posterior rounded, usually close ; umbones apart, eared ; hinge area triangular, cartilage pit central ; adductor impression lateral, large, double ; pedal scars two, small.

L. zealandica, *Sowerby*, *P.Z.S.*, 1876, *p.* 754, *pl.* lxxv., *f.* 1. Shell broad, thick, rather inflated, radiately ribbed, slightly gaping on each side ; front side obliquely produced and concavely flattened, forming an oblong lunule terminating below the middle in a decided angle ; the other side obliquely rounded ; ribs eighteen in number, rather square, thick, scaled, sometimes of a reddish-brown color ; interstices between the ribs smooth, concave, equal in width to the ribs ; auricles small, sloping ; umbones acute, incurved (Sowerby).
This is the *L. squamosa* of former lists.
Stewart Island.

L. angulata, *Sowerby*, *Thes. Conch., Reeve's Conch. Ic.. f.* 13. Shell ventricose, white, obliquely sub-trigonal ; anteriorly angular at the ventral margin, very finely radiately striated ; posterior ventral margin finely dentated (Sowerby).
North Island. Panama and New Caledonia. S. Australia. (Angas).

L. japonica, *A. Adams, P.Z.S.*, 1863, *p.* 509 ; *Reeve, Conch. Ic.,* *f.* 21. Shell ovate, ventricose, broad, rather straight, nearly equilateral, rayed with numerous strong, rather sharp ribs ; ventral margin scarcely obliquely produced ; hinge margin broad ; auricles nearly equal ; umbones produced (Sow.)
Stewart Island. Japan.
Of the same form as *L. bullata*, but smaller and with smooth rays.

FAMILY—SPONDYLIDÆ.

Mouth with foliaceous lips ; palps short, oblong, pointed. Mantle freely open, the margins thickened, and furnished with numerous rows of tentacular cirri, many of which are truncate, and end in a smooth convex surface ; gills large, equal, separate. Foot small, cylindrical, truncated, ending in a disk, from the depressed centre of which issues a small, cylindrical tendon terminating in a small, oviform, fleshy mass. Shell irregular, attached by the right valve, radiately ribbed, spiny, or foliaceous; hinge with two strong teeth.

Genus, PLICATULA—Lamark.

Shell inequivalve, plicate, irregular, attached by the beak of the right valve; beaks not eared; hinge with two strong diverging cardinal teeth in each valve, with an intermediate cartilage pit.

P. novæ-zealandiæ, *Sowerby in Reeve's Conch. Ic., f.* 1. Shell thin, white, depressed, leafy at the sides; plaits numerous, obtuse, here and there divided, dentiform at the margin (Sowerby).

The ribs are so divergent, that those near the dorsal margin are at right angles with the central.

New Zealand. (British Museum).

FAMILY—ANOMIIDÆ.

Mouth with narrow, plain lips, confluent with the gills; palps obsolete. Mantle wide open, except at the hinge, with a double pendent margin, fringed with short cirri; no ocelli; gills two on each side, unsymmetrical, united posteriorly, and suspended by two falciform membranes; outer gill lamina, furnished with a broad reflexed margin. Foot small, cylindrical, expanded at the end and grooved. Sexes distinct; generative organs combined with the right mantle lobe. Ventricle exposed, not perforated by the rectum. Byssus large, laminar passing through a nearly complete foramen in the right mantle lobe, and attached by a powerful muscle to the centre of the left valve. Adductor moderate; pallial line continuous. Shell largely indented or with a variously formed opening near the summit of the inferior valve, for the passage of the adductor muscle, which is attached to a plug that adheres to foreign bodies.

Genus, ANOMIA—Linnæus.

Shell not eared, upper valve with three sub-central muscular scars; the anterior upper lobe of the notch separated from the cardinal edge; plug entirely shelly, and quite free from the edge of the notch.

A. stowei, *Hutton, C.M.M., p.* 83. Sub-orbicular, thick, solid, lower valve smooth; yellowish-white; interior dark green; notch large, ovate, anterior lobe widely separated from the cardinal edge; muscular impressions two only, strongly marked; upper large, broadly oval or sub-orbicular; lower much smaller on the posterior lower edge of the larger, and confluent with it, sub-orbicular.

Diameter, 3·5.

Picton.

A. alectus, *Gray, P.Z.S.,* 1849, *p.* 117; *Reeve, Conch. Ic., f.* 28. Irregular, upper valves convex, reddish, internally pearly; lower valve

green, internally green; upper scar large oblong; lower scars two, large, rather smaller than the upper one, close together but not confluent, the lowest one the largest (Gray).
Stewart Island. Peru.
A doubtful determination.

A. cytæum, *Gray*, *P.Z.S*, 1849, *p.* 115. Shell sub-orbicular smooth; internally reddish, upper muscular scar very large, sub-cordate; lower two, sub-orbicular, smaller, nearly equal sized; the upper in the notch of the upper (sic.) one; the lower hinder close to lower hinder' edge of the upper one; sinus in lower valve large (Gray).
Stewart Island. China.
A very doubtful determination.

Genus, PLACUNANOMIA—Broderip.

Shell not eared; upper valve with two sub-central muscular scars; the anterior lobe of the upper notch agglutinated to the cardinal edge; plug shelly at the top and near the body to which it is attached, and with horny longitudinal laminæ below and internally.

P. zealandica, *Gray, Dieff, N.Z.,* ii., *p.* 260 ; *Reeve, Conch. Ic.,* *f.* 4 ; *Voy. Erebus and Terror, pl.* 3, *f.* 10 ; *Chenu, f.* 984. Sub-orbicular, white, smooth; upper valve with distant radiating grooves; internally dark green; upper valve with two confluent scars; upper oblong, longitudinal, lower rather small and more transverse; thin, translucent (Gray).
Stewart Island to Auckland.

P. ione, *Gray, Proc. Zool. Soc.,* 1849, *p.* 123 ; *Reeve, Conch. Ic.,* *f.* 6. White, laminar; edge of the laminæ with small, slender, elongated processes; interior green; lower muscular scar small, round, on the lower hinder edge of the larger one; sinus or perforations large (Gray).
Stewart Island. Australia. Tasmania.

FAMILY—OSTREIDÆ.

Labial appendages triangular, connected round the mouth by a plain membrane; palps separate from the gills. Mantle entirely open, the edges double, and each bordered by short tentacular fringes; no conspicuous ocelli; branchial leaflets not doubled on themselves. Foot obsolete. Shell inequivalve, inequilateral, irregular, close and fixed by the inferior valve, which is the largest, or free; beaks central, straight ; adductor impression single, behind the centre ; hinge toothless.

Genus, OSTREA—Linnæus.

Irregular, attached by the left valve ; upper valve flat or concave, often plain; lower convex, often plaited or foliaceous, and with a prominent beak; ligamental cavity triangular or elongated; herma-phrodite.

O. edulis, *L. Reeve, Conch. Ic., f.* 8 ; *O. purpurea, Hanley,* *Conch. miscel. pt.* 3 ; *O. chilœnsis, Sowerby in Reeve's Conch. Ic., f.* 33 ; *O. virginica, C.M.M., not of Lamark.* Ovato-orbicular, upper valve flat, laminated with imbricating scales; lower rugged, wrinkled ; liga-ment pit small, triangular; muscular impression large, lunate, scarcely hollowed ; purplish, white near the hinge ; interior yellowish or greenish white, margin purple, waved.

Diameter about 2.

Common. The mud oyster. Australia and Tasmania.

Very variable in shape and color.

O. discoidea, *Gould, U.S. Ex. Ep.,* xii., *p.* 463 ; *Reeve, Conch. Ic., f.* 26 ; *O. lutaria, Hutton, C.M.M., p.* 84. Shell rounded, flattened, finely striated, whitish-brown, rayed with pale purple, sub-equivalve ; hinge small ; lower valve convex, muscular impression very large ; upper valve much compressed (Sowerby).

Pelorus Sound ; Catlin River.

A doubtful identification; perhaps the same as the last.

O. glomerata, *Gould, U.S. Ex. Ep.* xii., *p.* 461 ; *Reeve, Conch. Ic., f.* 52. Shell thick, irregular, sharp ribbed, with the margin dentated or lobed, very inequivalve ; upper valve opercular, compressed. wrinkled with thick concentric laminæ; lower valve cucullated, purple, white within edged with purple or black ; lateral margins denticulated ; hinge generally attenuated, produced pointed (Sowerby).

The Rock-Oyster of Auckland ; not found further south.

O. reniformis, *Sowerby ; Reeve's Conch. Ic., f.* 57. Shell thick, elongated, narrow, laterally arched, whitish, inequivalve ; upper valve compressed, flattened, a little leafy towards the margins, edged within with purple ; lower valve deeply excavated, ventral margin straight, muscular impressions blackish-purple (Sowerby).

The rock-oyster of Dunedin is referred with great doubt to this species.

Class—Brachiopoda.

Body protected by a bivalve shell applied to the dorsal and ventral surfaces of the animal. Head none. Mouth with two long cirriferous arms; no branchiæ, respiration being effected by the lobes of the mantle. Sexes distinct or united.

ORDER—ARTICULATA.

The two valves united by a hinge ; the ventral valve generally with teeth, which are received into sockets in the dorsal valve. Two adductor and two divaricator muscles ; the latter running obliquely from the ventral valve to the median, or cardinal, process of the dorsal valve.

FAMILY—TEREBRATULIDÆ.

Shell minutely punctate ; ventral valve with a prominent beak, perforated by a foramen, for the passage of the peduncle. Foramen partly surrounded by a deltidium of one or two pieces. Oral appendages entirely or partially supported by calcified processes, usually in the form of a loop, and always fixed to the dorsal valve.

Genus, WALDHEIMIA—King.

Foramen complete ; loop elongated and reflected, attached to the hinge plate ; median septum of the smaller valve elongated.

W. lenticularis, *Deshayes. Mag. Zool.,* 1841, *t.* 41 ; *Reeve, Conch. Ic. (Terebratula), f.* 4. Orbicular. smooth, red ; margins even ; beak small, recurved ; foramen small ; deltidium conspicuous ; loop elongated, reflected.

Length, 2 ; breadth, 1·83 ; height, 1·17.
Cook Strait to Stewart Island.

Genus, TEREBRATELLA—D'Orbigny.

Loop elongated, reflected. attached to the hinge plate, and also to the longitudinal septum by processes given off at right angles from the crura, near the centre of the valve.

T. cruenta, *Dillwyn ; Reeve, Conch. Ic. (Terebratula), f.* 20 ; *T. rubra, Sowerby ; T. zealandica, Deshayes.* Rounded, ventricose, ornamented with radiating dichotomous ribs; orange-red, deepest at the lines of growth; margins crenulated; dorsal valve with a central, longitudinal depression; beak somewhat produced, lateral ridges distinct; area large, rounded; foramen large, complete; deltidium large; loop elongated, doubly attached.

Length, 1·5; breadth, 1·6; height, 1.

Cook Strait to Stewart Island.

T. rubicunda, *Solander; T. sanguinea, Q. & G., l.c.* iii., *p.* 556, *pl.* 85, *f.* 6-7; *Reeve, Conch. Ic., f.* 27; *T. inconspicua, Sow.* Shell somewhat triangularly ovate, deep red, or colourless, pale towards the beak, beak tumidly produced, rather erect, foramen large, sometimes entire, sometimes with the deltidium divided; valves gibbous, flexuously channelled in the middle; apophysis elongated, conspicuously doubly attached (Reeve).

Common. Auckland Islands. Chatham Islands.

Genus, MAGAS—Sowerby.

Shell with a reflected loop attached near the bend to a very prominent central septum.

M. evansii, *Davidson, P.Z.S.,* 1852, *p.* 77, *pl.* xiv., *f.* 7-9. Subovate, with a few unequal bifurcating ribs; pale red; beak tapering, slightly recurved, with well-defined lateral ridges; foramen incomplete; deltidia small; area flattened; dorsal valve rather flat; loop elongated, doubly attached; septum produced, nearly touching the opposite valve.

Length, ·33; breadth, ·3; height, ·13.

Possibly the young of *T. cruenta.*

Genus, WALTONIA—Davidson.

Oval, smooth, punctate; valves convex; margins sinuated; beak truncated by a large incomplete foramen; deltidia separate; loop reduced to two simple lamellæ, furnished with oral processes, and attached to a prominent central septum.

New Zealand only. Only one minute specimen is known in the Paris Museum, and in it the loop may possibly have been broken away; if so it should be referred to *Terebratella.*

W. valencienni, *Davidson, Ann. Nat. Hist.,* 1850, *pl.* 15, *f.* 1. *Reeve, Conch, Ic., f.* 31. Small, oval, red, smooth, with the margin fimbriated, the plaits radiating in front, diverging at the sides; dorsal valve nearly flat; ventral valve convex; beak prominent; foramen large and incomplete; deltidia dis-united.

Length, ·2; breadth, ·17; height, ·1.

Probably the same as *Magas evansii.*

Genus, BOUCHARDIA—Davidson.

Apophysary system anchor-shaped, consisting of an elevated central plate, to which are affixed two short lamellæ.

B. cumingii, *Davidson, P.Z.S.,* 1852, *p.* 78, *pl.* xiv., *f.* 10-16; *Reeve, Conch. Ic., f.* 29. Shell somewhat pyriformly ovate, thick, flexuous at the margin, whitish, tinged with rose; beak acuminately produced, but little incurved; foramen small, entire, terminal; deltidium obsolete, area impressly concave, rather rough; valves equally convex, sides callous within; loop doubly attached, septum large, anchor-shaped, callous (Reeve).

New South Wales. (Angas.)

Probably my *IV. tapirina* (Cat. Tert. Moll. p. 36) is this species; it must not be confounded with *Terebratulina cumingii,* David. from China, which is very different.

Genus, KRAUSSIA—Davidson.

Sub-circular, with a nearly straight hinge line; beak truncated; foramen large and round; deltidia small, disunited; beak laterally keeled; hinge area flat; dorsal valve longitudinally depressed; internal skeleton consisting of a small forked process arising from the septum, near the centre of the valve.

K. lamarkiana, *Davidson, P.Z.S.,* 1852, *p.* 80, *pl.* xiv., *f.* 22-23; *Reeve, Conch. Ic., f.* 34. Sub-orbicular, striated with fine bifurcating ridges, light yellow; hinge area well defined, flat; foramen large, incomplete; deltidia small; dorsal valve with a central longitudinal groove; apophysis central, bifurcating; margins of the valves thickened internally and spinulose.

Length, ·25; breadth, ·25; height, ·12.

Australia. Tasmania.

FAMILY—RHYNCHONELLIDÆ.

Animal free, or attached by a muscular peduncle issuing from an aperture situated under the extremity of the beak of the ventral valve. Arms spirally rolled, flexible, and supported only at their origin by a pair of short, curved, shelly processes. Shell, structure, fibrous and impunctate.

Genus, RHYNCHONELLA—Fischer.

Trigonal, acutely beaked, usually plaited; dorsal valve elevated in front, depressed at the sides; ventral valve flattened, or hollowed along the centre, hinge plates supporting two slender curved lamellæ; dental plates diverging.

R. nigricans, *Sowerby, Thes. Conch.,* i., *p.* 342; *Reeve, Conch., Ic., f.* 1. Thin, irregular, longitudinally ribbed; margin crenulated. Brown or blackish.

Length, ·7; breadth, ·8; height, ·4.

Not uncommon in the South. Chatham Islands.

Class—Polyzoa.

Alimentary canal suspended in a double walled sac, capable of being partially protruded ; mouth surrounded by a circle of hollow ciliated tentacles ; animals always composite.

ORDER—PHYLACTOLÆMATA.

Lophophore bi-lateral ; mouth with an epistome.

Sub-Order—Lophophea.

Arms of lophophore free or obsolete. (Fresh water.)

FAMILY—PLUMATELLIDÆ.

Zoarium rooted.

Genus, PLUMATELLA.—Bosc.

Zoarium confervoid, branched, composed of a series of membrano-corneous tubular cells, each of which constitutes a short ramulus with a terminal orifice ; branches distinct from one another. Lophophore crescentric, with two long arms.

P. aplinii, *Macgillivray,* *Trans. Royal Soc. Vic.* 1860, *p.* 204. Zoarium adherent, creeping ; cells cylindrical, with a distinct keel ; aperture oblique.
Homebush Creek, Malvern Hills, under stones. Australia.
I have only examined dried specimens, but Macgillivray says that the tentacula are about sixty, and the statoblasts elongated. It approaches very near to *P. emarginata* of Europe.

ORDER—GYMNOLÆMATA.

Lophophore orbicular, or nearly so ; no epistome. Marine.

Sub-Order—Cheilostomata.

Polypide completely retractile ; evagination of tentacular sheath perfect ; orifice of cell sub-terminal, of less diamater than the cell, and usually closed with a moveable lip or shutter ; sometimes by a contractile sphincter ; cells not tubular ; consistence calcareous, corneous, or fleshy.

FAMILY—CATENICELLIDÆ.

Zoarium divided into distinct internodes by flexible joints, internodes formed by a single series of cells.

Genus, CATENICELLA—Blainville.

Cells arising from the upper and back part of the lower one by a short corneous tube, all facing the same way, and forming dichotomously divided branches of an erect phytoid zoarium ; cell at each bifurcation geminate ; each cell with two lateral processes usually supporting an avicularium ; ovicells either sub-globose and terminal, or galeriform, and placed below the opering of a cell in front.
This is altogether a southern genus.

(a.) Fenestratæ.
Cells fenestrate in front ; ovicells terminal.

C. ventricosa, *Busk, Cat. Pol. Brit. Mus., p.* 7. Cells oval, compressed ; avicularia wide, sometimes supporting a cup-like cavity, sometimes a closed broad conical spine, fenestræ seven, with fissures radiating towards a rounded central pore ; front of cell studded with minute acuminate papillæ ; back smooth, sometimes spotted. Dirty white ; 3 or 4 inches long.
Lyall Bay. Bass Straits, 45 fathoms.

C. hastata, *Busk, l.c., p.* 7 *; C. bicuspis, Gray, Dieff, N.Z.*, ii., *p.* 293. Cells oval ; fenestræ seven to nine, disposed in a crescent, with fissures radiating towards the median line ; avicularia supporting large, pyramidal, pointed, hollow processes, compressed and perforated before and behind by five or six small circular pores. Yellowish-white or reddish ; 3 or 4 inches long.
Lyall Bay. Bass Straits, 45 fathoms.

C. aurita, *Busk, l.c., p.* 8. Cells oval or sub-globose ; avicularia large and strong, two blunt processes, the upper the longer, on each side of the opening in front ; fenestræ five, around a central one.
Cook Strait (Lyall). Campbell's Island. Bass's Strait.

C. cribraria, *Busk, l.c., p.* 9. Cells sub-globular, compressed, more or less alate ; avicularia large, without any superior appendage, and prolonged downwards into elevated lateral alæ ; fenestræ numerous, small, round, equidistant, the outside ones larger ; a minute central pore.
Lyall Bay. Bass Straits, 45 fathoms.

C. margaritacea, *Busk, l.c., p.* 9. Cells oval or sub-globular, much compressed ; avicularia short and broad, supporting a deep, cup-like cavity ; fenestræ five, large, with fissures radiating upwards ; lower margin of aperture notched in the middle ; back of the cell minutely sulcate ; sulci short, interrupted, irregular.
Lyall's Bay. Swan Island. Australia.

(*b.*) Vittatæ.

Cells furnished with a narrow elongated band or " vitta " on each side ; without fenestræ ; ovicells galeriform, not terminal.

C. perforata, *Busk, l.c., p.* 10. Cells elongated oval ; avicularium processes large, perforated at the base, or by several openings ; vittæ long, wider below, lateral ; surface in front papillose.
New Zealand (Hooker, Lyall, Darwin). Tasmania. Australia.

C. ringens, *Busk, l.c., p.* 10. Cells ovoid or sub-globular ; avicularia usually very unequal, the larger one gaping ; vittæ anterior, broad ; surface in front smooth.
New Zealand (Dieffenbach). South Africa.'

C. elegans, *Busk, l.c., p.* 10. Cells elongated ovoid ; avicularia large and projecting, without any superior appendage ; vittæ narrow, sub-lateral, surface in front papillose.
Port Cooper. Banks Peninsula. Bass Straits, 47 fathoms. South Africa. Port Dalrymple.

C. cornuta, *Busk, Voyage of Rattlesnake,* I., *p.* 361. Cells oval; avicularia in most cells wholly transformed into long pointed retrocedent spines, on one or both sides, in others into shorter spines or unaltered ; vittæ linear, extremely narrow, entirely lateral, and extending the whole length of the cell from the base of the avicularium. Surface in front smooth. Yellowish-white.
New Zealand (Darwin). Bass Straits.

(*c.*) Simplices.

Without vittæ or fenestræ.

C. scutella, *Hutton ; C. alata, Hutton, C.M.M., p.* 89; *not of Wyv. Thomson.* Cells ovate, narrowed below ; lateral processes projecting horizontally and forwards from the whole length of the cell ; · mouth round, simple, with a thickened rim, placed in the upper part of the cell ; surface smooth, with a single median pore (fenestra?), and occasionally another on each side of it.
Lyall Bay.

C. geminata, *Wyv. Thomson, Nat. Hist. Rev.,* 1858, *Q.J.M.S.* 7, *p.* 147. Axial cell, geminate. The secondary cell developed alternately on either side of the axis. Axial cells, pyriform ; a large gaping avicularium on the angle opposite the secondary cell ; secondary cell giving off by a terminal horny tube a single wedge-shaped peripheral cell ; cell mouth, large ; a deep notch in the centre of the lower lip ; in the primary and secondary axial cell four or five blunt spines surround the upper margin of the mouth, which is surmounted in the peripheral cells by two longer ear-like processes ; front of cell tuberculated.
A small species epiphytic on red algæ.
New Zealand (Dr. Joliffe). Australia.

C. carinata, *Busk, Voyage of Rattlesnake, Vol.* I., *p.* 363. Cells oval, narrowed at each end; lateral processes (without avicularia ?) projecting horizontally outwards from the side of the aperture, which is nearly central; mouth with a small tooth on each side, and below it a triangular space with three strong conical eminences; a few scattered papillæ on the surface of the sides and back; ovicelligerous cells geminate.

New Zealand (Dr. Joliffe). Bass Strait.

FAMILY—CELLULARIIDÆ.

Zoarium divided into distinct internodes by flexible joints; internodes formed by two or more cells in a row; cells disposed in the same plane, forming linear branches of a dichotomously divided, phytoid, erect, zoarium.

Genus, CELLULARIA—Pallas.

Cells bi-triserial, more than four in each internode; oblong or rhomboidal, contiguous; perforated behind; without avicularia or vibracula.

C. cuspidata, *Busk, l.c., p.* 19. Upper and outer angle produced into a strong spine; a single perforation behind; a cuspidate spine on the summit of the median cell at each bifurcation; ovicell smooth.

Lyall's Bay. Australia.

C. monotrypa, *Busk, Voyage of Rattlesnake, Vol.* I., *p.* 368. Cells oblong, narrowed below, with a single perforation in the upper and outer part behind; opening oval. margin smooth; a short spinous process at the upper and outer angle; a sharp, short spine in the middle of the upper border of the middle cell, at a bifurcation; ovicell (?) in form of a very shallow excavation in the upper part of the cell in front.

New Zealand (Darwin). Bass Strait.

Genus, MENIPEA—Lamouroux.

Cells oblong or elongated, attenuated downwards; imperforate behind, sometimes with a sessile avicularium on the upper and outer angle; one or two sessile avicularia on the front of the cell below the aperture.

M. cirrata, *Gray, Dieff, N.Z.,* ii., *p.* 292. Cells pyriform, constricted below, six in each internode, one of the lower usually more or less aborted; usually one large lateral avicularium to each internode; three marginal spines very long and strong; anterior avicularium single, its upper border toothed.

New Zealand (Dr. Sinclair). South Africa.

M. buskii, *Wyv. Thomson, Nat. Hist. Rev,* 1858, *Q.J.M.S.,* 7, *p.* 151. Cells, elongated, attenuated downwards, three in each internode; cell-mouth, large, oval, oblique, the lower third filled up by a tuberculated calcareous plate; upper lip prolonged, and fringed with from four to five spines, attached to the lip by horny joints, and one of them, usually the second from the outer edge, very long, curved, and pod-like; there is often an additional spine on the upper and inner margin of the cell-mouth; operculum spine, strong and clavate, stretching upwards and outwards from the lower and inner lip of the cell-aperture; connecting horny tube between the internodes, double; ovicell, spherical, with a richly granular surface, imbedded among the cells, on the cavities of two of which it encroaches.

New Zealand (Dr. Joliffe). Tasmania.

Genus, SCRUPOCELLARIA—Van Beneden.

Cells rhomboidal, with a sinus on the outer and hinder aspect; each furnished with a sessile avicularium at the upper and outer angle, and with a vibraculum placed in the sinus on the outer and lower part behind; aperture oval or sub-rotund, spinous above, with or without a pedunculate operculum; cells bi-serial and numerous at each internode.

S. scruposa, *Linnæus.* Cells sub-elongate, narrow; aperture elliptical, with three or four spines above; ovicell smooth.

Lyall Bay. Europe.

S. scrupea, *Busk, Ann. Nat. Hist.,* 2nd *Ser., Vol* 7., *p.* 83, *pl.* ix., *f.* 11-12. Cells rhomboidal, truncated above and below, sinuated behind; aperture sub-oval, margin a little thickened, armed above with four or five spines; operculum peduncled, reniform; ovicell, cucullate, sub-appressed, smooth.

New Zealand. (Dr. Joliffe). Europe.

Genus, EMMA—Gray.

Cells in pairs or triplets; opening more or less oblique, sub-triangular, partially filled up by a granulated calcareous expansion; a sessile avicularium generally on the outer side below the level of the opening.

Found only in Australia and New Zealand.

E. crystallina, *Gray, Dieff. N.Z.,* ii. *p.* 293. Cells in pairs; one, two, or three spines on the outer edge, the central usually the longest and strongest.

Bass Straits, 45 fathoms.

Parasitic upon *Polyzoa,* &c.; circinate, branched; branches irregular, divaricate; the opening of the cell triangular, very obliquely placed.

Lyall Bay. Campbell Island.

E. tricellata, *Busk, l.c., p.* 28. Cells in triplets; three or four long spines on the upper and outer part, a small spine on the inner and lower part of the margin of the aperture.

New Zealand (Hooker). Bass Straits. Campbell Island.

Parasitic upon *Catenicella,* &c. Habit long, straggling.

A ii.

FAMILY—SALICORNARIIDÆ.

Zoarium divided into internodes by flexible joints; internodes formed by cells disposed around an imaginary axis, forming cylindrical branches of a dichotomously divided erect zoarium.

Genus, SALICORNARIA—Cuvier.

Front of cell depressed, surrounded by an elevated ridge, by which the surface is divided into more or less regular rhomboidal or hexagonal spaces ; no aperture ; avicularia disposed irregularly.

S. farciminoides, *Johnston, Hist. Brit. Zooph., p.* 355. Front of cell rhomboidal, or hexagonal with a straight side at top and bottom, sometimes arched above ; cells in the same series contiguous ; surface granular ; avicularium distinct from and above a cell, rostrum immersed, mandible semicircular.
Europe. South Africa. Australia.

S. malvinensis, *Busk, l.c., p.* 18. Front of cell arched above, very acute below ; cells distant in the same series ; surface smooth ; avicularium replacing a cell, rostrum immersed, mandible wide, large, triangular, pointed.
South America. Falkland Islands.

Genus, ONCHOPORA—Busk.

Cells, ventricose, coalescent ; not boardered by a raised margin ; ovicells, inconspicuous.
New Zealand only.

O. hirsuta, *Lamx., Hist. des Polyp. cor., p.* 126, *Pl.* ii., *f.* 4. Front of cell rhomboidal, margin raised, surface granular ; cells in the same series distant ; a long corneous tube at the base of each cell.
Lyall Bay.

FAMILY—SCRUPARIADÆ.

Zoarium continuous throughout ; cells uni-serial.

Genus, ÆTEA—Lamouroux.

Cells tubular, erect, scattered, rising from a creeping fistular fibre adnate to a foreign base ; aperture terminal, or sub-terminal.

Æ. dilatata, *Busk. Ann. Nat. Hist.,* 1851, *p.* 85. *pl.* ix., *f.* 14. Cells cyathiform at the apex, curved, ringed, aperture largely dilated, sub-orbicular. (Busk.)
Torres Strait (?) (Quekett.) Foveaux Straits. (G. Joachim.)

Genus, BEANIA—Johnston.

Zoarium confervoid, sub-corneous, or calcareous; cells arising one from another by a slender filiform tube; cell open in front, the edges of the opening furnished with hollow spinous processes arching over the opening; mouth terminal, with a denticle on each side.

B. swainsoni, *Hutton, C.M.M., p.* 91. Zoarium erect, phytoid, dichotomously branched, sub-corneous : cells sub-continuous, one arising from the top of another ; costæ eight to twelve.
From the collection of the late W. Swainson.

FAMILY—CABEREIDÆ.

Zoarium continuous throughout, erect, or flexible, dichotomously divided into ligulate bi-multiseral branches, on the backs of which are vibracula, or avicularia, one common to several cells ; avicularia sessile.

Genus, CABEREA—Lamouroux.

Back of the branches covered with large vibracula, which are placed obliquely in two rows, diverging in an upward direction from the middle line, where the vibracula of either side decussate with those of the other ; avicularia, when present, sessile on the front of the cell.

C. boryi, *Andouin, Busk, l.c., p.* 38 ; *Selbia zealandica, Gray, Dieff, N.Z.,* ii., *p.* 292. Cells bi-serial ; aperture oval ; pedunculate operculum expanded principally downwards, and sometimes sending off a process to the opposite side of the aperture ; a single spine on the inner side springing from the peduncle of the operculum ; two marginal spines on the outer side of the aperture ; ovicell large, arcuate ; vibracula ovoid, setæ serrated.
Lyall Bay. England. South Africa. South America. Cumberland Island.

C. lata, *Busk, l.c., p.* 39. Bi-multiserial ; marginal cells with a single sub-apical spine ; central cells without marginal spines ; setæ serrated.
Australia.
Perhaps a variety of *C. hookeri, Johnston, Brit. Zooph., p.* 338 (Busk).

FAMILY—BICELLARIIDÆ.

Zoarium continuous, erect, dichotomously divided into narrow ligulate, bi- or multiserial branches; no vibracula ; avicularia, when present, pedunculate and articulated.

Genus, BICELLARIA—Fleming.

Cells turbinate, distant ; aperture directed more or less upwards ; several spines, marginal or dorsal.

B. tuba, *Busk, l.c., p.* 42. Aperture round, looking almost directly upwards ; a digitiform hollow process below the outer border, supporting two or four long incurved spines ; two or three other long curved sub-marginal spines behind or above the aperture, none below it in front ; a solitary spine on the back, a short way down the cell ; avicularia very long, trumpet-shaped, arising from the back of the cell.
Lyall Bay. Bass Strait, 45 fathoms.

Genus, HALOPHILA—Gray.

Cells continuous, attenuated downwards, much expanded upwards, with a large plain aperture ; unarmed.
Australia and New Zealand only.

H. johnstoniæ, *Gray, l.c.,* ii., *p.* 292. Cells obliquely truncated above, with a short spine on the outer angle ; aperture large oval ; margin slightly thickened. Pale gray.
Lyall Bay. Bass Strait.

Genus, BUGULA—Oken.

Cells elliptical (viewed behind). closely contiguous, bi-multiserial ; aperture very large ; margin simple, not thickened ; avicularia, when present, pedunculate and articulated.

B. neritina, *Linnæus ; Busk, l.c., p.* 44. Cells quadrangular, lengthened, with a truncated summit, the angles projecting.
Lyall Bay. Australia. Auckland Islands. Red Sea. Rio de Janeiro.

B. dentata, *Lamouroux, Busk, l.c., p.* 46 ; *Acamarchis tridentata, Krauss.* Cells bi-serial, oblong, rounded at each end ; aperture oval ; three marginal spines on the outer side, and one on the inner ; avicularia lateral, capitate ; ovicell superior, cucullate, blue. Gray or blue (Busk).
New Zealand (Hooker, Lyall). Australia. Tasmania. South Africa.

B. prismatica, *Gray, l.c.,* ii., *p.* 292. Zoarium rather rigid, compressed, dichotomously branched, erect, reddish-brown ; cells, distant, alternate, cylindrical ; aperture, entire, produced into a dentiform angle at the outer margin, from which a keel descends obliquely to the inner and lower corner of the cell ; ovarian cells, globular, white, situated in a single row on the front of the zoarium.
Motanau, Canterbury ; and Ocean Beach, Dunedin. (F.W.H.)

Genus, MUSCARIA—Hutton.

Cells multiserial, arranged back to back on both sides of the branches.
New Zealand only.

M. armata, *Hutton, C.M.M., p.* 93. Branches robust, flattened ; cells oval, convex, arranged in longitudinal rows which are divided by elevated ridges ; cells in the same series contiguous ; a long curved smooth spine by the side of every alternate cell ; aperture small, transverse, oval, the lower lip prominent. Avicularia ——(?).

Zoarium about an inch in height, brown. When viewed by transmitted light, pale brown, with the lips of the aperture dark brown.

Motanau. On the roots of *Bollenia australis*

FAMILY—FLUSTRIDÆ.

Zoarium flexible, expanded, foliaceous, erect, sometimes decumbent and loosely attached ; cells multiserial, quincuncial or irregular.

Genus, FLUSTRA—Linnæus.

Cells contiguous, on both sides of the frond.

F. papyracea, *Ellis* ; *Busk, l.c., p.* 48. Cells oblong, slightly enlarged upwards, a short marginal spine at each upper angle ; avicularia fusiform, situated on the right or left marginal spine ; olivaceous, in places pinkish.

Lyall Bay. Britain.

Genus, CARBASEA—Busk.

Cells continuous, on one side only of the frond.

C. pisciformis, *Busk, l.c., p.* 50. Cells (viewed behind) elongated, truncated at both ends, contracted at the waist ; in front pyriform, much expanded in the middle, contracted at the top and tapering downwards, slightly expanding again at the end; aperture large, occupying most of the front of the cell ; ovicells immersed, marked with radiating lines.

New Zealand. Cook Strait. Tasmania. Australia.

C. episcopalis, *Busk, l.c., p.* 52. Cells pyriform, cylindrical or barrel-shaped ; back marked with transverse rugæ ; aperture circular, superior ; ovicells lofty, keeled ; avicularia none ; pale stone colour.

Lyall Bay. Bass Strait, 45 fathoms.

C. indivisa, *Busk, l.c., p.* 53. Frond semicircular, undivided, sub-plicated ; cells oblong, surface behind granulated; ovicells —— (?). avicularia none (Busk).

New Zealand (Hooker).

P. cyathiformis, *Macgillivray, Trans. Phil. Inst., Victoria,* 1859, *p.* 97, *f.* 2. Zoarium infundibuliform, with the cells on the inner surface, white, translucent ; cells pyriform or oval, smooth, arranged in radiating series ; avicularia none ; aperture lunate, not extending across the front of the cell.

Lyall Bay ; on *Catenicella.* Australia.

Genus, DIACHORIS—Busk.

Cells disjunct, each connected with six others by tubular processes ; frond sometimes partially adnate and decumbent.
A southern genus only.

D. magellanica, *Busk, l.c., p.* 54. Cells semi-erect, open in front, oval ; mouth circular, with a thickened and raised margin ; a pedunculate and articulated capitate avicularium attached to the margin of the cell near the top on each side ; ovicell ——(?) (Busk).
New Zealand (Lyall).   Straits of Magellan.
Frondose, with cells on both sides, also loosely adnate.

D. inermis, *Busk, l.c., p.* 54. Cells decumbent, boat-shaped, entirely open ; two short marginal spines on each side near the top ; ovicell ——(?), avicularia ——(?) (Busk).
New Zealand (Lyall).   Straits of Magellan.

D. buskiana, *Hutton, C.M.M., p.* 94. Cells semi-erect, membranous, oval, open in front ; mouth circular, with a projecting lower lip, and often a small nodule in the centre ; nodule and lower lip granulated, the rest finely transversely striated ; connecting tubular processes short, about eleven to each cell.
Lyall Bay.
Encrusting seaweeds, loosely attached.

FAMILY—FARCIMINARIIDÆ.

Zoarium continuous, erect, flexible, dichotomously branched ; branches cylindrical, the cells disposed round an imaginary axis.

Genus, FARCIMINARIA—Busk.

Corneous, flexible ; margin of cell much raised ; aperture occupying the whole front of the cell ; ovicell cucullate.
A Southern genus only.

F. aculeata, *Busk, l.c., p.* 33. Sides of the cells within the margin beset with furcate spines ; ovicell cucullate, external ; surface aculeate (Busk).
New Zealand (Lyall).   Tasmania.

F. blainvillii, *Lamouroux ; Gray, l.c.,* ii., *p.* 293. Sub-quadrangular, formed of four series of ovate convex cells, with an oblong margined mouth, and scattered with flexible root-like fibres (Gray).
New Zealand.   (Dr. Sinclair.)

FAMILY—GEMELLARIIDÆ.

Zoarium continuous, dichotomously branched ; branches with cells in opposite pairs.

Genus, CALWELLIA—Wyv. Thomson.

Cells in pairs, joined back to back ; each pair of cells arising by tubular prolongations from the pair next but one below it ; each pair having a direction at right angles to the next ; at a bifurcation, each cell of the primary pair giving off a secondary pair ; ovicell, sub-globular, placed immediately above and behind the posterior margin of the cell aperture.

New Zealand and Australia.

C. bicornis, *Wyv. Thomson, Nat. Hist. Rev.,* 1858, *Q.J.M.S.,* vii., *p.* 153. The only known species.

Genus, DIMETOPIA—Busk.

Cells joined back to back ; aperture oblique ; each pair facing at right angles to those above and below ; at a bifurcation, the pair being disjoined, each of the disjoined cells gives off a secondary pair.

Australia and New Zealand only.

D. spicata, *Busk, l.c., p.* 35. Cells infundibuliform ; margin thickened, with numerous equidistant, elongated, acute spines ; white and transparent, forming thick tufts about 1½ to 3 inches or more in height ; color pink when alive.

Lyall Bay. Bass Straits, 45 fathoms.

D. cornuta, *Busk, l.c., p.* 35. Cells contracted below the middle ; aperture oblique, wide above ; a strong conical process on each side above ; one or two long projecting spines in front, inserted below the margin ; branches narrower than the former ; yellowish ; tufts loose.

Lyall Bay. Bass Straits, 45 fathoms.

FAMILY—VINCULARIDÆ.

Zoarium rigid, calcareous, unarticulated. Cells disposed alternately round an imaginary axis, forming dichotomously dividing branches. Surface of polyzoary not areolated.

Genus, VINCULARIA—Defrance.

Branches of zoarium not tubular ; front of cells surrounded by a raised border, arcuate above, nearly straight below ; ovicells, immersed, opening above the mouth of the cell upon which they are placed.

V. neo-zelandica, *Busk, Q.J.M.S., N.S.,* i., *p.* 155, *pl.* 34, *f.* 5. Zoarium simple, rooted at the base by radical tubes ; areæ of cells sub-pyriform ; anterior wall perforated ; margins smooth ; orifice arched above ; lower lip with a broad central denticle.

New Zealand. (Dr. Lyall.)

FAMILY—MEMBRANIPORIDÆ.

Zoarium membrano-calcareous, or calcareous, expanded, encrusting, sometimes foliaceous, contorted and sub-erect. Cells horizontal, quincuncial or serial.

Genus, MEMBRANIPORA—Blanville.

Cells more or less irregularly disposed, or quincuncial, with raised margins, a greater or less extent of the front membranaceous and flexible.

M. membranacea, *Linnæus, Busk, l.c., p.* 56. Cells oblong, with a short blunt spine at each upper angle.
Lyall Bay, on *Fuci*, etc. Europe. Australia.

M. pilosa, *Linnæus; Gray, Dieff. N.Z.,* ii., *p.* 292 ; *Johnston, Brit. Zooph., p.* 280. Cells prolonged below ; a moveable spine or vibraculum below the lower margin of the aperture, sometimes aborted ; an irregular number of marginal spines ; wall of cell cribriform.
Lyall Bay. Europe. Australia.

M. lineata, *Linnæus; Busk, l.c., p.* 58 ; *Johnston, l.c., p.* 349. Cells oval, separate, the margin armed with numerous slender spines, erect or bent inward.
Europe. Greenland.

M. tessellata, *Hutton, C.M.M., p.* 96. Cells oval, arrangement quincunc, front rounded above with the sides and bottom flat ; margin rough with short projecting denticulations ; interspaces granular ; ovicells rather flat, granular.
Common, incrusting dead shells, etc.

M. brunnea, *Hutton, C.M.M., p.* 96. Cells broadly oval, with a single spine at the centre of each side projecting over the front ; ovicells flattened with a median ridge ; a cup-shaped avicularium on each side just below it ; brown.
On *Turritella rosea.*

M. cyclops, *Busk, l.c., p.* 61. Front of cells oval ; margin very much raised, beaded ; a single avicularium below the aperture.

M. magnilabris, *Busk, l.c., p.* 62, Front of cells oval ; upper margin semicircular, much raised ; moveable lip very large, occupying the entire semicircular upper third of the front of the cell, remainder of the front of cell depressed, membranous or semi-calcareous, punctured
South Africa. Atlantic.

Genus, LEPRALIA—Johnston.

Zoarium adnate, crustaceous, spreading from a centre in a more or less circular form; composed of contiguous or connected, calcareous, decumbent cells, the walls of which are complete in front.

1. *With Avicularia.*

L. reticulata, *Macgillivray; Busk, l.c., p.* 66; *Johnston, l.c., p.* 317. Cells ovato-ventricose; interspaces punctured; mouth raised, with a thin margin and a channelled sinus in the lower lip, two to three spines on the upper margin; a central avicularium immediately below the mouth; mandible acute; ovicell globular, punctured, its opening bounded below by the meeting of its sides above the avicularium.
Britain.

L. angela, *Hutton, C.M.M., p.* 96. Cells ovate, immersed, with radiating grooves; mouth sub-orbicular, the lower lip prolonged into a deep spout-like projecting sinus; a spoon-shaped avicularium on each side just below the mouth, directed horizontally outwards; ovicell large, globose, granular.

2. *With Vibracula.*

L. ciliata, *Linnæus; Busk, l.c., p.* 75; *Johnston, l.c., p.* 279. Cells ovate or sub-globose, surface granular, an elongated acuminate vibraculum on one side of the body; a semilunar pore, frequently on an eminence, in the middle of the front of the cell above the centre; mouth with from five to seven spines; lower lip straight, entire; ovicell globose; surface granular.
Britain. Mediterranean. America. Australia.

L. lyallii, *Busk, l.c., p.* 75. Cells oval; walls thin, verrucose, or rugose; mouth raised; margin thickened, with a spout-like sinus in front, and five to six spines on the sides and above; a small vibraculum on many of the cells, on one side near the top (Busk.)
New Zealand. (Lyall.) On *Fuci.*

3. *Without Avicularia or Vibracula.*

(a.) With oral spines.

L. variolosa, *Busk, l.c., p.* 75; *Johnston, l.c., p.* 317. Cells oval, immersed or sub-immersed, usually disposed in linear series; punctured or areolated round the margin, granular (sometimes punctured) in front; mouth rounded or sub-quadrangular, with two to four close set spines quite at the summit; lower lip with a projecting mucro and an internal bifid denticle; ovicells deeply immersed, also areolated round the margin.
Lyall Bay. Britain.

L. nitida, *Busk, l.c., p.* 76; *Johnston, l.c., p.* 319. Cells ovate, raised in front; wall composed of four to nine ribs on each side, the spaces between which are filled up by a diaphanous membrane; mouth with four to six oral spines; ovicell sub-globose, surface granular.
Britain.

L. ventricosa, *Hassall; Busk, l.c., p. 78; Johnston, l.c., p. 305.*
Cells distinct above, or raised, immersed at the base, ventricose, ovate
or sub-globose ; mouth sub-orbicular, with a thickened raised margin ; a
bifid denticle on the lower lip, and four (rarely more) marginal spines ;
surface granular or irregularly striated ; usually a pointed or broad
mucro in front of the mouth ; ovicells globular, prominent.
Lyall Bay. Britain.

L. urceolata, *Hutton, C.M.M., p. 97.* Cells large (·04 inch),
ovate, ventricose, immersed behind ; surface finely granular without any
pores ; mouth simple, scarcely thickened, sub-orbicular, lower lip
straight ; from four to seven spines on the upper margin.
On dead shells.

L. cancer, *Hutton, C.M.M., p. 97.* Cells ovate, sub-immersed,
separated by depressed lines ; surface coarsely granular ; lower lip produced into a mucronate hollowed process, which covers the mouth, and
is transversely striated ; a short blunt incurved spine on each side of the
mouth ; in the fertile cells the lower lip is not mucronate but rounded,
and the spines are absent ; ovicells globose, coarsely granular.
Lyall Bay. On *Fuci.*

L. pellucida, *Hutton, C.M.M., p. 97.* Cells ovato-ventricose,
smooth, thin, translucent, a pore in the centre ; mouth nearly terminal,
oblong, transverse, with four or five long spines on its upper margin ;
ovicell ——(?). On *Fuci.*

(b.) Mouth without spines.

L. pertusa, *Busk, l.c., p. 80 ; Johnston, l.c., p. 311.* Cells ovato-
ventricose, or rhomboid, immersed, separated by a raised line, punctured ;
mouth orbicula, or narrowed below, and with a small tooth on each side ;
margin scarcely thickened, unarmed ; usually with an irregular perforated
tubercle below the mouth ; ovicell globose, punctured ; purple.
Britain. Australia (?).
On dead shells and corals.

L. areolata, *Busk, l.c., p. 82.* Cells sub-ovate or diamond-shaped,
depressed, quite immersed, quincunicial, outlines marked by raised
lines ; surface granular ; mouth sub-orbicular, with a sinus below and a
raised thickened margin.
Straits of Magellan, 10 to 20 fathoms.

L. malusii, *Busk, l.c., p. 83 ; L. biforis, Johnston, l.c., p. 314.*
Cells ovate, frequently truncate at each end ; front, especially round the
margin, punctured with numerous stelliform pores ; a central lunate
pore ; mouth rounded above, straight below, sometimes armed with
three to four oral spines, sometimes forked ; ovicells smooth, sometimes
porcellanous, grooved round the upper border, adnate to the front of
the cell above.
Britain. South America. Falkland Islands.

L. hyalina, *Busk, l.c., p.* 84 ; *Johnston, l.c., p.* 301. Cells sub-cylindrical, elongated or compressed and raised in front, sub-erect, the wall thin, transparent, and smooth ; mouth circular, frequently with a contracted often sub-tubular sinus below, the upper or posterior margin much raised, sharp ; ovicell globular, erect, free, punctured.

Britain. California. Greenland. Cape of Good Hope. Falkland Islands, but not New Zealand.

Var. D.—A sinus on the lower lip, and one or two low tubercles in the centre of the cell below one another.

Lyall Bay.

L. grandis, *Hutton, C.M.M., p.* 98. Cells large (.04 inch), ovate, ventricose ; surface shining, sub-granular, often with one or two longitudinal wrinkles, and with distant pores ; mouth simple, slightly thickened, sub-orbicular, with the lower lip flattened ; ovicell——(?). Pale brown.

Common on dead shells.

L. vellicata, *Hutton, C.M.M., p.* 98. Cells immersed, areolate ; mouth higher than broad, rounded at the top and contracted in the middle, the lower lip arched slightly upwards, and raised ; ovicell globose, areolate.

FAMILY- CELLEPORIDÆ.

Zoarium composed of cells more or less vertical to its axis or plane, heaped together, or irregularly overlying each other.

Genus, CELLEPORA—Fabricius.

Zoarium calcareous, rigid, adnate, or erect ; composed of urceolate, sub-erect, contiguous cells heaped together irregularly, or arranged quincuncially ; an ascending rostrum on one or both sides of the mouth, furnished with an avicularium.

C. pumicosa, *Linnæus; Busk, l.c., p.* 86 ; *Johnston, p.* 295. Glomerous ; cells heaped, ovate or pyriform ; mouth orbicula ; rostrum large, pointed ; avicularium on the internal aspect, oval ; ovicell small, decumbent.

Lyall Bay. Britain. California. Bass Straits.

Forming small white balls on *Sertularia*, &c.

C. bispinata, *Busk, l.c., p.* 87. Cells ovate, elongated, surface granular ; mouth orbicula ; rostrum anterior, with a very minute avicularium on one side ; two long oral spines on the opposite margin ; brown.

Tasmania.

C. mamillata, *Busk, l.c., p.* 87. Cells ovate, ventricose, immersed, forming an incrusting polyzarium, the surface of which is studded with mamillary projections ; mouth orbicular ; rostrum large,

conical, with a large avicularium on the internal face, sometimes a conical spine on the opposite side of the mouth.
Patagonia.

C. ampliata, *Hutton, C.M.M., p. 99.* Massive, free; cells agglomerated, vertical, smooth, ovate, with a row of large punctures round the margin ; mouth ovate or sub-orbicular, thin.
Lyall Bay.

C. agglutinans, *Hutton, C.M.M., p. 99.* Massive, free, enclosing serpulæ, &c. ; cells agglomerated, vertical, finely granulated, ovate ; mouth sub-orbicular, lower lip flattened, sometimes produced into a short incurved spout.
Lyall Bay. South Australia.

FAMILY—ESCHARIDÆ.

Zoarium erect, rigid, foliaceous and expanded, lobate or reticulated ; cells disposed quincuncially in the same plane on one or both sides of the zoarium.

Genus, ESCHARA—Ray.

Zoarium foliaceous and expanded, or branched and sub-linear ; cells on both surfaces back to back, immersed, coalescent, horizontal to the plane of the axis.

(a.) More or less expanded, foliaceous.

E. unicornis, *Hutton, C.M.M., p. 99.* Zoarium expanded ; cells short, with a few large pores on the surface; interstices finely granulated; mouth sub-orbicula, flattened below, lower lip produced into a rather incurved spout ; a single spine on the right or left side of the mouth.

E. flexuosa, *Hutton, C.M.M., p. 99.* Foliaceous, infundibuliform, much waved, springing from a broad base ; cells elongated, granular, separated by one or two rows of pores ; mouth transverse, oval ; a large spoon-shaped avicularium in the centre, below the lower lip.

(b.) Divided into branching lobes.

E. platalea, *Busk, l.c., p. 90.* Cells ovate, acute inferiorly, with a depressed area below the mouth in front, at the bottom of which is a simple pore ; avicularia irregularly scattered over the polyzoarium, rare, with a spoon-shaped mandible.
Australia.

E. lichenoides, *Milne-Edwards; Busk, l.c., p. 90.* Cells ovate, punctured in the centre by three to four stellate pores, which soon coalesce into a single apparent opening; mouth sub-orbicular; a small prominent avicularium on each side immediately below the mouth, looking outwards.
Australia.

Genus, RETEPORA—Lamark.

Zoarium foliaceous, reticulate, infundibuliform or contorted, sub-pedunculate; cells decumbent, opening on the upper surface only.

R. cellulosa, *Busk, l.c., p.* 93; *R. reticulata, Johnston, l.c., p.* 353. Zoarium turbinate or crateriform, undulated, curled; cells sub-cylindrical; surface smooth; mouth sub-orbicular; lower lip projecting, with an avicularium on one side; surface strongly vibicate; a papilli-form avicularium at the lower angle of the fenestræ; white.
Chatham Islands. Europe. Cape Horn. Australia.

Genus, HEMESCHARA—Busk.

Polyzoarium foliaceous, contorted, or laminar, composed of a single layer of cells disposed quincuncially, and opening on one surface only.

H. fairchildi, *Hutton, C.M.M., p.* 100. Cells ovate, immersed, granular, punctured round the edge; mouth simple; lower lip straight or with a sinus; occasionally with an avicularium on one side of the mouth; ovicell globose, granular; white.
Cook Strait.
Forming an easily detached crust on dead shells.

Sub-Order—Cyclostomata.

Cells tubular; orifice terminal, of the same diameter as the cell, without any moveable apparatus for its closure; consistence calcareous.

FAMILY—CRISIIDÆ.

Zoarium divided into distinct internodes, usually connected by flexible joints; attached by horny tubes.

Genus, CRISIA—Lamouroux.

Cells in two rows, sub-alternate; aperture entire.

C. patagonica, *D'Orb., Voy. Amer. Merid., Polypiers, p.* 7. Cells 9-19, straight, very distinct; branches arising from second or third cell; joints black.
Lyall Bay. S. America.

C. edwardsiana, *D'Orbigny, l.c., p.* 7; *Busk, Cat. Cyclost. Polyzoa in B.M.* (1875,) *p.* 5, *pl.* ii., *f.* 5-8. Cells 2-3 in each internode, curved forwards; dorsal surface of internode convex, and usually ridged transversely; branches arising from the first or lowest cell in the internode; one or other of the cells in each internode usually armed with a long jointed spine; ovicell lateral, pyriform (Busk.)
Lyall Bay. Australia. S. America.

Genus, MARGARETTA—Gray.

Cells disposed in four rows, back to back, each pair facing at right angles to those above and below ; furnished with long bristles.

M. barbata, *Lamark, Anim. sans vert.*, ii., *p.* 178 ; *M. cereoides, Gray, Dieff. N.Z.*, ii., *p.* 293, *nec Cellaria cercoides, Ellis.* Cells immersed, the mouth only projecting ; surface granulated ; mouth not thickened ; a long bristle on each side of the mouth ; white or pale brown ; in time the bristles fall off, but their position can always be recognized by a cup-shaped depression.
Lyall Bay. Cape of Good Hope.
The only species of the genus.

FAMILY—IDMONEIDÆ.

Zoarium erect, simple or branched ; branches continuous, cylindrical or sub-compressed, free or anastomosing.

Genus, IDMONEA—Lamouroux.

Zoarium ramose, branches dichotomous or irregularly divided ; free or anastomosing ; mouths of cells disposed in parallel, transverse or oblique, usually alternate, rows on each side of the front of the branches, which are angular or carinate in the middle.

I. giebeliana, *Stoliczka, Reise d. Novara, Palæ., p.* 115, *pl.* xviii., *f.* 4-6. Dichotomous, branches depressed, anastomosing ; cells irregular, sometimes single, sometimes in series of three or four, and sometimes in clusters of four to eight ; mouth round, raised ; both surfaces minutely punctate ; branches elliptical.

I. radians, *Lamark, Hist. Anim. sans vert., 2nd ed., p.* 279; *Busk, l.c., p.* 11, *pl.* vii., *f.* 1-4. Zoarium usually procumbent, stipitate, sometimes sub-erect ; branches, dichotomous, radiating more or less regularly in a circular form from the centre, very angular in front ; dorsal surface, perforated ; cells, one to four in each series, the innermost the longest ; aperture (when quite perfect) bi-labiate.
New Zealand and Australia.

Genus, HORNERA—Lamouroux.

Zoarium ramose ; branches dichotomous and free ; cells opening on one side only of the branches, which surface is marked with wavy anastomosing ridges, in the more or less rhomboidal interstices of which the openings of the cells are situated.

H. striata, *Milne-Edwards ; Stoliczka, Reise d. Novara, Palæ., p.* 107 ; *pl.* xvii., *f.* 8-11. Zoarium cespitose ; branches cylindrical, not reticulated ; mouths of cells disposed more or less regularly in longitudinal series, small, orbicula, those towards the lower part of the branches with a raised, slightly thickened, annular border, which is sometimes produced into an acute angle on one side ; a pore above and below the mouth ; anterior surface marked with smooth reticulated ridges, forming nearly regular diamond-shaped areolæ ; posterior surface sulcate, the sulci usually diverging obliquely from an imaginary median line, and finely punctate ; surface between the sulci smooth or sub-granular.

Genus, RETIHORNERA—Kinchenpaur.

Zoarium foliaceous, composed of sub-parallel branches connected by transverse tubules, so as to form an expanded frond with quadrangular fenestræ.

R. foliacea, *M'Gillivray ; Busk, l.c.,* *p.* 19, *pl.* xiii., *f.* 1, 2 ; *R. squamosa, Hutton, C.M.M., p.* 101. Foliaceous, waved, infundibuliform, reticulated ; mouths of the cells sub-orbicula, with a raised and scarcely thickened margin ; interspaces finely granulated and with slightly raised, scaly, longitudinal lines ; back finely granulated, with slightly raised rather scaly lines ; fenestræ small ; branches compressed ; white or pale brown.
Chatham Islands. Australia.

R. gouldiana, *Busk, Crag Polyzoa, p.* 95. Foliaceous, infundibuliform, waved, reticulated ; mouths of the cells sub-orbicular, with a slightly raised and thickened margin ; interspaces coarsely granulated ; back finely granulated and lightly striated ; fenestræ small ; branches cylindrical ; white.
Chatham Islands. Australia.
Perhaps identical with the last species, but the cells are nearer together.

Genus, PUSTULIPORA—Blainville.

Zoarium ramose, branches cylindrical, clavate or terete ; composed of tubular cells, which open on all sides of the branch.

P. parasitica, *Busk, loc. cit., p.* 21. *p.* xvii., *f.* 1-2. Zoarium about a quarter inch high, usually formed of one to three branches, short and truncate ; cells, usually deeply immersed, and very slightly prominent, except in very young specimens ; colour, brown, with white spots.
Bass Straits.
Always parasitic upon a species of *Catenicella.*

P. haastiana, *Stoliczka, Reise d. Novara, Palæ., p.* 102, *pl.* xvii., *f.* 4-5. Branches erect, close, anastomosing, in thick masses with the ends truncated to the same spherical surface ; sub-cylindrical ; cells distant, marked with longitudinal lines ; mouth slightly prominent, recurved, sub-orbicula, margin thickened ; white.
Common.

P. purpurascens, *Hutton, Trans. N.Z. Inst.,* ix., *p.* 361. Irregularly branched; branches spreading, slender; cells numerous, granular; mouths projecting, recurved, slightly contracted; purplish.

P. porcellanica, *Hutton, C.M.M., p.* 102. Branches slender, spreading, smooth; cells rather distant, wholly immersed, orifice suborbicular, neither raised or margined; branches cylindrical, sometimes anastomosing.

In fresh specimens the surface is coarsely pitted and the orifice slightly raised.

Lyall Bay. Australia.

Genus, CINCTIPORA—Hutton.

Zoarium erect, ramose; branches dichotomous or irregularly divided, free, cylindrical; cells immersed; mouths attached to the stem and to one another, forming circles round it; cell walls thin, punctured internally.

New Zealand only.

C. elegans, *Hutton, C.M.M., p.* 103. Cells arranged quincuncially, minutely granular, the septum between two cells prolonged upwards into a narrow rib running up the centre of the tube in the row above; white.

FAMILY—TUBULIPORIDÆ.

Zoarium depressed, or massive, adnate, orbiculated, or lobed.

Genus, TUBULIPORA—Lamark.

Zoarium adnate or decumbent; entire or divided into lobes or branches; cells partially free and ascending, radiating from an eccentric point.

T. glomerata, *Hutton, C.M.M., p.* 103. Encrusting, irregular, wart-shaped, thick; tubes crowded, irregularly placed.

Perhaps identical with *T. fungia* Couch., from Europe.

Genus, ALECTO—Lamouroux.

Zoarium adnate, creeping, irregularly branched; cells in single series or disposed in more or less irregular transverse rows.

A. racemosa, *Hutton, C.M.M., p.* 103. Large, branched; cells in clusters of from two to ten together, irregularly placed.

A. disposita, *Hutton, C.M.M., p* 103. Slightly branched, irregular; cells prominent, arranged in parallel rows; margin defined.

FAMILY—DISCOPORELLIDÆ.

Zoarium discoid, sometimes confluent, adnate or stipitate. Cells distinct or closely connate, intermediate surface cancellated or porous.

Genus, DISCOPORELLA—Gray.

Zoarium sessile or adnate ; discoid, centre usually elevated or sub-conical, rarely depressed ; cells, horizontal, usually disposed in lines radiating from the centre, sometimes irregular.

D. ciliata, *Busk, l.c., p.* 31, *pl.* xxx., *f.* 6. Discoid ; cells uni-serial, 4-6 in each row ; diameter of mouth less than that of the inter-stitial cancelli ; peristome, much produced on one side, nearly vertical, divided into several (2-4) long, acute, slender spines.
Cape of Good Hope.

D. novæ-zealandiæ, *Busk, loc. cit., p.* 32, *pl.* xxx., *f.* 2. Dis-coid, cupped ; cells, tubular, projecting, connate in uni-serial radii ; peristome bifid ; central area (unoccupied by cells) depressed ; cancelli, large, becoming smaller towards the periphery.
On *Catenicella.* (Dr. Lyall.) S. Australia.

Genus, DEFRANCEIA—D'Orbigny*.

Zoarium stipitate; capitulum cupped ; cells disposed in elevated rays extending to the margin of the cup; central portion of cup and interserial spaces cancellate ; outer surface of capitulum and stem pitted or smooth.

D. dentata, *Hutton; T. stellata, C.M.M., p.* 103, *not of Busk.* Capitulum broadly expanded, lobed, and curled ; cells in elevated branching rows, which form a denticulated margin to the lobes ; mouths slender, erect, rather closer towards the margin, but ceasing altogether before reaching it.
Stewart Island.

---

* The name of this genus is too much like *Defranchia* (Millet.)

APPENDIX.

A.

Remarks by Dr. v. Martens on some Shells sent to the Royal Zoological Museum, Berlin*.

Euthria lineolata, from the Auckland Islands, is the same that I have named *E. lineata*, var. *pertinax*, on account of the transverse ribs persisting into the penultimate whorl.

Risella, from Auckland, is *R. nana*, Lamark.

Scalaria lineolata, Kiener. Not *lineolata*, but perhaps it may be *S. tenuilirata*, Sow. ; Reeve, Conch. Ic., f. 118.

Diloma gaimardi, Phil. I suppose that this is *Trochus sulcatus*, Wood, ind. test. supp., f. 40, and perhaps also *Tr. lugubris*, Gmelin ; Chenu, Conch. cab., vol. v., f. 1571, but I doubt very much its being *Tr. cingulatus*, Quoy and Gaimard, which is the same as *gaimardi*, Philippi.

Trochus pupillus, Gould, is very interesting to me ; it appears to prove that Gould was right in giving New Zealand as the locality for his species, and that the shells from N.W. America, taken for it by several authors, is another species.

Patella magellanica, from Campbell Island. I do not think that this shell can be united with *magellanica* ; it is *P. luctuosa*, Gould.

Nacella cantharus, from Dunedin. Not that species, but probably some variety of *radians*, Gml.

Lima squamosa, Lam., from Foveaux Straits. The exotic species allied to the European *L. squamosa*, are in much confusion, and I dare not pronounce a definite opinion concerning them ; but I cannot think that the New Zealand shell is *squamosa*, and I would name it *sp. affinis*, *squamosæ*, until further elucidation, which will necessitate a thorough examination of the Red Sea and East Indian specimens.

---

* These remarks were received too late to incorporate with the text.—F. W H.

Mytilus dunkeri, from Auckland and Campbell Islands. Probably not *dunkeri,* but, in my opinion, *chorus* Molina, which comes from Chili, and therefore another Austral. circumpolar species.

Modiola securis, Lam (?) Dunedin, brackish water. May be a variety of *Mytilus ater,* Zelebor; the difference in the shape is not great. *Modiola securis,* is quite a doubtful species, which cannot be made out but by the examination of the original specimen.

B.

Since the manuscript of this catalogue was sent to press, the Otago Museum has received from Mr. J. Brazier of Sydney, and from Mr. W. Legrand of Hobart Town, valuable collections of Australian and Tasmanian marine shells; and from Captain Beddome and Mr. Petterd equally valuable collections of land and freshwater shells.

I have compared Australian and New Zealand specimens of the following, and can find no specific difference between them : *Polytropa succincta, Polytropa striata, Tritonium australis, Tritonium spengleri, Tritonium olearium, Ranella leucostoma, Ranella vexillum, Cassis pyrum, Cassis achatina, Littorina cærulescens, Nerita atrata, Bankivia varians, Lepidopleurus longicymbus, Bullina lineata, Lucina divaricata* (with Tasmanian specimens,) and *Modiola australis.*

Patula coma. This species is quite distinct from *H. diemenensis.*

Amphibola quoyana. This is certainly not an *Amphibola.* It is properly called *Ampullarina* by Australian Conchologists.

Gadinia nivea. This may be the same as *G. conica,* Angas (P.Z.S., 1867, p. 115,) for specimens received from Mr. Brazier shew that it is not always so conical as represented by Mr. Angas.

Trophon paivæ. In New Zealand specimens the spiral ribs are further apart.

Voluta kaupii, Dunker. Mal. Bl., x., 1863, p. 145; Novitates, t. 22, f. 1-2.
Hab. New Zealand (?)
I have seen no description of this shell.

Erato lactea. This may be the same as *Marginella muscaria,* but it is paler in colour.

Littorina luctuosa. Mr. Tenison-Woods considers that this species is identical with *L. cincta.*

Patella magellanica. I have compared this with specimens in the Otago Museum from Kerguelen Island : they are very different. Dr. Kidder considers that the Kerguelen Island species is *P. magellanica.* If he is right, Reeve's figure and description must be very inaccurate.

Anatina tasmanica. New Zealand specimens are higher in proportion to the length, than those from Tasmania.

Tellina deltoidalis. In Australian specimens there is in the left valve a posterior lateral tooth, which is absent in New Zealand specimens. Also in Australian specimens the anterior cardinal tooth of the left valve is not much broader than the posterior, and in the right valve the anterior cardinal is obsolete; while in New Zealand specimens the anterior cardinal of the left valve is much broader than the posterior, and the anterior of the right valve is distinct, although small. In Australian specimens also the posterior dorsal margin is not so rounded as in New Zealand specimens, and the anterior dorsal margin is flat, instead of being concave. These differences are quite enough to separate the two species.

Artemis subrosea. Specimens have been sent from Tasmania by Mr. Legrand. After careful comparison I can see no difference. In *A. japonica*, according to Reeve, the area of the ligament is more widely excavated, and the striæ incline to become lamellated at the sides.

Callista multistriata. Our species differs from that of Tasmania in being proportionately longer, and in the shell being much thinner. Specimens of *C. disrupta*, from Queensland and from N.S. Wales, are in the Museum. It is quite distinct.

Mytilicardia excavata. A comparison with a specimen from Port Jackson shews that New Zealand specimens are not so deeply sinuated below; the anterior ribs are more numerous, and the posterior ribs never seem to have the large scales found in Australian specimens; but I have only seen rubbed shells. It may be the same as *M. tasmanica* (Tenison-Woods,) published in the Pro. Royal Society of Tasmania, 1875, p. 161.

Barbatia pusilla. This appears to be distinct from *B. donaciformis*, as pointed out by Reeve. Dr. v. Martens is, I think, right in regarding our species as *B. donaciformis*. I have compared a valve with a specimen of *B. pusilla*, from Port Jackson.

Pecten australis. The ribbing on New Zealand specimens is finer than on those from Australia; but the difference is hardly sufficient to constitute another species.

F. W. H.

INDEX.

SYSTEMATIC LIST

OF THE

SPECIES

DESCRIBED IN THE

CATALOGUE OF MARINE MOLLUSCA, 1873,

WITH THE

CORRESPONDING NAMES GIVEN TO THE SAME SPECIES IN THE PRESENT WORK.

NOTE.—In the first column the names are given in order of the former Catalogue ; the second column shows the names adopted in this manual. When a blank occurs, it shows that the species has been altogether dropped out of the lists.

Cephalopoda.

Octopus lunulatus, Quoy.
Pinnoctopus cordiformis, Quoy et Gaim. — Pinnoctopus cordiformis.
Argonauta nodosa, Sol — Argonauta tuberculata, Shaw.
Onychoteuthis bartlingii, Le sueur. — Onychoteuthis bartlingii.
Ommastrephes sloani, Gray. — Ommastrephes sloani, Gray.
Loligo australis, Gray.
Sepioteuthis lessoniana, Féruss. — Sepioteuthis lessoniana, Féruss.
    ,, major, Gray. — Sepioteuthis bilineata Quoy & Gaimard.
Sepia apama, Gray.
Spirula lævis, Gray. — Spirula peronii, Lamarck.
Nautilus pompilius, Lamarck.

Pteropoda.

Hyalea affinis, D'Orb. — Hyalea affinis, D'Orb.
Dentalium pacificum, Hutton. — Dentalium pacificum, Hutton.

Heteropoda.

Ianthina exigua, Lamarck. — Ianthina exigua, Lamarck.
    ,, ianthina, Linnæus. — ,, communis, Lamarck.
Carinaria australis, Quoy. — Carinaria australis, Quoy & Gaimard.

Gasteropoda.

Murex zealandicus, Quoy. — Murex zealandicus, Quoy.
    ,, lyratus, Lamark. — Trophon ambiguus, Hombron & Jacquinot.
    ,, octogonus, Quoy. — Murex octogonus, Quoy.
    ,, eos, Hutton. — ,, angasi, Crosse.

Gasteropoda—continued.

Fusus pensum, Hutton.
,, australis, Quoy.
,, zealandicus, Quoy.
,, mandarinus, Duclos.
,, dilatatus, Quoy.
,, varius, Lamarck.
,, stangeri, Gray.
,, traversi, Hutton.
,, corticatus, Hutton.
,, plebeius, Hutton.
,, inferus, Hutton.
,, 'lineatus, Quoy.
,, linea, Martyn.
,, littorinoides, Reeve.
,, duodecimus, Gray.
,, bicinctus, Hutton.
,, vittatus, Quoy.
,, triton, Lesson.
,, nodosus, Martyn.
,, ,, var B.
Pleurotoma novæ-zealandiæ, Reeve.
,, trailli, Hutton.
,, lævis, Hutton.
,, albula, Hutton.
Lachesis sulcata, Hutton.
Daphnella letourneuxiana, Crosse.
Triton variegatum, Lamarck.
,, australe, Lamarck.
,, spengleri, Chemnitz.
,, acclivis, Hutton.
Ranella leucostoma, Lamarck.
,, vexillum, Sowerby.
Buccinum maculatum, Martyn.
,, zealandicum, Reeve.
,, ,, var. B.
,, costatum, Quoy.
,, luridum, Hutton.
,, lævigatum, Quoy.
,, cinctum, Quoy.
,, testudineum, Quoy.
,, gradatum, Deshayes.
Nassa rutilans, Reeve.
,, nigella, Reeve.
,, novæ-zealandiæ, Reeve.
,, corticata, Adams.
Purpura haustrum, Martyn,
,, textiliosa, Lamarck.
,, succincta, Lamarck.
,, rugosa,'Quoy.
,, scobina, Quoy.
,, quoyi, Reeve.
Ricinula iodostoma, Lesson.
Oliva erythrostoma, Lamarck.
Ancillaria australis, Quoy.
,, pyramidalis, Reeve.
,, obesa, Sowerby.
Voluta pacifica, Lamarck.
,, ,, var. B. (V. gracilis)
,, ,, var. C.
,, ,, subplicata, Hutton.
,, ,, kirki, Hutton.

Fusus spiralis, Adams.
Neptunea zealandica, var.
Neptunea zealandica, Quoy.
,, caudata, Quoy & Gaimard.
,, dilatata, Quoy.
Trophon stangeri.
Trophon stangeri, Gray.
Neptunea (?) traversi, Hutton.
Trophon paivæ, Crosse.
,, incisus, Gould.
,, inferus, Hutton.
} Euthria lineata, Chemnitz.
Euthria martensiana, Hutton.
Trophon duodecimus, Gray.
Euthria bicincta, Hutton.
,, vittata, Quoy.
Neptunea nodosa, var. C.
,, nodosa, Martyn.
,, ,,
Drillia novæ-zealandiæ, Reeve.
Pleurotoma trailli, Hutton.
Drillia lævis, Hutton.
Pleurotoma albula, Hutton.
Lachesis sulcata, Hutton.
Defranchia luteo-fasciata, Reeve.

Tritonium australis, Lamarck.
,, spengleri, Chemnitz.
,, olearium, Lamarck.
Ranella leucostoma, Lamarck.
,, vexillum, Sowerby.
Cominilla maculata, Martyn.
,, nassoides, Reeve.

Cominella funerea, Gould.
,, lurida, Philippi.
,, virgata, Adams.

Cominella testudinea, Chemnitz.

Nassa rutilans, Reeve.
,, nigella, Reeve.
,, novæ-zealandiæ, Reeve.
,, corticata, Adams.
Purpura haustrum, Martyn.
Polytropa textiliosa, Lamarck.
,, succincta, Lamarck.
,, squamata, Hutton.
,, quoyi, Reeve.
,, scobina, Quoy. & Gaimard.
Ricinula iodostoma, Lesson.

Ancillaria australis, Sowerby.
,, pyramidalis, Reeve.

Voluta pacifica, Lamarck.
,, ,, var. B. elongata.

Voluta gracilis, Swain.
,, kirki, Hutton.

Gasteropoda—continued.

Mitra obscura, Hutton.
,, aurantiaca, Lamarck.
,, nucea, Gronovius.
Marginella albescens, Hutton.
,, vittata, Hutton.
Columbella zebra, Gray.
,, rubiginosa, Hutton.
Cassis pyrum, Lamarck.
,, achatina, Lamarck.
Dolium variegatum, Lamarck.
Lamellaria indica, Leach.
Natica zealandica, Quoy.
,, vitrea, Hutton.
Scalaria zelebori, Dunker.
,, lineolata, Kiener.
Obeliscus roseus, Hutton.
Chemnitzia zealandica, Hutton.
Odostomia lactea, Angas.
Eulima chathamensis, Hutton.
Conus zealandicus, Hutton.
,, distans, Hwass.
Strombus novæ zealandiæ, Desh.
,, troglodytes, Lamarck.
Struthiolaria gigas, Sowerby.
,, nodulosa, Lamarck.
,, nodulosa, var. B.
,, scutulata, Desh.
,, vermis, Martyn.
Cypræa arabica, Linnæus.
,, caput-serpentis, Linnæus.
,, tessellata, Desh.
,, punctata, Linnæus.
Trivia australis, Lamarck.
,, coccinella, Lamarck.
Cancellaria trailli, Hutton,
Trichotropis inornata, Hutton.
Cerithium bicarinata, Gray.
,, alternatum, Hutton.
,, subcarina, Sowerby.
,, kirki, Hutton.
,, cinctum, Hutton.
,, exilis, Hutton.
,, minimus, Hutton.
Littorina cincta, Quoy.
,, diemenensis, Quoy.
,, vilis, Menke.
,, pyramidalis, Desh.
,, luctuosa, Reeve.
,, novæ zealandiæ, Reeve.
,, bullata, Martyn.
Risella kielmanseggi, Dunk.
Rissoa rugulosa, Hutton.
,, nana, Hutton.
,, subfusca, Hutton.
,, plicata, Hutton.
,, purpurea, Hutton.
,, impolita, Hutton.
,, rosea, Hutton.
Turritella rosea, Quoy.
,, fulminata, Hutton.
,, vittata, Hutton.

Mitra obscura, Hutton.

Marginella albescens, Hutton.
,, vittata, Hutton.
Columbella zebra, Gray.
Mitra rubiginosa, Hutton.
Cassis pyrum, Lamarck.
,, achatina, Lamarck.
Dolium variegatum, Lamarck.
Coriocella ophione, Gray.
Natica zealandica, Quoy.
Lunatia vitrea, Hutton.
Scalaria zelebori, Frauenfeld.
,, lyra, Sowerby.
Obeliscus roseus, Hutton.
Chemnitzia zealandica, Hutton.
Odostomia lactea, Angas.
Eulima chathamensis, Hutton.
Conus zealandicus, Hutton.

Struthiolaria papulosa, var. C.
,, papulosa, Martyn.
,, ,, .
,, australis, Gmelin.
,, inermis, Sowerby.

Cypræa punctata, Linnæus.
Trivia australis, Lamarck.
,, coccinella, Lamarck.
Cancellaria trailli, Hutton.
Trichotropis inornata, Hutton.
Cerithidea bicarinata, Gray.
,, alternata Hutton.
,, nigra, Hombron & Jacquinot.
Acus kirki Hutton.
Bittium terebelloides, v. Martens.
,, exilis, Hutton.
Triphoris angasi, Crosse.
Littorina cincta, Quoy.
,, cærulescens, Lamarck.

Littorina luctuosa, Reeve.
,, novæ-zealandiæ, Reeve.

Risella melanostoma, Gml.
Rissoina rugulosa, Hutton.
Barleeia nana, Hutton.
,, subfusca, Hutton.
Rissoina plicata, Hutton.
,, purpurea, Hutton.
Barleeia impolita, Hutton.
,, rosea, Hutton.
Turritella rosea, Quoy.
,, fulminata, Hutton
,, vittata, Hutton.

Gasteropoda—continued.

Turritella pagoda, Reeve.
  ,,   symmetrica, Hutton.
Siphonium lamellosum, Hutton.
Vermetus cariniferus, Gray.
Cladopoda zealandica, Quoy.
  ,,   rosea, Quoy.
Siliquaria lævigata, Lamarck.
  ,,   australis, Quoy.
Phorus onustus, Reeve.
Calyptræa maculata, Quoy.
Trochita tenuis, Gray.
Crypta costata, Desh.
  ,,   aculeata, Lamarck.
  ,,   contorta, Quoy.
  ,,   unguiformis, Lamarck.
Hipponyx cornucopiæ, Lamarck.
Nerita atrata, Lamarck.
Turbo smaragdus, Lamarck.
  ,,   ,,   var. B.
  ,,   rubicundus, Reeve.)
  ,,   granosus, Lamarck)
  ,,   undulatus, Reeve.
Imperator cookii, Lamarck.
  ,,   davisii, Stowe.
  ,,   imperialis, Lamarck.
Liotia shandi, Hutton.
Adeorbis varius, Hutton.
Rotella zealandica, Chenu.
Trochus gibberosus, Chemnitz.
  ,,   viridis, Gmel.
Chrysostoma fulminata, Hutton.
  ,,   simulata, Hutton.
  ,,   inconspicua, Hutton.
  ,,   rosea, Hutton.
Polydonta tuberculata, Gray.
  ,,   chathamensis, Hutton.
  ,,   tiarata, Quoy.
  ,,   tricarinata, Lamarck.
Labio zealandicus, Quoy.
  ,,   hectori, Hutton.
  ,,   cingulatus, Quoy.
  ,,   subrostrata, Gray.
Euchelus bellus, Hutton.
Diloma nigerrima, Linn.
Thalotia.
Zizyphinus tigris, Martyn.
  ,,   selectus, Chemnitz.
  ,,   cunninghamii, Gray.
  ,,   spectabilis, Adams.
  ,,   scitulus, Adams.
  ,,   punctulatus, Martyn.
Cantharidus iris, Chemnitz.
  ,,   purpuratus, Lamarck.
  ,,   elegans, Gmelin.
Elenchus dilatatus, Sowerby.
Bankivia varians, Beck.
Monilea zealandica, Hutton.
Gibbula sanguinea, Gray.
  ,,   nitida, Adams.
Haliotis iris, Lamarck.
  ,,   australis, Lamarck.

Turritella pagoda, Reeve.
Eglisia symmetrica, Hutton.
Siphonium lamellosum, Hutton.

Cladopoda zealandica, Quoy.
Stephopoma roseum, Quoy.

Siliquaria australis, Quoy.

Trochita novæ-zealandiæ, Lesson.
Trochita scutum, Lesson.
Crypta costata, Desh.

Crypta monoxyla, Lesson.
  ,,   unguiformis, Lamarck.
Hipponyx australis, Lamarck.
Nerita atrata, Lamarck.
Turbo smaragdus, Martyn.
  ,,   ,,   var. B.
Turbo granosus, Martyn.

  ,,   undulatus, Chemnitz.
Calcar cookii, Lamarck.
  ,,   davisii, Stowe.
  ,,   imperialis, Lamarck.
Turbo shandi, Hutton.
Fossarina varius, Hutton.
Rotella zealandica, Hombron and Jacquinot.

Margarita fulminata, Hutton.
Gibbula simulata, Hutton.
  ,,   inconspicua, Hutton.
Margarita rosea, Hutton.
Anthora tuberculata, Gray.
  ,,   chathamensis, Hutton.
  ,,   tiarata, Quoy & Gaimard.

Diloma æthiops, Gmelin.
  ,,   hectori, Hutton.
  ,,   gaimardi, Phillipi.
Trochocochlea subrostrata, Gray.
Euchelus bellus, Hutton.
Diloma nigerrima, Chemnitz.
Thalotia conica, Gray.
Zizyphinus granatum, Chemnitz.
  ,,   selectus, Chemnitz.
  ,,   cunninghami, Gray.
  ,,   spectabilis, Adams.
  ,,   scitulus, Adams.
  ,,   punctulatus, Martyn.
Cantharidus iris, Gmelin.
  ,,   zealandicus, Adams.
  ,,   purpuratus, Martyn.
Elenchus dilatatus, Sowerby.
Bankivia varians, Beck.
Monilea egena, Gould.
Gibbula sanguinea, Gray.
  ,,   nitida, Adams.
Heliotis iris, Martyn.
  ,,   rugoso-plicata, Chemnitz.

Gasteropoda—continued.

Haliotis virginea, Lamarck.
„ cunninghamii, Gray.
„ nævosa, Desh.
„ albicans, Desh.
„ cruenta, Reeve.
„ zealandica, Reeve.
„ stomatiaformis, Reeve.
„ pulcherima, Desh.
Fissurella squamosa, Hutton.
„ rubiginosa, Hutton.
Lucapina monilifera, Hutton.
Emarginula striatula, Quoy.
Tugali elegans, Gray.
„ parmaphoroides, Quoy.
Parmophorus australis, Lamarck.
„ unguis, Linnæus.
Tectura pilcopsis, Quoy.
„ fragilis, Quoy.
Patella inconspicua, Gray.
„ margaritaria, Chemnitz.
Patella octoradiata, Hutton.
„ tramoserica, Lamarck.
„ stellifera, Lamarck.
„ imbricata, Reeve.
„ pottsi, Hutton.
„ flava, Hutton.
Nacella radians, Gmelin.
„ flexuosa, Hutton.
„ carli, Reeve.
„ stellularia, Quoy.
„ argentea, Quoy. }
„ floccata, Reeve. }
„ affinis, Reeve.
„ cantharus, Reeve.
Chiton concentricus, Reeve.
„ canaliculatus, Quoy.
„ pellis-serpentis, Quoy.
„ sinclairi, Gray.
„ quoyi, Desh.
„ sulcatus, Quoy.
„ longicymbus, De Blain.
„ circumvallatus, Reeve.
„ areus, Reeve.
„ contractus, Reeve.
„ stangeri, Reeve.
„ empleurus, Hutton.
„ rudis, Hutton.
Tonicia undulata, Quoy.
„ rubiginosa, Hutton.
Acanthopleura ciliata, Reeve.
„ cælatus, Reeve.
„ nobilis, Gray.
Acanthochætes biramosus, Quoy.
„ porphyreticus, Reeve.
„ ovatus, Hutton.
„ hookeri, Gray.
Katharina violacea, Quoy.
Cryptoconchus zealandicus, Quoy. }
„ monticularis, Quoy. }
Buccinulus kirki, Hutton.
„ albus, Hutton.

Heliotis gibba, Philippi.

Haliotis cruenta, Reeve.
„ zealandica, Reeve.
„ stomatiaformis, Reeve.

Fissurella squamosa, Hutton.
Patella rubiginosa, Hutton.
Lucapina monilifera, Hutton.
Emarginula striatula, Quoy.
Tugalia parmophoidea, Quoy & Gaimard.

Parmophorus unguis, Linnæus.

Acmæa pilcopsis, Quoy & Gaimard.
„ fragilis, Chemnitz.
Patella inconspicua
„ denticulata, Martyn.

„ tramoserica.
„ stellifera, Chemnitz.
„ reevei, Hutton.
„ redimiculum, Reeve.
„ flava, Hutton
„ radians.
„ flexuosa, Hutton.
„ affinis, Reeve.
„ stellularia, Quoy.

„ pholidota, Lesson.

„ affinis, Reeve.

Chiton concentricus.
Lepidopleurus canaliculatus.
Chiton pellis-serpentis, Quoy.
„ sinclairi, Quoy.
„ glaucus, Gray.
„ sulcatus, Quoy.
Lepidopleurus longicymbus, De Blain.
„ circumvallatus, Reeve.
Chiton arcus Reeve.
Lepidopleurus contractus, Reeve.
Chiton stangeri Reeve.
Lepidopleurus empleurus, Hutton.
„ rudis, Hutton.
Tonicia undulata, Quoy.
„ rubiginosa, Hutton.
Mopalia ciliata, Sowerby.
Acanthopleura cælatus, Reeve.
Chætopleura nobilis, Gray.
Plaxiphora biramosa, Quoy & Gaimard.
Acanthochites porphyreticus, Reeve.
„ ovatus, Hutton.
„ zealandicus, Quoy & Gaimard
„ violacea, Quoy & Gaimard.

Cryptoconchus porosus, Burrow.

Buccinulus kirki, Hutton.
„ albus, Hutton.

Gasteropoda—continued.

Aplustrum lineatnm, Wood.
Cylichna striata, Hutton.
Bulla oblonga, Adams.
,, quoyi, Gray.
Haminea obesa, Sowerby.
Akera tumida, Adams.
Philine angasi, Crosse (?)
Aplysia sp. ind.
Doris carinata, Quoy.
Onchidoris tuberculatus, Hutton.
Æolis longicauda, Quoy.
Onchidella nigricans, Quoy.
Peronia patelloides, Quoy.
Siphonaria dimenensis, Quoy.
,, zealandica, Quoy.
,, scutellum, Desh.
,, funiculata, Reeve.
,, australis, Quoy.
,, denticulata, Quoy.
,, cancer, Reeve.
,, obliquata, Sowerby.
,, spinosa, Reeve.
Melampus commodus, Adams.
,, adamsianus, Pfeiffer.
,, zealandicus, Adams.
,, costellaris, Adams.
,, sulcatus, Adams.
Cassidula mustelina, Desh.
Amphibola avellana.

Bullina lineata, Wood.
Cylichna striata, Hutton.
Bulla oblonga, Adams.
,, quoyi, Gray.
Haminea zealandica, Gray.
Akera tumida, Adams.
Philine angasi, Crosse.

Doris carinata, Quoy.
,, wellingtonensis, Abraham.
Phidiana longicaudata, Quoy.
Onchidella nigricans, Quoy & Gaimard.
,, patelloides, Quoy & Gaimard.
Siphonaria obliqata, Sowerby.
,, sipho, Sowerby.
,, sipho.

,, australis.

Siphonaria cancer, Reeve.
,, obliquata.
,, spinosa.
Melampus commodus, Adams.
Tralia adamsianus, Pfeiffer.
Melampus zealandicus, Adams.
Tralia costellaris, Adams.

Amphibola avellana, Chemnitz.

Lamellibranchiata.

Barnea similis, Gray.
Pholadidea tridens, Gray.
Teredo antarctica, Hutton.
Aspergillum novæ zealandiæ, Lamarck.
Saxicava arctica, Linnæus.
Panopæa zealandica, Quoy.
,, solandri, Gray.
Corbula zealandica, Quoy. }
,, catlowæ, Reeve. }
,, adusta, Hinds.
Anatina tasmanica, Reeve.
Lyonsia vitrea, Hutton.
Thracia novæ zealandiæ, Reeve.
Neæra trailli, Hutton.
Myodora striata, Quoy.
,, ovata, Reeve.
,, brevis, Stuchbury.
Chamostræa albida, Lamarck.
Mactra discors, Gray.
,, murchisoni, Desh.
,, scalpellum, Desh.
,, donaciformis, Gray.
,, æquilatera, Reeve.
Hemimactra ovata, Gray.
Mulina notata, Hutton.
Darnia pusilla, Hutton.
Lutraria deshayesii, Reeve.
,, lanceolata, Reeve.

Barnea similis, Gray.
Pholadidea tridens, Gray.
Teredo antarctica, Hutton.

Saxicava australis, Lamarck.
Panopæa zealandica, Quoy.
,, solandri, Gray.

Corbula zealandica, Quoy.

Corbula adusta, Hinds.
Anatina tasmanica, Reeve.
Lyonsia vitrea, Hutton.
Thracia novæ zealandiæ, Reeve.
Neæra trailli, Hutton.
Myodora striata, Quoy.
,, ovata, Reeve.
,, plana, Reeve.
Chamostræa albida, Lamarck.
Mactra discors, Gray.
,, murchisoni, Desh.
,, scalpellum, Desh.
,, donaciformis, Gray.
,, æquilateris, Desh.
Standella ovata.
,, notata, Hutton.
Mactra scalpellum, Desh.
Zenatia deshayesii, Reeve.
Vanganella taylori, Gray.

Lamellibranchiata—continued.

Zenatia acinaces, Quoy.
Raeta perspicua, Hutton.
Vanganella taylori, Gray.
Psammobia stangeri, Gray.
,, lineolata, Gray.
,, zonalis, Lamarck.
,, affinis, Reeve.
Hiatula nitida, Gray.
,, siliquæ, Hart.
,, incerta, Reeve.
,, nitens, Tryon.
Tellina albinella, Lamarck.
,, deltoidalis, Lamarck.
,, sublenticularis, Sowerby.
,, decussata, Lamarck.
,, lintea, Hutton.   }
,, subovata, Sowerby.   }
,, tiaconica, Desh.
Mesodesma chemnitzii, Desh.
,, cuneata, Lamarck.
,, ventricosa, Gray.
,, elongata, Quoy.
,, lata, Reeve.
,, ovalis, Reeve.
,, spissa, Reeve.
,, novæ zealandiæ, Reeve.
Venus tuberosa, Desh.
,, oblonga, Gray.   }
,, zealandica, Gray.   }
Chione lamellata, Lamarck.
,, yatei, Gray.
,, costata, Quoy.
,, lima, Desh.
,, stuchburyi, Gray.   }
,, dieffenbachi, Gray.   }
,, creba, Hutton.
,, mesodesma, Quoy.
,, gibbosa, Hutton.
,, paupercula, Desh.
,, alatus, Reeve.
Callista multistriata, Desh.
,, disrupta, Desh.
Dosinia anus, Philippi.
,, subrosea, Gray.
Cyclina kroyeri, Philippi.
Tapes intermedia, Gray.
,, fabagella, Desh.
,, galactites, Lamarck.
Venerupis reflexa, Gray.
,, brevis, Quoy.
Petricola serrata, Desh.
Cardium striatulum, Sowerby.
Venericardia australis, Quoy.
,, zealandica, Potiez.
Lucina divaricata, Lamarck.
Cryptodon sp. ind.
Mysia zealandica, Gray.
,, globularis, Lamarck.
,, novæ zealandiæ, Reeve.
Kellia cycladiformis, Desh.
Pythina stowei, Hutton.

Zenatia acinaces, Quoy.
Raeta perspicua, Hutton.
Vanganella taylori, Gray.
Psammobia stangeri, Gray.
,, lineolata, Gray.
,, zealandica, Desh.
,, affinis, Reeve.
Soletellina nitida, Gray.
,, siliqua, Reeve.
,, incerta, Reeve.
,, nitens, Tryon.
Tellina alba, Quoy & Gaimard.
,, deltoidalis, Lamarck.
,, disculus, Desh.

Tellina subovata, Sowerby.

Tellina tiaconica, Desh.
Mesodesma novæ zealandiæ, Chemnitz.
,, spissa, Reeve.
,, ventricosa, Gray.
Standella elongata.
,, lata, Desh.
,, ovalis, Desh.
,, spissa, Reeve.
,, novæ zealandiæ, Chemnitz.
Venus nodosa, Dunker.

,, oblonga, Hanley.

Chione lamellata, Lamarck.
,, yatei, Gray.
,, costata, Quoy.
,, lima, Desh.

Chione stuchburyi, Gray.

Venus creba, Hutton.
Chione mesodesma, Quoy.
,, gibbosa, Hutton.
,, paupercula, Chemnitz.

Callista multistriata, Sowerby.
,, disrupta, Sowerby.
Artemis australis, Gray.
,, subrosea, Gray.
,, lambata, Gould.
Tapes intermedia, Quoy
,, fabagella, Desh.
,, galactites, Lamarck.
Venerupis reflexa, Gray.
,, paupercula, Desh.
Petricola serrata, Desh.
Cardium striatulum, Sowerby.
Cardita australis, Lamarck.
,, zealandica, Potiez & Michaud.
Lucina divaricata, Lamarck.

Diplodonta zealandica, Lamarck.
,, globularis, Lamarck.
,, striata, Hutton.
Kellia cycladiformis, Desh.
Pythina stowei, Hutton.

G ii.

Lamellibranchiata—continued.

Solenya australis, Lamarck.
Gouldia isabella, Hutton.
Mytilicardia excavata, Desh.
Cardita tridentata, Say.
Mytilus magellanicus, Lamarck.
  ,, polyodontes, Quoy.
  ,, hirsutus, Lamarck.
  ,, smaragdinus, Chemnitz.
  ,, dunkeri, Reeve.
  ,, latus, Lamarck.
  ,, ater, zelebor.
Crenella discors, Lamarck.
Modiola albicosta, Lamarck.
  ,, securis, Lamarck.
Lithodomus truncatus, Gray.
  ,, gruneri, Philippi.
Pinna zealandica, Gray
Barbatia sinuata, Lamarck.
  ,, pusilla, Sowerby.
Pectunculus laticostatus, Quoy.
  ,, striatularis, Lamarck.
Nucula margaritacea, Lamarck.
  ,, strangei, Adams.
  ,, consobrina, Adams.
Leda australis, Quoy.
Solenella cumingii, Adams.
Pecten zealandiæ, Gray.
  ,, gemmulatus, Reeve.
  ,, picæ, Reeve.
  ,, dieffenbachi, Reeve.
  ,, multicostatus, Reeve.
  ,, radiatus, Hutton.
  ,, vellicatus, Hutton.
Vola laticostatus, Gray.
Lima squamosa, Lamarck.
  ,, bullata, Born.
Anomia stowei, Hutton.
  ,, alectus, Gray.
  ,, cytæum, Gray.
Placunanomia zealandica, Gray.
  ,, ione, Gray.
Ostrea purpurea, Hanley.
  ,, lutaria, Hutton.
  ,, virginica, Lamarck.
  ,, mordax, Gould.
Waldhemia lenticularis, Desh.
Terebratella cruenta, Dillwyn.
  ,, rubicunda, Sol.
Magas evansii, Davidson.
  ,, cumingii, Davidson.
Waltonia valencienni, Davidson.
Kraussia lamarkiana, Davidson.
Rhynchonella nigricans, Sowerby.
Crauia, sp. ind.

Solenya parkinsoni, Smith.
Crassatella bellula, Adams.
Mytilicardia excavata, Desh

Mytilus magellanicus, Lamarck.
  ,, polyodontes, Quoy

Mytilus latus, Chemnitz.
  ,, edulis, Reeve.
  ,, latus, Chemnitz.
  ,, ater, Frauenfeld.
Crenella impacta, Hermann.
Modiola areolata, Gould.
  ,, fluviatilis, Hutton.
Lithodomus truncatus, Gray.
  ,, gruneri, Reeve.
Pinna zealandica, Gray.
Barbatia decussata, Sowerby.
  ,, pusilla, Sowerby.
Pectunculus laticostatus, Quoy.
  ,, striatularis, Lamarck.
Nucula nitidula, Adams.
  ,, strangei, Adams.
  ,, sulcata, Adams.
Leda concinna, Adams.
Solenella australis, Quoy & Gaimard.
Pecten zealandiæ, Gray.
  ,, gemmulatus, Reeve.
  ,, picæ, Reeve.
  ,, zealandiæ, Gray.
  ,, multicostatus, Reeve.
  ,, radiatus, Hutton.
  ,, vellicatus, Hutton.
Vola laticostatus, Gray.
Lima zealandica, Sowerby.
  ,, japonica, Adams.
Anomia stowei, Hutton.
  ,, alectus, Gray.
  ,, cytæum, Gray.
Placunanomia zealandica, Gray
  ,, ione, Gray.
Ostrea edulis, Reeve.
  ,, discoidea, Gould.
  ,, edulis, Reeve
  ,, glomerata, Gould.
Waldhemia lenticularis, Desh.
Terebratella cruenta, Dillwyn.
  ,, rubicunda, Sol.
Magas evansii, Davidson.
Bouchardia cumingii, Davidson.
Waltonia valencienni, Davidson.
Kraussia lamarkiana, Davidson.
Rhynchonella nigricans, Sowerby.